PRAISE FOR *TIDES OF HONOUR*

"Graham has delivered a book that reads like a love letter to a time and place that figures largely in our national identity: Halifax in 1917."

The Globe and Mail

"Evocative of place and time, a novel blending tragedy and triumph in a poignant and uplifting tale that's sure to leave its mark upon your heart."

Susanna Kearsley, *New York Times* bestselling author

"Fans of Diana Gabaldon and other historical fiction/romance writers will lap this up for the classy, fast-moving, easy-to-read, and absorbing book that it is—with some Canadian history to boot."

Winnipeg Free Press

PRAISE FOR GENEVIEVE GRAHAM

"Readers weary of European-centric World War II dramas will delight in *Letters Across the Sea*, which centres on the courage and tenacity of Canadian soldiers, veterans, and home-front fighters. . . . A tender, moving tale."

Kate Quinn, *New York Times* bestselling author of *The Rose Code*

"One of my favourite historical fiction authors! Graham reveals our past—both the shame and the hope of it—in the truest possible light."

Marissa Stapley, *New York Times* bestselling author of Reese's Book Club Pick *Lucky*

"Inspired by a little-known chapter of World War II history—including Toronto's race riot at Christie Pits—a young Protestant girl and her Jewish neighbour are caught up in the terrible wave of hate sweeping the globe on the eve of war in *Letters Across the Sea*, a powerful love story from Genevieve Graham, bestselling author of *The Forgotten Home Child*."

49th Shelf

"I always look forward to diving into a Genevieve Graham novel because I know I'll be swept away by her meticulous evocation of the past, her memorable and wonderfully observed characters, and her unmatchable flair for shining a light into the neglected corners of our shared past."

Jennifer Robson, internationally bestselling author of
The Gown and *Our Darkest Night*

"Graham is a master storyteller with a gift to touch the heart. I'm so happy to have discovered her work."

Santa Montefiore, bestselling author of *The Temptation of Gracie*

"A page-turner. . . . Graham writes about ordinary people living at important moments in Canadian history, from the displacement of the Acadians to the Yukon Gold Rush to the Second World War. In *The Forgotten Home Child*, she ensures the British Home Children are remembered and honoured."

Winnipeg Free Press

"From icy gales on the Chilkoot Trail to the mud and festering greed in booming Dawson City, *At the Mountain's Edge* gives new life to one of the most fascinating chapters in Canada's history. Fast-paced and full of adventure, this novel is an exciting take on the raw emotions that make us human and the spirit required to endure."

Ellen Keith, bestselling author of *The Dutch Wife*

"Graham has immense talent when it comes to making our nation's history interesting and weaving a riveting story around historical facts."

Niagara Life Magazine

"Graham continues her worthy crusade of recounting pivotal Canadian history in this poignant story [about] the travesties of war both on the battlefield and the home front."

RT Book Reviews, on *Come from Away*

"The talented Genevieve Graham once again calls upon a fascinating true story in Canadian history to remind us that beneath the differences of our birth, and despite the obstacles we face, we're all human underneath. Vividly drawn and heartwarming, *Come from Away* is a beautiful look at the choices we make in the face of both love and war."

Kristin Harmel, *New York Times* bestselling author of
The Forest of Vanishing Stars

"At once dizzyingly romantic and tremendously adventurous, this novel also serves as a poignant reminder of the senseless toll the violence of war can take—and the incredible lengths of heroism humans will go to in order to survive and rescue the ones they love."

Toronto Star, on *Promises to Keep*

ALSO BY GENEVIEVE GRAHAM

Bluebird
Letters Across the Sea
The Forgotten Home Child
At the Mountain's Edge
Come from Away
Promises to Keep
Somewhere to Dream
Sound of the Heart
Under the Same Sky

Tides of

Honour

GENEVIEVE GRAHAM

Published by Simon & Schuster Canada

New York London Toronto Sydney New Delhi

Simon & Schuster Canada
A Division of Simon & Schuster, Inc.
166 King Street East, Suite 300
Toronto, Ontario M5A 1J3

This Simon & Schuster Canada edition August 2022

SIMON & SCHUSTER CANADA and colophon are registered
trademarks of Simon & Schuster, Inc.

For information about special discounts for bulk purchases,
please contact Simon & Schuster Special Sales at 1-800-268-3216
or CustomerService@simonandschuster.ca.

Interior Design by Erika R. Genova

Manufactured in the United States of America

1   3   5   7   9   10   8   6   4   2

Library and Archives Canada Cataloguing in Publication
Title: Tides of honour / Genevieve Graham.
Names: Graham, Genevieve, author.
Description: Simon & Schuster Canada edition. | Originally published: Toronto,
Ontario: Simon & Schuster Canada, 2015.
Identifiers: Canadiana 20210392509 | ISBN 9781668002063 (softcover)
Classification: LCC PS8613.R3434 T53 2022 | DDC C813/.6—dc23

ISBN 978-1-6680-0206-3
ISBN 978-1-4767-9053-4 (ebook)

To Dwayne, Emily, and Piper
and all my friends along Nova Scotia's Eastern Shore

When it is dark enough, you can see the stars.

—RALPH WALDO EMERSON

Prologue

Percival Johnson huddled in his coat, hiding his nose among the rough fibres of his scarf and squinting against the sunshine. The glare off the Halifax harbour was almost blinding, set against a backdrop of white, and the cold sky carried no clouds. It seemed only right to Percival that the morning of December 6, 1917, should be so beautiful, because today was his tenth birthday. He figured the whole world was probably smiling about that right now.

He glanced beside him at his friend George, then cast an eye over his shoulder, up the hill. "See that? Everybody's coming down since they lit up fireworks for my birthday."

"Right," George muttered. "We should go. We'll be late."

"Fiddlesticks. This is way better."

The ship across the harbour was now fully engulfed in flames. Once in a while a small explosion went off, shooting sparks into the pitch-black smoke hovering above the ship, and all the people gathered around the harbour made loud noises of approval. It was like a great big magic show, and the whole city had turned out to watch.

Both boys jumped at the next bang. "Whoa!" Percival exclaimed. "Did you see that one?"

George laughed. "Looked like the whole boat was going to blow up it was so big!"

"I know! Wow! This is brilliant!"

"You boys step back now," came a voice.

Percival smiled up at the gruff face looming over him. "Hey, Mr. Porter! Do you fellas have to put out the fire soon? I hope not. It's awful pretty."

The fireman shrugged. "Not much we can do from here. We'll wait until it floats closer. It'll probably burn itself out anyway."

"It's coming closer," George said.

"Sure is. It'll get louder, too," Mr. Porter replied with a nod. "Just you wait."

"The fireworks are for my birthday," Percival informed the fireman.

Mr. Porter chuckled and rubbed his hand on the boy's cap. "Surely they are, son."

The three of them stared out to sea and watched the burning ship draw ever closer to the shore, headed right to the foot of Richmond Street. Looked like the captain was aiming to land at Pier 6. They'd have to stop it before it touched, since Pier 6's pilings were all wood. Setting that on fire would make a big mess.

The fireman frowned down at the boys. "Shouldn't you be in school? It's after nine o'clock."

"Aye, we should," George said, glaring at Percival.

But Percival was not to be swayed. "Why, I'm sure the rest of the school is out here with us. It's so much more fun than reading, anyway."

"I *like* reading." George stepped back and tugged on his friend's sleeve. "Come on, Percy. Let's go."

Percival's expression flipped from gleeful to furious in that moment. "George Harris, you old stick-in-the-mud. I want to stay—"

In the next instant, the little boy's words were sucked from his mouth, along with every other noise in Halifax. It was as if the fire on board the *Mont Blanc* took a deep breath, preparing itself before it exhaled and obliterated everything in its path.

DANNY

– October 1916 –

ONE

The rocky shores of Halifax jutted from the sea, her buildings and trees appearing and disappearing like black angled spectres playing hide and seek in the drifting mist. Her dark profile came as a relief to the hundreds of hearts beating on board HMHS *Mauretania*. Seven days and nights on the Atlantic had been too long, and the passengers craved the security of solid ground.

The autumn air was cool, barely moving, the hovering mystery of fog undisturbed. As the ship neared the shore, Danny saw people wandering the hillside along the confusing grid of streets, small figures in black meeting up. He couldn't hear them over the grinding engines of the ship, but he knew they were talking, laughing as if they hadn't a care in the world. His gut twisted at the sight, though he knew it shouldn't affect him this way. He couldn't help it. What right did these people have to move with such optimism in their strides, to meet and walk and think nothing of what could happen in the next step? What right did the city have to so much life? So much hope?

Danny's parents were waiting for him when the tide washed the big ship into the Halifax port. They stood on the dock, two small figures wrapped in coats and scarves, waving. His father's other hand was tucked under his mother's elbow. They both stood tall, smiling, but Danny thought from that distance they looked older. Standing straight or not, they appeared a little stooped.

Coming down the ramp was awkward, as he'd known it would be. Danny was learning every day how to better manage the chunk of wood that was now his right leg, but he still leaned heavily on his crutch. He hated the leg. Hated the sores it wore on his stump. But he wasn't very well going to carry on his life hopping like a one-legged rabbit. That was for damn sure. So when the nurse had offered to show him how to use the crutch properly, Danny had listened and learned.

"Danny!" his mother cried, rushing forward. She stopped short two feet away from him, uncertain, her arms outstretched as if she were waiting to be thrown a ball.

"It's okay, Mother," he said. "It's just my leg, and it hardly pains me much anymore."

Her head tilted, catching the sunlight, and he saw grey strands threading in and out of her tethered hair. He didn't think those had been there before. Or had they, and he hadn't noticed?

"Oh, Danny," she said. Her eyes, wet with sympathy, flicked from his face to the place where his leg should have been. "Here, now. What a sin."

He shifted his crutch out of the way when she stepped forward and folded him against her, and he thought there was no better, no stronger place on earth than in his mother's arms. She had cried that other day as well, eighteen or so months past, watching him climb the ship's ramp along with Big Jimmy Mitchell and Fred Arnold. Back then they'd been a different kind of tears. And though he hadn't been around to see it, he knew she'd cried again when he'd written to her about his two best friends being shot to pieces in the muck. But he wouldn't think of that. Couldn't. Not today, at least.

For a moment he let himself hang on to his mother as if he were a little boy again, holding his breath to contain the sobs that pushed against the wall of his chest. He wouldn't cry. Wouldn't give in. Seemed awfully silly to cry, now everything was behind him.

"Son," Danny's father said, and his mother stepped to the side, sniffing into a worn handkerchief. Daniel Baker Sr. clasped Danny's hand in an iron, callused grip. "Good to have you back."

Daniel Sr. was a traditional man, a man who stood as if a pole had been slid into his spine. He was a fisherman and a Baptist minister, a man with such a strong belief that he expected that the sun rose or fell depending on how he carried himself. His father had worn his black suit today, the one he normally reserved for Sundays. He held his first-born's gaze for a moment longer than usual, and Danny felt suddenly like a child who had done something he couldn't remember, but whatever it was, it would require penance. He knew he was expected to meet his father's even stare, so he did. He saw pain there, certainly, and loss. But there was something else, he thought. His father looked hollow. Tired. And . . . disappointed?

"Damn fine to be back, sir," he said.

"Danny! Your language!" his mother exclaimed out of habit. Her lips pursed in an expression he remembered well, a frown she'd given him for as long as he could remember. From back in the days when he was small enough she could wash out his mouth with soap. But she hadn't done it often. Only when he hadn't given her a choice. His mother enjoyed laughing more than anything else.

God, Danny was tired. His body trembled from relief and exhaustion and hunger and grief. "Sorry, Mother."

Home. The familiar, aching face of love, half frowning at him for forgetting where he was.

Home. The filth of battle beginning to peel like the curls of old paint from the surface of his heart.

Home. No more waiting for shrapnel to shred his brain.

From the ship they went to the schooner, all nineteen feet of it waiting quietly at the dock's edge. Funny how land changed under a man's feet. One day Danny'd been running through grass and roots, the next marching up to his knees in sucking mud. Now he walked on weathered timbers, and the wood of his leg met the wood of the dock. The ground here was predictable. Familiar. Setting foot in the boat was like coming home all over again. The rocking motion caused by his weight welcomed him like a feather mattress, and he fell back into the rhythm he had always known, helping to haul in ropes and cinch them, feeling for the current and sensing the momentum—though his balance was precarious these days.

When the wind filled the sails and pointed them up the Eastern Shore, Danny sat and wondered if he really had just lived through a war. Or whether it had all been the most unimaginable of nightmares. The soft rocking of the boat and the sight of his father's back was a comfort, and since he knew there was a good six-hour trip to go, he let his head nod.

He woke a few times, but the exhaustion that had dragged him under kept him sleeping for most of the journey. When at last they approached his home, he awoke as if someone had tapped him on the shoulder, and he couldn't look away from the sight. The house seemed smaller than he remembered it. And fragile, as if a nor'easter might just pick it up and drop it into the sea. Danny figured it looked that way because in the back of his mind he could still hear artillery fire, could still see mounds of dirt blasting up around the yard like fireworks, could even imagine a shell obliterating the house, leaving nothing in its wake but a shattered chimney.

In a few months, as soon as they could pull together the money, he'd be introducing his beautiful Audrey to this place. How would he tell his family about her? She wasn't from the area, that's for sure, and sometimes the community could be tough on someone who came from away. To him, Audrey was incredible. How would they see her?

His mother dropped her hand onto his. "So good to have you home, Danny."

He'd tell her first. His mother always knew how to do things like that.

"We left your room exactly the same, son. I just tidied up. Dusted, you know? Put fresh sheets on for you."

"Thanks, Mother."

Ignoring their offers of assistance, he stepped awkwardly onto the dock and remembered how he'd never had to think about doing that before. The first time he'd ever climbed onto the dock was just about the same day he'd learned to walk. He could hop fences without effort, outrun any of the other kids, reach into that frozen ocean if the nets got tangled. All that was gone.

He turned back for his bag, then realized with dismay his father had already pulled it out and was carrying it for him.

"Hey, Dad. Let me get that, huh?"

Daniel Sr. gnawed at the inside of one cheek while he thought about the request. They both knew it was an important question, and Danny saw when his father made his decision.

"I've got it, son. Help your mother out of there, would you?" Without any change in expression, he headed toward the little white house, Danny's bag clutched in his hand.

Just like that, Danny thought, feeling a dark red pulse of fury ignite in his chest. Even as a little boy, his father had made him carry his own things and more. "Work like a man and you'll grow up to be a man," he had always said. A rather strange expression, since he was fated to be a man whether he worked or not, but he understood the sentiment. And he had always worked hard. He had outworked pretty much every other boy around, and he'd done it partially so he could see the glint of pride in his father's eyes.

So what did this mean? Danny wasn't going to be able to work like a man anymore? He was less of a man?

Yes, Danny thought. *Yes, it means exactly that.*

He offered his arm to his mother. She leaned slightly against him, then stepped onto the dock.

"Oh, Danny," she said. "Are you all right? Are you going to be okay with all this?"

He cleared his throat, which felt suddenly dry. "What choice do I have?"

"I've got fresh scones inside for you," she said after a moment. "And I'll brew some tea and give you a little extra honey. Just to sweeten it up, right?"

"Thanks." Some things never changed, *thank God.*

She cocked her head to the side, looking at him with so much pity Danny wanted to scream. The soft palms of her hands pressed against his cheeks, and her eyes searched his expression. But Danny stared back without exposing anything. He would not be pitied. He would not. There were boys over there hurt far worse than he was. There were better men than him who would never come back.

"You know what, Mother?" he said through a tight smile. "I'm going to have one of those scones because I've been missing your cooking for a very long time now. But I'm going to wait on the tea. What I really want is to go to bed. Sleep a few hours. Would that be all right?"

Her eyes flew open. "Of course, son! Let's get you inside."

They entered the house and Danny stopped, feeling like a stranger in his own home. Everything felt so different from before, though he knew nothing had changed. Nothing but him. While he ate the scone, his mother kept talking, and he nodded, barely hearing her over the panic rising in his head. They walked through the kitchen and stopped at the bottom of the stairs to the bedrooms.

"You know, Danny, we could move your things to the sitting room—"

"It's fine, Mother. Really. I've survived worse. And now . . ." He took in the endless staircase. "Now I just need to rest."

Her shoulders relaxed a little. "Of course, Danny. It's a long voyage. You'll feel much better when it's time for supper. I'm making your favourite. And your aunt and uncle are coming as well, bringing little baby George for you to meet."

But he slept through supper. He'd barely stripped off his tattered uniform and unhitched his peg leg before he collapsed onto the safety of his childhood mattress. He didn't hear his brother when he came in hours later, stood over Danny and studied the strange outline of his body under the wool blanket. He didn't hear his parents arguing and shushing each other. He didn't hear a thing.

He awoke in the dead of night. It was raining, the drops falling outside his window, ticking off the edge of the roof in an uneven rhythm. Danny was used to rain, both here and away. It was just about always foggy or rainy around East Jeddore. But goddamn it, Danny sure was sick of rain. Rain led to mud. Mud led to memories he didn't want to see. But whenever he sank back into sleep, they were waiting for him, fresh and insistent.

Danny scrubbed a hand over his face, hoping to wake up, shove the memories out. Out of habit, he turned his head on the pillow and looked across the room, momentarily forgetting where he was. He felt an unexpected jolt at the sight of his brothers' bunk bed and two of the boys sleeping in it. Three more slept in the next room. He heard his brothers breathing, almost in time with each other. The easy sound a relief to Danny after so many months of living a half life: too afraid to sleep, too exhausted to stay awake. Besides the boys' gentle snores, he could hear no other sound.

Danny's chest tightened. Then his throat. He slid the pillow from under his head and hugged it over his face, trying to muffle his sobs.

TWO

❧

The sun was hours away; October mornings were dark and cold.
Danny snuck out of bed as quiet as he could and reached for the oil
lamp, but his movements weren't soft enough. As he reached for the door
he heard the pattern of his brothers' breathing change. They were awake,
waiting for the stranger to leave so they could discuss him. Danny had
known it would happen. It broke his heart anyway.

The stairs creaked under his step, the crutch making a harsh clacking
sound against the wood. Not much he could do to keep that quiet. He'd
packed his wooden leg in his trunk before he'd fallen asleep, needing to
get away from it. Now the family would see what was left of him. Not
much. Better to get it all out in the open right away, he figured.

In predawn, the house looked different. Strange how it felt so foreign.
As if he'd been away ten years instead of almost two. He relit the fire, fed it
kindling until it snapped into action, then he stood and took in the flickering shadows of the kitchen. The place smelled wonderful, the air thick with
the sweet breath of yesterday's fresh bread. His mother made a few loaves
almost every day, and the smell of that bread was just one of the millions of
things Danny had thought about when he couldn't face the war a moment

longer. The bread in the trenches was hard as shale most of the time, until it was sunk deep in whatever stew or beans they had.

His mother's bread hid under a cloth on the counter, next to the knife block. Danny cut himself a thick, soft slice, then sunk his teeth into it, moaning quietly with ecstasy. He finished it off, then cut another slice. He considered the rest of the loaf but figured that wasn't quite fair to the rest of them.

Danny heard a small sound at the door. A scratching, then a soft chirp, almost apologetic.

"Cecil," he whispered, surprised at the sudden joy coursing through him.

Cecil's salt and pepper muzzle had turned almost pure white. The black Lab's eyes were milkier than they had been, and his hips wobbled with the stiffness of old age. But when Danny grabbed a coat off the hook and stepped outside, the dog's tail thrashed from side to side, and his ecstatic whines got louder and more excited. His smooth black lips pulled back in an approximation of a smile.

"Hey, boy," Danny said, and at the sound of his voice Cecil threw his head back as if he were about to howl, but Danny set his palm on the hard black skull and grinned. "C'mon, Cess. Let's not wake the whole house."

The sky was beginning to lighten, no longer an infinite black but a velvet indigo, readying the earth for the sun. The tides were low, retreating for another hour or so, Danny figured. As man and dog took their favourite path down to the sea, Cecil hobbled ahead, then circled back as if he couldn't believe Danny was there and had to keep checking. Danny stopped short on the outskirts of the rocky beach, admitting to himself that the slippery unevenness of the stones looked a little beyond his abilities for now. He leaned against a boulder he'd climbed as a boy, dropped his crutch, then slid down until he sat on the ground. Cecil was immediately at his side, licking Danny's face until he couldn't help laughing. God, it felt good to laugh.

"How are you, boy? Miss me?"

Cecil stared at Danny with adoration, his heavy black tail thumping in celebration. He sniffed Danny's hair, his coat, and finally his pants. He spent a little time snuffling at the stump, wrapped within Danny's pant leg.

"Yeah," Danny said. "That's something new, ain't it? I might give you a couple of shoes to chew on, Cess. I won't need 'em."

It was Sunday, so the fishing boat hugged the dock, resting for the day. The others would be getting out of bed soon, curious and eager to see their brother now that he was awake. Cecil lay down and drummed his tail on the earth, then rested his nose on Danny's foot. They stayed like that for ten minutes, the dog dozing, the man staring out at the receding tide, one hand on his companion's sleek black head. He breathed in, filling his lungs with crisp, salty air, welcoming back the cleansing stink of fish.

———

The Twenty-fifth Battalion's mascot, an underfed golden Labrador retriever, made her way through the soldiers, winding around sleeping bodies, sniffing for bits of food that didn't exist. She was a distraction.

"Hey, Minnie," Danny said softly. "How's hunting, girl?"

Her tail's constant wag sped up. She walked to Danny's side and nudged his hand. He didn't mind the lice on her—he probably carried just as many within the seams of his own shirt. He'd given up fighting them. He stroked her neck and she pulled closer to him, then curled up at his side.

"Good idea," he said. Danny stretched out as well as he could, then rested his head on Minnie's bony back. She sighed under him, and they both slept awhile.

Minnie died a few weeks later in Ypres. No one had given her a gas mask when that hateful yellow gas had spilled into the trenches.

———

Cecil's head jerked up. A low growl started deep in the loose folds of his throat.

"What is it, boy?" Danny slid back into the present. He tried to peer around the boulder, but he couldn't see from his position. Cecil's growl rose, and he scrambled to all four paws, hackles raised.

"Okay, okay," Danny said, rolling to his side so he could get up the way the nurses had taught him. "What we got? A porky?"

Cecil sounded furious, but Danny only chuckled when he spotted the intruders. Three young dogs loped down the trail toward them, tails wagging cautiously. They stopped a few feet away, their heads low to the sprouting grass as if scenting it for clues about this mysterious stranger.

"Who's this, Cess?" Danny asked. The dogs came closer at the sound of Danny's voice, optimistically wagging their tails. "Sit," he said, and they all sat. Danny lifted his eyebrows, surprised at the unexpected result. "Well. Don't you boys have good manners."

Cecil stopped growling and sat as well, but he kept his cloudy eyes trained on the other three. Danny wanted to crouch, get to know the dogs, but crouching was out of the question. Too awkward.

"Danny?"

The sun was starting to come up, and despite the lack of light he recognized his twenty-two-year-old brother, Johnny, standing on the path. Johnny was staring at him, a smile plastered on his face. Not a real smile, Danny saw. One he was trying real hard to hold in place.

It was difficult to believe he'd gone almost two years without seeing Johnny. The last time had been on that day at the pier, when Danny'd boarded the ship in his freshly pressed uniform. His mother had cried, his father had stood proud but stiff, trying to maintain a cool expression. The oldest of Danny's brothers had buzzed around him with envy and emotion, and the smallest two had sobbed until their baby blues turned red. After their father, Danny had been the man of the house. The one all the other kids followed. Then he had sailed to war, leaving them crying on the shore.

He and Johnny had been practically inseparable before the war. Now they were like strangers. Johnny seemed older, as though he'd become a man while Danny was away. For the first time Danny wondered what it had been like around here, worrying about him, making do without him.

He kept his voice soft, blending with the morning. "Hey, Johnny. Come here."

Johnny strode down the trail, trying to appear nonchalant, but his eyes were inexorably drawn to the missing leg. Danny let him look. He was going to anyway. Him and everyone else. Danny might as well make it easier on them.

Danny raised a sardonic eyebrow. "Do you want to see it?"

"I don't know," Johnny replied, lifting his gaze. "Should I?"

Danny shrugged. "It ain't pretty, but it's all I got now."

Danny propped himself against the boulder, then watched Johnny's face while he untucked the trouser where his leg should have been. For the first time, Danny worried about his brother's reaction. He undid the folds and hated the way his hands trembled while he did it. They always shook now, even when he was at ease. It seemed strange, to be scared of a little thing like what Johnny'd say after all Danny had been through.

Danny had to be calm. Reassure both of them. He rolled the material back, exposing the ugly pink skin at the end of his stump, about four inches beneath his right knee. The doctors had done what they could, patching it together, sewing it back up when it split apart. Scars crisscrossed like barbed wire, white against the pink.

Johnny stared at it, blinking hard. He didn't meet Danny's eyes.

"What do you think, kid?"

"Does . . . does it hurt?"

He didn't like the sound of Johnny's voice. It had been years since either of them had cried in front of the other, and Johnny sounded close to doing just that. Danny cleared his throat, more confident now that he was back in the older-brother role.

"Nah. Not anymore. Feels strange but hardly hurts anymore. Funny thing is, sometimes my foot hurts. The one that's gone."

Johnny drew nearer, examining the leg. He reached to touch it, then glanced apologetically up at Danny, who nodded.

"Go ahead."

Johnny poked it gently, then prodded a little harder in a few other places. "Feels like a leg still."

"Still is a leg," Danny confirmed. "Just a little shorter."

"Your knee still bend okay?"

"Oh yeah. But I ain't gonna outrun you like I used to, that's for sure."

Johnny took a seat on a facing boulder. "You never did," he muttered, focusing on Danny's face. His eyes flickered with emotions Danny needed to understand. But he knew better than to ask.

"What was it like?" Johnny asked, bold as always. "The war, I mean."

Danny's eyes shot toward the water, and a door slammed shut in his mind. Sweat dampened his palms in that instant, and he was desperate to change the subject.

"Hey, no problem," Johnny said quickly. "We don't have to talk about that."

"Who are these hounds?" Danny asked. His voice was strained, his throat constricted by the effort of holding back an unexpected wave of fear.

"Oh." Johnny frowned and pointed out the pups one by one. "That real dark one's Toby, the one with the white on his tail is Pops, and that's their sister, Betty. They live in the old shed out back. We think their mother got killed by a bobcat. They came through about a year ago and have been here ever since."

The pups got scraps for treats once in a while, but were mostly feral and hunted for their own meals, he explained. Cecil still retained ownership of the doghouse, three and a half walls and a good sturdy roof, packed tight with old blankets. Danny had built it when he was fifteen and Cecil was a puppy. Watching the faithful black lab shuffle arthritically toward the water, Danny realized ten years was just about all Cecil had in him. He was glad he'd come back in time to say goodbye.

Danny stuck a piece of grass in his mouth and chewed on the end. "So, Johnny. What's been going on while I was gone?"

THREE

Near the end of Danny's stay in the Cambridge Military Hospital in Aldershot, England, Captain Johnston had come by to check on him. He'd brought Danny's things, as well as two small boxes. On the top of each was stamped a name. One said Private James Mitchell, the other Private Frederick Arnold.

When Danny got home, he'd tucked the boxes under his bed. For two days they sat patiently between his shoe and his wooden leg, waiting for him to come to terms with what he had to do. By the following Sunday, the silent voices of his two best friends, the wild Irish boys of East Jeddore who would never see her shore again, had forced him to do something about them.

Danny packed the boxes into a sack he hung over his shoulder, then leaned on his crutch and stepped outside. It was raining, as it had been all night, and the mud wriggled down the road in streams like tiny snakes. Danny pulled his cap down and started up the slippery path to his best friends' homes.

From the outside, the Arnolds' house looked abandoned. He knew they were there, though, because he could hear a couple of kids laughing and a dog yapping. It wasn't that the house was in disrepair, it was just gloomy. Could have been the rain, could have been the need for paint. But Danny figured the sadness of the house went far deeper, and he'd never have to ask why. He shuffled up the front walkway, between the skeletal remains of weeds in Mrs. Arnold's unusually neglected flower bed and her unharvested potato patch, and knocked on the door.

It felt strange, standing there, waiting for one of the Arnolds to let him in. As boys they'd roared through that door, barely pausing to take off muddy shoes before thumping up the stairs to Fred's bedroom. Fred, freckled and carrot-coloured, always shared the wooden toys his uncle had made for him. They'd smashed carved horses and carts together, played with little-boy versions of guns. Fred had a huge collection.

The front door was a solid reminder of why he was here. Nothing would ever be the same. He stared at it until the latch clicked and the door creaked open. Mrs. Arnold stood before him, frailer than before, wiping beet-stained hands on her apron. She took one look at Danny and stepped backwards with a whimper.

"What is it, Alice?" came Mr. Arnold's voice, and something twisted in Danny's chest. Mr. Arnold's quick Irish accent was so much like Fred's.

It took her a moment, an inhalation that swept her glistening eyes from Danny's face to his remaining foot. Then she said simply, "Oh, William. It's Danny. Danny's come home."

"Good day, Mrs. Arnold," Danny said, cap in hand. Rain pattered on his head, soaking him through, but he didn't care. He felt safer standing in the rain than he did stepping inside the house.

"Oh, Danny," she said. Her chin quivered before she remembered to stand up straighter. "I'm ever so glad to see ye. Come in out of the rain, darlin'. Ye'll catch your death out there." She bit her lip and motioned for him to come in, then stood to the side so he could hobble through. In the old days he would have barrelled past her. Now he needed the width of the doorframe to contain his body, the sack over his back, and his crutch. Mr. Arnold appeared behind her, a taller, older, thinner version of his son.

"Welcome home, son," he said, and Danny knew how badly they wished they could have been saying those words to Fred instead of him.

"A spot of tea?" Mrs. Arnold asked.

"That'd be swell," he said, then he followed Mr. Arnold into the sitting room.

Everything looked exactly the same as it always had except for the large framed photograph of Fred sitting on the mantel. Fred in uniform, proud and raring to go to war. *Give those Germans a taste o' the Irish,* was what he'd said.

"Here you go," Mrs. Arnold said, carrying a tray of tea and apple tarts, just as in the old days. How strange. Danny already thought of them as the old days. Another lifetime. She placed the tray on a table between them, then she sat across from Danny, her hands linked together on her lap. She and her husband sat stiffly, an inch apart from each other. The Arnolds stared at Danny, and he stared back, not knowing how to start.

"Yer mother must be so happy to have ye home," she finally said.

"Yes, ma'am," Danny said. "She's learning to put up with me again, I figure."

"And yer fat'er, too. His sermons have oft remarked upon our sons being far . . . too far away."

Another awkward silence filled the room.

Danny cleared his throat. "I'm sorry Fred's not with me. Truly I am. I'm so sorry he isn't here."

Mrs. Arnold blinked a few times then smiled, but Danny saw the mother behind the mask. She was a little brown-haired woman, not particularly attractive, but efficient in an appealing way. Out of the three, she had been the one mother to always ensure the boys had enough to eat, but not always scones. The Arnolds had a small, hardy orchard, and Mrs. Arnold could work magic with that fruit. Besides all different kinds of apples, she grew rhubarb and plums, and from the bushes she plucked raspberries, blackberries, foxberries, and blueberries, which she made into jams and pies that disappeared quickly. Her daughters often brought the finished products to neighbouring homes, feeding the elderly and the infirm. It was every good Christian's responsibility, she had always said, to provide for those who could not—or would not—provide for themselves.

Her voice was soft when she spoke again. He'd never heard her speak like that. Maybe she reserved that tone for grown-ups, and it was the first time she'd used it with him. He would have preferred hearing her scold.

"Ye're a good lad, Danny. Oh, what I'd have given to have my boy here, but no matter how long the day, the evening will come. We will survive."

Mr. Arnold was frowning at Danny's remaining foot. "How's the leg?" he asked.

"No idea, sir. I'm sure it's having a fine time in France right now. I haven't seen it in months."

Mr. Arnold had never been overly fond of humour. He frowned. "'Twas the other one I meant, boy."

Danny's mouth twitched. "I know, sir. Sorry. It's fine, thanks."

"Thank you for the letter ye sent," Mrs. Arnold said. "Meant a great deal to us, it did, gettin' that letter from ye."

Danny cleared his throat. "I've, uh, I've brought you his things."

He leaned down to pull Fred's box from the sack, then stood, balancing awkwardly against the sofa arm without his crutch. They both rose, and Mrs. Arnold stretched out her hands. She brushed small, flickering fingers over the top of the box, then folded it against her breast as if it were a babe. Eventually she pried open the lid and peered inside. Both parents seemed to slouch at the same moment, like air leaking out of twin balloons.

"Oh, William," Mrs. Arnold whispered, beginning to weep. "What a sin. What a sin." Her husband came around from behind and wrapped his long arms around her, the box held between them.

A promise broken.

They forgot all about Danny, and he didn't wait for them to remember. He'd heard men cry before. Lots of men. He didn't need to hear the Arnolds' grief. He politely excused himself, then headed back outside.

It would be worse at the Mitchells', he knew. They had already had more than their fair share of loss. They lived the farthest from the Bakers, so when Danny had fallen or hurt himself in some unpredictable way, Mrs. Mitchell had been like a second mother to him. Danny's mother had done the same for Jimmy. In effect, they had both lost a son that day.

He was nervous about how this visit would go. Would they still think of him as Danny, or would they see him as the one who came home when Jimmy hadn't? Would they still love him, or would their familiar faces try to mask resentment? He would understand that. How many times had Danny wished he could have replaced Jimmy on that stinking field, taken that bullet himself?

The Arnolds' front door had been a faded white. The Mitchells' door was freshly painted as it was every other year, the trim a festive red to match the shutters. Floyd Mitchell would have been sure to do that, come hell or high water. It was Floyd's message to the world that the Mitchells were doing just fine, thank you very much.

There should have been music coming from within, the sounds of fiddles and singing. Every one of their twelve children had learned fiddle, including Jimmy. But three of them had died of pneumonia and Jimmy's older brother had drowned five years before the war had even begun. So the Mitchells were down to seven children. The next oldest child was seventeen, and she was a daughter, already married. The one blessing the Mitchells could count on was they wouldn't have to send anyone else to war in the next little while.

But Jimmy, big, jolly Jimmy, everyone's best friend, well, he was worth about four.

Danny stood at the door for a long time, lost in panic and grief. His throat felt thick and his hands shook, slick with rain and sweat. *God, Jimmy. This should have been you, bringing my stuff to my family. Not me, damn it. You, Jimmy.*

He couldn't knock. He couldn't see them, talk to them, look at them and not see Jimmy. He'd pushed the memories of his best friend to a safe little spot in the back of his mind, shoving them away every time they tried to pop back out. But Jimmy was front and centre now, grinning at him, joshing him about bein' chicken. *I ain't chicken. I just can't,* Danny told him.

Danny lowered the sack from his shoulder. He'd leave the box here for them to find. They'd understand.

But the door opened. How she'd known, Danny would never know, but Mrs. Mitchell was there in that moment, peeking through the door. When she saw Danny her face went white, then red, then she started to cry.

"Danny! Danny! Oh, my dear Danny! God has brought ye home to me, love. Oh, how I've needed ye here with me, Danny! Come in! Come in!"

She was at least a foot shorter than he, and she'd been rounder before, but she held him tight and they wept together, holding each other up.

"I'm so sorry, Mrs. Mitchell. I'm so sorry. I couldn't save him. I couldn't—"

"Danny. Danny. I've been awake every night since your letter." She reached up and swept her hands over his cheeks, drying his tears. "Let me see you. Oh, Danny. I've been prayin' for you to come home. I couldn't bear it, to lose you both. Come in, love, and sit. Come and warm your bones. I've such a yearnin' to hear your voice, lad. I've such a need!"

They went into the sitting room, which was nothing like the Arnolds', though it too featured a framed photograph of their son in full uniform. Jimmy's chest was puffed up, his cheeky grin breaking through the serious facade. That's how Danny wanted to remember him. Not heaving and jerking in Danny's bloody hands. Not suddenly still, with a tiny black circle cut through the centre of his helmet.

It was somewhat of a relief not to see Mr. Mitchell there as well. Jimmy had resembled his father, joked the same way. Mr. Mitchell had that same bumping laugh. Danny guessed he was probably out in the shed, most likely, thick hands slick with grease.

"Oh, look at yer poor leg, child. Look at t'at. What a sin. What a terrible sin. Does it pain ye? Can I get you somet'ing? Oh, dear, dear Danny."

Somehow it didn't bother him when she cooed over him like that, though he couldn't stand it from his own mother. It was like when he was small, and he took comfort from it. She bustled around him, keeping active, bringing cookies, touching his hair. Jimmy's had been coal black and straight as straw, but Danny's was brown, with a slight wave. When she couldn't think of anything else to do, she sat beside him and tried to hold her hands still in her lap.

"I brought his things," Danny said, laying the wooden box on her lap, but her hands clenched the soft white folds of her apron, avoiding the box. "The captain gave it to me when I was in the hospital. It's for you to keep."

She seemed to shrink. Everything but her eyes. They glowed with such sadness Danny wanted to run, to get away from it. But she needed him.

"You know what, Mrs. Mitchell?" he said. He put his hands over hers, trying to still the tremors—his and hers. "There's nothing in here that is Jimmy. I mean, sure. There are things, like photographs, notes, they gave us each a Bible, and there's maybe a lucky coin or something. But the real Jimmy? He's right there." He pointed at the photograph. "And he's in my head." He put both hands to his ears and pressed hard as emotions swelled inside him, but he was helpless to stop them. "He's always in my head." He clenched his teeth, blinking hard. "God, I miss him."

Mrs. Mitchell placed the box on the chair beside her. This time it was she who reached for Danny's hands and held on tight.

"He's in mine too, Danny. I've been missing him and crying over him until I wonder there's a tear left in me head. But I t'ank God ye're here, darling. I'm so glad He sent ye home. When I look at ye, I remember so much laughter, so many times you t'ree caused trouble and made me shake me head wit' wonder when ye didn't kill yerselves with some fool game ye played. I see ye floatin' away in the ol' bateau, I see ye comin' in late at night, stinkin' o' fish. An' I see ye all dressed up in your fancy uniforms, all t'ree of ye when you were wit' Fred. But t'at's as far as I go." She squeezed his hands again. "We've a job to do now, Danny, you an' me. We've a need to make new memories. I'll watch ye grow up an' I'll wish he was wit' ye. I'll watch ye become a good husband an' father, an' I'll wish I could hold my own wee grandchildren on my knee. But first of all, I'll t'ank God every day that ye came home. Every single day."

She leaned forward and kissed his tear-soaked cheek.

"I miss him so much," he whispered.

"As ye should, darlin'. He would've missed ye just as much. He loved ye well, my lad." Her voice was soft. Tender. "He loved ye well."

A while later, Mr. Mitchell came into the room. He still wore a smile reminiscent of his son's, but it was subdued in comparison. The twinkle in his eyes had faded since Danny'd last seen him, but when Mr. Mitchell's eyes met those of his wife, it sparked back.

"Danny, me boy," he said. Danny stood and reached for a handshake just as Mr. Mitchell stepped back in surprise. "Jaysus, Mary, and Joseph, Danny. Where'd you leave your leg, man?"

"France, sir," Danny said.

Mr. Mitchell's eyes softened. He stepped closer and hugged Danny tightly against him, then he spoke into Danny's ear.

"We left a lot of t'ings in France, didn't we? Terrible trial for us all, t'at war. A terrible, terrible trial. Ah well. We'll be fine, though, given time. It's the turning of the tide, son. Nothin' to be done about it now." He hesitated a moment, and Danny knew the pain he was trying to bite back. Knew it so well. "But oh, we're that glad to see ye back, my lad. Welcome home."

FOUR

In the muted hour before daylight, Danny sat at the kitchen table by the oil lamp, a steaming cup of tea warming the palms of his hands. How strange that everything around him was exactly the same as it had been and he was so entirely different. Same creaking board on the floor, same rust stain by the window latch, even the same melody humming through his mother's lips as she worked around the kitchen. He was the only stranger here.

He stared into the teacup, losing himself in the soft white swirls as they rose from the heat, condensed on his chin. Now that the brutal shock of being back at home was easing, gentler thoughts had begun to surface. Hints of hope blinking through the clouds. He let himself remember the twinkle of pretty eyes. *Audrey.* He'd lost his best friends, his leg, and any innocence he might have had as a boy, but he'd found Audrey. She had become the one fixed thing in his life, the buoy he clung to when the blackness of memories lapped at him, threatened to swallow him whole. He loved her—or at least he assumed it was love, since she'd become the most important thing to him. Sometimes he felt slightly guilty when he thought about her. Had God—or whatever it was his father preached about at that pulpit—given her to Danny in exchange for what he'd lost?

It was five a.m., and his father, Johnny, and Thomas were out on the Atlantic, bringing in their catch. All but Danny. He could almost hear their conversations in his head, the hollow voices bouncing off the water as they toiled and teased, the simple, companionable way of men working hard. He envied his brothers the cold slice of the wind against their faces, the rise and fall of the deep swells, the occasional humps of whales gliding by in the summer months. He missed being one of the voices dropping into the fog.

Now he stayed home with his mother, along with the younger children. The little ones were all still asleep, oblivious to what would someday be their responsibility, but his mother clanged around in the kitchen, clearing up, getting the next meal ready to go. There was always something for her to do. She was a strong woman. He'd never once seen her look weak. No, that wasn't true. He'd seen it twice: when he'd headed off to war, and when he'd returned.

"How's your tea, Danny? Shall I top it up for you?"

He held up his empty cup. "Thanks."

She took it and filled it, then brought her own over and sat across the table from him. Mother and son eyed each other nervously, then she dove in.

"How are you feeling, Danny?"

"I'm all right."

"Do you want to talk about anything that happened over there?"

He frowned, his defensive wall rising automatically. "Like what?"

She blinked quickly, and he knew she'd noticed his swift reaction. Of course she had. She knew him so well. Her fingertips tapped against the side of her teacup. "You don't have to tell me anything that hurts, Danny. I can only imagine what it was like—we've read the papers after all—and I don't particularly want to know how horrible it was. But was there anything that you enjoyed? Anything at all that made you smile out there? Was every moment terrible?"

"No," he said carefully. "It wasn't all bad." He caught himself doing the same thing with his fingers as she was doing, then purposefully set them flat on the table. "I made some good friends over there. Of course most of them died," he said, raising one eyebrow, "but I hope a few are still alive."

His mother's lips drew into a little bow, and she glanced down, drying her hands on the apron covering her lap. "Do they live around here?"

"Yeah. Halifax. There was Tommy Joyce, for one. He was a good guy. Quality. And Mick was my buddy over there. He's a newspaper man. Always telling stories."

Her face was heartbreaking. He could see his own pain in her eyes. "I'm glad you had friends," she said.

"You had to have friends over there. Otherwise you'd lose your mind." His voice was cold. He hated taking it out on her, but she was there. She had asked.

Her gaze dropped to the tabletop.

"The best part of it was getting mail," he told her, needing to fill the empty space between them. He was nervous about having this kind of conversation, opening up a raw wound all over again, but a part of him wanted to tell his mother everything, let it all spill onto the table so she could clean it up as she always did. "When you sent packages it was a terrific surprise, and hearing the news made such a difference to me over there."

"I told your aunts and uncles to write to you. And Johnny did too, didn't he?"

"They all did. I really don't know what I would have done without those letters. It was some lonely out there. Oh, and . . ." He eyed his mother, teasing, daring her to ask.

"What?"

"Someone else wrote me letters."

"Oh? Who was that?"

"Her name's Audrey. Audrey Poulin."

His mother clapped her hands together and beamed at him. "You met a girl! Oh, Danny! I'm so happy for you! Tell me all about her!"

So he did. He explained how the soldiers had stopped to fix her wagon's broken wheel.

"Rain was coming, so Audrey invited us to sleep in their barn a few miles off. She and I struck up a conversation. Got to know each other pretty well." Those eyes twinkling for him, the soft pucker of her lips drawing into a smile, then closing again just before he kissed her . . . "In the morning the battalion had to leave, but she gave me her picture and address, and we started writing. Mom?"

"Mm-hmm?"

He hesitated, imagining Audrey's face. It had blurred slightly in his memory after so long but still hovered there in spirit. He focused on the brown curls that framed her pale face and the slow blink of her eyes.

"I fell in love with her. She's the most wonderful girl I've ever met. Beautiful and smart and unafraid. There I was in the darkest place on earth, and she was like the sun." He beamed at his mother. "So I asked her to marry me."

"Danny!" She leapt from her chair and was around the table before he knew it, her arms wrapped around him, her voice ringing with happiness. "Oh, my boy! My baby's getting married! So tell me more. Is she Canadian? Is she back here now? When will we meet her?"

He shook his head. "No, she's not Canadian." He watched his mother's reaction closely. "She's from England."

She tried valiantly not to react, but he saw the slight twitch of one eyebrow and steeled himself. He'd known this would be a little difficult. Not so much with his own family, but with the others in the area. Around here, everyone married neighbours.

"Well, that's nice," she said. He could practically see her planning out how to explain this slight complication to Danny's father. "And we will all be so happy to meet her. When will she come over?"

"I think in the summer. We need to raise the money for her transport first."

"We'll have her here before you know it. Oh, Danny! How wonderful!"

"You're gonna love her. And she's gonna love you, too."

His mother rolled her eyes, primping her hair as if he were a mirror. "Do you really think so? Oh, I'll have to make sure everything is perfect for her. But then again, she probably won't even notice what I do. She'll just be so happy to be with you it won't matter. Oh, Danny. I'm so happy for you. Your father will be thrilled."

Daniel Sr., as far as Danny knew, didn't have an emotional bone in his body. The first week he'd been home, his father had said very little. His mother was trapped between the two men's stubborn senses of pride, and Danny could see it was hard on her. She gave her husband nudges, encouraging him to talk with his son, but Daniel Sr. was resistant, and Danny refused to make it easy on him. He was tired of the way his father turned away whenever he limped into the room. He was tired of hearing his father ask Danny's brothers to do chores Danny used to do. He was tired of the silent scorn.

A couple of weeks after Danny got home, Daniel Sr. finally broached the subject. He had started to build a dinghy, so Danny took it over, deciding he could at least do that, figured maybe he'd feel a little more normal if he was being useful in some way. His father came down to help Danny get organized, and it was slow work, since Danny couldn't lift what he used to lift. He was strong enough, just didn't have the balance for it. But he was going to finish what his father had started, no matter how long it took. He always did. When they were done getting ready, they sat on a couple of stools and discovered Danny's mother had brought them each a lemonade. She'd set it on a table between them.

"That hits the spot," Danny said. He set down his glass and glanced around, wanting a smoke to go with his drink. The tobacco can sat on the grass by his father's feet, so Danny leaned forward to grab a pinch, then he drizzled it down the centre of a small white paper he pulled from his pocket. He licked the edge and twisted the ends closed.

"Mm-hmm. Sure does," his father replied, looking anywhere but at his son.

Daniel Sr. had never been a talkative man. He preferred to give sermons and turn away from unpleasant things. Like his crippled son. Danny let his father sit in the awkward quiet. He didn't offer anything.

The older man finally spoke while Danny lit the cigarette. "So, son. How are you finding being at home?"

Danny took a deep drag from the cigarette and a breeze wafted by, stirring the sparks from the tip. "I like being here just fine, sir."

The pause was uncomfortable again, but Danny said nothing. It had taken his father a long time to work up to this. Too long, damn it. The old man hadn't gone to war. He could suffer a bit.

"I imagine it's much different from how you've been living the past couple of years."

Danny nodded, his mind automatically going to the hungry, sucking trench mud that had swallowed his feet. Both feet. How he'd look down and see nothing below his thighs but sludge. He could still feel the frozen weights connected to those legs, hidden under that filth, and he wondered vaguely what had happened to the one he'd lost. They'd probably left it to rot in the mud. The thick, bloody mud that tripped men, holding them down until they drowned in it. After all, what difference did one man's leg make?

"Are you glad to be back?"

The man had no idea what Danny had seen, what he'd done. He had no images in his mind of death, blood, fire, screaming. All he saw was his son, who'd come home before a lot of other soldiers had.

When Danny spoke, his voice was shrapnel sharp. "You know I would have stayed if I wasn't hurt, right? You know I didn't just come running back with my tail between my legs. Or . . . pardon me. Behind my leg."

Daniel Sr. met his son's eyes, and the two men stared at each other until something in his father's expression collapsed. His whole body seemed to sag just a little, and tears shone in his eyes like sunlight off the sea. Danny had never seen his father like that. He looked much older than his forty-odd years.

"Is that what you thought, Danny?" His voice was almost a whisper.

It was too late for Danny to backtrack now. He'd said it, the words were out there, and goddammit, he'd meant them. "Doesn't matter. I'm back. I'll be just fine now."

His dad hung his head and pressed swollen fingers to his face.

Hauling nets and battling the sea for so long had invited arthritis into the man's hands and knees; Danny's own hands often felt stiff from the beginnings of the same affliction. When Daniel Sr. looked up a moment later, the familiar posture had resumed, his head held a little straighter, shoulders back. Danny sat up taller without even thinking about it. For just a moment, the men's eyes locked, and Danny was sure his father saw right through him. Then the older man blinked, and the contact returned to normal.

"I believe that, son," Daniel Sr. said, showing no emotion at all. "You're strong. Always have been. You'll be just fine now," he repeated.

AUDREY

— April 1916 —

FIVE

උ∿ච

Audrey hadn't seen many soldiers up close before. Not back here, in this quiet piece of land that never did anything. She'd seen the battalions from a distance, even heard explosions when the wind blew the right way. When she spotted a dozen or so men marching along the road, she knew they were headed off to war, just like Laurent, her cousin. Just like him, they marched with their backs straight, heads held high, their minds and hearts full of blind courage. And just like him they were unconcerned, apparently, with family left behind. Just like Laurent, very few of them, she expected, would ever come marching back.

She leaned over the broken wheel of her wagon and feigned interest in it, taking the opportunity to study these new men out of the corner of her eye as they drew near. Of course they would stop. What man wouldn't stop to help a woman in need? Then again, they were marching with purpose. Maybe they weren't allowed . . .

The officer up front gave her a little bow. "*Bonjour! Est-ce que nous—*"

It was painful, listening to him stumble through the language. She smiled gently. "I can speak English, monsieur, if it would be easier."

He beamed at her. "Well, that's great. For both of us. Now, may I offer some assistance?"

English. Such a relief to hear English spoken again after all this time. It wasn't *English* English, but at least the words were the same. Audrey glanced at her grandmère, who looked quickly away, hiding inside the folds of her black shawl. Céleste Poulin was from the old world, and she didn't trust anyone. Especially these days. Audrey took a deep breath. After living such a secluded life for the past ten years, she had to summon the courage to actually speak to a stranger. But she had no choice. She stepped forward, clenching her thick green skirt for reassurance.

"We would be most obliged, sir. My grandmère and I, we were coming from town and hit a bump." She gestured toward the wagon, hitched to their tired grey mare. The nag's sorry head drooped in the shadow of a tree, and Audrey felt strangely mortified by its ragged appearance. "The wheel came off."

She was distracted by the movements of two soldiers behind the officer. One was grinning directly at her, waggling his eyebrows with suggestion. Another was staring at her as well, but his expression was less aggressive. He appeared to be making an attempt to shut the other fellow up. Audrey smoothed down her skirt, feeling flustered. The second man was uncommonly handsome, an oddity in these parts—in her life, actually.

"Oh! Well," the officer said, giving a gallant bow, "we'd be happy to help." He turned toward the men. "Baker! Joyce! MacDonald!" he called.

The second soldier, the one she couldn't seem to peel her eyes from, set his cap on straight, then trotted toward the wagon with two others beside him. It appeared none of the men were strangers to fixing simple mechanical problems like this, so Audrey stood back to admire their handiwork. One went to retrieve the wheel, lying on its side on the road, while the other two leaned down and assessed the situation.

"Thank you so much, sirs," Audrey said.

The handsome soldier pushed his cap back and looked up at her, and in her mind she reached for her artist's palette. His eyes were the deepest shade of blue, a vivid, lush blue that made something in Audrey's chest take flight.

For a moment she forgot where she was, and her imaginary brush swirled a handful of crushed blue wildflowers and vinegar together, then she thickened the dye with yolk. She'd add in just enough charcoal, since she saw deep water, not flowers in the soldier's eyes. Mr. Black—*Richard* to her mother—had taught her that, how she must see the colour she wanted first, then study what she had already before adding a sprinkle of darkness or light. Never too much at once. The first time she'd made blue with Richard Black, she'd been small, maybe six. His big, stained hands had closed over hers like weathered gloves, showing her how to use a pestle and mortar, helping her make dust from ashes, then magically turn her dye from sky in the morning to sky at night. She'd watched the colour transform as she stirred, then she'd looked up at him in wonder, seeing the same colour reflected in his eyes. It always fascinated her that his last name was Black when everything she saw in him was vivid, breathing colour.

At night Audrey curled up between her mother and Richard, safe and loved, listening to him sing some old song to her.

> *"D'ye ken John Peel with his coat so gay?*
> *D'ye ken John Peel at the break of day?*
> *D'ye ken John Peel when he's far far away with his*
> *hounds and his horn in the morning?"*

Then his big hand would move to her mother's cheek, those blue eyes would hold her mother's. "*Ma chèrie,* Pascale," he'd say softly to her, but she'd shake her head.

"Only English, Richard," Pascale said, gesturing toward Audrey. "Teach us English."

The soft lines of his face would ease even further, then he'd quietly sing,

> *"Oh, promise me that someday you and I*
> *Will take our love together to some sky*
> *Where we may be alone and faith renew,*

And find the hollows where those flowers grew,
Those first sweet violets of early spring,
Which come in whispers, thrill us both, and sing
Of love unspeakable that is to be;
Oh, promise me! Oh, promise me!"

Then, one day, Richard was gone. At first Audrey had been confident they'd see him again, that he'd simply gone off seeking the solitude Audrey herself needed at times. But his blue, blue eyes, his unkempt black hair and matching beard never returned. Eventually another man came and took Pascale's hand, stepped into the place where Richard's shoes had been. And another after him. Pascale was never without a partner for long, but Richard was the only one who stayed with Audrey. The sadness that came to her mother's eyes every time Audrey asked about Richard made it too painful to press her further, but the question had never gone away. *Is he my father? Is he the reason I see colours and lines and shading everywhere I look?*

"Baker," one of the soldiers grunted, rolling the heavy wooden wheel ahead of him. Audrey's thoughts went back to the men on the road. "Eyes in your head, man."

The man at whom she'd been staring earlier jerked his gaze away, and she was delighted to see a warm flush rise up his neck and into his cheeks. He muttered something to the other soldier, who chuckled, but something about his tone assured her that it wasn't rudely meant.

With a groan, the men heaved up the axle. Two more came to help, squatting under the wagon and pushing up with their shoulders. They were strong men, but the sun was hot and they were sweating by the time the wheel was on. As they stood to go, the sunlight blinked out, blocked by a storm cloud, and a sudden gust flipped up the men's woolen coat-tails. Rain was on its way, and from the glower of the clouds, it didn't plan on settling into a mild shower.

"Yep," an older soldier from the group muttered. He was squinting up at the sky, assessing. "Soon then."

The soldiers walked back to their place on the road, and Audrey panicked. The man they'd called Baker was the last to go, but she wanted him to stay longer. How could she possibly meet a man like this, then lose him just as quickly? She glanced at her grandmère, trying to disguise her desperation.

"Peut-on dormir dans la grange ce soir?" she whispered. *"Il va pleurir."*

The old woman narrowed her eyes, dark with suspicion as always.

"Que ferait le Seigneur Jésus Christ? Aurait-il les faire dormir sous la pluie?" Audrey asked, playing the card Céleste couldn't fight. It didn't seem like too much to ask. They would come to no harm having a dozen men sleep in the barn, after all. The old woman nodded once, and relief surged through Audrey.

"Sir," she said, addressing the officer in charge, "it looks as if it shall rain tonight."

"Yep," repeated the man on the road.

She saw Baker glare at the weatherman, then turn back to her, apparently wanting to hear what she had to say. She imagined that—considering all the time these men spent together—they must miss simple conversation with other people. She could think of a million things to talk about with Baker. Anything to break up the monotony of her life.

"We have a barn two miles along this road," she informed the officer, tucking a light brown curl under her green head scarf. The rest of her hair she let bounce around her shoulders, but this one was getting in her eyes, bothering her. Especially now that the wind was picking up. "There is plenty of shelter for you and your men to spend the night, if you'd like."

The officer's neat black eyebrows lifted. "Oh. Well, I wouldn't want to impose, mademoiselle . . ." He left the sentence unfinished until she picked it up.

"Oh, it's 'miss.' My grandmère is French, not me. I am Audrey Poulin. I'm from Sussex," she said, feeling heat race into her cheeks. How wonderful it felt to be able to speak her own language again! "And I assure you, sir, that it would be no imposition at all. It is the least we can do to thank you."

The officer glanced back at his men, and Audrey couldn't miss the hope in their expressions. They seemed so tired. So worn down. She felt an urge to clean them, feed them, make them laugh.

"The loft has fresh hay," she assured them. "And we have extra blankets."

"If you're sure it's no trouble," Captain Johnston said. He frowned skeptically at the sky. "We'd be in your debt."

The soldier named Baker blew out his breath, then caught himself, but Audrey noticed. Even if no one else did, she did.

"Not at all, sir," she said, smiling at Baker and letting her eyes dance for him. "We are more than happy to help."

The ancient horse was painfully slow. Audrey feared she might die of embarrassment as she chirped it forward, tickling the reins against its swayed back. Her grandmère sat beside her up front, muttering antique obscenities into her scarf about Englishmen, accusing Audrey of who knew what with her eyes. Audrey had learned to take it all in stride these past ten years. The old woman's blood had always been thick with suspicion. Every time her grandmère cast eyes on her, she knew the old woman was reminded of Audrey's wild-hearted mother and her ill-fated dash to freedom. Sometimes Audrey wondered which had come first: her grandmère's bitterness or her mother's escape to England so long before.

The soldiers marched beside them, dutifully quiet, the only sounds in the air being the shuffling of tired leather soles and the crunching of hooves and wagon wheels over pebbles. The captain moved ahead to lead the horse around holes in the old road, and while Audrey knew she could have done it on her own, she was glad not to have to bother. She was tired of the horse. Of the wagon. Of the muttered black criticism constantly dribbling in her direction. Of the dead farmland that produced nothing anymore but misery now that there was no one left to work it.

Once upon a time Audrey had laughed out loud and danced, though other children her age had passed through her days like clouds. Her mother and Richard Black had been her best friends, and the lively musicians with whom they'd spent Audrey's early years had been more like playmates than adults. She'd never stepped foot into an actual school. Her friends had taught her how to speak English, and she'd learned to read by peering over Richard's shoulder when he read out loud from old books, regaling her with wild tales of adventure. Cold nights huddled together around a fire often consisted of individualized history lessons, when the friends remembered how things were different, when their parents and grandparents had done such and such. There was never any talk of Audrey learning mathematics, for none of them had a coin to add to another. But she learned music and song and art, and she'd known both friendship and love.

Even as her mother lay dying, she knew a kind of love. She sat by her mother's bedside for hours at a time, and at night her little back curled against her mother's chest. The tender fingers playing in Audrey's hair thinned, their caresses became vague. When her mother's beautiful, weak voice seemed to tremble more than form actual words, Audrey took over, telling the nighttime stories she knew so well. Her mother would sigh at the familiar tales, her warm breath tickling Audrey's neck just under her ear. The breaths tickled more slowly as sleep claimed her, and the twig-like fingers stilled in Audrey's light brown tangles. And still Audrey told the stories, needing to hear the endings said out loud.

She knew her mother was dying, though all the playmates denied it during the daylight. *Your mother will dance forever! Your mother will never leave you!* they said, and in her need for any kind of love, she forgave them all their lies. It ended up that none of them were quite loving enough to take her under their wing permanently after she became an orphan, but they did their duty by bringing the ten-year-old to her grandparents' farm.

Back then, life hadn't been as drudging or as dark. Her grandpère had run an active farm, and he'd spent a good deal of time teaching Audrey how to tend the animals while staying out of his wife's way. Young local men came to work when it was time for harvest, helping in the fields, and Audrey tested her fledgling flirting skills on a couple, but they left her alone. Once in a while her bossy cousin Laurent came to visit for a few weeks. He was five years her senior, and despite Audrey's arguments, he casually fell into the role of her big brother until it was time for him to leave again.

Laurent wasn't like her friends in England. He was serious and quiet, and his upper lip tightened to near invisibility whenever he was forced to hold in arguments. He never fought with their grandparents, and he quietly informed Audrey that it was not her place to argue with them, either. She must do as she was told, he said, and when she complained that their grandmère was a wicked, evil woman, he quieted her with one sharp look. He wasn't fun—he rarely laughed—but he was her mother's brother's son, and Audrey occasionally saw a flash of her mother in his one dimple.

Audrey had absolutely no wish to be alone with Céleste. She did what was required, cooking and cleaning, taking care of the old woman's demands, but when all was done, she infuriated her grandmère by racing outside to be with Laurent and grandpère. Audrey worked much harder out of doors, pretending to be a boy, stacking wood after Laurent chopped it, carrying heavy bags of feed and flour from the wagon to the barn or larder, but she didn't mind the work. At least she never had to suffer undue criticism when she was with them.

And when she was done with her work, Audrey painted. Using the soft edges of twigs and grass, bits of material, or her fingers, she created her own flowers and birds and trees, even tried to remember her mother through the strokes. Grandpère had patted her on the head, saying her art was very pretty. Sometimes he came back from the woods with a different berry or flower, adding to her paint ingredients. Whenever he did that, he bent at the waist and reminded her that although he knew painting made her happy, he didn't ever want her to show her creations to her grandmère. She would not appreciate them, he said, since she would consider painting to be an idle activity, a waste of time.

When Audrey was eighteen, a tree had fallen on grandpère. He'd gone hunting, and two days later Audrey had discovered him trapped under the heavy trunk. His hip had been fractured badly, and there was nothing anyone could do. She'd had to run for help a mile away, but by the time she returned to him, all there was left for the neighbour to do was cart him to the churchyard for burial.

Then the war had hit. Laurent had only ever hugged her once, and it happened on the day he'd come to the farm in his soldier's uniform, wanting to bid them adieu. He'd stared awkwardly down at her, and Audrey had never understood why they had both been so sad. After he left, though, he never came back. Audrey had no choice but to suffer her grandmère's grating old age all by herself. She had no other friends, nothing to do with her life but flee to the nearby woods and try to remember her mother's stories.

Her grandpère should have been more careful. He should have had her with him even, though she probably couldn't have helped him anyway. After he was gone, she missed his quiet presence, but she couldn't quite find it in her heart to forgive the old man, since his negligence had left her alone with dear, spiteful Céleste. And once everyone else was gone, the old woman had done her best to drain the life out of her granddaughter.

In Audrey's mind, Céleste and the war had killed everything. Even Audrey's art had changed. In the past she'd avidly collected petals, leaves, and berries, boiling and smashing them into the shades she desired, mixing them with either egg yolks and water or flour and water, depending on what was more available, then she'd captured the brilliant colours of the world flourishing in the fields and the forests beyond. Now if she wanted to play with anything other than greys or browns, she had to dig deep into her memory to find a model.

But as the wagon creaked along beside the marching men, she felt a surge of hope. Now that Baker had appeared, she had a new muse.

She wanted to talk with the soldiers—with Baker, really. And the more she thought, the more she became aware that it was something greater than a *want*. It was a *need*. She glanced quickly over and saw him talking with the man beside him, a shorter, darker fellow. They both were laughing at whatever Baker had said, but their expressions were light, happy. She focused her attention straight ahead again, enjoying the give and take of his voice. When she looked again, Baker's smile was for her, so she gave him one as well. All she wanted was for this damn horse to get moving, so she could find some excuse to speak with him.

It felt like hours before they arrived at their beaten-down house. Once it had been a bright, quick building, buzzing with efficiency and prosperity. But after her grandpère had died, and all the workers had gone off to join the army, the place had fallen apart with only the two of them left. For a while some of the villagers had stopped in to help, but Céleste and her anger had worn them down. They stopped coming, stopped caring. All that was left now for Céleste and Audrey was the old horse, a couple of stupid goats who ate anything and everything they could see—including Audrey's paper and pencils—and a healthy flock of talkative chickens. Other than that, the place felt as dead as the flat, ugly fields that stretched for miles all around.

Clouds slid in and the wind rose, tasting of rain. Ignoring Céleste's warning glare, Audrey stopped outside the barn and hopped off the wagon's bench, landing lightly on her worn brown boots.

"This way," she said. She led the soldiers under the overhang that extended outside the barn's door, then through the splintering doorframe. Céleste never came into the barn anymore. She hadn't spent much time there before, but now there was no cause for her to visit at all. So the barn was Audrey's, and she shared it with the cats and birds, the horse and goats. She kept her art and her hoarded supplies in a back corner of the building, sheltering it from her grandmère's disapproval, keeping it from being offended. Audrey's art was a private, delicate entity, an expression of lines, shades, and colours that came from somewhere she never shared. The colours came from nature, the paper came from generous salesmen who felt they could part with scraps, the brushes she'd made herself from twigs, straw, animal hair . . . even her own fingers and hair when she needed a specific texture. Céleste had no right casting a shadow over any of it.

"Shoo," she said, waving away the black and white cat always prowling the entry. The tom was skittish and missing half an ear, and he was the only cat uninterested in her touch. She didn't mind. It only made sense that, like her, the cats had their own lives to lead. They didn't necessarily want her involved. She understood that. She understood only too well.

The cat fled and a couple of doves panicked, flapping up to a higher rafter to better observe the battalion's arrival. The wind pushed against the wall, making the place tremble, but when Audrey checked, the soldiers didn't seem bothered by it. Nor did they appear to notice the somewhat stale smell. To them it must have seemed a welcome shelter. They climbed the ladder to the loft, dropped their packs, and settled in.

"I thank you," Captain Johnston said. "We shall be invisible to you, I promise. Now don't let us keep you."

"Nonsense," Audrey said, suddenly afraid of being dismissed. She glanced at Baker, but he was busy with the dark-haired soldier. "I shall put some food together for you."

"Oh, there's no need. We have our supplies—"

"It's easily done, sir." She dipped the smallest of curtsies, flushed with a new sense of purpose. "I'll be back within the hour."

Baker glanced up as she left, and this time she pretended not to notice.

The sky swirled in layers, looking impatient, and Audrey hurried to the house, determined to find something in their meagre stock. Eggs were always plentiful. Sausage, well, no. There was barely enough for Céleste and her. But she had made bread the day before, having planned to deliver a couple of loaves to the neighbouring farm, and she had made jam the week before that, so the soldiers would receive an evening breakfast.

From her corner, a silently furious Céleste watched her work.

"I must feed them," Audrey explained.

"Nous n'avons pas assez," her grandmère objected.

"We have enough."

"Non."

The eggs, scrambled with goat's milk for volume, hissed as she stirred. She left them and got to work on the bread, cutting it into thin slices and spreading a hint of butter over each piece.

"Yes."

Her tray stacked high, Audrey kicked open the door, then paused, ducking her head against a moist gust of wind. The cloth she'd used to cover the food flapped up, covering her face, then dropped. She held it down with her chin, then walked as quickly as she could to the barn and knocked on the door with one elbow. It creaked open, and the captain was quick to help, taking the tray and setting it on a wooden bench nearby. The soldiers used bowls from their own packs, and every one of them thanked Audrey as they turned from the ad hoc table. Baker came last, and at first she was disappointed that she'd had to wait. But when he served himself, then lingered beside her to talk, she understood. He got the least amount of food, and he'd done that on purpose, sacrificing the meal so he could spend time with her.

"This is very kind of you, miss," he said shyly.

She beamed. "Not at all, sir." He looked a little awkward, as if he weren't sure whether to talk or eat. She flapped her hand gently toward his bowl. "Please eat before the eggs get too cold."

He took a bite and chewed slowly, even closed his eyes briefly. He liked it, she could see. Warmth rose in her chest. "Nothing special," she said. "I imagine you get eggs all the time."

"No . . . well, yes, but these are delicious."

"Thank you, sir."

"Baker."

"Pardon me?"

"Private Daniel Baker," he said, then grinned sheepishly. He held out one tentative hand and she took it. It was warm, despite the chill in the barn. "I'm Danny."

"I'm Audrey."

"So good to meet you, Audrey."

She viewed him through the eyes of an artist, taking in every tiny dot in his cobalt blue eyes. Her gaze explored the splayed lines at the corners of those eyes, every one of them crusted with filth from the march. His strong chin and lean cheeks were dark with a few days' growth of beard, and now that his cap was off she was able to admire the gentle wave in his dirty brown hair. Her hand ached to paint its lines in a deep, warm sepia.

His gaze suddenly dropped to the floor, and she blinked, mortified. She hadn't even realized she'd been studying him. What must he think of her? But when he looked up again, he was smiling, and she saw some of her own embarrassment reflected in his handsome face.

"I . . . I'm sorry," he said.

"Whatever for?"

"I guess . . . I guess I was staring. It's just . . ." His voice faded while he searched for some kind of explanation.

Audrey saved him the trouble. "Where do you go after this?"

"I have no idea," he told her. "They'll probably send us back up front. They seem to like sticking the Canadians up front."

That explained the accent, she thought, regarding him with fresh eyes. This Danny wasn't just a handsome man, he was some kind of exotic species. "Canadian? I've never met a Canadian before."

"Oh, yeah. See? See this maple leaf?" he asked, fingering a small pin on his collar. She saw the leaf, noticed that it was well-worn, but mostly she focused on the broken nails of his strong fingers, on the angles of his knuckles and the way he handled the pin with a kind of tenderness. Pride, she assumed. Something about that gave her a small thrill. "That's Canada's emblem. Our uniforms are pretty much like the Brits', but those pins are ours. Oh, and we have our own pipers. You know, bagpipes?"

"Really? Why? You aren't from Scotland."

"Well, see," he said, "I'm in the Twenty-fifth Battalion, which is the boys from Nova Scotia. And a lot of our folks back home are Scottish, only they live in Canada now. Anyway, the pipes are kind of a symbol of that."

She raised an eyebrow, fascinated, which encouraged him to go on. "Yeah, and the pipers wear kilts. They sound fantastic when the guns are going."

"Do you hear the guns a lot, then?"

He nodded, then looked to the side. She understood. He didn't want to talk about that. But now she was afraid. Had she said the wrong thing? Had she ruined this?

"I'm sorry. I didn't mean—"

"Did you grow up here?" he asked, saving her this time.

"No. I've been here about ten years. I grew up outside London, but when my mother died, I came to live with my grandmère. I have no brothers or sisters, just my cousin Laurent, and he's in the army. I haven't heard from him in a long time." She hesitated. Simply because he wore a uniform, Danny was the closest she'd come to Laurent in a while. "I think about my cousin and I feel utterly helpless. I'm sorry, but I have to ask. Is it really so bad?"

"Yeah. It is," he told her.

They stood in silence, but Audrey didn't think it was awkward anymore. "Have you seen nothing good out there?" she wanted to know. "Nothing at all?"

"Not much," he said, sighing. "I miss the sea. I miss the quiet. Once in a while there'll be a pretty sunrise or sunset out here, but that's just about it." He smiled and gave a little shrug. "Of course, there sure are some pretty ladies out here."

"Are there?" she asked, blushing.

"Well, really only one," he admitted, and she watched all the blood rush to his face. *Then* it was slightly awkward, but it also carried a new, thrilling edge. She stepped to retrieve the tray she'd carried out, unsure of whether she wanted to flee or stay, but Danny stopped her by putting a hand on her arm. The warmth of his touch made her dizzy.

"Let me carry that for you."

"Oh, thank you," she said, letting him take it. "I just need to take it back to the house." Of course she didn't need to do anything in that moment, but this gave her a perfect opportunity to lead him away from the others, and she grabbed onto that chance with both hands. "It's starting to rain, so we may have to run."

"I can run," he said, curling one corner of his mouth. "Let's go."

SIX

❧

The rain was starting off slow, but she could sense a deluge coming. When they got to the door of the house, she stopped him with an apologetic smile and one hand on his arm. She didn't want him going inside. She couldn't imagine showing him where she lived. And the idea of letting her grandmère see him there, well, it just wasn't worth the battle.

"I'll be just a second. Wait here, will you?"

When she ran inside, Céleste was sitting at the kitchen table, glaring at her. "Send him back to the barn," she hissed in French.

"I won't. He just helped me carry this, and he's waiting outside. He'll go back to the barn when he's ready to go."

"You are acting like a whore."

Audrey slammed the tray down, shocked. "Grandmère! Have you lost your mind for good this time?"

"Shame on you. Every Sunday the priest speaks of the sins of the flesh, and I know he is talking about you. You and your mother."

God, give me strength! "The priest doesn't talk about anyone in particular, you know that. And I have not sinned!"

"The Lord calls you a sinner!"

"Ah!" Audrey threw her hands in the air, exasperated. "I am no sinner. Just because I want to speak with another person does not mean I am acting like a whore. How can you be so cruel? How can you speak to me that way? I am your granddaughter!"

The old woman squinted at her. "Because you are like your mother."

Audrey closed her eyes, prayed for patience. It would be easy to fly off the handle, and it would serve the old woman right, but right now all she wanted was to escape. To be with Danny.

"My mother was no whore," she said through her teeth. "She was a beautiful, happy, exciting woman who loved life. Do you know what I want, Grandmère? I want to enjoy *my* life. And that is precisely why I am leaving right now. So I can speak with a normal human being, not waste my time with a mean old witch."

The old woman spat more words meant to injure her, but Audrey didn't stop moving. She was out the door and smiling prettily at Danny as soon as she could get there. They were walking back toward the barn when the heavens opened. Danny ducked and turned toward the barn door, but she grabbed his forearm and tugged him in the other direction.

"This way," she said, and he followed her as she sprinted to the firewood shelter behind the house. The stack was low; they'd have to chop more firewood before the autumn winds closed in. For now it provided room to sit and wait out the rain pelting the walls.

"I know it's loud," she said, raising her voice over the din. "I hope you don't mind."

Danny sat beside her on the log pile. Not close enough to touch, but nearly. "Not at all."

She shrugged, searching for an explanation for why she'd led him there. "It would be even louder in the barn."

There wasn't much he could say to that, and they stared at each other wearing matching masks of shyness. Had coming here been a mistake? Could she save the moment, think of something to say? Anything at all? *A question. I should ask a question.*

"Tell me about Canada," she blurted. "Is it always cold?"

For the next half-hour they sat and talked, slowly at first, then picking up momentum, learning to laugh together as the rain eased. When the storm dwindled to uneven beats on the roof, their words slowed as well. The day had passed with the clouds, so it was becoming almost too dark to see each other. She wished she had brought a lantern, but she'd been in too much of a hurry to plan ahead.

With a sigh, he stood and faced her. "Thank you for letting us stay here tonight," he said.

She panicked. It sounded like goodbye. "I'm glad I could help."

"Audrey?"

He hadn't said her name throughout the conversation, and she loved hearing it now, hearing the simple syllables roll so easily off his tongue in his soft Canadian accent. His gaze made her nervous and brave all at once. She cocked her head to one side, waiting.

"I didn't mean to be forward earlier, saying you're pretty and all, but—"

"Oh, you were just being kind," she said, daring him to say more.

"I wasn't!" Then he grinned, lifting one wry eyebrow. "*Kind* isn't the right word. *Honest* is more like it. Truth is, you're the prettiest thing I think I've ever seen. And I wish—" She bit her lip—hoping, hoping— and he went on. "I was wondering if you had a picture I might have of you. So I can see something pretty every day."

She had no idea why tears rushed to her eyes in that moment, but she blinked them away. "Oh, Danny. That is so sweet." She glanced at the log beside her, then back up again, remembering. It had taken forever, but she'd drawn her own self-portrait a few months back, just needing something to occupy her mind. She'd stared in that small, broken mirror for hours, memorizing the freckles and curves she knew intrinsically, then translated everything to the paper. She rarely even looked at it now, but it had been a great accomplishment for her at the time. Could she give it to this stranger? Of course she could. Besides, this was no stranger. Not really. "Yes, I have a picture. I'll give it to you in the morning."

It seemed as natural as the wind for him to lean in at that moment and kiss her lips. She didn't resist, didn't move away.

"Sleep well, Audrey," he murmured.

She couldn't move anything but her eyes, and they blinked open slowly. As if she was just waking up. "I will," she whispered. Her lips tingled. She wanted more, but he was stepping away. "And you, too. Sleep well, Danny."

He walked her around to her door, then said a quiet good night and turned toward the barn. She watched the slender line of his back as he faded into the night, saw the burst of pale yellow light when he opened the barn door and went inside.

Audrey unlatched the door of the house, wishing the hinges didn't squeal so loudly, but it didn't matter. Céleste was sound asleep in their shared room, snoring and smacking her lips as she rolled to one side. Audrey made her way through the familiar dark, skimming her fingers along the trunk and pulling out her nightgown. She hung her rain-dampened clothing over the table at the foot of her bed and slipped into the chilled white cotton, still dazed from the touch of his lips.

In the morning, a distinct chill existed in the air between Audrey and Céleste. Her grandmère was not pleased at the prospect of serving breakfast to the battalion, but Audrey insisted despite the old woman's angry mutterings. They set bowls of steaming oatmeal and cups of tea on the covered porch, and the men claimed their breakfast with gratitude, then withdrew to eat by the barn. Audrey, most of her hair covered by a white kerchief, stirred a spoonful of precious honey into Danny's oatmeal when she thought no one was watching. Danny saw her do it, though. His eyes were on her, a warm, supportive touch she could feel. When she snuck a peek she could see he looked tired, yes, but not overly so. She couldn't blame him—she wasn't sure she'd slept a wink. But she kept her smile bright and pretty and natural, and she laughed with the men as if nothing out of the ordinary had happened. As if she hadn't been kissed a few hours before by this wonderful man, this hero.

The grass was too wet to sit on, so the men stood in a rough circle, eating. One by one, the Canadians carried the bowls back inside the house and handed them to Audrey. When Danny offered his, she made sure their fingers touched again, wanting to feel that delicious sizzle race through her veins. When he touched her, her blood felt alive. Electric. She wanted more.

"Have you had enough, sir?" she asked, tilting her head to one side like a sparrow.

"I, em—" He shook his head as if he were trying to clear confusion from his mind. Could he feel as dazed by her as she did by him? Could it be? "Yes, thank you. Plenty. Better than I've eaten in a long while." Céleste, tidying up the kitchen table behind her, emitted a "hmph," and Audrey glared back at her. The old woman only frowned, then "hmphed" again. She made a big production of drying her wrinkled hands on the dishcloth, eyeing them both with deep suspicion, then she folded the cloth and left the room.

As soon as she was gone, Danny took Audrey's hands in his. "Thing is," he said quietly. "I don't want to leave you. I can't understand it, but I feel like I need to stay, to be with you."

Audrey's stomach flipped, and she reached for the tea. She hated the tears pressing behind her lids. Hated the thought of his leaving. Couldn't stand the idea of watching him march off to get killed while she stayed here to rot with her grandmère. *Let's run! We could hide somewhere,* she thought desperately, then dismissed the impossible thought.

She poured tea for him but didn't meet his eyes. It was too difficult. She couldn't say goodbye. Not yet. "Milk? Honey?"

"Nah. Black's good. Thanks."

She held out the cup, and the steaming surface shimmered with her trembles. When he reached for it, she held it between them. "Will you write to me, Danny?" she whispered.

"Whenever I get the chance." He sipped his tea, then closed his eyes in appreciation. "This is so good. And hot. Nothing like the sludge we drink in the trench. That stuff you can practically chew."

"I like you, Danny," she blurted. "I really do. Do be careful, won't you?"

"I will, Audrey." He lifted her hand to his lips and kissed her knuckles, holding her gaze the whole time.

Captain Johnston's voice carried into the kitchen. "Baker!"

"Sir?" Danny called back.

"Come on, son. We're shipping out now. Say your goodbyes and let's go."

Danny's grin was forced when he faced her again. "Guess that's it," he said.

"Please be careful, Danny."

"I always am, Audrey."

"Even more now, all right?"

"All right." He stepped closer, and she could swear the air hummed between them. "What I really want, though, is for *you* to be careful. Don't trust soldiers, Audrey. None of them. Soldiers are crazy."

"I trust you."

"Okay, well . . . I guess you can trust me." He paused, then touched her cheek with the backs of his fingers. She closed her eyes, feeling like a happy cat. She practically purred when he touched her.

"I guess it makes no sense, but I'm plain crazy about you," he said softly, then leaned in to kiss her. His lips were soft but not shy. When he pulled away, she leaned in for another. Then he rested his forehead against hers and whispered, "I'll be back for you, Audrey. I promise."

"Kiss me again, soldier," she whispered, and he did. "I will wait for you," she said, then she turned toward the kitchen counter. She slid open a drawer and pulled out a small sheet of paper, then a pencil. She scribbled the postal address in town and thrust the paper at him. "Mail comes to here. And I'll send letters to the Twenty-fifth Battalion, right?" She tapped her temple with the pen. "I'll remember."

Danny read the address on the paper, then folded it and tucked it inside his jacket. Then, shy again, she reached into her apron pocket and pulled out the portrait of herself. She peeked at it, said a silent farewell, then handed it to him.

"You sure are pretty," he said, then flipped the picture over.

To Danny. Please be careful. Audrey.

He opened one of the packs that hung from his waist and pulled out a small tin can that smelled strongly of tobacco. The picture fit perfectly into the lid.

"My writing's not too neat," he said, tucking the can back into his pack.

"I'll understand," she assured him.

"I've never been much good at spelling, neither."

"Don't worry."

He kissed her again, then she touched the straps crossing over his shoulders as if ensuring they were secure. She skimmed her fingers over each one of the nine buttons on his jacket, then reached for the mess tin hanging on the outside of his pack. She held up one finger, asking him to wait, then turned to the pantry and brought out a small sack of buns, which she set inside the tin.

"Thank you," he said.

"You can share."

"I will. Thanks." They stared at each other, and she knew he was trying just as hard to memorize her features as she was with him. Her mind's brush swirled over the dark line of his eyebrow, skipping over the scar that cut the line neatly in half. She had just the brown for it.

"Audrey?"

"Yes?"

"Thanks. Thanks for everything."

Her chin quivered awfully, and tears threatened. When he saw it, Danny slumped a little, his eyes wide with concern. He folded her into his arms again, and she wished she could crawl inside his coat with him, hide there, be safe there.

"I will wait for you, Danny," she repeated, then he was gone.

The last brown coat disappeared over the hill of the road, but Audrey still didn't move. *One second more,* she thought. One more second where she could pretend they were still standing in the same place, breathing the same air. Just one more moment with his deep blue eyes inches from hers, gazing into her soul.

Then she spun and raced back toward the house, her skirt flapping behind her as she went. She didn't say a word, didn't want to interfere with the pictures pulsing through her mind. Paper. She needed paper. And charcoal for now, though paint would be added later. All different hues, from white to yellow to red, and a touch of cobalt blue for his eyes and for the shading beneath them. Right now it was imperative that she capture every line, every curve of his handsome face, bring back the light in those eyes, the shy charm in his smile. In her mind she recalled how he'd lifted his cap and a brief spark of sunshine had brought to life a gentle hint of gold—*raw umber,* she thought—about halfway back, blending into his brown waves. Then he'd replaced his cap with one hand, tugging on the brim with finger and thumb, shadowing his brow. She'd wanted to knock it back off, see if he'd laugh or get angry, but the pride in his expression held her back from causing mischief.

He was a noble man, her Danny. Noble and proud and handsome, and such a hero. She knew it deep in her soul, though she knew none of it at all. They'd spoken of nothing of consequence, mostly. And yet her spirit sang with a new certainty. Her charcoal floated over the curve of one dark brow and her memory brought back its width and particular angle. Slightly different from the right side, she recalled, because of that little scar cutting through.

SEVEN

Letters arrived stained, creased, sometimes in a bunch, sometimes straggling in after an excruciating lapse of weeks. But he wrote. She'd feared at first that he wouldn't, knowing his mind and body would be busy with far more important things than her. But he kept his word. The first letter arrived and she squealed like a child, running all the way home with it clutched in her fingers. As he'd said, his printed words were messy, sometimes short and distracted. She didn't care.

May 2, 1916

Dear Audrey,

I hardly know how to start this letter. I don't write much. I suppose I should tell you a bit about me. I live in Nova Scotia. I'm a fisherman, like my dad and his dad before. I'm saving up for my own boat, but it'll be a while before that happens. Fishing's pretty much all I know, other than hunting and logging, and I guess that's what I'll be going home to when this is all over. It's hard work, but what isn't? We usually get up at around four in the morning, and sometimes it's so awful cold you wonder how you can even move your hands, but it's all worth it. My family and I live right on the sea, and when it gets stormy it's pretty much the most beautiful place in the world, to my way of thinking.

It was a bit strange, coming way out here and having everything be different, but I thought it would be the right thing to do. You know, fighting for the good guys and all that. I thought it'd be exciting, too. Well, I was right about that part, but I could do without most of the excitement now, to be honest.

I just had my twenty-fifth birthday the other night. The fellas found a candle and stuck it in my supper. I have seven younger brothers and a dog named Cecil, but he's real old, so I don't know if he'll still be there when I get home. I hope so.

The boys here are pretty jealous, now that I've been telling them about you. They all wish they'd met a beautiful woman, but I told them that even if they did, she wouldn't be as beautiful as you.

Anyway, like I said, I'm not real good at letter writing, but if you write to me, maybe I can answer some of your questions. I apologize for the poor writing, but it's been raining, so my hands are cold and it's hard to hold the pen proper. My hands are always cold out here. I remember that yours were warm. Until I hear from you, I am

Yours affectionately,
Danny

His hands had been solid and warm, too. She remembered that, how hers had felt immediately safe once they touched his. Now all she wanted was to keep him safe. And to feel that warmth again.

Spring moved into summer, and his letters became her reason for rising in the morning. Sometimes they didn't arrive for a couple of weeks, sometimes she came from town with a thin stack in her hand. She answered faithfully, sending out note after note, trading eggs for paper and stamps. She told Danny about her life before the farm, and when she couldn't hold it in any longer she gently complained about the awful things her grandmère said on a daily basis. Some days she sat outside, far from the house and barn, and just let the sweet summer days flow through her pencil.

Before Danny's letters came, no one had ever asked Audrey what *she* wanted. Danny did. So she asked herself the same question. It took a moment to get started, to think outside of what she knew, but then her eyes went to a soaring bird overhead and she couldn't stop. When the breeze lifted the hem of her skirt and kissed her knees, she closed her eyes and imagined he was there, holding her hand, listening, nodding encouragement, and she let the words come, found someone who cared about her dreams of seeing new things, meeting new people, saying she wanted to paint it all.

Through the summer weeks the health of Audrey's grandmère rapidly deteriorated. Not surprising. Audrey often wondered if self-imposed misery could kill a person in the end. She sometimes speculated on what her grandpère had been like earlier when he was younger, because her mother was nothing like this bitter old woman. Their daughter, Pascale, had laughed more, danced more, and when Audrey painted, her mother had celebrated every brush stroke. Here the paintings were hidden away in boxes for fear of their getting tossed into the fire for practicality. Audrey had learned that the hard way.

Pascale Poulin had been twenty years old when she'd run from her mother, escaping the life for which she'd never been born. She had always been a mystery to Céleste, who never understood her daughter's need for a life far from the farm. The girl loved people, loved laughter, but trapped on this remote farm the best she could do was flirt with the neighbouring boys they hired to help at harvest time. But the harmless flirtation hadn't been enough for her, apparently, because one day after the fields had been put to rest for the winter, a couple of the young men had driven up in a wagon and said they were moving to England to open a store, and would she like to come? Pascale had raced inside to stuff her things in a bag, then she'd hopped onto the back, waving goodbye to her parents and grinning as the wagon bumped away down the old road.

"She never said nothing to me but goodbye," Céleste repeated throughout Audrey's existence. "No word of thank you. That girl was a whore and a waste of time. A waste of my life."

When she'd been ten and had first arrived at the farm, Audrey had felt sorry for the old woman. She couldn't imagine the pain of having a daughter run away like that, riding off with a group of men without so much as a thank you to her parents after all they'd done. On the other hand, she did think it rather harsh for her grandmère to call her own daughter a whore and say she'd wasted her life on her. Audrey's opinion soon changed. Within six months, she knew for certain that Pascale had done the only sane thing by running that day.

But now it was up to Audrey to care for the old woman as if she really did care, because no one else would, and Audrey couldn't imagine anyone existing entirely on their own. She guessed she did care a little. As the old woman's feeble limbs rose from her bed less and less often, Audrey supposed she would eventually miss her in some way, though she had trouble imagining that.

Audrey milked the goat, who had waited at the door, bleating for attention, then poured the milk into two metal cups. The warm drink fortified her, gave her strength enough to go back inside, cradle the birdlike neck, and urge a few sips through her grandmère's grey lips. But it came back out in a weak explosion. *"Non,"* Céleste wheezed. "No more."

"You must drink," she tried.

"I will do as I please," the old woman huffed in French. She narrowed her eyes in a benign attempt to appear dangerous. "Just like your mother."

Audrey sighed, overwhelmingly tired of this argument. "All my mother ever wanted was to enjoy her life. She tired of your lessons and lectures. She wanted to dance."

"And she died of that," she snapped.

"At least she died happy. I know she was happy because I was with her. I want to be happy like her."

"Then you are stupid, just like her."

Tears surged into Audrey's eyes, but she blocked them. This wasn't the first time she'd heard that from her dear grandmère. "Drink," she said again.

"*Non.*"

Audrey rose and stepped away from the bed, then pulled the brown wool blanket over the stubborn old thing. "Fine," she said. "Good night."

She wasn't ready to lie down in her own bed against the other wall. The thought of falling asleep beside her grandmère's gurgling, wheezing breaths made her slightly queasy. The night was muggy, made soggy by a light drizzle, so she decided she would sit in the woodshed where she'd sat with Danny that night. She would dream of him and let the weather cool the burn in her chest. As she stepped through the doorway, her grandmère spoke again.

"You are just like her. I have accomplished nothing. I die an empty old woman."

Audrey blinked up at the grey sky, letting the mist soothe her hot cheeks. The only way she knew she was crying was because her tears were warm where the rain was cool. But she still didn't know *why* she was crying. An hour later she went back into the house and stopped short just inside the door, listening. The horrible, rasping breathing had stopped.

EIGHT

Audrey was twenty, the same age as her mother had been when she'd run away to England to start her life over again. Audrey knew next to nothing about how to deal with the finality of her grandmère's long-awaited death, so—just as with her grandpère—the neighbours took care of it all. Céleste Poulin was buried in the churchyard a mile away from the farm, and Audrey was left alone. The air felt clearer now, cleaned of the poisons the old woman had spat at her for the past ten years. Audrey could do as she pleased, think as she pleased, and no one would accuse her of being the devil's spawn, *le frai du diable.* It was liberating.

It was also lonely. She was somewhat surprised to find that she was slightly afraid now that the black nights were devoid of Céleste's laboured breathing. After all, it wasn't as if the old woman could have protected them from any threat when she'd been around. Audrey supposed she'd really always been on her own, but the constant disapproval had provided something of a shield. That was gone now. The world was open to her. Where to begin?

The first thing she did was open all the boxes and free her artwork from its prison. Soon every spare place in the house was taken up with her pictures. Then she tied on a thick, stained apron and brought out her paints and easel. She set them up wherever she damn well chose to set them up: in the house, in the barn, out of doors. She preferred the open air because the fumes gave her a headache, sometimes made her light-headed. If it rained, though, she stayed inside, painting images from memory or things she saw in the room. When the sun bloomed, she went outside. Now that she was on her own, she could choose to paint anything she wanted, but she often returned to the faces of the animals. Portraits of cats and kittens multiplied, popping up on the walls alongside a close-up of the horse's resigned expression and a particularly inspired tableau of the new baby goat frolicking in the yard out front. Trees, grass, rocks, stumps—everything was reborn on paper or silky smooth birch bark, lovingly coaxed from her brush.

She didn't want to waste fuel at night by lighting lamps or candles. That meant she couldn't paint, couldn't read—though that didn't really matter. She'd already read their meagre supply of books many times, and they were in French, anyway. She lay in the silence of her bed, envying the crickets, wishing she too had something to sing about.

There had to be more she could do.

In the morning she walked to town to check for mail. A letter from Danny had arrived, and she grinned while she opened the envelope.

June 30, 1916

My dearest Audrey,

I'm so sorry to hear about your grandmother's passing. I suppose people say it can be a blessing, but it's never a blessing for the folks left behind. I wish I was there to comfort you. I hope you know that I'm thinking of you, like I do all the time.

Audrey, as tragic as it is, your loss gives me all the more reason to ask you something I've been thinking about for a while. Truth is I'm kind of afraid to ask. If I do, you might either be real angry at me being so forward, or you might love the idea. But the thing is, if I don't ask, I'll never forgive myself. Now seems like as good a time as any.

I don't want you to stay here. Especially not now that you're alone. I want you to come to Canada. I'm not sure if getting to know you through letters and all is the right way, but the thing is, I've fallen in love with you, Audrey. I want to marry you and have a family. I wish with all my heart that I could be on one knee in front of you, asking, but I can't. I promise to do it right when I see you again.

Please make me the happiest man in the world, Audrey. Come to Canada and be my wife. I remain

Yours most affectionately,
Danny

I've fallen in love with you.

How was it possible for simple words scrawled in a messy hand, written on stained and crumpled paper, to make her feel as if she'd left her body? As if she'd sprouted wings and flitted over the old farmhouse, where she could flip and fly wherever she wanted? He loved her. He *loved* her. He wanted to marry her, have a family. Could it be? Could love happen like this? Through a shockingly short courtship and a box full of scribbled letters?

Of course it could. She'd known it in the first moment she'd caught his eye. She'd seen something in that face, in the set of his shoulders, heard something in the awkward first words between them. And she'd known she would only ever love him.

She was staring so hard at the paper, rereading his words, that she tripped on a stick lying on the road, but she righted herself and didn't look back.

Come to Canada.

That was a whole other idea, one that she'd never really considered before. That would mean learning a whole new way of life, being around people with different accents, different opinions, different . . .

everything. It wasn't that she was afraid, really. She'd never been a timid girl. But this was a big step.

She would think more on that aspect later. For now she wanted to bask in the glory of the idea of the thing. He loved her. She would see him soon, and she would wear her prettiest gown, and they would make beautiful children, and live happily ever after on the quiet shores of Nova Scotia. They would grow old together.

She knew nothing about the sea. So much to learn!

Would it be such a strain for her to go to Canada? Would it really be that difficult? She'd moved from the wild, unpredictable life her mother had led her through in England, then landed with a crash in this godforsaken farm in the nowhere middle of France. She'd survived that.

The physical voyage itself would be a challenge. Audrey's whole life had been spent either on this flat piece of farmland or wandering Sussex, and she barely remembered the wagon ride in between. She'd seen the sea while crossing the Channel, but the idea of going all the way to Canada was impossible to envision. She'd have to go on a great ship, obviously, then sleep among strangers aboard something that rocked and swayed with the tide.

Kind of a metaphor for her own life, she mused, since she'd never had any choice but to rock and sway, move with the tide. Any anchor she might have had was thrown by someone else, not her. Did she dare draw it up and start fresh? Was she brave enough to steer toward that distant place on the horizon?

Canada. It almost seemed like an imaginary world, it was so far away. In truth, she knew nothing about it other than what Danny had written in his brief letters. She supposed it couldn't be all that different from here, since he fished and hunted and did what most men here did as well. What might there be for her in Canada? On one hand, she almost didn't care. It couldn't be worse than it was here on the farm, all alone and desperate for human contact. She would have to go somewhere. But Canada? Did she need to make such an extreme departure? What did she know of Canada? What did she know of Danny, really?

When the soldiers had stopped there for the night, Danny had shown her his little pin, the maple leaf. The road where she walked was shadowed by vivid green, evidence of that same tree. Uneven grey bark bumped under her fingers, drawing paths, colliding, running away. Like long grey rivers without a care in the world, flowing upstream until they burst into pointed sprays of colour, celebrating the sky. Now the silver maples were green, but when October came, the world would mellow with them, head inside to warm by the fire when the leaves rustled their vivid yellow leaves.

She imagined maple trees must be at least as glorious in Canada as they were here, since the army had pinned them so proudly to their soldiers' chests. It was encouraging to think that if she did go to Canada, she might one day walk alongside these magnificent trees again, might paint them again. As much as she craved a new life, a tiny voice inside begged for some kind of landmark.

Danny had mentioned bagpipes too, which made her smile. Noisy, brash things which she imagined might just be the perfect accompaniment to gunfire and bombs.

It had been months since they'd heard anything from Laurent, and that note had been brief. What if he came back when all this was over and found the place abandoned? What then? Did she even have the right to do this? He was older than she, and it got her wondering. Even though he'd barely lived there, was this more his place than hers?

War changed things, she reminded herself. What was right before might not be right anymore, and if she was making a mistake, she would probably have to answer for it another time. Laurent was gone. Something deep inside told her he'd never come back. And that reminder was only a quick, brief twist on her heart, since she'd resolved herself to that probability on the day he'd set his shoulders and strode from the farm, looking so strong and brave.

All around her, people were loading up wagons and abandoning their land, unable to work it now that the war had taken over. No one was left to work the farms since the young men were all in trenches, and their remaining families were starving. Winter would come sooner than anyone was ready, and it would be a long, terrible winter, she knew.

One of the goats spotted her as she approached the barn. He ambled over, complaining about the lateness of breakfast or something. Audrey had too many eggs now for one person, and too much milk. She should sell the animals. And if she sold the animals, what was holding her at the farm?

"What do you think, little one?" she asked, scratching the knobbly black head. "Should I go to Canada?"

The world was changing. It was time for Audrey to change as well.

She had very little to pack. A few dresses, her art supplies, all Danny's letters, and enough food to last for a few days. Just until she got to the city. She also had the little tin box her grandmère had thought secret, filled with a healthy amount of money. Not a fortune, she knew, but something to get her started at least. She wouldn't be homeless.

———

The first thing she had to do was write a reply to Danny, the man she wanted to marry more than anything else on earth.

NINE

She hadn't thought London would be so big. Or so busy. The driver shifted beside her, leaning forward to ease his back, and she scanned the street. Even though the day was ending, the pace here was over-whelming—a constant stream of black hats and coats, the clattering of wheels and engines, an all-consuming cast of grey looming over the cov-etous fingers of cathedral steeples. The towns in Sussex had been large, she remembered, but they had nothing on this circus. Of course, she could have gone there, to her mother's old world, but something had driven her farther north. Maybe, she mused, she needed something big because she was destined for something big. The thought made her grin, and she was startled when a gentleman on the street lifted his top hat and smiled in return.

"Where to, miss?" her driver asked, weaving around a pothole.

"I need a place to stay. Is there a hotel or something nearby?"

"O' course." He chirped to the pair of horses jingling ahead, who looked as tired as Audrey felt. But the days of travel had led to this, and her blood sang with excitement. London. She was on her own in *London*. What an adventure!

Just over twenty years ago, Pascale Poulin had done this, too. Had her nerves vibrated as Audrey's did now? Had Pascale clung to her travel mates for balance the way Audrey gripped the bench? Had her mother ever regretted trading in the quiet, the solitude, the sweet, calm, fresh air for this madness? If she had, she'd adjusted. Somehow she'd created a life with strangers, and she'd met someone, even brought a healthy, happy baby into the world. And though their life in the streets had been unsettled and meals had been unpredictable, the days and nights had been warm with affection. Nothing like the frost that had always emanated from Audrey's grandmère.

Audrey wasn't sure if she was terrified or just excited. Everything moved so quickly, a natural chaos created from unnatural fabric.

Pascale had been strong. Audrey would be strong. And one day soon she would stand beside Danny, and he would be so proud of her for what she'd dared to do.

Despite the rain, she set out walking in the morning, exploring the endless streets and windows. After a couple of hours the rain had settled into a relentless drizzle that worked its way into her bones until she was simply too cold to go on. She would either have to return to the hotel or figure out something else. She cast an eye toward a café, wondering. Did women go into these places and sit by themselves? Was that considered all right? A church, she knew, was different. Anyone could go there. But a social setting like a café? Everyone she'd seen going in or out of those places was either in a couple or in groups of two or three, huddled beneath combined umbrellas.

She paused before the large window. Inside, a stove burned, pumping beautiful orange heat into the room. It looked comfortable, with probably a dozen white-clothed tables, most of them occupied. She jumped when the door burst open beside her and a couple of women stepped outside, beautiful in their tailored suits, giggling under large brimmed hats. Audrey desperately wanted a hat like that. She'd seen them everywhere, decorated by either gemstones, ribbons, feathers, or flowers, in all colours and sizes. What she wanted was a deep red velvet with a ruby-like gem on the front, with all the ribbon gathered around it like a frame. She'd already seen it in the store window a few doors down. She'd been sorely tempted but had reluctantly walked away, knowing it was too much to spend. It made sense to find her way around this city first, maybe get a job, though she had no idea what she might be hired for.

What could she do, after all? Her schooling was practically non-existent, though she could certainly do the basics, like read and write. She supposed she could take care of children, maybe cook, possibly tutor French and art, but there wouldn't be much call here for a girl with great talents at milking goats or shovelling out chicken coops. For ten years she'd done all that, and though she'd dreamed of escape, she'd never let the thoughts go much further. After all, that could only lead to disappointment.

A shadow of a figure danced through her memory, attached to a laughing, skipping child. Had her mother ever held down a job? She didn't think so. Certainly not for as long as Audrey had known her. But she'd been a wonderful mother, teaching her daughter to make do, make the best of what she had.

She recalled one night, when Audrey had been around nine years old, her mother had wrapped her in blankets for the night, then touched her cheek gently and said she would be gone for the night. Audrey had never been left alone the entire night before.

"*Non, Maman! Restez-ici!*"

Pascale had touched her daughter's lips with one gentle finger, saying, "Shh, Audrey. You are safe. This is not the only tent here."

It was true; they had many friends here, but still . . . "I want to come with you."

Her mother let out a slow breath, and her eyes filled with sympathetic tears. "You are a big girl now. And sometimes Maman must do things without you. I will be back in the morning."

"No! I cannot—"

Pascale lifted her delicate chin and rolled her shoulders slightly back as she got to her feet. Audrey still remembered how brave her mother appeared to her in that moment. How brave, and how deeply sad.

"*Ma chérie,*" she said, stepping away from Audrey. "*Nous sommes des femmes. Nous faisons ce que nous devons pour survivre."* We are women. We must do what we must do. "I will see you in the morning, and we will have a lovely day tomorrow."

Pascale was never a prostitute. Audrey knew that. She'd seen those working women with their dead, glassy eyes, and her mother was not like that. She did not eagerly sell her body to support herself and her daughter, but as Audrey matured, she understood that certain things could be bought and sold when needed. Within their little, ever-evolving group, sex was simply part of a barter system. A practical way to survive when you had nothing else to trade.

After Richard disappeared, Pascale and Audrey moved on, finding a fire someplace, endearing themselves to a friendly face or two. They never had much, but they had each other. At the time Audrey hadn't known they'd needed more, hadn't wondered how they paid for food, or where her new little coat had come from. She was a child, oblivious. And all the while, her mother had been doing what she needed to do, quietly, patiently, earning what she could.

Audrey understood, but it didn't take away the shame she felt when she remembered those days. She swore she would never be reduced to living that way ever again.

The two women still walked toward her, laughing between themselves. One clutched the other's arm, keeping them close and dry under one umbrella, and Audrey stepped to the side of the walkway so they could pass. At the last minute they stopped, and one of the women handed her a piece of white paper.

"Here, love. You might want to come see us tonight." She stared, confused, and the women gave her matching smiles. "Seven-thirty. Come early for a good seat."

Audrey watched them walk away, and when they stopped to hand someone else a piece of paper, she read the one they'd given her. It was for some kind of meeting, it appeared, though she had no idea what it meant. *Suffragette*. What on earth?

She shivered then made up her mind as a cab drove by, spraying water that landed far too close for Audrey's liking. Sucking up her pride, she walked into the café and glanced around. To her relief, after a few curious looks, no one paid her any attention at all. She took the last available table, settling in quietly and keeping her eyes averted from the strangers. When the waitress appeared, Audrey ordered a tea and biscuit, then sat back and relished the warmth as it travelled through her. From here she could watch the business of London from a safe place, and while she found it exciting to be among so much, it was intimidating as well.

"Pardon me, miss."

Audrey glanced up, surprised. Two women about her age stood by her table, their coats shiny with rain. "Yes?"

"Would it be a terrible inconvenience if we were to share your table with you? All the others are taken, and we were hoping to enjoy a nice spot of tea. It's frightful out there."

"Of course you may sit with me. I'm not wonderful company, but you're welcome to it."

"Lovely," said the second woman, and the two took the seats across from her.

"Jean Saunders," she said. "So pleased to meet you."

Audrey felt unaccountably shy. She didn't think she'd ever been shy before, but something about this woman spooked her. She supposed it was because the woman didn't appear to have a nervous bone in her body.

Jean cleared her throat and crinkled her nose. "And you are?"

Flustered, Audrey took her hand, feeling dangerously close to tears. "I'm so sorry. I'm new here, you see, and terribly tired. I believe you're the first person to say hello to me in days, other than the doorman, that is."

Jean's other hand closed over hers, and her brow creased with concern. "Oh my poor dear! Well, Marjory and I will just have to take care of this, won't we, Marjory?"

"Most certainly," said her friend, offering her hand as well. "Marjory Buckins. Shall we just guess at your name?"

Audrey flushed. "Audrey. I'm Audrey Poulin. I'm . . . I've only just arrived from France."

"How lovely." Marjory's smile was wide and warm. She was darker than her friend, with brown eyes that seemed to be moving all the time, studying the other tables, the door, everywhere she could look. "Lovely indeed." Those dark eyes focused momentarily on Audrey. "What were you doing in France?"

"Oh, I lived there. But I live here now. Or, at least, I hope to live here, at least for a while."

"What does that mean?" Jean asked. "*Do* you live here?"

Audrey blinked. "Well, I suppose so. I'm staying at the Bedford Hotel at the moment. I have to figure out what I'll do next."

"Are you here to work?"

"I'm sorry?"

"Work," Jean said. She spoke slowly, as if addressing a child. "You know. As a munitionette?"

Audrey had never felt so stupid and small as she did in that moment. *Munitionette*? That was the second new word she'd heard in the past hour, and she snuck a quick peek at the paper beside her plate, wondering if she'd misheard. Maybe it was the same word, but she'd forgotten. No. The other word was *suffragette*. She swallowed back what she could of her embarrassment and shrugged.

"I have no idea what you're talking about, I'm afraid."

Marjory reached over and patted the back of her hand where it lay on the table, and Audrey noticed with horror how ragged her own cuff was. When her hand was released, she tucked both hands safely under the table, out of view. "Don't worry yourself over that, dearie. Jean's only talking about the factories. They're hiring hundreds of women, you see, and a lot of them are coming from far away. So she thought perhaps with your coming from France, you might be planning to do that."

"Oh! Women are doing men's jobs?"

"No, no, darling. We're doing our *own* jobs," Marjory said with a chuckle. "Just so happens the men did them before we did."

"So . . . they get paid?"

"Yes," Joan said, "and it's good pay too, I hear. That's what Sophie said, wasn't it, Marjory?"

Marjory nodded, then placed their order when the waitress stopped by.

Audrey waited until the waitress had left. "Do you work there?" she ventured.

"Not there," Marjory said, "but that's only because we're already working at the post office. We only just got off our shift."

"Oh!" Jean suddenly exclaimed, reaching for the paper by Audrey's teacup. "Are you going?"

"I . . . I don't know. A woman handed me this outside, and I—"

"Do you know what it is?" Marjory asked. Audrey shook her head. "That's all right."

Jean jumped in. "We are fighting for a woman's right to vote."

"And not just that. It's about democracy and justice for all. Equality."

Audrey raised her eyebrows, listening, hoping something they said would soon make sense.

"Do you know that men are paid twice what we're paid for doing the same job?" Jean crossed her arms and leaned back with a little huff. "It's not as if we're asking for charity. Just equality."

"I didn't—"

"Women all over the world are pulling together, demanding justice," Marjory added.

"That's right," Jean confirmed.

Marjory continued with vigour. "They're being imprisoned, going on hunger strikes, being forcibly fed. Treated like animals, really. It's horrendous."

Audrey felt as if she were watching a tennis match, looking from one woman to the other.

Jean turned her bright smile on Audrey. "So you'll come tonight?"

Audrey could think of nothing else she'd rather do. In fact, she could think of nothing else she might have done anyway. "Of course. You'll have to give me directions, though."

They finished the pot of tea, then ordered another and sat for a companionable hour, sheltered from the miserable London day, and Audrey made the first two friends she'd had in years.

TEN

A few hours later, Audrey, Marjory, and Jean were in the thick of dozens of women, listening to speeches, learning what was being planned. Audrey was fascinated with the stories, and her mind couldn't help but return time and time again to her mother. How she would have loved these women! How she would have jumped in with both feet and danced to their speeches! She imagined her up there, probably wearing a ruby red gown, her long black hair shining, her eyes alive with rebellion.

"Deeds, not words!" she would have cried, leading the charge. "Equal pay for equal work!"

Audrey had been only a child when her mother died, fading away before her little girl's eyes in a clinic set up for folks like them. People without true homes. Her mother had been an actress, a dancer, a gypsy who held men captive with one slow blink. She had been fearless and free. Right up until the end, when the horrible, hungry illness had stolen the twinkle from her eyes. Audrey wondered if her mother had known about this movement back then, or if it had even been going on when she was alive.

Throughout the meeting, her hand skimmed over the back of her flyer, her pencil busy with curves and shadows. She mentally catalogued the colourful outfits, the expressions of the women, planning how she would paint it all. For she would have to do that, she knew. She wanted to remember this occasion, and painting everything she saw was how she kept her memories vivid.

The meeting ended after they arranged for another one and told everyone present about a protest they were planning for the following Tuesday afternoon. Audrey wrote the date and time at the top corner of her drawing, sorry the evening was at an end. A few heads nodded; they'd be there. More prevalent, though, were the mutterings of women who said they'd be too busy at work to show up.

"Will you be there?" Jean asked. "We can't, can we, Marj?"

"No. That's during our shift. What about you, Audrey? Will you be at work?"

"I . . . I don't work," she reminded them. "Though I suppose I should find out about that. I won't be able to afford living at the hotel forever."

"What do you do, Audrey?"

She shrugged. "I can do anything, I suppose. I worked the farm practically on my own for the past six years, I cooked and cleaned, I—"

"Gracious, girl! You can draw!" Marjory exclaimed, leaning close to stare at Audrey's renderings. Audrey automatically tried to cover the drawings. "Why I've never seen such beautiful drawings, have you, Jean?"

Jean pulled Audrey's protective hand away, and her beautiful eyes widened. "So lovely. Such a pity you can't be paid to paint, or you'd be rich!"

"That's all right. I only paint for my own eyes."

"That's a waste," Marjory snapped. "You should share your gift."

Audrey sorted her papers so the art was buried beneath blank sheets. "No, really. But thank you for your kindness."

Jean and Marjory exchanged a glance, then shrugged simultaneously. "Fine then," Marjory said. "We'll find you some kind of job, though."

"Job?" Another woman stopped beside them, overhearing. "Looking for a job?"

"Yes," Jean said. "For our friend. She's new in town. Do you know of something?"

"I do, as a matter of fact. At the Brunner-Mond munitions factory."

Marjory's brow lifted with concern. "Not very safe."

"Nonsense," the woman said. She brushed a speck off her coat with one hand. "It's perfectly safe."

Audrey frowned. "Munitions? Working with weapons? You mean for the war?" She pictured Danny, remembered how she'd run her fingers over the buttons on his uniform. She pictured her cousin, walking away for the last time, so cocky, so proud of himself. How could she possibly work with weapons?

Except these weapons were *for* Danny.

"Of course," she was told. "Very good pay, you know."

"Where?"

"Down at the Royal Docks in Silvertown. I hear they're hiring just about anyone right now."

Money. She needed money to survive, obviously, but the thought of even more, of saving toward that steamer to Canada . . .

"I'm interested. Thank you very much." She wrote down the directions, then headed back to the hotel, making plans as she went.

———

She was hired on the spot and given a pair of earth-coloured overalls—which felt scandalous until she noticed none of the others seemed to notice—then sent off with a group of women who showed her the machines. The room was black for all intents and purposes, a metal cave seeping with grease, echoing with the clang of pipes and hammers. Women in aprons and overalls worked around the room either at tables or on metal pipes that twisted like gnarled branches of an ancient, dead tree. Audrey held her breath against the clogged air, feeling trapped as the door closed behind them.

"Just breathe," one of the women told her. "You get used to it after a while."

"How can you?" she whispered, feeling close to tears. "How can you come back here every day?"

"Because it could be worse, couldn't it?"

Audrey stared. "How could it possibly?"

"We could be with our boys in them trenches," volunteered a woman with a heavy Scottish brogue. Her cheeks were blackened and her apron filthy, but her eyes sparkled. "They be breathin' in dirt and blood and explosives, just hopin' to catch another one of them foul breaths."

Audrey clutched at the wall, her stomach lurching. She felt sick at the thought of the trenches, sick at the stink of the factory, sick at her own weaknesses. She wiped away a runaway tear, realizing too late that her hand was sticky with grease.

"Hush, Frances. You're upsetting the girl."

"Ah, there ye go," Frances said, her teeth startlingly white in her filthy face. "Now she's officially one of us. There ain't no goin' back now."

Audrey frowned, puzzled, until the woman came over, still smiling kindly. She took out a cloth, stained beyond saving, and dabbed at Audrey's cheek.

"Like a battle wound, aye? Never ye mind that. The black won't never quite leave your skin, I'm afraid. Tears won't wash it off neither, missy. But now you're like the rest of us. Greasy canaries, they call us. But we're proud of that, we are. We be doin' our part."

If she'd needed more reason to stay at the job, that was it. Yes, she would do her part.

Day after day she rolled out of bed at five in the morning, joining the army of women packed onto the tram, marching into the sweltering factory. She'd left the Bedford and moved into the barracks where most of the other factory women worked. It was easier, moving with the crowd, and the rent wasn't bad. The barracks took away her privacy, but she soon felt comfortable among the colourful mixture of women from all walks of life. They were doing what they could, and they all got along for the most part. As well as hundreds of women could get along, she supposed.

The tram dropped them off outside the factory's gates, and the ocean loomed beyond that. She'd heard the ocean had a strong smell, but it was nothing against the stink of the two rival sugar refineries located nearby.

After her first experience of choking over the stench, Audrey wrapped a woolen scarf over her nose and mouth, and it didn't bother her as much.

When the workers boarded the tram at the end of the day, she rarely managed to snag a seat, but if she did, she used the opportunity to press her nose against the window and watch the pawnshops go by, noticing how the items in the windows rarely changed. Loose women stood on the roadside, their made-up faces fogged by warm clouds of breath. Occasionally, if she got lucky, she spied an exotic foreigner—or at least "exotic" was how she liked to think of them—hunched in corners, just like the locals, against the cold.

Her lungs and nostrils eventually hardened against the acidic stink of the air in the factory, but the shiny black ooze of the place haunted Audrey's dreams, spilling over her memories of yellows, blues, and greens, drowning the red of wild roses in the fields at the farm. The sun hadn't yet risen when she went into the building, and it had retired for the night by the time she walked out, dragging her feet but holding her head high. Autumn was in the air, its cool grey a dull canvas, though no colours appeared in contrast. Everything was grey these days. Grey or black. Especially now that summer was gone. How she tired of it. Back at the farm the trees would be turning, soon the ground would be littered by gold. There would be apples. And fresh eggs. The maple leaves would sweep underfoot, made slippery by the cool autumn rains. She could almost smell them . . . But she mustn't think that way. She'd made a choice and moved on.

Besides, she made her own colour, didn't she? When she closed her eyes she could see every shade, and the moment she was free to grab her paints, she did. Trees, water, grass—anything with a hue found its way to the paper. Danny appeared time and time again, but she wondered if she'd unwittingly changed his features at all over time. It was difficult, not having a photograph for reference, though she'd drawn his likeness often enough. Sometimes she questioned her pencil, wondered if it were taking creative licence, but she let it happen anyway. Even drawing an approximation of him felt good. When the other girls saw what she could do, saw how she brought life to a flat image, they sat for portraits. Subtleties of eye colour and slopes of individual jawlines were puzzles she craved, and the women were happy to model for her. Audrey never asked them for money, but the women compensated her by saving up and picking up supplies when she ran low. She told them painting was an escape, and that was the truth.

When she wrote to Danny, telling him everything about London—her job, the weekly suffragette meetings, and her new friends—she finished off by saying that she was being paid well at the factory, and it was all going into the box under her bed labelled *Canada*. He wouldn't have to worry about paying for her passage, and she wouldn't arrive at his parents' home dressed like a gutter rat, either. She'd make him proud of her, as she was proud of him. Oh, what a pair they'd make when they were finally together!

She fell asleep thinking of him, wondering where he was, but she tried to banish the vision of him in the trenches. She'd seen photographs of what it was like there. The newspaper printed some, and she hadn't looked away quickly enough. They wrote about soldiers dying or coming home broken. She'd seen soldiers around the city too, bandaged or hobbling on crutches. Or both. She'd even seen one who screamed like a madman on the street corners, reliving the nightmares, ducking under his hands from invisible explosions, then weeping with loss. *Not Danny,* she prayed. *Let him be just the same as when we met. Perfect in every way.*

He'd spoken of his parents, of his seven brothers, of his old dog. She knew his father preached when he wasn't fishing, and his mother made the best bread in the world. Sometimes, from his descriptions, Audrey could imagine a pat of golden butter melting in the middle of a slice, almost inhale the curl of steam rising up in the lamplight. He'd told her about the cold Atlantic swells, how he rode them like a teeter-totter on those dark days when storms came in fast. It didn't take much to imagine him there, feel the rise and fall under his legs as he stood solidly on deck, fighting for balance. How she loved to see him there in her mind, and see how he'd come in after fishing, soaking wet, frozen to the bone and exhausted, wanting only to come in and get warm with Audrey. They'd sit by the fire, and if his family wasn't there, she'd warm him with more than blankets.

Those kinds of thoughts lulled her into a mellow, dreamy smile, but the reality behind them brought her back. What did she really know about him, this man with whom she'd promised to spend the rest of her life? They'd seen each other for less than twenty-four hours, kissed a handful of times, and almost overwhelmed the post office. Was it enough? Could a lifetime of conversations come from so little?

What choice did she have? Stay here in London? No. As fascinating and as exciting as this city was, Audrey had found something vastly more intriguing between the lines of Danny's letters. He would be feeling the same hesitation, wondering what on earth he was doing, proposing to a woman he barely knew. And yet . . . something had happened on that night they'd met. Sure, it was true she hadn't met a lot of other men, living as remotely as she had, and it was possible she could have made a connection with anyone in that battalion. But it had been Danny. From the moment their eyes had touched on each other on the road beside that wonderful! blessed! broken wheel, it had been Danny. It would always be Danny, and if anyone asked her to explain why, she wouldn't know what to say.

Every Tuesday night she saw Marjory and Jean at the women's meetings, and since they worked at the post office, they often brought her mail from Danny. Audrey kept quiet, paying attention, but her thoughts always dwelled on the possibility of his letters.

After one meeting adjourned, Jean handed her two more letters, both bearing Danny's uneven printing. Audrey clutched them to her chest and closed her eyes, with him in that moment. Or as close as she could get.

"Well? What do they say?"

"Jean! Mind your own business. They're from her sweetheart. I don't think you'd be sharing letters from Simon with us, would you?"

"I might," Jean said, brow raised. "He does write saucy letters, though. They might shock your sense of propriety, my darling Marjory."

Her friends giggled then turned away when Audrey stuck one finger into the envelopes and slit open the first of the letters. Short missives containing nothing of any consequence, just a reaching out, a sharing of words, meant to help them both feel as if this were a perfectly normal courtship. This idea of his surviving in a muddy trench and her slaving in a greasy black hole, miles and miles apart from each other, would have to suffice for now. But someday . . . someday there would be no need for pen and ink. Someday there would be no need for words at all. They could just be together and be whole.

July 10, 1916

Dear Audrey,

Your parcel arrived yesterday, and boy oh boy, were we happy to dig into that! After we're done our weekly rations, a fellow can get awfully hungry. Do you make those ginger snaps yourself? Because they sure are delicious. Maybe someday you could bake some and we could eat them together, hot out of our own oven. Doesn't that sound sweet as candy to you? It does to me.

Sometimes we get moved out for a few days to the wagon lines, near where they keep the horses. That's where they have canteens where we can spend some of our money. We get 60 cents a day, which my friend Mick says is about 2 shillings. Last time I was back there I had ham and eggs nearly every evening. The meal cost my whole day's pay, but why worry? I haven't got anyplace else to spend it. Eggs are 13 cents each, which I suppose isn't too dear, but at home we have our own chickens, so I'm not used to having to buy eggs.

The weather has been uncommonly beautiful lately, which sure makes things easier. The mud gets a chance to dry a bit, and the boys like to take off their shirts or socks just to feel the sun on their skin. When the sky is clear like this, the air is fairly alive with planes.

I hope the weather near you is just as pretty as you are, if that's possible. I remain

Yours affectionately,
Danny

The second envelope was made of a stiffer, whiter paper, different from every other envelope she'd received from him. It made her curious. Was he somewhere new? His writing looked tired, even messier than usual, and she hoped that wherever he was, he was getting some well-deserved sleep.

August 12, 1916

My dearest Audrey,

This letter is the hardest thing I've ever had to write. I am in a hospital. I'm alive, but I have lost part of my right leg. Shell blew it clean off last week. Never even heard it coming.

I can't say what I'll be able to do for work when I get home, and I'll be getting home soon, because they called me a "Canada." If a fellow gets wounded but not too bad, he's called a "Blighty case." That means he can go back to the line after he's well. But I'm a "Canada case." In a way I'm happy about that, because I never want to see another explosion for as long as I live. But I'm leaving my leg behind, and that's what hurts the most.

No, that's not true. What hurts the most is that I'm letting you go, Audrey. Meeting you was the best part of my life, and I have loved getting your beautiful letters and packages. But you deserve a man who can take care of you. With only one good leg, I can't. I'm not much good for nothing anymore. So this letter is goodbye.

I've known I loved you from the first time I set eyes on you. I still do, and I wish you a wonderful life. I don't want you to feel bad for me. I want you to have a good life, with a good husband and a house full of kids.

With all my affection,
Danny

DANNY

– August 1916 –

ELEVEN

***

She had held both his hands before he left, squeezed his thick, strong fingers inside her little ones. *I like you, Danny, I really do. Do be careful, won't you?*

Something had changed in Danny in that moment. Something warm had stirred in his chest. Of course he knew to be careful, sure. At least as careful as a man could be when bombs exploded randomly around him. But there was something about the way she watched him, with hope in her eyes and . . . a guarded, unspoken promise. As if it really *did* matter if he made it back or not.

"I will, Audrey."

He watched her expression as he lifted those fingers to his lips and gently kissed them. Her eyes, so intense and earnest, melted into a kind of liquid joy, and in that moment he felt more like a man than he'd ever felt during any filthy, cussing, fighting, killing, hunting time in his life. From then on, all he wanted was to see those eyes do that for him again.

It seemed like so long ago. He'd fallen back into line after that, and Fred was staring pointedly at him, one bright red eyebrow lifted. Jimmy shot him a dirty look. "Lucky bastard."

Danny, Jimmy, and Fred trudged into the Somme along with the rest of the regiment. The Germans were wearing down the French in Verdun, so the British and Canadian troops were there to back them up. Talk was the Battle of the Somme was the biggest battle they'd ever face, and though the men were painfully aware of the dangers ahead, they couldn't help but step a little quicker as they came toward the action. The Fighting Twenty-fifth came in with a chip on their shoulders. Earlier that summer, the First Newfoundland had gone in, fronting the attack. Out of the eight hundred soldiers, fewer than seventy men had come back. Maritime boys stuck together. That kind of carnage was personal to Danny and the other Nova Scotians.

Once he was there, Danny thought the fighting at the Somme might never end. He couldn't look away from Parker, whose whispers never stopped leaking out of his mouth, nor the tears from his eyes. Then there was Johanson, whose attempt to blow off his own hand and get sent home had failed. Instead, the man had been left undoctored, the stumps of his fingers had gangrened, and he had died shaking with fever.

The artillery was a constant, booming across the maze of trenches in No Man's Land so the earth vibrated beneath their feet, shaking the mud from the walls. It seemed the Canadians were always the first to go over the top. They'd zigzag between the barbed wire blockades, shooting and being shot, there one moment and gone the next, swallowed up by an incoming shell and the resultant geyser of dirt vomited by the earth.

Danny witnessed the men fall, one after another. And every time he returned to the trenches at the end of his shift, he sat with Fred and Jimmy, holding Audrey's picture and thanking God for letting him see one more sunset.

"Ye'll be wearin' that portrait down to nothin'," Fred ribbed him.

"Poor lass. She's obviously got a touch o' the fever, thinkin' ye so high an' mighty."

"Shut your mouth," Danny shot back, though he loved their banter. "You're just jealous."

"Damn right I am," Jimmy muttered, and lit another cigarette.

After a while, the three of them decided Audrey's portrait was a lucky charm. Before they lined up to start fighting, Danny took it out and each of them touched her face lightly. She was their guardian angel, her gentle smile soothing and promising all at once. Danny liked the idea of that, of her watching over the three of them. Her being an angel of sorts seemed to bring her even closer to Danny.

But there was only so much her image could do.

Danny worked hard, shovelling in the trench, filling sandbags, carrying ammo and other supplies where they needed to go, cleaning and oiling his Ross, hoping it wouldn't self-destruct in his hands as it had with some of the other guys. Rain had set in a couple of days before, and his section of the trench pooled with putrid, muddy water so his boots made sucking noises when he walked. Each man had to do two hours of guard duty every night. Sometimes those nights went well into the next day, because often the dead of night was the best time to surprise the enemy. Sometimes nothing happened, and on those nights all the men battled were the lids falling closed over their bloodshot eyes.

On one of those endless nights, Jimmy, Fred, and Danny were on patrol while the others slept. Nothing was going on. Not a breeze, not a whisper. The three friends sat a few feet apart from each other, fighting to stay awake, and Danny gazed up into the stars, trying to focus on something. If he could just keep his mind occupied, he'd be okay.

They'd learned about shellings long before that night. A fellow could hear a shell coming and sometimes duck in time. But maybe Danny'd been nodding off. Maybe his thoughts had been on the gentle blue of Audrey's eyes or the soft coolness of her fingers curled around his, because he didn't hear anything that night. By the time the murderous whistle pierced his consciousness and he'd flopped onto his stomach as he'd been taught, it was almost too late.

Instantly that focus he'd sought arrived, shocking him with the same suddenness as the shell that struck the earth moments later. It was followed by another, this time accompanied by the rapid onslaught of gunfire. Danny clutched his rifle and shot back without thinking, firing blindly, seeking out his friends when the next blast lit the night. Jimmy was twenty feet ahead of him, doing the same thing, and their eyes met.

"Where's Freddie?" Danny screamed.

Jimmy put one hand to the side of his helmet; he couldn't hear Danny over the noise. Danny ran toward him, shooting and ducking.

"I said," he yelled as he got closer, "where's—"

The falling shell stole his voice and, blessedly, most of the sounds around him. His ears rang from the impact, and dizziness swelled as he fell into the mud. An odd, warm sensation wrapped around his leg, as if a blanket had landed on it, and when he tried to get up, a fire roared through him, searing and burning invisible flames up his pant leg, igniting his gorge. He screamed and retched, unable to comprehend what was happening, not knowing what to do next. The reek of smoke, of cooking meat was inside his skin; the roaring pain was white, pure white. Ice shocked against the wound when a breeze came, bringing a new agony. He couldn't hear his own screams over the booming of the guns. Then the fire was back, and Danny didn't think he could take any more.

"Danny!" Jimmy dropped to his knees beside him, vivid rivers of red lining the faded whites of his eyes. "Jaysus, Danny! Your leg!"

After a stunned moment, Jimmy whipped off his belt and cinched it around Danny's leg. "Ye'll be fine," he informed him. "We'll just get ye back."

Danny reached for something to say, but he was lost. His lips moved without direction. How could this be happening?

He and his best friend were staring at each other, Jimmy's eyes wet with unfamiliar tears, when Jimmy was struck. He flew back with the impact so his toes pointed skyward right around Danny's ear.

"Jimmy?"

His big friend was wheezing bad, but Danny figured that was good. It meant he was still breathing. Clenching his teeth against the exquisite pain shooting up his leg, he rolled to his belly and dragged himself up to Jimmy's body. His friend's arms and legs had flung apart when he'd fallen. Like a huge starfish from one of the lobster traps they'd hauled in together so many, many times. Now Jimmy moved one of those arms, slowly reaching toward his chest. Or maybe it wasn't slow. Maybe it only felt slow because Danny had a feeling he knew what was coming. Jimmy fumbled with the side of his jacket, then folded back one edge to reveal the hole that was killing him.

"Jesus Christ, Jimmy," Danny murmured. He pressed his hand on his friend's chest. The iron tang of fresh, pulsing blood filled his sinuses and gagged him at the back of his throat. "You look like one of them trout we used to gut in the harbour."

And Jimmy laughed. Danny felt the movement under his hand, the familiar bumping motion Jimmy made when he laughed. Like a bike with a twisted wheel.

"Screw you," Jimmy said, then he spat, his broad grin red with blood. "You're like a lobster that's lost a claw." His body shook, and the bumping laughter turned to shudders that rattled up through his clenched teeth. A tear squeezed from the corner of Jimmy's eye, avoided a blob of mud, meandered toward the ground. Danny grabbed Jimmy's hands, gripping them hard for reassurance. Reassurance for himself or Jimmy, he didn't know.

"Jaysus, Danny. Jaysus," Jimmy said, squinting a little. "I'm so god-damn cold."

Strange. Jimmy's blood didn't scare Danny nearly as much as the shivering. Jimmy had never been cold on the boat, no matter the season or the wind. He was always the one to razz Danny for being such a baby.

"Freddie's gone," Jimmy whispered, closing his eyes, "and I'm goin' with him. Can't trust the lad on 'is own, never could." His face contorted, hit by a wave of agony, and a foreign kind of wheeze whistled from his cracked lips. When he opened his eyes again, they were deep and dark as the ocean, and they were terrified. "You watch yerself, Danny."

The pain eased from Jimmy's face after his next breath, and Danny screamed, grabbing Jimmy's arm, then throwing himself over top of the still-warm body, shielding his old friend, clinging to him, feeling so afraid, so terribly afraid.

The boys in the trench were up and awake by then and returning fire. Machine guns swept the lines, dropping men where they stood, but the Fighting Twenty-fifth kept coming, rolling out of the trench like the furious, bayonet-wielding inhabitants of an anthill.

Boom. Boom. Boom. The guns pounded, roaring over the earth, pelting him with mud, jarring his leg.

"Beat it, Danny! Get out of the way!" he heard Mick holler, but there was nothing Danny could do. The fire in his leg and the inconceivable grief were melting him, loosing him from himself, tearing at his guts. It was like nothing he could ever have imagined. He lay across Jimmy's body, too shocked to cry, barely able to breathe.

Sounds and images took on the shape of the guns' echo, and the air in his head thickened. Everything in the world slowed. The booming and rat-a-tat and screaming faded and he felt cushioned, *soft, Audrey, safe, home . . .*

Another shell hit fifty yards away and he was back, jolted into the pain. *Gonna die here.*

I'm so sorry, Jimmy.

Danny fought the fire, rolled onto one side to see the damage.

There it was, the mutilated body of a man like many he'd seen before, but now it was his own. An explosion lit up the night and he stared at his muddy boot, six feet away. The leg above it had been neatly severed, still bleeding despite Jimmy's tight leather belt. A clean slice, he thought. Need a good, sharp blade to make a cut that clean. *Maybe they can just sew it back on.* Sure. Sure they can. He laid his cheek back in the muck and forgot all about the war.

———

Rough hands, fingers digging under his arms and ribs . . . *No no no leave me here. Please please leave me here . . . I'll be fine here . . .*

The stretcher carriers were as gentle as they could be, but Danny had to be moved. Shelling had stopped temporarily, and a brief period of time existed during which the wounded could be collected and possibly saved. They ignored the sounds Danny made, the pleading, begging prayers. They'd heard it thousands of times before. Those who could fight again, the men with cuts, bruises, lesser injuries like missing fingers or toes— had been taken off the field first and readied to fight another day. They'd come back after that for Danny and others who were closer to death. They would return later, if the shelling didn't start again, for those who had lost the fight. *Don't forget Jimmy and Freddie!*

The stretcher dipped and bumped under the grip of the bearers, and Danny's jaw set so tight he thought his teeth might splinter. Didn't matter. He was going to die anyway. They stopped at the regimental aid post, where Danny was lifted from the stretcher and laid on a table. The stretcher disappeared from view, and the carriers went back for more.

A doctor bent over Danny, his blood-smeared hands flitting around the mangled leg, bending down to get a better view.

"Uh-huh," the doctor muttered.

"Tell me," Danny managed to say.

"You'll live, soldier," the doctor said. "But you'll live with half a leg, I'm afraid. I'm going to bind you up and give you some morphine. You'll go from here to the CCS. They'll be able to take better care of you there." He turned. "Bart!"

A smaller man jogged over, unfolded Danny's arm and jabbed a needle into his vein. Danny flinched, then blinked up at the doctor, trying not to cry.

"This'll make it stop?"

Of course not. It'll never stop. Not until I'm dead.

"For now, soldier. They'll have more when you get to the CCS." He patted Danny's shoulder and gave him a smile he had probably used a thousand times on boys like Danny. "You're a brave man, son. Your country is proud of you."

It took five minutes for the morphine to pass through his heart and travel around his limbs, to dull the throbbing pain. The world slid a little farther away, and Danny closed his eyes, trying to think of home. Of what they'd be doing right about now. Would the tide be in or out? His brothers would be yanking in the traps, laughing or cursing as they worked. He could practically see them. Dump the lobsters into the crate, bait the traps, drop them into the hungry sea, paddle back in time for lunch. Mother would have soup, and there'd be toast—

Hands grabbed him, loaded him back onto a stretcher. The carriers were laughing, talking to each other about something Danny couldn't quite grasp. The morphine pressed against his eyelids, but he forced them open, needing to see. The stretcher bumped as it slid into the back of a covered wagon, and Danny tried not to scream. He focused on what he could see, not what he was feeling. Around the inside of the wagon were benches loaded with the walking wounded. The floor had room for two stretchers, and one was his. Danny didn't recognize the bloodied soldier in the next one, but even if he'd known him before, he might not have recognized him now. Half of the man's face had been wrapped in rapidly darkening bandages, one arm was severed at the shoulder and more bandages covered his chest. A gurgling sound came from the man's gaping mouth whenever he breathed. Made Danny think of the bubbles a lobster blows when he's taken from the sea. And that made him think of Jimmy.

"Everyone in? Let's get this show on the road!" called the driver. When he got the okay, the driver chirped to the pair of horses and the wagon jolted forward. Every man in the wagon cried out, clutching at their injuries, and one man near the back threw up over the half door.

The wagon moved at a snail's pace, dipping into craters, slipping on mud. One of the injured started humming a song, and a couple of them joined in. Danny didn't know the song, but he liked the sound. He chuckled at a few of the words. The morphine was doing a fine job, keeping the pain at bay, keeping his mind dulled. Some of the other men on the benches couldn't sing. A few of them were crying. Danny could hear the snuffling, the occasional gasp when the big wooden wheels hit another bump. The man on the stretcher wasn't crying, he didn't think. All he could see of him was bandages.

Someone lit a cigarette, and Danny's stomach twisted. What he would do for a smoke right then. It must have been obvious on his face, because next thing Danny heard was a hoarse voice to his right.

"Smoke?"

"God, yes," Danny said, looking up toward the voice.

Because of the lack of light within the wagon, Danny couldn't see the man's face until he leaned forward and offered the cigarette. Danny tried to raise himself closer to a sitting position, at least to support himself on one side, but his leg was having none of it. So Danny accepted the cigarette, stayed horizontal, and breathed in, welcoming the rush of smoke as it travelled through his system.

"I'm Danny," he said, handing the cigarette back. "Thanks."

The other man nodded, bringing the cigarette to his own lips. "Happy to oblige. Henry's the name."

"You're English, huh?" Danny asked, his mind flashing on Audrey.

Henry's smile faded into the leathery skin of his face. It could have been the morphine, but Danny thought the man's stubbled cheeks seemed almost nonexistent, shadowed as they were by the chiselled bones of his face. His fleshed-out skull framed eyes like black diamonds. When he blinked, Danny wondered where one might mine for something like that.

"Tough luck about your leg," Henry said.

Danny didn't say anything for a bit. He couldn't sit up, so he couldn't see the damage, but that was okay. He'd see it soon enough.

"Guess it could have been worse," Danny said.

Henry offered the cigarette again, and Danny saw how the Englishman's hand shook. Like an old man's hand. But Henry didn't appear to be much older than twenty-five. Same as him. Danny brought the cigarette to his mouth, paying close attention to his own hand. Did it shake too? Yes. Constantly. Like Cecil's leg when he scratched the old dog's furry belly in just the right spot. He wondered how long that shaking had been going on. Had he left more than his leg on the battlefield?

"Been here long?" Henry asked.

"Sixteen months," Danny said. "Sixteen months too long. But who's counting?"

"She's a terrible war, ain't she?" Henry asked, though he wasn't looking at Danny when he asked.

At some point along the uneven path, the man lying beside Danny starting screaming. It started out of nowhere. One moment they were bumping along, the next moment the prostrate man was arching his back, flailing his one remaining arm in the air, head thrown back so

Danny saw the roof of his mouth when he screamed. They stopped the wagon and a medic jumped in to see what could be done, but the man died quite suddenly. The medic pulled a sheet over the body, and Danny noticed all the other men staring down at him.

"Hey, boys. Don't look at me," he mumbled. "Just 'cause I'm lying here doesn't mean I'm following him."

Scattered laughter bounced around the wagon, and as Danny sank back to sleep, he heard one man say, "You'll make it home yet."

The sleep that came upon Danny was no longer a vague suggestion. It sucked him in, like the ocean undertow. His last thought rose from the depths, *I'm sorry, Audrey,* then he slept until the wagon stopped again.

TWELVE

"Baker?" the orderly called. "Daniel Baker, Twenty-fifth?"

Danny pushed up onto his elbows. "Here, sir."

"Two letters today, son," the man said, handing over a couple of worn envelopes. Danny nodded his thanks, but the man had already turned away, seeking the next person.

The first was from his mother. Of course Danny's parents knew all about his leg. The army called the casualty list every night to the next of kin, so they'd known within twenty-four hours. His mother had sent a parcel of candy and a sweater. Navy blue. He was glad to see the sweater, because he had no idea where any of his other clothes or personal things were. He hoped someone would bring them in before it was time to head home. It hung a bit loose on him—Danny hadn't eaten much over the past year and a half—but it was warm. Especially over the hospital gown. And despite the miles and miles of separation, it smelled like home.

He slipped his finger through the cut in the envelope and popped it open so he could pull out the single piece of paper. His mother's writing wasn't neat and tidy like other women's. Danny could picture her leaning over the paper, fountain pen in hand, loose brown hair tumbling over her forehead. She had been born left-handed and had spent years stubbornly trying to get her right hand to cooperate, to follow her mind around the curves of letters. Her missives weren't long, but he knew she spent a long time writing them, thinking through what she wanted to say so she could be economical with the words.

Danny rolled to the side and leaned on one elbow, holding the letter with the other hand. His leg was a constant throbbing, but less so now than it had been before. At least the repair to his stump had gone smoothly. No infection. He glanced down out of habit, a tiny voice in his mind wondering if he might have been mistaken. Maybe the leg would be there this time. But no. Everything from just below his right knee was gone. The doctor had said it was a relatively simple operation, since Danny had already done most of the work out on the field.

August 17, 1916

My dearest son,

Your father and I are only happy to know that you are alive. We will do what needs to be done when you are home. Your father and I can hardly wait to meet you in Halifax. Please keep me informed as to the blessed day of your arrival.

We await your reply, our hearts alight with joy at the prospect of seeing you soon.

All our love,
Your devoted parents

Danny folded the letter and slipped it back into the envelope, then held it against his chest. Tears welled, but he swallowed them down. For the longest time he had wanted to go home. He had missed everything about that old chunk of rock. But the idea now . . . the thought of being at home but being only part of a man . . .

Fact was, he was afraid. People he had always known would stare, their eyes dark with sympathy and fascination. His brothers would back away as if he were a stranger. How could he go home?

Danny sighed and closed his eyes, cooling their heat beneath his lids. He shuffled the envelopes so the second one was on top, then opened his eyes again.

Audrey. His heart leapt at the familiar curls of her letters. What would she say? He had wondered if she would answer at all after his last note. Oh, that had been a hard one to write. Had she seen the dark circles left by his tears, or had they disappeared into the paper? She had been the one hope he'd had for bettering his life. Now that hope was gone. Taken by a piece of metal.

"Audrey," he whispered then very carefully opened the envelope. A sprig of a dried flower tumbled out, and he caught its tiny buds before they could roll off the bed. His fingers squeezed the flower into dust as he read.

August 16, 1916

My dearest Danny,

I am torn to pieces by your note. I cry every night thinking of you in the hospital. I cannot bear to think of you in pain.

I read your letter so many times, hoping you didn't mean what you said.

Danny, I love you, too. I wish I could say it to your face. You think I only love what you were before, but you're wrong. I love what you are now, leg or no leg. You're mad if you think I will be happier without you.

If you still want me, I want to come to Canada and be your wife. We shall do fine. I can work hard, and you will feel better over time. You will learn how to live again.

If you still want me, Danny, please write and tell me what to do.

I love you, Danny. I don't know how to live without you anymore.

Audrey

He read the letter again; then, ignoring the familiar streak of pain that jolted up his body as he moved what was left of his leg, he leaned back and stared up at the ceiling. He laid the letter flat on his stomach, keeping both palms open on it. She loved him? She still wanted him? He brought the letter up and held it with both hands above his face so he could read it again.

I love you, Danny. I don't know how to live without you anymore.

A tear rolled down the side of his face, blurring the words on the page. He lowered the letter to his chest and closed his eyes.

"Thank God," he whispered.

———

He spent six weeks in the hospital learning what he'd become. Six weeks getting to know the peg leg and crutch that would accompany him for the rest of his life. Six weeks of lying in a hospital bed among fellow cripples. Then they sent him home, where he battled every day with the urge to write back to her, persuade her to change her mind. He had nothing to offer her. Beautiful Audrey, with her zest for life, would be swallowed up by his agony. But he never put that in writing. He needed her as he'd never needed anything in his life. She would bring life back to him. She would become life itself.

THIRTEEN

Man was not meant to stand on one foot. He wasn't a damn heron. Sure, he had the crutch, but it wasn't the same thing. It wasn't the other half of him, just a substitute off to the side. But the peg leg rubbed his skin raw. It hardly seemed worth the pain. He still had to use a crutch. After a while he left the peg at home and tried to get past the scrutiny of people who had never before seen a man with one leg. At least it was finally spring. Still slippery, but easier going.

Before the war, Danny had been one of the boys. He'd laughed and teased and was constantly in the thick of things. Now he was most content when he was in the shed, working with wood, away from everyone else. He liked being on his own, away from prying eyes. It was a relief that his family had finally stopped staring. Especially his mother. God, the pain in her eyes was too heavy for him to bear. Her big, first-born son with all the promise in the world. Only half was left. What a waste. Johnny'd have to step up now.

Didn't seem to matter what Danny did, at least three of the littlest Bakers were usually clustered around him. Didn't even matter what they talked about. Could be the weather, could be the neighbour's cat, the one that broke into the henhouse and killed half a dozen birds in one night. Could be the big dock spider they'd trapped.

"Don't you boys ever have anything better to do than bother me?" Danny snapped one day.

Artie, Ross, and little Harvey exchanged a quick glance, then Artie shrugged. "Don't think so," he said.

"Tell us a story, Danny," Harvey asked.

Danny was sitting on a log, carving slices from a stick, trying to come up with some kind of practical model for a new peg. Harvey sat on the grass in front of Danny, crossing his legs as if he were in school.

"A story?" Danny asked, peering up from the bit of birch in his hands. He set aside his project for the time being, hoping if he just gave the boys what they wanted, they'd eventually leave him alone.

"Yeah," Ross agreed. "Tell us something we've never heard before."

"From the war," Artie suggested.

"Yeah," said Ross. "You never tell us nothing about the war, Danny."

"What do you want to know?"

The boys shrugged.

"Okay," Danny said. "But first, Artie, take my knife and cut me that willow branch."

Artie took the little blade and ran obligingly to the tree Danny indicated. "This one?"

"The thicker one. Next to it, see? Think you're strong enough to cut through that?"

The little boy puffed out his chest. "I'm strong enough."

"Sure you are. Bring it over when you're done." Danny scratched his chin, realized he'd forgotten to shave that morning. "A story, huh?" He sorted through the thoughts in his head, searching for something he could tell. Artie brought him the branch and Danny cut it short with one quick slice.

"Well, there was one fellow over there you boys would have liked," Danny said.

"Is he still there?" Ross asked.

"Yeah. I think he is." He hoped he was. He hoped he wasn't buried somewhere. "His name's Mick. He's from Halifax. He worked with the newspaper there. He's a funny guy, Mick."

"What did he look like?" Harvey asked, eyes round.

"Well, kinda like Johnny Hartlin, you know? Shorter than me by about six inches, wiry like a rope. But he could take the biggest guy down with his fists. He was quick." Danny stopped, lost in thought. He stopped whittling and sat stone still until Artie jerked him back.

"Danny?"

"Right. Right," Danny said, blinking. "Well, you know about the Jerries, right? The Germans? Just as soon shoot you through the eyes if they could. But Mick, he loved 'em."

"Why?" Harvey asked.

"Do you want me to tell this story, Harvey? Or do you want to ask questions?"

"You can tell it," the little boy decided.

"Okay," Danny said. He started carving again. "Well, with Mick, see, whenever there was quiet, he would shout out to them Germans, ask if they wanted to come play checkers. If they wanted to come on over and have a party with us."

"Really?"

"Yeah," Danny said, chuckling. There were so many things he wanted to forget. But it was bittersweet to realize there were still a few he wanted to remember. "He only did it when it was a clear night, so they could hear him good. Well, one night he got it into his head that they were being rude, not coming over to have a party. He was some funny, that boy. Well, Mick, he takes a peek through the scope—that's the thing that let us see what was happening outside of the trench, see? Anyway, there was nothing going on that night. It was Christmas Eve 1915, and there was kind of a truce going on or something. We didn't hear nothing. So Mick, he gets going. He figures we should have a Christmas Eve party. He could make this ridiculous duck call with his hands, and he was just going with that."

For a moment his brothers saw a real smile. He was painfully aware that they hadn't seen one out of him since he'd gotten home, eight months before.

"So Mick takes a peek then climbs up the wall. He gets up top and yells 'Merry Christmas, Jerry!' then he turns around and drops his drawers."

The boys gasped, then hooted with laughter. "He didn't!" Artie exclaimed.

"He did indeed. He did indeed. Well, the Jerries, they started making noises like you boys are doing right now. Mick was dancing away up there, and all of a sudden there's a shot, right? Just one, though. Not like machine-gun fire. Just one shot to get Mick's attention. Mick, he freezes. Then one of the Jerries yells out in his German accent, 'Put that thing away! Ve don't vanna see dat ass on Christmas Eve!' and Mick hollers back 'It's the best thing you'll see this Christmas, boy!' and then everyone was laughing. We could hear 'em laughing in the other trench, which was real strange. But it was a great night. Like no one wanted to kill anyone on Christmas Eve."

"Did you kill anyone, Danny?" It was Harvey again, asking for truths with his little-boy innocence.

Danny frowned at the carving in his hands. He didn't want to have to explain, to tell this trusting little soul what his big brother had done.

"Sure he did," Artie said quickly. He shoved Harvey's shoulder. "You know that. Dad already told us that."

"But did you really?" Harvey asked.

"Oh yeah," Danny said, resigned. "I killed a lot of guys."

"What was that like?" Ross asked. "To shoot a guy?"

Danny frowned. "Why would you wanna know that?"

Ross shrugged. With his gaze on his little brother, Danny stabbed his wooden leg with the carving knife. It didn't bother him, but the boys gasped and paid very close attention after that.

"Killing a man is a terrible thing, Ross. A terrible thing no one should ever have to do. But the thing is, when they put you out there, when you're up against the other guy, well, you just know he's gonna kill you if he can. So you gotta stop him first. I stopped a lot of guys."

"What about your foot, Danny?" asked Harvey.

"What about it?"

"Where is it?"

"I don't know. Here you go. What do you think of this?"

He passed Artie the five-inch piece of finished willow and the boy scowled at it, uncomprehending. Danny took it back and blew into one end, lighting up Artie's eyes. The little boy reached for the toy.

"It's a whistle! That's so—"

"Is it like killing a rabbit?"

All of them stared at Harvey. Then Artie and Ross shifted their attention to Danny, wanting to know, silently thanking their baby brother for being the one to ask the hard question.

"Harvey, do you think it'd be like killing a rabbit?" Danny leaned toward the little boy and locked onto the innocence of his eyes. He clutched Harvey's arms and held on tight when the boy tried to squirm away. Danny wanted no misunderstanding when he gave this lesson. "Would the rabbit be like a man? Would the rabbit have family that he cared about? Tell me, Harvey, have you ever seen a rabbit's thoughts before he died?" Harvey shook his head like mad. "Know why? It's because rabbits don't have thoughts. They think only two things: eat and run. Men are just like you. Men have thoughts and memories and futures. They love people, just like you do. They have a mother back home waiting to pour them lemonade and mend their britches. And one day they go out there and somebody tells 'em to shoot that other boy."

The whistle was forgotten. Harvey blinked.

"Now here's a question for you, Harvey. For all you boys. Say you're that man, and you meet another man who's just like you. Say that other man is pointing a gun at you, and you're pointing one at him. One of you's gonna shoot first. Say it's you. You watch him look at you like he can't believe you just did that. Like you were a buddy who just took something away. Something real important. You see his last thoughts. You see him saying goodbye to his family, his friends, and his future. Then you watch him fall down. And no one ever sees him get up again."

Not even a bird chirped. There was no one left on earth besides Danny and the three little boys.

"So the question is, Harvey, is it worse for the guy that's been killed or for the guy who has to spend his life remembering how he killed that other man?"

The boys didn't have an answer. Danny hadn't expected one. He let Harvey go, and the little boy shuffled out of his reach. Danny yanked the knife out of the peg and pointed it at each boy like a finger. Not a threat, but making a definite point.

"Don't you boys ever go to war, you hear me? Don't you ever go. Folks can call you all sorts of names, but don't you listen. There's plenty of other things a man should do that don't involve killing another man." Danny's words came fast now, punctuated by tiny blasts of spittle. "You know what we were fightin' for? Artie, you're the oldest. Do you know what we were fighting for?"

Artie was ten. Up until this moment he had considered himself to be grown up. Right now he looked very young. He cleared his throat. "We was fightin' the Jerries, right, Danny? So's they don't take over the world?"

"Yep. That's what they tell you. That you're saving the world from these fellows. But the truth is, when you fix that bayonet in your gun and go over the top, you're saving no one but yourself. And what you're fighting for? Well, shucks. It's maybe twenty yards of dirt. And not even good dirt."

Harvey's blue eyes filled with tears.

"Don't you cry now, Harvey," Danny said. "Big boys don't cry."

Harvey sniffed.

Ross, the tough guy, cleared his throat. "But we gotta go to war when they say so."

"Do you?"

"Sure," Ross said. "Or else they put you in jail."

"Yep," Danny said. "Or worse. But I tell you what, Ross. I'll never go to sleep again without seeing the eyes of all those men I killed. All those boys who were just doing what they were told. And those boys? They'll never go to sleep again."

"Father said he's proud of you," Artie said after a moment.

"Does he? That's good to know." Danny looked away, couldn't let them see the shame in his eyes. "I ain't."

FOURTEEN

Danny had always liked working with his hands, sorting through nets and traps to get at the creatures caught within. He'd been out a few times since returning home, standing on the boat, leaning on his crutch as he hauled in the nets. The waves caught him, tossed him to the floor of the boat a few times, until he gave in and decided to revert to the slower process of handlining, bringing in a smaller but more valuable catch of cod.

He, Thomas, and Johnny eased into a spot they'd used for years.

"Grease the line, Danny. We'll check depths."

"You do it. I sharpened the hooks last night."

Johnny grunted and smeared grease on the anchor, then dropped it in, counting the fathoms with each disappearing knot.

"Where are we?" Danny asked.

"Seventeen," Johnny replied, hauling the anchor back up. Gravel stuck to the anchor, confirming they'd hit the shoal. Anything close to twenty fathoms gave them a good chance of coming home with a fair catch. The cod would be here if they were anywhere.

Sure, it was fishing. But it wasn't what Danny thought of as fishing. It wasn't rolling over deep, black waves, their crests white with warning. It definitely wasn't clinging to the mast when the Atlantic reminded men of her power. What they were doing now seemed like either old-man fishing or little-boy fishing. Danny wondered which one he was supposed to be.

He'd gone out a few times with the oldest two of his younger brothers, Johnny and Thomas. He knew they preferred to use nets to pull in the haddock, but they slowed the process down for him. The rough seas were too much for Danny to handle.

"I seen that Mary Tracey watching you," Thomas told Johnny as the boat rose and fell, riding a long Atlantic swell. "Like a cat on cream, she is."

"As she should be," Johnny replied. "Who is there around here with looks like mine?"

Danny yawned loudly. "That big sow in Webber's barn has your look," he suggested.

"Oh, and aren't you the funny one," Johnny drawled, rolling his eyes.

"That's what the ladies tell me," Danny replied.

Johnny and Thomas exchanged a grin.

"What?" Danny asked, feigning disinterest.

"Mother said you have a girl," Thomas blurted. "That she's coming here to marry you."

"Uh-huh," Danny said. "That's right."

They let the saltwater breeze clear the tension from the air before Thomas continued with the interrogation. "What's she like? Pretty?"

"Prettiest I ever seen," Danny said, and smiled. "Her name's Audrey. She's smart and feisty, you know? Like she's not going to take no business from nobody. And she sure does think the world of me, for whatever reason."

Johnny snorted. "Can't say she's that smart if she thinks that."

"I can still shove you over," Danny warned.

"Can you? Or would you topple in there with me?"

"Oh, now who's being funny?" asked Danny. "Do I have to remind you of the spearing event?"

Johnny'd been only eight when they'd set out in two smack boats that day, hunting for flatfish, or flounder. The flat-bottomed boat they used for clamming and lobstering also worked for flatfish, and their mother had sent her two oldest on a mission. Jimmy Mitchell had gone, too. The trick was to kneel, lean in with the spear at the ready, then stab the mud. Had to be quick and accurate. But waiting for the fish to peek out of the mud could be a lesson in patience some days, and Johnny never had much of that.

"I did tell you not to stand up," Danny reminded him.

"Haven't we been over this?"

He chuckled. "I'll never forget that, seeing you hugging that spear after you launched it deep into the mud, lost your balance, and the boat skipped out from under you. You were like a porcupine up a tree."

"And you were a big help."

Danny grinned even wider. "Hell, Jimmy was laughing so hard I didn't think he'd be able to turn the boat around to pick him back up."

"Wish I'd been there," Thomas said, laughing.

"You were barely walking."

"Hey! I was six!"

Danny winked at him. "Exactly."

Thomas jigged his line hard, setting the fish, then pulled steady with long strokes. A shiny foot-long cod, hooked in the belly, flopped from the hook. Thomas grabbed the slippery body, freed it, then dumped it on the floor between them. His hook was lowered back into the black water within seconds. That was good. Meant they were right over a school.

"Vinny's brother's going to enlist," Thomas said, his eyes on a screeching gull overhead.

Danny said nothing, just gave his line an experimental tug.

Thomas continued. "Floyd says he wishes he was going, too. He's seventeen. He thinks that's old enough." He hesitated. "I do, too."

Johnny's eyes shifted to watch his older brother's reaction. Danny sighed.

"Sure, I guess it's old enough, Tommy. To die. To lose a leg or an eye or something. To see your buddies blown to meat. Tell you what. I reckon I'm as tough as any of those boys over there. Tougher than a lot of them. And I would cry most every night, wishin' I was here with you brats. If it was up to me, I'd end the war tomorrow, so you'd never have to go. Neither of you."

The gull was still shrieking, but the wind had changed. The water was still, slow and soothing, like a cradle after the baby has fallen asleep.

"Ain't biting much," Johnny said.

"Nope," his brothers replied.

The gull dove, focused and unafraid, hitting the surface of the water with jarring suddenness. Then he floated, like the decoys the hunters used each fall. As though he were carved from wood. The boys sat likewise.

"So she's pretty?" Thomas asked after a few minutes.

"Uh-huh," Danny said. "You'll see her soon."

———

Later that night, Danny and Johnny sat on the edge of the dock, smoking and listening to the spring peepers fill the night with their chirping. Johnny cleared his throat.

"You need money for Audrey, don't you?" he said. Both of them knew there wasn't much Danny could do about that.

"I'll need it when she gets here."

Johnny's dark eyebrow flicked up. "And how's she getting here?"

It was tough to say it out loud. Tough enough to think it, but even tougher to hear it said. He looked into the darkness, not wanting to see Johnny's reaction. "She's got a job in London. Working in a munitions factory."

Turns out he didn't have to see him to feel Johnny's surprise. "A job?"

Danny took a deep drag on his cigarette. There was no breeze, so when he and his brother exhaled, the smoke sat in front of their faces like fog over the cove. Something flopped in the water, grabbed an evening snack off the surface, then plunged below.

"She said she wanted to."

"And you let her?"

"Who am I to order her around?" he snapped, then he sniffed and lowered his voice. "She has to make money anyhow, I guess. She has no family."

Johnny seemed to accept that. "Okay. So when's she coming? It's been a while."

"Yep. At this rate I may be an old man before she gets over here."

"Poor girl," Johnny said. "You're ugly enough now. Wouldn't want to see you when you're old."

"Always so funny, little brother."

———

Plans went ahead, despite the fact that her arrival was still a ways off. Daniel Sr. approached Danny one morning with the first step. "I've been thinking," he said. "You and your wife'll want your own room, I expect."

Danny grinned, a little sheepish. "I'd think so, sir."

"I've ordered some lumber, and I thought you and I could build it on this side of the house," he said, gesturing. "So your wife can see the ocean when she wakes. Do you reckon she'd like that? The view?"

"Oh, yes sir," Danny assured him. "She's a real queen, my Audrey, sir. She loves everything. You'll see. And she's the prettiest thing—"

"That's fine, son," his father said, lifting an eyebrow. "No need to discuss her virtues. I'm certain she has many. I was only wondering if she'd like the view."

"Right. Sorry, sir." He chuckled to himself. "I get carried away thinking about her sometimes. Yes. She'd love it."

"Good. So we'll build it here, cut through that wall for the door, fashion a window this way, and maybe a separate entrance." He looked at Danny without the slightest hint of pity. "I'll expect you to pull your weight, son."

"You can count on me, sir."

It became a spring project, with Johnny and the younger boys pitching in as well.

Someday they'd live in more than a room off to the side. Someday they'd build their own house, though he'd keep it nearby. Even if he had two legs, it didn't make sense for Audrey and him to break new land since his grandfather had already made a good start on it. Besides, when his father could no longer hoist in a net, when his mother hadn't the strength to do things on her own, Danny and his brothers would be nearby. Family stayed close. Always had, always would. For now, a room in his father's house would do.

After a difficult but determined first day, he stayed up late by the oil lamp, writing to Audrey, telling her what they'd done. It was a good time for Danny, getting back into daily routines. He wore his peg leg while he worked, covered by his trousers, and though it was uncomfortable and hot, it gave him better balance. It also kept the others' eyes off him and on the work at hand. He leaned into the boards when he needed support and occasionally forgot he was missing anything at all. Almost.

DANNY

— June 1917 —

FIFTEEN

Passengers swarmed off the newly completed Pier 2, shuffling along the concrete wall for what seemed like miles, just to get their papers stamped. The floor was awash with faded hats, coats, and bags, everything wallowing in browns, greys, and blacks. Bright colours were out of fashion these days, dulled by the war. Everyone was in mourning for someone.

Danny was so excited he fairly shook. They'd waited so long for this, it was hard to believe the day was here. He stared out at the people, imagining her arms around his neck, remembering the sweet touch of her lips, but he had a lurking fear he wouldn't recognize her when she finally arrived. It had been so long, after all.

He needn't have worried. Through all the bodies and bags, Danny could still spot Audrey. It had been over a year since he'd seen her, but his eyes picked her out like a hawk on a mouse. He didn't remember her being so tiny, and he worried that when he finally held her, he'd crush her in his enthusiasm. Then he thanked the Lord that he had seen fit to take Danny's leg instead of his arm. He needed to hold her.

She wore a brown belted dress that was styled like a coat. A line of dark buttons ran down its length, from her oversized collar to just beneath her knees. Topping it all was a small yellow hat, like a lid over a pot of bubbling brown curls.

What had she been wearing that day they'd met? He couldn't recall. That had been the one and only other time he'd ever seen her, apart from her picture, that is. A white kerchief over her hair, he remembered that.

He'd hardly dared to dream of her coming to him after all this. Like a nightingale willing to fly into a battlefield. He'd fallen in love with a crazy bird, hadn't he?

"Audrey!" he called, leaning on his crutch and waving along with hundreds of other welcoming arms. She couldn't hear him. He knew that. But if he celebrated her arrival even in this little way, it seemed to bring her closer.

Someone shoved past Danny, accidentally kicking his crutch. Danny stumbled, cursed, and glared at the offender's receding back.

"Watch your bloody step," he growled.

"Excuse me," a woman beside him said coldly. "I'm sure you can control that kind of language, can you not? There are ladies and children here, sir."

He glanced at the children at her feet, then back at her. All three were staring at Danny's stump, their faces twisted with disgust.

"Excuse me, kids," Danny said. He waited for her to look up, then he slowly added, "Ma'am."

He smiled, but it was a dark smile that dared her to say another word, that said, *Judge me all you want, lady. I lost this leg fighting for your freedom.* Something about that smile must have had an effect, because her scowl dropped. She stepped back, tugging her children into the crowd. *That's right,* he thought as loudly as he could. *You* should *be scared.*

He peered back toward the lineups, and his heart gave a little jump when he couldn't spot Audrey right away. He scanned the coats he knew were ahead of her, behind her, beside—ah, there she was. Her yellow cap stood out among all the drab browns, like a daffodil poking through wilted grass. She was crouched down, talking to a little boy in an oversized blue cap. It appeared as though she only had one bag with her. That was just fine because the schooner they were taking wasn't very big, and it was a good, long ride to East Jeddore. At least the weather was good and the wind was up.

He was glad she'd come out mid-summer. Summer in Nova Scotia was a gorgeous palette, and he knew she'd love it. The bunch of day lilies he clutched, all wrapped up in a pink lace ribbon his mom had suggested, were soft, feminine, and pretty. Just like Audrey. It was beautiful. It was all beautiful. The trees and the water, the blue of the sky. It was all a man needed. That, and a good wife.

Maybe they'd get married right away, under the huge oaks in his parents' yard by the sea. Why spend time in separate bedrooms when they could be living together as man and wife?

Man and wife. It hardly seemed real. On the day they'd met, they'd been two frightened souls in the middle of nowhere, and he marvelled it had come to this. They'd met one day and parted the next, but he'd known. She'd known, too. That's just the way it was. And now he was standing at the pier, vibrating with impatience. He was like a kid at a candy shop, waiting for his turn to grab a treat.

His family would all come to the wedding, and that would include a lot of aunts and uncles. He couldn't invite any of his friends, because they were either still fighting overseas or they were dead. He'd written to the boys in the battalion but hadn't heard back. He wondered if they'd opened his letter in a trench and read it out loud while they huddled around an insubstantial fire. Had they laughed over it in someone's bombed-out basement? Had they kept it and used the paper to roll cigarettes?

Soldiers stood in a wall of uniforms around Audrey, looking as if they needed protection more than she did. Their haunted eyes darted around the pier, lost without the burn of smoke and stink of death. Danny knew that confusion. Felt it every day. Sometimes when he awoke in the mornings, he panicked, fooled by the silence of the room. When he heard nothing, his first thought was that maybe he'd died. He'd often wondered if death was better than the alternative.

Some of his own kind were drifting in now, men on stretchers and crutches, bandaged like mummies. They were marched or carried up to the top floor, where a small hospital had been set up for those who couldn't go another step without help. Danny felt sick, watching them. His eyes found their injuries first, then scanned their faces, wondering if he might recognize one of the thousands he'd seen at the front. He never did.

Some of the boys were very young. Young, but with the spirit twisted right out of them. Danny knew that pain as well.

He peered back toward where he'd last seen Audrey and realized she'd moved right up to the front of the line. He limped closer, trying to avoid squishing anyone's feet with his crutch.

"Audrey!" he called, and her head spun, curls bouncing as she searched for him. He waved. "Over here, Audrey!"

"Danny!" Her smile was beautiful. Radiant. She shuffled in place as if she wanted to run to him, but the woman behind the desk was taking her time. "I'm coming!"

She bent over the desk and signed whatever needed signing, grabbed her bag, and ran toward Danny.

At first he just stared at her, paralyzed. It felt unreal, seeing her right there in front of him, in his own country, his own place. She stopped two feet away. One small hand nervously tugged the curls hanging onto her neck.

"Please don't look at me like that, Danny," she said. "Say something."

"I—" Danny wanted to oblige, wanted to say something and quit acting like such an idiot, but he was tongue-tied.

"Danny?" She frowned. "Is it all right that I'm here?"

"God, Audrey," he managed at last. He thrust the flowers toward her, then started forward, leaning on the crutch, wanting so badly not to look awkward. She was there first, her arms around his neck, her lips on his as if they'd always belonged there.

"What?" he said, leaning away from her. "Are those tears, Audrey? Are you cryin'?"

She snuffled and backed away, scrambling in her handbag for

a handkerchief. "Oh, I beg your pardon. I have a cloth somewhere but I—"

"Forget that. I'm only teasing. Come here, will you? I've wanted to touch you for so long!"

Her arms went back around him, and he grabbed her waist. The crutch snugged under his arm, but he didn't need it. She was holding him, he was holding her, and he felt as if he could run and jump again, fly through the forest paths as he'd done for twenty-five years before this. Her brown dress was rough, like the calluses on his fingers, a lighter wool than his uniform had been. It carried with it the smell of the sea, of travel, and of the grime she'd picked up along the way. He liked everything about it. It made her more real to him. And less fragile. He kissed her for so long he thought he might run out of breath.

"I can hardly wait to introduce you to my folks and my brothers. You'll be stayin' in the new bedroom until we—" Words bubbled up his throat, nervous, excited, unstoppable. Champagne behind a cork. "But I already told you that in my letters, didn't I? I can't believe I wrote so many letters. I never used to write. Anyway, it's a nice room. My father and I just finished it. I hope you'll be comfortable in it. It's just down the hall from the room that I share with some of my brothers. And my mother is planning a big supper for tonight, so I hope you're hungry. She's a pretty good cook. I think we're having cod and potatoes. We've got a ways to go to get home, so she sent some scones. Are you hungry? Maybe you're thirsty? Do you want to walk around town a bit before we head home?"

Audrey's eyes were dancing. "You are amazing, Danny."

He hesitated. That was unexpected. "I'm amazing? Well, shucks."

She giggled. "I am very, very happy to be here."

"I'm talking too much, aren't I?"

"No," she said. "Never enough. Tell me more." She flapped a hand at the crowds behind her. "I've listened to these people and their problems all the way here. Now I only want to hear you."

"You're easy to talk to, Audrey. Maybe that's why they came to you."

"Maybe. But it was a long trip, and the whole time I was feeling so sorry for people, I hardly had time to get excited about coming here." Her smile flashed. "But I'm here now. Would you take me home, Danny?"

Danny closed his eyes for a moment, savouring her request, then opened them. "Would I take you home? Well, you tell me: is the ocean wet?"

She frowned and tilted her head, then tossed it back and laughed. "Oh, Danny. I've missed you."

She didn't once drop her eyes to his missing leg. Not once. He wondered if she'd even noticed. He decided to say something. Make it easier.

"I'm not gonna be like those folks on the boat. I'm not gonna tell you any sad stories," he said, holding both her hands, the flowers between them. "I want you to be happy."

"Danny, I know about your leg. If you want to talk about it, I want to talk about it. If you don't, that's fine. It's just that all those strangers, well, I didn't care about their stories. They weren't important. Yours are important."

She was so pretty. For months he'd held on to the portrait she'd given him that morning so long ago, and he'd been determined not to forget her features, but the cool black and white lines couldn't bring him the blue of her eyes or the way they'd captured him on that very first day. Now those eyes dimmed with exhaustion, and he couldn't blame her. He swung her bag onto his shoulder, the one without the crutch. She opened her mouth, then shut it again. She knew him well enough by now to know he wouldn't want help. Not with that, damn it. He was still a man. He was glad she didn't ask.

"Let's get you home and settled, okay? I bet it'll feel good to sleep in a real bed."

SIXTEEN

Danny awoke and stared at the bottom of the bunk overhead, listening to his brothers' snoring and thinking of Audrey. She had settled into the addition, the room they would eventually share as man and wife.

His wife. What a thought. Shouldn't come as such a surprise, he knew, that time had transformed him into a man, but sometimes he couldn't help but wonder at that. He'd just turned twenty-four when he headed to war with his friends, all of them proud and cocky and full of spice. He'd felt invincible. Different from how he'd felt before, when his idea of fun was taking girls out on a boat, sitting out with sunsets, introducing them to rum. Girls had been an empowering kind of a thing for him, a diversion. They'd looked up to him—even the ones he'd known since he was little—and when they blinked nervously at him, he felt like a king. Helen Crockett, with her tangled blond curls, had been his first kiss. She was a couple of years older, a little more experienced, and it had torn him in half when she'd batted her lashes for George Hartlin a week later. He'd found solace in the arms of Anna Mitchell, then moved on to her cousin, Mary. He and Mary had held hands on and off for about six months when he'd been twenty-three, and he'd known she wanted more. But how could he have committed to something like marriage? The families had waited, suspecting he'd take the next step soon, but he'd surprised them all. When Mary gave him an ultimatum, he'd replied with a kiss and wished her well. Even presented her with a wedding gift when the time had come.

Now he could hardly wait to get married. He rolled over and squinted at the clock, then lay back and puffed out his breath. Four-thirty a.m. His father and brothers would be pushing the boat into the water, dropping the nets, hauling them back in again. The rest of the house was quiet. Too early for Audrey to be up yet. He could picture her tucked under the covers of what would become their bed, the blanket layered gently over her body. Was she a light sleeper? Did she lie perfectly still all night or did she roll around while she dreamed? What would it be like to lie beside her? To touch her in the dark, to close his eyes and kiss the soft curve of her neck, her breasts—oh, he had thought about that a lot.

He closed his eyes again. He should have gone fishing this morning, if only to occupy his mind. It was going to make him crazy, lying here, waiting for the rest of the house to get up.

With nothing else to think about, his mind travelled across the sea. Four o'clock meant it was about eight o'clock over there. Plenty of time for the boys in the battalion to have eaten their breakfast, popped on their helmets, and gotten blown to kingdom come. Tommy Joyce had still been there on Danny's last day; Tommy and Mick had been on that offensive, he remembered. When his captain had come to bring his personal items, as well as those of Fred and Jimmy, Danny hadn't asked how many men had survived that day, and the captain had offered nothing. But Mick had tossed a note into the box. "See you in Halifax," it said. *Wouldn't that be something,* Danny thought.

An early-rising bird called outside his window, and Danny stared at the ceiling. He wasn't going to get any more sleep, he could tell. He sat up and swung his leg and stump to the side of the bed, pulled on some trousers and a shirt, grabbed his crutch, and headed toward the kitchen. He lit the small lamp by the sink and it bloomed to a yellow glow, casting shadows where there'd been nothing a moment before. He wasn't hungry, but he picked up the bread his mother had left out for him. She must have known he'd be restless. Danny boiled water and poured himself a cup of tea, then he leaned against the counter and sipped.

At the end of the dark hall, a door handle clicked. Danny tilted his head but couldn't see anything.

"Danny?"

Audrey. She was awake and whispering his name so as not to wake anyone else.

"There she is," Danny said quietly, trying to sound relaxed. She edged down the hall toward him, and he could hardly wait for the lamp to bring him her features.

When it did, Danny felt warm all over. She looked a little rumpled by sleep, one cheek still lined by her pillow, and her hair tumbled lazily over her shoulders. She wore a different dress this morning, of course. Her travelling dress would be in need of a good rest. Her eyes were wide open, though, and blinking at him.

"I couldn't sleep a minute longer," she whispered.

"Me either," he said, keeping his voice low. He didn't want anyone else to wake up and disturb this perfect moment. "Want tea?"

"Yes, please," she said. "And do I smell bread?"

"Help yourself. Mother makes it all the time. She knows I have a weakness for it."

She cut a slice of bread while he poured steaming tea into a small white cup. He had tried to find the nicest one for her, but they all had tiny cracks and chips around the edges. The china had been around a long time. Crossed the sea, even. Just like Audrey. He slipped the cup into her hands, and she sighed as her cold fingers soaked in the heat.

"That smells good," she said, then tried a sip, but it was still too hot. Her eyes travelled around the kitchen, and she smiled, seeing her own drawings on display along the counter wall. She'd sent him beautiful depictions of trees, cats, and birds, and they'd helped tide him over when the war had threatened to obliterate his memories. He'd shown them to his mother, who had fallen in love with them. She'd ironed out the folds and pinned them along the wall.

"Hope you don't mind," he said. "You sent them in your letters."

"I remember."

"And when I showed them to my mother, she kind of insisted . . ."

She bit her lip. "So sweet of her. It's nice seeing them here."

"I think it's her way of saying you're already a part of our family."

Her eyes sparkled in the lamplight, and she reached out to touch a picture she'd done of her farmhouse. "Seems so far away," she said quietly.

He didn't want her to dwell on the past. "Let's sit," he said. "We could go outside, but it's still pretty cool. We'll see when the sun comes up."

He led her into the sitting room and waited until she took a spot on one side of his mother's old sofa, a homemade, dark red monstrosity with curving oak arms. Audrey sank into it, and Danny moved in beside her so their knees touched. There was an awkward silence at first, as if neither knew how to start. As always, it seemed the easiest way was to begin with the basics.

"Did you sleep okay?" he asked.

She smiled, seeming relieved that he'd spoken first. "I did, thank you. It's a lovely room."

"Well, I guess I'll be finding that out for myself soon enough," Danny said, then bit his lip, unsure of how she might react. Fortunately, it seemed she was good and ready for it.

"Oh, yes," she said, and her eyes lit in a way that made him want very badly to kiss her, but he restrained himself and waited for her to say more. "I've thought about that for a long time, Danny. About getting married. I still can't believe it's true, but I'm so, so happy you chose me to be your wife."

"I chose you? How can you say that?"

She fiddled with the folds of her skirt, pleating them between nervous fingers. "It's only, well . . . a man like you could have any woman he wanted."

Helen Crockett's seventeen-year-old lips puckered in his memory, and an unexpected pang of guilt hit him when he recalled the trust in Mary Mitchell's dark eyes. But that was all in the past.

"Aw, Audrey. You're being silly. There's nobody but you. Never really has been. I mean, well, sure, before I met you, but never since."

"Now stop it, Danny." She reached for her tea and took a sip.

"You're even prettier when you blush."

He watched her, captivated by the action of her throat, the light dusting of freckles that shifted when she moved her nose.

"Don't stare at me. Didn't your mother ever teach you that? I'll spill my tea all over your mother's beautiful rug if you keep watching me like that."

"Sorry," he said, but he wasn't. "It's just hard to believe you're really here. Aren't you tired from that trip? It's a long one. I remember that. And uncomfortable."

"I am, and I'm sure I'll feel it more later," she admitted, "but I wanted to see you. I imagine the journey was worse for you. With your leg, I mean."

He swallowed the bitter answer that sprang to his lips. He didn't want to think about his leg. She was perfect, he was not, and thinking about the leg did nothing but make him angry.

"Let's not talk about me," he said.

"All right," she said easily. "But we'll have to think of something else to talk about so you won't just look at me that way." Her tone scolded, but the smile beneath it was warm and receptive. "Tell me about this place. Tell me about your brothers."

Sometime over the next two hours, during which they barely paused to take a breath between words, Danny's mother came into the kitchen and tried to be quiet. Danny knew she was there, shuffling in the background, but didn't make any sign. From the amount of talking the couple did, it seemed the letters they had sent each other over the miles and the months hadn't quite covered everything. If Danny said something, Audrey was transfixed, asking questions, and when Audrey said something, Danny understood it immediately.

He couldn't remember ever being so happy in his entire life.

A crash in the kitchen broke the spell, followed by a distressed, "Oh, no. Look at what I've done. I'm so sorry, you two! I didn't mean to interrupt, but it seems I—"

Audrey and Danny poked their heads into the kitchen and saw his mother, pink-faced with embarrassment, taking out a broom to collect the scattered shards of a serving platter. Audrey was on her knees in an instant, picking up the larger pieces and piling them in her hands.

"Oh, just leave that, Audrey dear. You'll cut yourself."

"No, no," Audrey assured her. She picked up a large shard and sighed. "Oh, that's too bad. Such a lovely plate."

"You think so? How kind of you. Yes, my mother gave it to me long ago."

"Lovely," Audrey repeated, examining it up close. Mrs. Baker took the piece from her. "What a fine way to welcome you! Get you working right away! Well, at least let's get you some breakfast."

"I'm not afraid of hard work, Mrs. Baker. I hope you'll keep me busy."

Danny leaned against the kitchen wall, arms folded, and watched his two favourite women in the world as they got to know each other. This was going to be just fine, he thought. Just fine.

SEVENTEEN

On Sundays no one ever did any work other than the mandatory cooking and cleaning up afterwards. So a couple of Sundays before their wedding, Danny took Audrey for a walk, carrying the paints and paper she'd begged him to bring. He wore his peg leg so it would be easier for him to wind through roots and grass along the same forest path he could have cut through blindfolded as a boy. She followed him down to a stream near Arnold's Lane, fed by Abbiecombec Lake, and he reached back to squeeze her hand when he spotted a doe standing knee-deep in the water. Audrey stood as still as the animal, delighted. Further on, a frog plopped into the water nearby, and Audrey jumped, startled, then dissolved into giggles. Danny stepped into the edge of the cool water and scooped up the creature. The little claws scrabbled inside Danny's hands when he trapped it, then he held it up so she could touch its soft, smooth skin.

The day couldn't have been more perfect. Sunshine burst through the leaves, dappling the water, and Audrey sighed with contentment.

"Have you ever seen anything so beautiful, Danny?"

"Yeah, I have," he said, keeping his gaze on her. When she wrinkled her nose at him, he released the frog back into the water. "What?"

"Oh, please. Just look."

Danny grinned. "I am."

Her expression told him she had wanted to argue but changed her mind. Instead, she leaned in and kissed his lips, long and slow. He wrapped his arms around her waist and pulled her tight against him.

He eventually let her go but felt vaguely empty in the moment they lost contact. "Shall we sit here for a bit?"

"Can I paint you?"

He grudgingly sat while she wove his likeness into their surroundings. He was getting used to doing this for her, though it had been somewhat uncomfortable in the beginning. It gave him an opportunity to revel in the knowledge that she was studying him, concentrating on aspects of him that even he had probably never considered. She made him feel important.

"Where's that frog?" she teased. "We could put him on your head, and I'll paint you both."

"I reckon he's out catching flies for his wife."

"Which is what a good husband does. Did you bring any food?"

"I did."

"Good. I'm hungry."

Danny stretched. "Worked up an appetite looking over my fine physique, did you?"

"You're terrible. What a tease."

They had a light lunch then dug into an apple pie Mrs. Mitchell had brought over. When they were done, they sat quietly, watching the water, and Danny rested his head on her shoulder, as if it was the most natural thing on earth. As if it belonged there.

"Amazing, isn't it? The way life turns out?" he mused.

Audrey smiled. Danny could see the subtle motion from the corner of his eye. She reached into her bag and took out one of the white squares of paper she used for painting, then held it in front of him.

"You see that?" Audrey asked.

"Mm-hmm," Danny said, feeling lazy and nuzzling closer.

She flung the paper into the water, saying nothing.

"Hey! What you go and do that for?" He pulled his nose from the soft curve of her neck so he could watch the white square rotate with the current.

"When I was a little girl, my mother said our lives are like that. We're the paper, see?" She turned to see if he was watching, then gazed back at the water, satisfied. "And life is like this stream. We start out clean and white and perfect, and we float on top of the water. Some of us carry important words and thoughts, others just float. But life—the water— always wins in the end. No matter who we are, we'll only float until the river pulls us under, or until we rot from beneath and fall apart."

Danny watched the paper as it disappeared over a tiny rapid, bumping on rocks, spinning over the edge. Then he blinked at Audrey, saying nothing, thinking she was the smartest, most perfect human being in the world.

She leaned her head on his shoulder this time. Her voice was soft. "You know, Danny, I saw you fighting."

He wanted to sit up straight, guard himself from the idea of war, but he didn't, because she was so obviously comfortable. And she had brought it up, so he was curious. "How could you have seen that?"

"From far away at night. Perhaps it wasn't you, but I thought of you just the same. The whole sky lit up. It was almost pretty from far away." Her voice drifted with memory, soft and sad, and she reached for his hand.

He stroked the back of her knuckles with his thumb and rested his head on the soft pillow of her hair. The drifting water and its reflections flowed beneath them, and Danny wished they could sit there forever. Somehow it was easier this way. If he could share the pain from the war with her, maybe he'd feel better about everything. And maybe it helped her as well.

"No matter how pretty it might be, I couldn't smile for it," she said, then she lifted her head so they were face-to-face. Her eyes shone with tears. "I tried to see the beauty, but I cried every time. I prayed so hard, Danny. I prayed you were nowhere near where all that was happening. I wanted you to run away. Even if . . . even if I never saw you again, I wanted you to be safe. Far away."

"I wouldn't have left you there."

"Oh, I know. But I did wish for it in a way." She wrapped her hands around his arm and snuggled closer. After a moment she sniffed then spoke again. "You know, I think perhaps my mother's story of the paper is a little wrong. The war was more like an entire box of paper thrown into the ocean during a storm. And all the paper was ruined at once."

"Audrey?"

She sniffed again. "Yes?"

"You and I, we've lived through hell. But you're here now, with me, and I'm gonna take care of you. I think what we gotta do is think about what's ahead of us, not behind. Sounds easier than it is, but I think since we did this together, we can help each other."

"I know. It's only—"

"Come here, my love." He pulled her to him and kissed her, and he knew she felt the electricity buzz through them just as he did. "I can't do it without you."

EIGHTEEN

They got married two weeks later under a thick green umbrella of oak leaves, and every day leading up to their wedding was spent in anticipation. When Danny wasn't working, he was by Audrey's side, holding her hand, listening to her stories and telling his own. He kissed her in the morning, kissed her at night, kissed her any time he could get her alone. She asked endless questions about anything at all, but never once about the war, and he knew she was only waiting for him to tell her in his own time. He would tell her one day. Not yet, though. He needed this time so he could feel better about everything. Right now she was life to him, a sun that dazzled over everything else. He didn't want to talk about death.

She told him about England, about the stink of the factories that hung over everything, clinging to her nose, her lungs. The way she spoke was the way she moved a paintbrush, and he clearly saw the way she and the other women had lived, stuffed into their bunks at night like salted fish in a bucket, sleeping like the dead. She raved about the suffragette women and their exciting plans, insisting on possibilities even when he called them hopeless optimists.

Audrey loved her new country: the quiet colours of the ocean on a peaceful day, the calm, rolling sound it made as it reached toward the shore. When storms rolled in, her eyes flashed with the lightning, and she drew closer to him with the the thrill of the wind, the crash and rumble of an angry sea. True to her promise, she was a hard worker, pitching in with anything that needed doing. Danny watched her learn, picking up new ways of doing things, and he admired Audrey's quiet, occasional suggestions to his mother. It was obvious from the start that the two would get along well. It hadn't really been a worry, but it was a relief.

On the day of the ceremony, Danny's mother flitted like a humming-bird, wanting everything perfect for her first son's wedding. She was in her element pulling the event together. It was a beautiful July afternoon, and while great maples and birches stretched over the party, providing much-needed shade, just enough breeze kept the mosquitoes off. The sun sparkled on the still harbour, and songs rose from within the forest: birds and bugs enjoying the day. All the neighbours were invited; some brought fiddles, one even brought a set of bagpipes. Everyone brought food. The folk of the Eastern Shore were always looking for reason to celebrate, and Danny's wedding was more than enough.

The newly married couple weren't hungry. They stood off to the side for most of the day, accepting congratulations and best wishes, but mostly speaking quietly to each other, celebrating in their own way. When the sun set, the party continued, but no one expected the newlyweds to stay. As Danny led Audrey into the house, he laughed off an appropriate amount of teasing, especially from his brothers and friends. The younger boys were just as loud in their catcalls but had no idea what they were saying. Danny didn't mind. As long as no one said anything derogatory about his sweet new wife, everything was good.

The new room was small but large enough for a double bed and a dresser and enough space to move easily around the sides of the bed. Danny's dream was to construct an entire house elsewhere on the property, but he would need to make money if he was going to be able to afford that. He'd built the dresser as a wedding gift for Audrey, even added the luxury of a large mirror on top. Audrey had sewn green striped curtains for the window, and she had drawn them closed.

"Come to bed, Mrs. Baker?" Danny asked, stepping into the room.

From the hallway, Audrey smiled into the dark, a soft look in her eyes that he wanted to see better. He lit an oil lamp so the room warmed with a dim, gold glow, then he stood back toward the window when she came in. She latched the door behind her, then leaned against it, her hands behind her back. Neither said a word, only stared at the other. Outside, the sounds of laughter continued, a fiddle started up, accompanied by a whoop as dancing began.

"Are you scared of this, Audrey?"

"I think so," she said quietly. "I feel strange."

"Me too," he said, then gave her a crooked smile. "Not sure how it'll go when I only have one leg to balance on."

She stepped toward him, since they'd found it was easier for her to come to him than the other way around. She stopped halfway across the room, fidgeting with the folds of her skirt as she'd done on that first morning after she'd arrived. He had thought she was beautiful then, but now she took his breath away. She had made her own wedding gown—a pale blue skirt that touched the ground under a modest bodice—modelling it after photographs she had seen in a catalogue. It was a practical dress, one she would wear after her wedding day as an everyday dress. For now, though, it was a special dress, and Danny could tell she was afraid to take it off.

Danny's mother had tied Audrey's hair on top of her head, then decorated any stray curls with a matching blue ribbon. He was used to seeing her hair down, bouncing around her shoulders. Her neck looked smooth and vulnerable like this, and he wanted to curl his fingers around the back of it.

Danny had worn the peg through the day, using it mostly to fill in the pant leg and keep the curious neighbours' focus off him. He ached to take it off, but he would have to remove his trousers in order to do that. Neither of them had moved yet in that regard. Obviously someone was going to have to start taking off clothing.

He stepped closer to her, and her eyes searched his. When they were a foot apart, he stopped and did what he'd wanted to do all day, circling the back of her neck with his fingers. She closed her eyes and leaned against his hand, and he pulled her to him.

They kissed slowly, tasting this new person who was their spouse. *For better or for worse.* She felt warm against him, and a thrill ran down his body with the knowledge that she was entirely his. *In sickness and in health.* That he could touch her and make love to her as he had dreamed, and it would be just fine in the sight of God. *For as long as we both shall live.* His other hand slid down her back, travelling along the line of buttons—he counted eight—that fastened the gown from neck to waist.

"Can I help you with your gown?" he whispered.

"I'm scared, Danny."

"No need, Audrey. I won't let nothing hurt you. Ever."

Her forehead creased suddenly, and just as quickly her eyes filled with tears.

"What is it?"

She swallowed hard and blinked. A lone tear dropped. "Promise me, Danny? Promise you will never, never, never leave me." Her eyes moved between his, searching. "Please, Danny. I would die."

He took her face in his hands and felt his own eyes tickle with tears. "Never be afraid, Audrey. You're my world. I'm nothin' without you."

"Don't leave me," she whispered again.

He shook his head slowly. He needed her to understand. She was everything. Without her, well, he couldn't even imagine the possibility anymore.

"I won't. Please, Audrey. You gotta know. I'll never, ever leave you."

AUDREY

– August 1917 –

NINETEEN

It had never taken Audrey long to make friends in the past. Trouble was, there weren't that many people for her to meet in such a small area. So once in a while Danny took her for a walk down what passed for a road around Jeddore, bringing her around to meet more of his relatives. It wasn't something he did often, because the wear of the crutch under his arm was so painful. She knew he didn't want her to see that he suffered, but late at night, when they settled into their bed, she saw the redness, the bruising and blisters, and she felt immediately sorry that she'd dragged him so far.

But Audrey had a thirsty soul, drinking in air and colours and shapes and detail the way anyone else would need water. Fortunately, Danny seemed to understand that. As often as possible, he took her out in his boat, paddling her down the shore so she could take in the beauty of the place. And it was *so* beautiful. So peaceful. Back in Silvertown she'd seen the ocean beyond the factory, but this was nothing like it. The only sounds here were the gulls and the surf, rolling over the rocks, retreating back into the sea. The trees were vast, never-ending, and the ground by their roots was a carpet of moss, constantly changing colours and textures. It wasn't deep soil, he'd told her. That's why so many trees were uprooted during storms. Not much for them to grab on to when the autumn gales blew, and he promised her they did. The idea of those storms worried her a little, but for now she was convinced there was nowhere on earth as lovely as this. Everything begged to be painted.

"Look at those rocks, Danny. See how they face into the water? Like they're talking to each other. And the birch in the shade. It's almost smiling!"

She knew he didn't see it like she did, but he played along, enjoying her excitement. She was grateful for that—more than he could know. The only other people to have ever shared her love of art were Richard Black and her mother. Her grandmother had shoved it away, treating it as if it were poison. But not Danny. He loved her. He wanted her happy, and she couldn't seem to convince him that she was. She truly was. Nothing made her happier than seeing his strong, lightly stubbled jaw tighten with affection for her. And when his eyes were on hers, she felt herself drifting, losing touch with her surroundings, felt whatever stretched between them sucking her farther in, and she went with it, wanting to be so close to him she became a part of him.

For Audrey's first birthday in Canada, Danny bought her paper and paints. He'd even saved up to buy her the precious sable brushes she'd gushed over in a catalogue. He also built her an easel just like one he'd seen in that same catalogue. From the apprehension in his eyes and the way he opened and closed his fists, she knew he was concerned that she wouldn't like his gifts, but what a fool he was. He hadn't expected her tears of joy. And when she cried, his eyes shone as well. Now, whenever they returned from their voyages up and down the coast, she disappeared into their bedroom, took out the art supplies, and spent hours recreating what she'd seen.

Sometimes he watched her paint, but mostly he left her alone, and she appreciated that as well. She liked to melt into the pictures the way she melted into his eyes, and she couldn't do that when her attention was divided between her two loves. When she finished a painting, he always came to admire it. He said they were beautiful. Not the exact, perfect renderings his grandfather had once done in charcoal, he told her. Hers were less rigid. As if she saw *beyond* the lines and colours. One day when he came in late from working with his brothers in the boat, she drew him while he slept. He'd had no idea until she presented it to him three days later, the muted colours on the paper as restful as his face had been, lost in dreams.

"Gee, Audrey. This is amazing." He stared at it. "Huh. Is that really what I look like?"

"Yes," she said slowly, squinting critically at the paper. "Except you're much more handsome."

Their bedroom walls were soon covered by her paintings. Danny carefully cut, sanded, glazed, and assembled frames for each one.

"You'll have to stop soon, Audrey," he teased. "We don't have any more walls."

"I guess so," she agreed with a shrug. "Or maybe I'll just trade the frames around."

"Yeah," he mused, distracted. He scratched his head. "Hey, you know what? Could you do a portrait of Mother?"

"Of course."

When it was done, a smooth, feminine likeness of the older woman rolling out dough in the kitchen, Danny's mother was so moved, she suggested Audrey hang her new pictures all over the house, brighten the plain walls. From the corner of Audrey's eye she saw Danny nod smugly to himself, making her grin. So that was how he'd thought it might turn out. He set to work building more frames.

One Sunday, a couple of weeks and many paintings later, Danny's aunt and uncle came visiting from Oyster Pond at the head of the harbour. Their schooner lay low in the water, heavy with their load of six children, ranging in age from a few months to ten years. Johnny and their father helped the family onto the dock, then led them into the yard where Danny and Audrey stood. Danny's mother stood at Audrey's other side.

"Georgina," she said, pulling her sister into an embrace. The infant caught between them gave a squawk and clung to his mother's neck. "I feel like I haven't seen you in so long."

"Too long, Helen," the woman agreed. "I'm so sorry we couldn't make it to the wedding. The children were too ill to get out of bed, and I'm afraid I wasn't much better."

"I'm only glad you're all recovered."

"As am I! And you, well, you've been so busy with things, welcoming your dear boy home again. Where is he? Where's my little Daniel?"

Danny appeared at her side. "Nice to see you, Auntie Georgina. You're looking lovely as usual."

"Daniel!" She handed the baby to her sister, then reached for Danny, but she didn't step toward him. Instead, her eyes went to his stump, hidden inside his folded trouser leg. Audrey saw the woman's nostrils flare slightly. It made her want to step between them, demand the woman's apology. But she behaved, settling for the slight touch of her fingers against Danny's where they fell at his side.

His aunt folded her hands together at her waist and smiled sweetly at him. "So good to see you again, dear nephew. I know your parents must be overjoyed to have you home."

"And it's wonderful to be home," Danny said, hiding the annoyance Audrey was certain he'd felt at the slight. His fingers folded over Audrey's as he led her forward. He stood tall, proud as a peacock. "Auntie Georgina, I'd like to introduce my wife, Mrs. Audrey Baker, recently arrived from England."

Georgina's gaze went to Audrey, who met it bravely. "Lovely to meet you, Mrs. McWhidden. I've heard wonderful things about you and your family."

Danny's mother cleared her throat from behind them, her subtle sound of support. She'd told Audrey ahead of time that she loved her sister—Danny assured her he did too—but said Georgina wasn't exactly the most down-to-earth person she knew. In fact, where Danny's mother's dream in life was to see her family happy, Georgina had purposefully married a wealthy, older man and had spent her energy with the well-to-do whenever possible.

"I'm pleased to meet you, too." Georgina tilted her head. "England? I didn't realize—"

"Audrey and I met in France, but she's English. She saved my whole battalion from going hungry one night."

"Oh, Danny," Audrey objected. "It was nothing like that."

"Yes, it was. You're too modest, my love. Truly, Auntie Georgina. The woman's a hero."

"And we love having a daughter," his mother added, making Audrey blush deeper.

"Well, then. Welcome to the family, my dear."

The men spent most of the day sitting and talking, smoking and eating. Audrey and the ladies alternated between the kitchen, the care of the children, the yard, and the dining room. When the work was done, Danny's mother pulled Audrey aside.

"Are you having fun, darling?" she asked.

"I am," Audrey assured her. "These are lovely people, and it's a beautiful day. How could I not?"

"I'm so glad." She peered out the window at the others. "Audrey, I'd like to ask you for a different kind of help, if you don't mind."

"What can I do for you?"

"I'd love for my sister to have one of your paintings. Georgina was admiring the lovely picture hanging in the sitting room—of the oak and that little bird? Oh, you know the one. Well, I hope it's all right with you. I'd like to give it to her as a gift."

"A gift? You would?" Audrey was thrilled with the compliment. "Of course it's all right with me. That's wonderful she should like it so much. But it is only a tree!"

"Maybe so, maybe so. But you know, Audrey, I don't know anyone who can paint quite like you do. I'm awfully proud of you as a daughter-in-law but also as an artist. Tell me—would it be a terrible inconvenience, Audrey, if I were to ask you to do a portrait of the McWhidden family? I'd love for my sister to hang it in their fancy house for everyone to see—"

"I beg your pardon?"

"—and I'm hoping you can do it without their knowing. A surprise, like."

Audrey frowned, unsure. "I've never done a portrait with more than one person in it."

"Oh, you'll manage. You'll do fine. Just think of them as a group of trees. All different kinds of trees. You're good with trees. Do it so they aren't aware. I'll distract them as well as I can." She winked. "Now run along and get your easel, dear. I'll wait for you outside. Thomas!" she called her son through the door. "Thomas, come here a moment and help Audrey, would you?"

Audrey collected her paints and papers, then sat on a stump just to the side of the group, trying surreptitiously to spot distinctive features in each one of the McWhiddens. Thomas carried the easel outside and set up the tripod in front of her.

"You want it here?"

"That's perfect, Thomas," she said.

"What are you painting?"

She darted a quick glance at her mother-in-law.

"Thomas, come. Leave Audrey alone now."

Thomas glanced suspiciously between the canvas and his mother.

"Don't worry, Thomas. I'm only painting trees. You're not missing a thing."

She did a vague outline of each of the McWhiddens: three girls, two boys, the baby, and the parents. The two young sons could have been twins, they were so similar. The eldest was about a foot taller, but that was the biggest difference. Black hair cut short over tall brows and deep brown eyes. Not overly thin; healthy for their age. They were pretty simple to paint. The three eldest were sisters. Unlike their brothers, they were all quite different and required a little more concentration. Mrs. McWhidden, a small woman, and the obvious source of her boys' colouring, held her baby son in her arms. He was a round, soft-faced boy. If he hadn't had his stubby legs wrapped like a hug around her waist, he might have been too big for his mother to carry.

Audrey couldn't see Mr. McWhidden at first, so she got to work on the others, playing with poses, adding in facial expressions as she went and leaving a spot for Mr. McWhidden at the back. He was a tall, barrel-chested man with short blond curls and blue eyes. When she was ready, Audrey glanced around and spotted him sitting apart from the others, talking with Danny and Daniel Sr. It seemed Joseph McWhidden was asking Danny questions, and his posture suggested he was fascinated by Danny's responses. Audrey let her gaze slip to her husband and lost her concentration.

Danny was slightly pale. He was leaning a little away from Joseph, as if trying to escape the barrage of questions. He lifted his cigarette to his lips and inhaled while staring at the sea, then smoke leaked out of his nose as he nodded at something Joseph said. He looked so sad, Audrey thought. So far away. She wanted to run to him, to bury him in her arms and keep him safe from the world. But he was a man, and a man who could defend himself well enough, leg or no leg. Danny turned to Joseph and said something, his expression revealing nothing. Then all three men regarded Danny's stump, and Audrey gripped her paintbrush hard, feeling afraid for him. Would he rant at them for asking things that were none of their business? Or would he disguise his anguish, let it float away with the smoke?

As if sensing her gaze, he met her eyes from across the yard. She saw the lift in his shoulders, the deep breath he took at sight of her. He smiled, and she thought what an amazing man he was, to be able to move through all that. She was the luckiest woman alive.

"Would you like some lemonade?" Mrs. Baker had come up beside her, filled to the brim with curiosity.

"That would be lovely," Audrey said.

"How's the painting going?"

"It's coming along."

"Do you think you can finish it by the time they leave tonight?"

Audrey frowned. "Oh no, I'm sorry. This will take time to complete, and then the paint will still be wet for at least a week."

Mrs. Baker slumped slightly, then pursed her lips, thinking. Audrey saw when the answer came to her. "That'll be perfect. I'll be able to give it to her for her birthday." After she left, Audrey set to work, swirling in colours, adding details, fitting Mr. McWhidden in so he watched over them all. The man behind the family. The afternoon flew by. Audrey got up to help with supper, but Mrs. Baker sent her back outside to paint.

She was just finishing up when she heard the distinctive shuffle of her husband behind her.

"Hey, beautiful," he said.

"Hello, Danny." She turned toward him, and he leaned in for a kiss. He smelled like cigarettes, which she didn't really like, but she didn't say anything. The kiss was all she needed.

"What you working on?" he asked. "You've been busy most of the day with that."

"Your mother asked me to paint this for the McWhiddens. It's a surprise. What do you think?"

He leaned over her shoulder, his eyes scanning the characters on the paper. He let his attention dwell on each individual separately, then he shook his head. Her heart sank.

"What?" she asked, concerned. "It's only just starting out, but I think—"

"I don't know how you do that," he said, and just like that she was happy again. "I could tell it was the McWhiddens from miles away. You're so good at that. I'm the luckiest man in the world to have such a talented wife."

She set her forehead against his. "I was just thinking how lucky I was to have you."

"Nah. You could have been much luckier. Found yourself a rich man with two legs, for starters."

"I suppose," she said, squinting at the picture and dabbing a smudge of peridot in one corner. She reached for a rag and cleaned the brush before touching another colour on the palette. "But then I wouldn't have been happy."

He snorted and kissed her neck. "You're crazy. Comin' for supper?"

"Yes. I think—" Another swipe of olive, a flourish in a background tree. "I'm done for now. We can leave it here to dry in the breeze."

The painting was presented exactly six weeks later when the McWhiddens returned for Georgina's birthday celebration. Danny had set it inside a strong oak frame, and he presented it with great ceremony after supper while Audrey sat back, beside herself with nerves. The children made sounds of interest, then came in close to figure out who was who. Mr. McWhidden leaned over their heads, commenting on what fine likenesses they were.

Georgina McWhidden, was—as Mrs. Baker had hoped—entirely moved by the gift. Her hand fluttered weakly at her face, and Audrey saw tears shine in the woman's eyes.

"Oh, Audrey," she said, her voice a little ragged. "This is the most beautiful gift. I can't accept such a wonderful thing, can I? It seems . . . too much. I've never seen anything like it." She turned to Mrs. Baker, who beamed with pride. "You know, we took the family to a photographer in Halifax last year. That was really quite an ordeal, having to sit so still for a very long time. Think of that, with all these children! But the photograph is, obviously, in black and white. This is a hundred times prettier. And we didn't have to sit still, even. Oh, it's so artistic! How ever did you manage it?"

Audrey smiled, relieved to the soles of her feet. This had been, beyond any doubt, the most labour-intensive thing she'd ever done, but she'd enjoyed the process immensely. "You have a beautiful family, Mrs. McWhidden. It was easy to paint them so."

Georgina McWhidden pulled out a handkerchief and dabbed at her eyes. Her husband, having stepped away until he stood behind her, laid a reassuring hand on her shoulder. "There, there," he said.

The McWhiddens said they planned to hang the picture in their front hall, so anyone coming to visit would see it there. Mrs. Baker already had told Audrey what a well-to-do house they had, with their velvet wallpaper and dark oak banisters leading up to a second storey, and they even had one of those newfangled iceboxes—inside the house! Audrey loved to imagine her picture there, at home among those beautiful things.

TWENTY

A note came the next week, delivered by a boy Audrey didn't recognize. Incredibly, the missive was from Madame Eleanor Hartlin of the nearby Hartlin Settlement. Eleanor was the grande dame of the area, descended from some of the original settlers from England, and she reportedly lived her life as if she lived in an English castle, surrounded by doting family and only the finest of things. She must have been closing in on a hundred years, Audrey had been told. She had given birth to sixteen children, fourteen of which had survived. And those fourteen had gone on to multiply like rabbits, prompting houses to pop up all around the area.

Danny's mother was wide-eyed when the note arrived. "What could it be? A note from Mrs. Hartlin? Why, that's unheard of! Open it quickly, Audrey. I'm fading away with curiosity."

Audrey pulled out a piece of white paper on which neat—though a little shaky—black letters were inked.

My dear Mrs. Daniel Baker Jr.,

I am in acquaintance with the portrait you recently painted of Mrs. Georgina McWhidden and her family. It is an exceptionally handsome painting and you are to be commended on your considerable talent.

I should like to commission you to come to my home and paint my likeness. I shall not reside on this earth forever, and I enjoy the idea of my portrait hanging over the family hearth as a reminder after I am gone.

I shall pay you three dollars and fifty cents if I am satisfied with your work.

Please respond by sending a note through this messenger, my great-grandson, Nolan Hartlin.

With sincere thoughts,
Madame Eleanor Hartlin

Audrey and Mrs. Baker exchanged a look of absolute shock.

"Three dollars and fifty cents?" they exclaimed together. Both women snapped their jaws shut, but their eyes were round with amazement.

"She must not mean that," Audrey said, shaking her head and reading over the note again. "That much for one painting? I can't—"

"You sure can, love!" Mrs. Baker practically jumped up and down with excitement. "This is wonderful! Soon people from all over are going to be asking for their portraits to be done. Go tell Danny. He'll be thrilled. Congratulations, Audrey!"

Audrey found Danny in the shed with Johnny, sharpening saw blades. The two didn't seem to talk much—or if they did, Audrey rarely heard their conversations—but they seemed content just to be together.

"Danny?" she called into the shed.

"Oh, hey, Audrey," Danny said, smiling out of the shadows.

"Could I speak with you?"

"Of course. Here, Johnny. You finish this one, and I'll be back to help with the other one." He grabbed his crutch and hopped toward her.

"You are even lovelier than usual, wife of mine. What has you lit up like a Christmas tree?"

"Oh, Danny. The most exciting thing has happened."

She told him about Mrs. Hartlin and her proposal, and of his mother's dreams for future commissions. Danny frowned while she talked, but didn't interrupt.

"So? What do you think?" she asked.

"What do I think? Well, what else can I think? I'm proud of you."

His smile lacked enthusiasm, and some of the wind escaped her sails. That wasn't the reaction for which she'd been hoping. "What is it?" she asked.

"Hmm? Oh, nothing."

He sat on a stump beside her and stared out at the water. Audrey watched his profile, wondering—as she so often did—what he was thinking. More and more lately he seemed to drift from her, his thoughts going to a private place where she wasn't invited. It hurt. She couldn't deny that. But she had to give him room, she knew. He had a lot of recovering to do, a lot of memories to get past. She'd heard of that, of soldiers falling apart, unable to handle the postwar world. Some of them even ended up in insane asylums, she'd heard. Not that Danny was anywhere near that bad. It's just that, well, she had started to miss the warmth of his eyes more and more.

"I don't need to say yes if you think—"

He turned his head quickly. "I never said that," he snapped. She blinked at his unexpected tone, then Danny clicked his tongue. "Sorry," he said, his voice back to normal. "No, no, Audrey. I think it's fantastic, you painting and all. Folks *should* pay you. You're great at it."

"Then . . ." She looked away from him, letting her gaze go toward the sea as he had. "What's wrong?"

"No, really. It's great. It's only . . . the thing is, I'd feel better if you didn't have to work."

It was worse than she'd thought. When their eyes met, she saw hurt swimming in the depths of his that she hadn't seen before, and she suddenly understood why. It had been hard enough on his ego that she'd paid for her own passage to Canada. She knew he, as a man, wanted to be the valiant knight and whisk her across the sea all on his own, but reality had stepped in. The tragedy of his loss was one part of that reality, but the other was her job. She was aware some people were uncomfortable at the idea that she'd even had a job, but because of it, she'd been able to afford coming to Canada. She'd wanted to help—but the truth was a man like Danny didn't want help. Especially with money. He'd been forced to swallow his pride once already, and she knew it had carried a bitter taste.

Danny went out fishing sometimes, hauling lobster traps when the sea was calm enough that his precarious state of balance wasn't constantly threatened. He could manage some fur trapping if he didn't have to stray too far into the dense bush. He could hunt, but not much. He'd mostly given up on his wooden leg, finding it cumbersome and uncomfortable, since its edges chafed the tender pink skin of his scars. And when he walked in the woods, his crutch caught on protruding roots, catching him off guard so he stumbled. He was frustrated and embarrassed

Working with wood seemed to help. Danny had perfected the technique of making picture frames, then gone on to build a new boat, with Johnny and the other boys as assistants. He often spent all day by the dock, sanding, painting, hammering. He even sold a small boat to a neighbour. When his hands were busy, Danny was happy. Sometimes Audrey sat with him, talking or painting or saying nothing at all. But occasionally he went out by himself and she left him alone, seeing the shadows loom behind his eyes. In those times she knew his mind had travelled back and landed in France. She tried comforting him during those dark hours, but he became someone she almost didn't know. He turned from her, abrupt and cruel, his handsome face twisted with bitterness. If he spoke a word during those times, it was cold and impersonal.

Since she'd arrived, they'd looked after each other, making do as equals. The possibility of her making money tipped the scale.

Audrey wasn't sure what to do. The truth was they could use the income.

"Danny?"

He looked up at her, and she saw the wound tearing through his spirit. She bled for him, wishing she could take his pain. The one thing she absolutely could not do was show him even a blink of pity. He would hate her for that.

"I'm going to go and help your mother with the washing-up. Would you like something to drink?"

He offered the semblance of a smile. She took it and walked away. Mrs. Baker was waiting for her inside the house, and together the two women composed a letter of acceptance to Mrs. Hartlin.

A candle lit their room, flickering as the wind cut through tiny holes in the wall. Audrey had never known such gales in her entire life. This land seemed ruled by the wind. Some nights it shrieked against the wall so their bed shook, and she buried her face in her pillow, trying to prepare herself for the moment when the place blew down on their heads. Danny assured her they were safe, that the house had stood for decades through much worse than this. But that wind sometimes screamed in the worst way, sounding like a cross between the gulls that circled overhead most days and the terrified screams of children.

It howled again tonight, and she huddled under the blankets, waiting for Danny. The tone of the voices in the kitchen was subdued now that the children had gone to bed. She heard Mrs. Baker laugh once, but it was brief. Daniel Sr.'s voice rumbled, but she couldn't make out what he said. Then she heard Danny say good night and shuffle down the hall toward her. *Thump step thump step.*

The bedroom door creaked open, and Danny stepped in. She had cut his hair the day before, and now one side stuck straight up. He had evidently been out in the wind. She watched him get ready, brushing his teeth, then sitting on the bed so he could peel off his shirt and trousers, pulling on the wool pyjamas she had sewn him for his birthday.

Sometimes, watching the lean lines of him lit by the hope of one candle, she remembered how strong he had been. She remembered him as a soldier, young and unharmed and crazy about her. Even after he lost his leg he had been a beautiful man, one she loved to touch and paint. Lately, though, sadness drained his body. It made him much older than he really was.

She didn't say anything as he slid under the blankets. They lay in bed, and she felt all alone, staring up in the dark.

"I'm sorry," he said softly.

She turned her head on the pillow, surprised. His eyes still gazed at the ceiling. "What for?"

"For being rotten to you. I'm not myself these days. You know what? We need the money. I'd be a fool to ask you not to do this. It's more money than I could ever make. It's just that, well . . ." He took a deep breath and set his chin as emotions surfaced. Audrey held back, knowing he needed to do this on his own. If she touched him he might stop. "I had such big dreams, you know? Before all this happened I could have—"

He stopped talking, and she felt his shoulder press against hers when he swallowed.

"You mustn't give up, Danny. I love you, and I'll do whatever you ask of me, but I can't stand seeing you like this. Where is the light in your eyes? Where's the smile that made me want to kiss you from the first moment I saw you?"

He didn't say anything.

"We'll think of something you can do, Danny. You just need to feel proud of yourself again."

He rolled onto his side and cupped his fingers under her chin so she couldn't look away. Not that she would have. She craved these kinds of conversations. She needed his voice, his words.

"You know, you are the best thing in my life, Audrey. You make me see things the way I should see them. I just have so many things in my head lately about how I'm letting you down. How I let everyone down. Everything has changed. Everything is so much harder than it was supposed to be."

"I'll always be here to help you," she promised. "Always."

He leaned toward her, and she met him halfway, kissing him gently until she felt the strength build between them. His hands slid the length of her body, his fingers strong on the places he'd come to know. He was hungry, and she fed him. She leaned into him, the trusting curl of her body showing him he was all the man he ever needed to be.

In the morning, Audrey got up to visit the outhouse then returned quietly to their room, not letting the door squeak. He was awake though, lying in bed and looking up at the ceiling's wooden beams.

"Good morning, beautiful," he said, sounding groggy. He stretched his arms over his head. "Sleep well?"

She wrinkled her nose and blushed. "You know I did."

Audrey crossed the room and drew open the curtains, letting the sun stream into the room. He'd taken out her braid the night before, and now her curls tickled down her back, reaching for her waist. She wore a cotton nightdress, and she knew he could see the line of her body through its thin material. It gave him pleasure to see her in that way, and all she wanted was for him to be happy. He smiled when she turned toward him, but when he stretched out a hand, she shook her head.

She climbed into the middle of the bed, sitting up so she could still see the view of the sparkling ocean outside the window, and set one hand gently on his stump. Not with curiosity but with a calm sort of possession. As if it were the most natural thing in the world. Danny stiffened at her touch, embarrassed, and she felt his immediate urge to pull away. She'd expected the impulse, and she didn't release him. It was so important that he feel what she was doing. Her fingers slid smoothly over the scars, holding him in place while he gripped the sheets.

"Audrey." His hoarse whisper was urgent, pleading, but she didn't say anything, just kept gazing out at the sea, touching his leg.

Eventually the grip of his fingers on the bed relaxed slightly, and she put both of her hands on the rounded edge of what remained of his leg. She squeezed, gentle but firm, then started moving her thumbs in circular motions over the ugly lines.

From the corner of her eye she saw Danny's eyes almost roll back in his head, and she imagined the waves of pleasure washing through him at her touch. Pain and relief all in one. She kept on, saying nothing but giving him peace as he'd never imagined.

Eventually he opened his eyes, and the calm behind them raised tears in her own.

"Why are you doing that?" His voice was hoarse.

"Do you like it?"

He sighed and closed his eyes as she massaged the forgotten muscle beneath his knee. "You have no idea how much I like it." This time when his eyes opened, she saw pain. Not from what she was doing but from the hurt in his heart. "But you don't have to. I mean, it's pretty horrible just looking at the thing. It must make you ill, touching it like that."

"You still don't know me, do you, Danny?" she asked gently. "I want to give you pleasure. And touching you gives me pleasure as well. I see nothing horrible here. I'm touching a part of you, a part which never left you. It's still your leg, and I love every piece of you."

"Fat lot of good it does me, this thing," Danny said with a snort.

Her thumbs dug in a little deeper, and his eyes fluttered closed. "This is something small I can give you," she said, needing him to understand. "I can take away the bad and give you the good for a while. If you had an entire leg, would I be able to give you this?"

"That's a funny way to think of it."

She shrugged. "I suppose. That's how I think of it."

For a moment he simply breathed and she imagined swirls of pleasure swooping through his mind like chickadees flitting from tree to tree.

"Sure do love you, Audrey," he whispered.

"I know," she said with a smile.

DANNY

— October 1917 —

TWENTY-ONE

October grabbed the mercury and squeezed it down to temperatures Danny knew well. The frozen air carved lines of ice which divided the harbour, the curves constantly drawn and redrawn by razor-edged winds. Gusts rattled the windows and roared through the trees until they hit the walls with a boom, shaking the foundations of the house.

Danny's wife had never experienced a Canadian winter before. He saw the lines of worry on her face when they blew in hard, but he also saw her fine-boned jaw clench with determination. If everyone else was calm, she would be, too.

She was stronger than he was in every way, and he envied her. She seemed to grow braver by the day, while Danny felt his courage crystallizing with the cold. He was a cripple. He would never be able to give her the world, which was what she deserved.

He lay awake for a long time, listening to her fall asleep. Hours later he awoke to darkness, the still of the air telling him morning was far away. Audrey lay awake beside him. He could tell by her breathing, though he could also tell she was trying very hard to be still.

"You okay?" he asked.

"Oh, I'm sorry. I didn't mean to wake you."

"I don't mind. Are you okay?"

She rolled toward him, and he felt the pressure of her head against his arm, asking in. He lifted it so she could pass underneath and lay her head on his chest, then he lowered his arm so it fell across her side, pulling her closer, keeping her safe. She didn't say anything for a while.

"Do you ever have trouble sleeping?" she asked.

Danny thought about all the nights when he never caught a wink. When his mind echoed with pounding guns and screams. When his memory showed him nothing but corpses he had been forced to use as stepping stones. When he first saw his leg, lying in the gore, six feet away from where it was supposed to be. How he reached for the leg in his dream. How it was never within his grasp.

"Sometimes," he admitted.

"I do," she said. "Sometimes I think I hear the cannons. Sometimes I dream of the planes, those big ugly planes that tore up the sky, and they're circling down to chase me, but I have nowhere to run."

"Is that what woke you tonight?"

She nodded slightly, and strands of her soft brown hair slid over his chest. "There were soldiers, and they shot you dead . . . but you weren't really dead. You got up and tried to reach my hand, but we kept moving farther apart. Oh, Danny. It was awful. I was all alone."

Her hair was soft against his chin, tickling it, and he kissed her brow. "You okay now?"

"I'm all right. I'm safe with you."

Danny tightened his hold on her, but it was more to comfort himself than to reassure her. He wanted to keep her safe, sure. But he'd never admit to her how often he looked to her for stability, for sanity. She was wrong. It wasn't he who kept her safe. It was she who kept them both alive.

He pressed his lips into her hair and stroked it as she began to doze. He saw the planes, the cannons, the soldiers, the guns, the blood, the oily smoke choking the air . . . and he saw the space between Audrey and him widening. He didn't even try to sleep.

He had never meant to let his disappointment see the light of day. He didn't want her to know. But it simmered so close to the surface sometimes, he wasn't sure he could keep it under the lid. As much as he tried to control himself, sarcastic remarks and quick, unnecessary snarls had begun to spit out and sizzle in the air between them.

Most of the men nearby had gone off for the winter, headed into the backwoods to fell hardwood and sell it to the mill. It was a strange life the shoremen led: half a year in the water, half a year in the bush. Neither job worked for Danny anymore. These days he was useless at anything he'd ever done before.

When he awoke, Audrey was usually there, waiting for him. If he woke up feeling fine, he saw the love in her eyes. He knew deep down that she didn't care if he had any limbs at all. Other times he was cool toward her, wallowing in self-pity, and she would curl up near him but give him room. She never went too far away.

Johnny had started bootlegging a few months back, and he'd made great money on the water while Danny lolled about being Audrey's pet. He'd suggested the idea to Danny, but when he mentioned it to Audrey, it was obvious she didn't like the idea. She was frightened by the stories she'd heard, about ships sinking or getting shot down. About Johnny's friends who had ended up in jail. About men getting killed. And she was right to be afraid. But Danny'd had enough of feeling financially impotent. He was sick of standing back, watching their tiny coffer grow penny by penny without any help from him. He couldn't fish, couldn't trap. He could work with wood, but fishermen were suffering so much these days, no one could afford to buy a new boat. They patched their old ones up instead. Not that they'd buy one in the winter anyway.

And there was no damn way Danny was going to spend the rest of his life making frames for Audrey's pretty pictures.

Johnny came to him one day with a different idea.

"There's an opening at the docks," Johnny told him. Through his connections, Danny's brother knew everyone who was anyone in Halifax. "It's perfect for you and pays pretty well."

Danny stared the gift horse in the eye. "Why hire me?"

"Because you're my brother. Family's important with these guys, and they trust me. That means they're trusting you."

Danny tilted his head and glared at Johnny, thinking it through. Yet another reversal in roles. He wasn't particularly happy at having to depend on his younger brother, but deep down he was proud of Johnny. He'd grown up just fine and had friends in all the right places, friends who would stand up for him if they were needed. And so far Johnny'd avoided being sent off to Europe. He didn't seem even remotely interested in the war. Why would he be? Johnny was making all the money he needed right here.

"What's the job?"

"It's at the docks, managing inventory. Watching shipments and keeping track, you know? Being the ears and eyes."

"Just not the leg."

"Right."

"I'm in."

Audrey wouldn't be happy. She'd said she never wanted to move from the Eastern Shore. But Danny had no choice. He was treading water where he was, and he couldn't keep his head above the tide for much longer. Maybe she wouldn't be quite as upset when he told her he was on the docks instead of a rum-runner's ship. But they'd still have to move to Halifax, which she didn't want to do. She'd had her fill of city life in London. He understood that.

In the end, he figured out how to make her happy—or at least relatively happy. It was the art. Always the art.

"There are folks in the city who can afford to hire you on, Audrey," he said one night. They lay in bed and she was snuggled up against him, warm and soft after their lovemaking.

"Oh?" she said. She yawned and tickled his chest with her fingernails, drawing figure eights around his nipples. Goosebumps rose over his body, and he let the sensation distract him.

"So you'd be at the docks, and I would paint? We could both make money?" She sounded vaguely pleased, as if she were rolling the thought around in her mouth, seeing how it tasted. "That sounds good. We could make enough money so we could come back here, right?"

He sighed. "You really don't want to go?"

"Oh, Danny." Her hand dropped flat on his chest. "You know I'll go anywhere you ask. But I love it here by the sea. So quiet and beautiful."

"But we need money, and I'm not making much. You've already painted for everyone out here. You need new customers. Rich ones."

She smiled, but he read the warning in her eyes. "Don't say we're doing this for me, Danny. I'd rather live here with nothing than get rich in a dirty city."

He knew she meant it, but his mind was already made up. He was so tired of feeling useless around his parents' house. He wanted to build a home for the two of them but couldn't afford the lumber. If he could only get some money, he could do whatever he wanted. He decided to play his last card. The one he knew was unfair for him to play.

"Oh, well. Maybe we won't then. Schneider's always looking for help with the rum-running."

The minute the words left his mouth, he knew he shouldn't have said them. She would have gone anyway. He felt even worse when she shot him a furious glare.

"You know I'd do anything to keep you off those foul boats," she muttered.

"Good," he said briskly, needing to change the subject. "Johnny's friend Franco says he knows of a guy with a few houses to let, and maybe Johnny can bunk with us for a while."

He didn't like the bullying tone of his own voice, and he knew she didn't, either. But it had to be done. He'd had enough of heading upstream with a sieve as a paddle.

"I'm going to sleep," she said. She rolled away from him, pulled the blankets up to her neck.

"Fine," he said, trying to sound nonchalant. "You have a good sleep. We can talk more in the morning."

She said nothing. For a while he just stared at the profile of her body, snug and separate from his, and wondered what he'd just done.

———

A week later, Danny, Audrey, and Johnny rented a small, two-bedroom furnished house in Richmond, a ragged section of Halifax. The place belonged to one of Johnny's bosses, and it was nothing much—actually, it was less than that—but it was near the docks, close to where Danny and Johnny needed to be. Johnny wouldn't always be there, since he was out on the sea running rum quite a bit these days, but Danny was happy to have him there. And Audrey loved Johnny, too. They had gotten along like brother and sister from the beginning.

True to his word, Johnny did seem to know just about everybody. When he first brought Danny to the docks, he introduced him to Charles. Charles was in charge of security, and he was Danny's direct boss. Danny's job was a mishmash of things, including overseeing and keeping track of everything being loaded and unloaded at Pier 6, occasionally pitching in if they were a man short, and standing up to troublemakers. He took to wearing his peg again, wanting to keep his disability hidden for as long as possible. It'd be hard for Danny to intimidate a man while leaning on a crutch.

On his second day at the job, Charles introduced him to Stan O'Malley, who in turn presented him to Pierre Antoine, the company's owner, the businessman with all the connections, the guy everyone called the "top dog."

Both Johnny and Danny took off their caps as they were introduced. O'Malley stood silently off to the side, his expression blank. Mr. Antoine was about a head shorter than Danny, with jet black hair and a sturdy build. He wore a long black coat that Danny thought might have cost an entire month's rent or more. The man regarded Danny shrewdly before saying a word. Then he nodded briefly, as if he'd made a decision.

"Welcome to Halifax, Monsieur Baker," he said, smiling vaguely. "You are my new inventory manager, I understand."

"Yes, sir. Thank you for the opportunity."

"This is a very important position, you understand."

"Of course. You can count on me, sir."

"I'm sure I can." His eyes went past Danny and touched on Johnny.

"You come highly recommended, though I understand you do not have any qualifications."

"My brother's a hard worker, Mr. Antoine," Johnny assured him. "He won't let you down."

The sharp gaze returned to Danny. "I will be receiving regular updates on your progress, Monsieur Baker. As important as I believe it is for us to help family, you must understand that I run a business. If you do not carry out your responsibilities to my expectations, you can easily be replaced." Mr. Antoine reminded Danny of a bird he'd seen in a book one time. A peacock. All bustled up, full of bravado, parading around like a politician, using his polished French accent as a tool. Then again, it must be working for him, because he was obviously successful.

Just behind Mr. Antoine, Danny spotted Audrey approaching. She was carrying a small bag in her hand, and he recalled that he'd forgotten to bring his lunch that morning. Antoine didn't miss Danny's moment of distraction. He turned to see what might be interrupting their conversation, and Audrey gave them both a shy smile.

"Sorry to interrupt," she said.

Danny held out his hand, and she shuffled to his side. "Mr. Antoine, this is my wife, Mrs. Audrey Baker."

"Nice to meet you, sir."

The businessman's transformation was startling. He was suddenly all charm. He held out his own hand, and Audrey glanced at Danny with a question in her eyes. He lifted his eyebrows, giving an approximation of a shrug, and she set her hand in Antoine's. The Frenchman lifted it to his lips and kissed her knuckles.

"*Je suis enchanté, Madame Baker,*" he said gently, and she blushed that delicious shade of pink Danny loved to see, though he wasn't especially happy to see her do it for another man.

"*Merci beaucoup,*" she replied. "*Vous êtes très aimable.*"

He would have to ask her about that later, Danny decided, find out what she'd said. When Antoine finally released Audrey's hand, Danny took it and wound his fingers through hers. "My wife is an artist."

Antoine's brow lifted. "Ah! *Une artiste!* What do you paint, madame?"

"Just about anything, sir, but recently I have been painting portraits of people."

"*Vraiment?* Perhaps you would paint my family."

"I would be honoured."

He considered Audrey closely, having apparently forgotten all about Danny for the time being. "Would you come to my house? Meet my wife and show us some samples of your work?"

Audrey appeared delighted. Danny stared at her, realizing how long it had been since she'd really smiled like that. Lately her expression had seemed strained.

"I would love to," she replied.

"Excellent. Bring your supplies as well, and we can start immediately if we like what we see." He faced O'Malley. "Give Monsieur and Madame Baker my address. I shall see them in the morning, early. That way, Monsieur Baker will have plenty of time to get back to work after he brings his wife." His eyes found Danny's. "Yes? This is fine?"

"Certainly, sir."

"You see how we like to work in my little company? We help each other's families. It's good for business."

It was difficult for Danny, swallowing his pride, but the army had drilled respect into his head. "Yes, sir, and we're grateful for your help."

It was the right thing to say. Mr. Antoine nodded at him, then at Johnny, and finally touched his hat and gave Audrey a small bow. "Until tomorrow," he said, then he walked briskly in another direction, followed by a couple of note-taking employees. O'Malley and Johnny headed toward the docks, leaving the couple alone.

Audrey positively glowed. "What do you think?"

What could he say? "It's fantastic! Didn't I say you'd be painting here? And I don't think you can go much higher than Pierre Antoine."

"I'm so excited! I'll have to pull together those samples for him." Her fingers linked and she held them under her chin, beaming like a little girl. "Oh, Danny, you were right. This is going to be wonderful for us both."

"Of course it is." He tilted his head, regarding the bag she carried. "That for me?"

She blinked, confused, then remembered. "Oh, yes. You forgot your lunch. I wanted to come and see you anyway. It's awful, being alone in that little old house, you know."

"I know. But I'll be home in a few hours, then you can show me what you're planning to bring tomorrow morning."

She flung her arms around his neck and kissed him. "Thank you, Danny."

He never tired of that, of the way she loved him. His arms tightened around her waist and pulled her close. He kissed her again, trying to be discreet since dockworkers milled around them, then he lowered his lips to her ear.

"You can show your appreciation later, my love," he hinted, and she pulled away in mock surprise.

"Why, Mr. Baker. I'm shocked!" But she couldn't hide her grin, and her eyes danced just for him.

"Sure you are. Go on now. I'll see you back at the house later."

She kissed him again then headed back up the street. Danny watched her go, slightly uncomfortable with the fact that the bounce in her step might not be because of him. He wanted her happy, and he knew she wanted to paint, to contribute to their income, but a small part of him was still reluctant to accept that. On the other hand, if she did a good job on the Antoines' portrait, that practically guaranteed Danny's position on the docks. He would just have to adjust his way of thinking, he decided.

The next morning, Danny carried her easel and paints to Pierre Antoine's house, kissed her at the door, then limped back down the hill to the pier without a word. He had seen the man's dark brown eyes slide over Audrey's body when they'd arrived, yet Danny had left her there. What else could he do?

———

Halifax was a bustling, crowded city, peopled by factory workers and owners, prostitutes and bootleggers, and frequented by shiploads of soldiers and sailors. Hundreds of ocean-going ships passed through the

Halifax harbour, many of which carried war supplies for the British and French. On sunny days there was nothing like it, with the vast blue of the water reflecting endless golds and reds of sloughing trees. He imagined it would be even prettier in the summer, when Citadel Hill was awash in green. One sunny day in Halifax could most likely bring a smile to anyone's face.

On the other hand, there seemed to be more grey days than blue lately. And when the city was awash in fog or drizzle, the whole world faded into tired, colourless features. It was hard to feel optimistic on days like that. What bothered him the most, though, was how that grey seemed to leech colour from Audrey's face.

The money that both he and Audrey were making, as he'd been promised, was pretty good. He did his job, keeping track of shipments, occasionally helping to unload, intimidating guys from the other side of the docks when it was called for, and watching out for the rest of his team. Danny was becoming a popular fixture on the docks. Johnny had introduced him to all his friends and coworkers, and Danny'd connected with a few real characters, like the monster Irishman named Red, the Italian boxer Franco Solieri, Mad MacDonald from Scotland, and a couple of others he'd like to keep on his side. None of the men he knew now were the kind he'd bring home to his mother for Sunday night supper, but then again, that kind of fellow might not survive on the docks. With so much shipping action going on, there had been some fights, but though Danny had been hired for his cold countenance and ability to stand up against troublemakers, he avoided confrontations. He knew himself too well. Yes, he could pull the trigger if it was called for. But once his fists started flying, they were hard to stop. More than once Johnny had had to pull him off an unlucky longshoremen who had taken one look at Danny's wooden leg and thrown a miscalculated challenge in his direction.

Audrey, on the other hand, didn't appear to have any friends. For weeks she spent every day painting at the Antoine house, and when she got home she was usually too tired to want to go anywhere. Not that they could really afford to go out anyway, and here in the city that was the only real option. It was different from back on the shore, where they could just drift in a boat or cuddle together under the stars.

Over time Audrey became quiet, withdrawn, and he knew the squalor of the area was killing her. What choice did he have? At least she was painting, though even that didn't appear to be enough. When she looked wistfully down the street toward the sea, he knew she was having trouble seeing any other colours but grey.

AUDREY

– November 1917 –

TWENTY-TWO

Audrey had lived a lot of lives. As a child she'd wandered alongside her mother, dancing and dining through the poorest places in Sussex. She'd been happy, she remembered, but she'd known hunger and rough living. When the sickness had taken her mother away, Audrey had become a slave of sorts to her grandmère, tending the big, lonely farm. After that death, Audrey had stumbled with exhaustion through the munitions factory, her fingers black as pitch and frozen into painful, solid lumps, courtesy of the London winter.

Then life had changed again. She'd come to Canada with her heart open wide. Jeddore had been cold and windy and beautiful with a wild, uncaring abandon, and in the summer the sun had baked down on them, its warmth almost as loving as the people around her. She had never wanted to leave.

Now she was in Halifax, another different world. A world that offered so many choices.

In a way, having options was a new concept to Audrey. As a child she'd followed her mother, learned that even the woman she worshipped could make mistakes. On the farm she'd had no choices, but the understanding of her restrictions had only squeezed her creativity into a more volatile package. Escape hadn't been an option—since she had no idea where she might run—but it had become the only possible path to take after she'd met Danny. He had blinded her to any others.

Then she'd been adopted by Danny's family, and oh, why bother to choose any other life? It was beautiful there, most of the time, and she was happy.

But Danny wasn't. She'd known he needed to do something to redeem himself in her eyes, to make enough money to be a "real" husband, yet she'd chosen to close her eyes, pretending to be blinded again. She tried to tell him life would be all right in their home in East Jeddore, that somehow they'd get by just fine. She'd lied to them both, and he'd been forced to choose.

Now Halifax spread before her, showing her people and ideas she'd never considered before. She tried to keep busy, tried to figure out which direction to take, but one rainy morning when she was not at the Antoines' house, she headed out with absolutely nothing on her mind but escape from the drab, lonely existence in their miserable house. She wandered into downtown Halifax and was drawn to a large, ancient cathedral called Saint Mary's. The entry was a giant set of heavy oak doors, miniature in comparison to the massive granite walls surrounding them. Audrey heaved open one door and the thick black hinges creaked gently, welcoming her inside.

The church was dark within, like a cave. Then the flickering glow of candles caught her eye, and her mind registered a blend of cadmium orange and yellow paints come to life. She moved farther into the building and found herself lost in magnificence. It felt wrong, dripping like a rag before all this splendour, so she slipped off her hat and dropped her hand so that the limp material hung at her side. She hoped it wouldn't drip all over the soft, burgundy carpet, but she felt somehow more respectful this way.

A tray of small candles greeted her at the centre aisle, some lit, some with only blackened wicks. It felt like an invitation to venture within, but she stood beside them a few moments longer, her jaw hanging open in awe as she gazed upward. The ceiling rose in a series of marble arches, and within those forms had been painted the most beautiful pictures she'd ever seen. Her eye followed the paths of the arches, marvelling, and a thought came to her that this place couldn't be the product of a regular builder. The lines and colours could only have sprung from the heart of an artist.

She knew others would claim it had been created by God. Audrey didn't know enough about that to either argue or agree. Her mother had despised the restrictions of the Church, and her mother's mother had used those same restrictions to smother them both. Audrey supposed her grandmère would call her a sinner, say she had no right to be in this sacred place, but Audrey didn't care. She had needed shelter, and here it was, more beautiful than she could have imagined.

A few people sat in the benches, scattered in solitary silence, but no one knew her. She felt liberated; she had nothing to apologize for here. Not wanting to make a sound lest she disturb others, Audrey stepped silently along one of the side aisles, taking her time, savouring the windows with their glass renderings of saints and sinners. She assumed their colours would come alive on a sunny day. As it was, they only hinted at the colours soldered within the frames, and the effect made her cold. She shivered, hugging her coat closer as she moved toward the front of the church. It would be glorious up there, she knew. She'd seen the sheen of gold from the entryway at the back of the church, but she promised herself she wouldn't peek at the altar yet. She wanted to take it all in at once. When she finally arrived at the front, she dropped her eyes to her feet and kept them there until she reached the centre of the floor.

When she was ready, she opened her eyes and exhaled. The rain couldn't touch these colours, couldn't detract from the intricate, perfect sculptures, their gold skins warming over more small flames. In the centre, suffering in an endless, voiceless agony, stretched the body of Jesus, nailed on a wooden cross. She liked that, how the artist had brought in the simplicity of the wood, to contrast with the gold. Above everything rose more arches, more spindles stretching toward heaven. In that moment, Audrey wondered if there actually could be a God. Not some old man with a long white beard, not a tortured soul on a cross, but a spirit somewhere, a presence. And if that were so, she was certain the art in her came from that presence. That God. She might not believe in heaven and hell or the saints, but she believed in her art.

"Thank you," she whispered.

She chose a seat a few rows back, where no one else was, and lowered herself onto its hard wooden bench. She liked how she felt so tiny here, just a speck in the middle of all this, and yet she felt as if she belonged. The walls and ceiling swirled with figures which came alive in her mind, opened their painted veins and bled for real. She examined one woman's face, and wondered at the golden circle painted around her head. It didn't appear to be a crown, so she assumed it represented a halo. The woman looked so desperately sad. Captivated by her expression, Audrey stared at her, wondering who she was, and what could have happened to take the life from her eyes in that way. How could anyone be so unhappy?

An image came to her then, of Danny. She saw him in the muddied fields of France, his lovely brown hair covered by a helmet. He blinked, so she did too, and a tear escaped one of her eyes. Then his expression changed, reflecting the sadness of the woman she'd seen in the picture, and Audrey's heart melted.

"Oh, Danny," she whispered. "You will be fine. You and I will have a wonderful life." *God, if you're there, please let that be true.* A flutter of nerves deep in her belly warned that it probably wouldn't be that easy. *I'll be there for you, Danny*, she promised, then she rose and walked back to the entrance of the church.

She had come in seeking shelter, had stayed long enough to be awed by the beauty, and now she stood at the exit, cloaked in sorrow. Was it supposed to happen this way? Was she supposed to come into a place of worship and lose hope instead of gain it?

She didn't want to go back home. Not yet. Disappointment pressed against her chest. She'd wanted so much—expected so much from this, her first visit to a place of religion. If God was art, she accepted that he was in her soul, but she didn't plan to come back and visit him anytime soon. The ups and downs of being in his house were too hard on her heart.

Her hat had dripped dry along the way, and when she put it back on her head, it was cool and damp but no longer sopping wet. She buttoned up her long black coat, put her hands on the oak doors, and pushed out into the rainy day.

All she'd ever wanted was to be beside Danny, to laugh with him and see the love in his eyes. She'd been willing to go anywhere, do anything to be with him. What was she supposed to do now that just about everything she loved about him was gone? He rarely smiled and never laughed. Not with her, anyway. He drank. He stayed out nights with his rough friends, and worse, he often brought them home to sleep in their tiny home. Except how could she call it a home? To Audrey's way of thinking, a home was a place where hearts beat in unison, where weak, rattling walls could be overlooked because love kept them strong. There was no unison in their house. No harmony, either. Just the day-in, day-out ache of heartbreak.

It reminded her a little of France, of surviving her grandmère's smothering misery. Except she'd never known love with Céleste. That made this time even worse.

When Johnny was around, he settled easily into the company Danny kept, since he was a rough sort as well. Strong like his brother, with a rich, dark laugh. But Johnny, even when he'd had too much to drink, didn't carry a contagious sadness with him. He didn't wear the smothering cloak of anger Danny wore. Johnny was a comfort to her, a friend, though she couldn't ask him for help. She'd tried once, but he'd only shrugged.

"He has to do that on his own, Audrey," he said. "You gotta remember that Danny's seen and done things that don't just go away. But he'll come around. Best not to mess with it."

In Jeddore, she'd sometimes lain in bed, waiting for the morning sun to light their room so she could watch Danny sleep. She knew the moment he awoke, knew he was sensitive to her own breathing patterns. His eyes would open first, and if it was a particularly lucky day, he was on his side and they opened to her. Before either of them said a word, it was understood and mutual: *I love you. You are my world.*

Sometimes, lately, he wasn't even there in the morning. He passed out in the living room with his friends or fell asleep with his head on the kitchen table, snoring loudly with the effects of too much rum.

Oh, she wanted to understand. She wanted so badly to be the answer he sought, the comfort he so obviously needed, but he turned away from everything she offered. The war had been planted deep in Danny's mind. Its roots had twisted and spread voraciously, unearthing more terrifying, loathsome memories. From those roots grew clinging vines of self-hate and self-pity, which had bloomed into an armour so thick, he could no longer see the sky. All of it was fortified by the unavoidable sight of his stump.

What would have happened if he'd come home in one piece? Would he still have gotten caught up in this vortex and left her to watch helplessly from the side?

She'd watched other women cope with their husbands' depression. Some had joined their partners in the dark, drinking and fading into the broken, mouldy shadows of Richmond. Some peered nervously from behind cracked-open doors, their eyes swollen from tears, even blackened by fists. What she hadn't seen was a woman who stood up for herself, who dared to make something of her life even if her husband had quit on his own.

She couldn't talk reason to Danny anymore. Couldn't make him see. Any attempts to do that had been cut short, ending with his storming from the house without a response. He seemed bent on keeping to this path, too stubborn, too shackled by self-defeating pride to reach for the lifeline she threw time and time again.

If she couldn't save him, she still had to save herself. As much as she loved him, and as much as she knew that deep down he still loved her, it appeared she'd have to do this on her own. Audrey was still young, and she had no intentions of allowing herself to ease into the acceptance of her life as it was now. She would not skulk in the dark, hiding from his callous words, his accusatory glares. While every nerve in her ached for the solid anchor of his arms wrapped around her, she would not beg.

Growing up, she'd moved from place to place, moment to moment. She'd never had any real, defined dreams for her future—other than moving to Canada and marrying Danny—but it made no sense that she shouldn't have any. The world was changing. She'd learned that from the women in London, and though Halifax was smaller, she didn't believe it was any less progressive. She would find proof, and she would do something about it.

Antoine's wife, one of the few women she'd met, would be no help in that regard. She was the perfect example of someone Audrey didn't want to be: weighted down by all her children, satisfied with a vague belief that her job in life was complete. The woman sat around with nothing but complaints, and Audrey had never seen her with anyone outside of the house.

Her husband, however, had vast connections. He was enthusiastic, intelligent, and innovative. He was charming and handsome and the centre of the city, as far as she could tell. She liked that Antoine had asked her to bring samples of her work before he asked her to paint his family. It was professional, and it made sense for a man who was so good in business to ask for references of a sort.

It seemed like another lifetime, but only a few weeks had passed since Danny had carried her things, then left her at the ornately carved front door. She had stepped inside the Antoines' grand house on a blast of cold November wind and fumbled with apology as the maid took her coat. Everything about the house, from the outside in, seemed extravagant and thrilling, leaving her searching for words. She gripped the wooden handle of her bag; the artist in her burned to get it all down on paper.

"This way, please," the maid said in a soft French accent, and she led Audrey to the front sitting room.

A large woman was there already, sitting like an overgrown toad on a sturdy chair, studying Audrey through belligerent eyes.

The little maid introduced the two. "Madame Antoine, may I present Madame Audrey Baker, the artist."

The toad blinked. "Charmed. Lily, get Monsieur Antoine."

"Of course, madame."

Audrey and her hostess regarded each other in silence, and Audrey fought the impulse to run. Under the weight of the woman's scrutiny she felt completely out of place. She stood before a woman draped in jewels, surrounded by lush furniture and elaborate trimmings, witnessing a manifestation of wealth she'd never imagined.

Madame Antoine's flat little eyes examined her, blinking up from under her thin-plucked brows. "Do sit. You're making me uncomfortable."

Four chairs and one central table took up most of the room. "I'm so sorry. Anywhere in particular?" The woman shook her head and the stack of curls pulled to the top of her head bobbed. Audrey took the chair farthest from her, then sat straight and prayed the master of the house would be a little less intimidating.

"So you paint."

The woman's rhetorical question was unexpected. "Um, yes, madame. I do my best."

"And where are you from?"

"England. I lived a while in France, then I came across and have been living in East Jeddore."

Madame Antoine's face was blank. "Where?"

"East Jeddore? On the Eastern Shore."

The older woman stared at her a moment, her expression unreadable. "One of those little fishing villages, I expect. And you have painted for whom in the past?"

Audrey was so nervous, she decided to overlook the slight. "Well, mostly I paint for my own pleasure, but I have painted for a few families near my husband's home." She smiled sweetly, hoping to ease the tension. "I was very fortunate to be hired by Madame Eleanor Hartlin."

"Hartlin?" She sniffed. "I don't know the name. Should I?"

Audrey was struck by an odd sense of pity for the woman and her baseless belief in her superiority. To her, Audrey was nothing, as was everyone else not fortunate enough to be in her husband's circle. "I wouldn't think so, madame. She is quite an elderly woman but an impressive one nonetheless. She lives in Hartlin Settlement—"

"There's a settlement of Hartlins?" She rolled her eyes. "No, dear. What I wanted to know was if you'd ever painted for anyone here."

"*Non, mon coeur.* Madame Baker has only just moved to Halifax." Mr. Antoine breezed into the room and offered a hand to Audrey. He never even glanced at his wife. Audrey stood, but he waved her back down. "Oh no, please. It is an inhospitable day out of doors, and you must make yourself comfortable now. Madame Baker, I am *absolument* charmed to see you again."

Lily appeared with tea, and Audrey concentrated on keeping the delicate china safe. She brought her lips to the rim but pulled away from the heat.

"This is lovely," she said through the steam. "Thank you."

Pierre Antoine beamed at her. "Thank you for coming to see us. Especially in this weather." He sipped his tea without seeming to notice its dangerous temperature. "Now," he continued, "I hope you don't mind my getting right to business."

"Of course not, sir."

"As I mentioned before, my dear wife and I are interested in having our family's portrait done by a professional, and I have been told you have quite a gift."

"That's very kind, sir."

"Not at all, not at all." His eyes went to the bag at her feet. "Are those the samples of your work I requested?"

"They are. I hope this is what you were imagining. I'm afraid I don't have a large collection. Most of what I've painted recently covers my mother-in-law's walls," she admitted, reaching for the bag. She'd brought a few paintings she'd done of Danny and one of his mother, then she pulled out some pencil sketches of both landscapes and people.

"Ah. Your husband," he said, holding the pictures in front of him. He moved to show his wife, but she only flicked an eyebrow and looked uninterested. Pierre Antoine didn't appear to notice her reaction. His eyes were fixed on Danny's likeness. "Quite a handsome man. And your portrait reflects his character as well."

That was an odd comment, she thought. "You've heard something of my husband, sir?"

Pierre Antoine's eyes twinkled. "But of course. You know, a man such as myself has spies everywhere." He winked, but Audrey wasn't sure how to take his statement. How could he know Danny's character? He chuckled. "Not to worry, *ma chère*. I do not speak of espionage. All I know is that he is a hard worker who was injured in the war. And now, well, now I know he has a talented and most beautiful wife."

His wife sighed with ennui and glanced over one shoulder, away from them both.

Audrey blushed but didn't look away. "Thank you, sir."

He watched her eyes for what felt like a moment too long, and she shifted uncomfortably. He nodded. "*Bien*. I have decided. You will paint our family's portrait. Can you start today?"

TWENTY-THREE

Pierre Antoine was called away from their portrait sitting more than once since he was needed for some sort of business, but he always returned and encouraged Audrey to continue. It took her weeks to complete the portrait, and though she was exhausted by it, she enjoyed the process so much she almost wished it could have gone on longer. Antoine sang her praises with the melodic enthusiasm of a Frenchman, and when she suggested it was time for her to move on, he contracted her to do individual portraits as well, offering more money than she could ever have expected.

"This way," he explained, "when I am dead, they will not all have to fight over this one painting, *n'est-ce pas?*"

Other than when she sat for the portraits, Madame Antoine made herself scarce. When Audrey asked, he waved his hand, dismissing the question. "She is unwell" or "She needs quiet for her delicate condition" were his common replies, and eventually Audrey stopped asking. She preferred it this way anyway. Pierre Antoine had become a good friend, talking with her about people he knew, asking about her own story. They were on a first-name basis. He said she was a breath of fresh air, that her conversation helped him forget the day-to-day troubles of business. She had come to trust him, even opened up one time and mentioned that Danny was having difficulties adjusting to city life, which was taking its toll on her as well. When he looked concerned, she quickly assured him Danny was well enough and healthy, always able to work hard, because she knew Pierre was the real boss of the docks. One word from him and Danny could lose his job. That would destroy everything.

After her portrait of the family had been hung on a prominent wall of their living room, he invited her to sit in one of the large armchairs and quietly admire it with him. She knew every brushstroke, every shade of colour from memory, but she tried to see it from his perspective, wanting to understand what he saw.

"I very much admire your talent and skills, Audrey. You are so young, and yet your artwork seems somehow wiser than is possible for your years. It is a . . . *je ne sais quoi*. I do not understand the craft, but I do appreciate art when it is done well." He sat back and crossed his legs, smiling with fascination at her. "You must have made your teachers proud."

She had to laugh. She'd become entirely comfortable around him by this point, even looked forward to the times when he came and sat behind her, watching her paint. "Oh, no. I had no teachers."

"But this is amazing!" He stared again at the painting. "You are *superbe, ma chère! Incroyable.*"

Her cheeks bloomed. She couldn't deny that his compliments and his obvious interest in her work made her feel good. He was rich, he was handsome, and he was probably about ten years her senior. When she left his house every day and went back to Richmond, she faced quiet evenings with a man who reacted entirely the opposite way around her. Danny was always tired, always morose. Lately he smelled more of alcohol than he did of his own scent, and she couldn't remember the last time he'd complimented her. When had they last made love?

Pierre leaned forward and gently rubbed his handkerchief across her cheek, then showed her the evidence: a smear of cadmium lemon paint left behind. She blushed. "I must be a mess," she said, pressing her hands to her cheeks.

He chuckled fondly and tucked the handkerchief back in his pocket, then set his hand on the arm of her chair. "A party. I shall throw a dinner party this coming Saturday night, which is . . ." He frowned, thinking. "*Ah, oui.* The second of December. It will be in honour of you, *ma chère*, and everyone will come to see *ma petite artiste*. They will see what you have created, and they will all hire you to paint for them. This is a wonderful idea, yes?"

She stared at him, struck dumb. The idea was terrifying in the most exhilarating way.

"You are teasing," she scolded.

"I am not! Twenty, maybe twenty-five people will come and they will all fall in love with you." His eyes softened, and his hand slid from the chair's arm. It settled on top of her hand, warm and confident. "How could they not?"

He waited expectantly, eyes shining. The gentle pressure of his hand on hers set her heart racing, stirring up a confusing mixture of giddiness and guilt. A party for her? When she thought back on her life, she couldn't remember anyone ever doing something like this, something so completely on her behalf. Oh, Danny was full of compliments for her—or at least he had been—and she knew he loved her. Danny had always praised her artwork, made frames, encouraged her. He'd viewed painting as something she did out of love for the art—which also happened to bring in an unexpected income when they needed it.

What he didn't understand was that she didn't paint simply for the love of it. When Audrey disappeared into the art, something within her was freed. All her life, when she'd needed to express herself, she'd run to her paints. What Pierre was suggesting with this party was saying so much more in her eyes. For Pierre to even think of organizing something so grand, he must somehow understand how vital the act of painting was to her. He was honouring her, opening a window and encouraging her to grow wings, letting her fly beyond what she'd known before.

Of course, not only had Pierre given her a level of respect she hadn't anticipated, with this party he would basically guarantee her future in painting by inviting his friends to meet her. What an amazing friend she'd found in Pierre.

He was grinning to himself, doing calculations. "Oh yes," he said. "I know exactly who would appreciate such a fine evening. It will be all the talk!"

Her whole body tingled with pleasure at the thought. People coming in their fancy clothes, wearing expensive jewellery, seeing her as some kind of special artist? She hadn't even known it had been a dream of hers until this moment, when it was being offered to her on a silver platter. She opened her mouth to agree, then stopped herself, suddenly mortified.

She had absolutely nothing to wear to an event such as he was planning. Even her wedding dress had been worn down to a sad grey, and she had no baubles with which to dress it up. And what of Danny? What would he wear?

She glanced down at Antoine's hand and he withdrew it, but his enthusiasm remained.

"Well, my dear? What do you think?"

"Oh, Pierre. You are a wonderful person to offer this, and I am overwhelmed by your generosity. It's just . . ." She took a deep breath and panicked, trying not to fuss with her skirt, but it tangled between her fingers. She mustn't cry. She *mustn't.* "I'm afraid I cannot, sir."

He sat back abruptly, shocked. "Why ever not?"

He must see it, but for whatever reason he was choosing to overlook the obvious. How could she admit it out loud, that she simply didn't belong in that kind of company? That she longed for it, wanted so badly to meet these exciting people, touch their silks and satins, maybe even make a friend. To know that she'd come from so little and was so close . . .

Her eyes dropped to the floor. "I . . . I have nothing to wear, Pierre. Nothing suitable."

He shrugged, obviously nonplussed. "It will be on Saturday. Today is Monday. You have time enough."

She had thought her cheeks were on fire before, but it was all suddenly so much worse. "No, sir, I cannot. You see—"

"Ah!" he said, eyes widening. He jumped to his feet and moved toward his desk, pulling open a drawer and writing on a small card in one swift movement. "But how ignorant of me! *Je m'excuse!* Please, allow me. This soiree is my idea to begin with, and I would not have the guest of honour uncomfortable because of my oversight."

He tucked the card into an envelope bearing his name and told her to bring it to a particular dressmaker in the city. Audrey was to choose whatever she desired, and the dressmaker would bring the bill to Antoine. She objected, embarrassed at the very idea, yet ecstatic at the same time. Fortunately, he insisted with his customary charm then called a cab to bring her home. He also wrote down her address, promising to send another cab to her house to pick up both her and Danny on the night of the party.

She could hardly think on the cab ride home. The whole idea was ridiculous, she told herself, and yet it was happening, wasn't it? He would be sending out invitations in the morning, he had said.

It was dark when she got home. Winter had come quickly, pulling down temperatures, forcing lamps to light earlier every evening. Audrey didn't like being alone in the dark, and Danny no longer came to get her if she was late. He assumed she'd be fine, since she was under the care of the great Pierre Antoine.

Their sad little house was unlit on the outside, and only a dim hint of gold flickered from within a front window. Audrey stood outside the door and stared at it, holding Antoine's card in her gloved fingers. She felt weak at the thought of telling Danny about the invitation and about the dressmaker. He already hated how much charity she accepted from the family. Just the week before she'd brought home a coat for Danny. It had been too worn for Antoine, but it would have fit Danny. Winter was coming, and he'd need something, but he'd had too much to drink by the time she'd gotten home. When he'd caught sight of the beautiful black coat, he'd promptly thrown it out on the street. She'd gone out to retrieve it in the morning, but it had already been claimed by a more practical soul.

The air had teeth tonight, and she clenched her own together, knowing she couldn't stand out there all night, dreading the encounter. The door swung open when she turned the knob, and she stepped inside, keeping her coat on. It was too cold inside—as she'd known it would be—to go without.

"Danny?"

He didn't answer, and she hoped he was asleep. She hated the times when he was passed out with his arms like a pillow on the kitchen table. It had only happened twice, but she'd hated it. Once he'd left a cigarette burning between his fingers while he slept.

She stepped into the kitchen, but he wasn't there. At least no one else was, either.

"Danny?"

"In here." His voice was oddly quiet. It came from the bedroom.

"You're ready to sleep already? It's early yet."

"I have nothing else to do." He was sitting up in bed, wearing a tired undershirt untucked over a loose pair of dark grey pants. The smoke from his cigarette rose straight up in a thin line, then drew squiggly circles up high. He looked tired. "I was just waiting for you."

Something in his voice made her feel so sad. She heard no antagonism, no defensive edge. It was like the way he'd spoken to her once upon a time, when she'd felt important to him. How long had it been since he'd made her feel special? Why did it feel as if they'd been married twenty years now instead of only a few months?

"Sorry I'm late." His mellow mood made the question of Pierre even more difficult to bring up. She didn't want to break the spell settled over the room, but she couldn't hide from the conversation, and who knew when they might speak civilly again? "Mr. Antoine wanted to speak with me about my painting."

It hadn't really been about her painting, but she could say it was. At least that way it wouldn't start out as a confrontation. Regardless, she braced for his response.

"Is he happy with it?"

She was taken by surprise at his gentle reaction. So often just the mention of Antoine roused snarls from him. Encouraged, she settled in on the bed, brushing up against his arm with her own, hoping for more.

"Oh yes. He's very happy. He hung it right in the living room." She held out her hands in front of her, demonstrating how it would hang right at eye level. "And he . . . he's planning to throw a dinner party to show it to all his society friends."

"Ooh la la," he said with a wry grin. "They'll all be talking about you now. Wonder what they'll say."

This was the tricky part. "Actually, Danny, he's invited you and me as well."

He searched her eyes for the punchline. When he didn't see anything change in her reaction, he barked out a laugh. "Oh, that sounds just right. You and me with the high and mighty. Come on, honey. Why would he invite us to something like that?"

She knew he was right, that they couldn't possibly fit in, but he didn't have to be so negative about it. "He wants to help my career. He says I have a lot of talent and I deserve recognition. If they all see it, and if they all meet me, he thinks they all might just hire me to do their portraits."

He set the cigarette between his lips and inhaled, let the smoke out slow. "I don't see why I'd have to be there."

"Because you're my husband is why!"

His shrug was small, noncommittal. "I'm not going."

"What? Why not?"

She hated the smile he gave her, that cold, arrogant sneer he reserved for a special kind of insult. Based on his expression, she knew his response before it came, and she already knew what her own answer would be. "Because I'm not."

"Well, I am."

"No, you aren't."

"It's a party in my honour, Danny. You should be proud of me, happy for me."

He adjusted his body on the bed so he was facing her, and his eyes softened. "Oh, you know I'm proud of you. Always have been. But you gotta know those people will look down on you. You know what they're like. You'll just be the entertainment for the night. *See that poor little fisherman's wife? You know he only has one leg, don't you?*"

She turned her face away, close to tears.

"Don't go, Audrey." He was almost begging, but she didn't give in. This was her dream even if it wasn't his. "Don't let them play with you like that. You're better than that."

A sob escaped, and she let him have it, all her frustration in one long exhalation. "Why do you have to be so mean, Danny? Why do you do all you can to ruin things for me? All I want is a little happiness." Her hands clenched into fists, and she felt the sharp press of her nails against her palms. "I want to see people enjoy my paintings. I want to meet new people. I want to try new things. But you always make the pretty things ugly. You want to keep me unhappy."

"No, I don't."

"You do! Every time I come home and tell you something good, you find something suspicious about it or you twist it around so it's about you. Why do you have to do that?"

"That's who I am."

She sniffed and wiped her cheeks with the back of her hand. "That's a lousy reason. You're being very selfish."

He didn't say anything at first, and his gaze slid to the foot of the bed. He'd taken off the peg and the empty pant leg gathered near his other knee.

"You didn't use to be selfish," she added quietly.

"Maybe not." He opened his mouth, as if there was something he wanted to say. Something he was fighting to keep back. "Maybe it's not being selfish. Maybe I want to protect you."

"You just want to keep me to yourself."

His expression was unsure. As if he didn't know whether or not he needed to defend himself on that point. "Is that so wrong?"

Oh, it broke her heart seeing him this way. All she'd wanted in the past was for him to hold her, protect her, love her. She hadn't cared if there was another person in the whole world. He'd made her laugh, he'd thrilled her, and at times she felt as if he were too good to be true. How could anyone love her as much as he did? But that love had turned upside down. Now he was drowning in his own despair, and he was pulling her under with him. She could barely breathe.

"Yes," she whispered. "You have to let me be happy, Danny."

She didn't know what she'd hoped for, maybe for him to slump just a little, to suddenly see the light and apologize, to beg for her forgiveness. And she'd give it to him, if only she could see that love back in his eyes. She'd give it all to him in that instant.

But he didn't. He stood up, hopped to his crutch, and yanked on his old coat. She heard the door latch behind him, and it was the loneliest sound she'd ever heard.

TWENTY-FOUR

⁎

She went to the dressmaker the next morning after Danny had gone
to work. He hadn't come home until three hours before he had to get
up, and they hadn't spoken a word to each other all through those long,
cold hours. Audrey had closed her eyes, refusing to cry, but all the time
she craved his touch and had to fight the urge to slide closer, press her
back against his. But he hadn't moved toward her. He hadn't reached for
her at all.

So she stepped into the street outside their little house just after ten
o'clock, Pierre's little card tucked in her pocket. She had no idea if she
would actually use it, if she would be brave enough to do as he had so
generously suggested. But the very idea of walking into a store she had,
until then, considered out of bounds, and maybe even walking out with
a purchase appealed to her on many levels.

It was quite a distance to the shop on Hollis Street, and she was glad
she'd worn her thick winter coat. Snow clouds were closing in.

The little store was called Nanette's Boutique. The front was white
with a big, beautiful window out to the street, and two breathtaking
gowns were on display, one in light pink with ivory lace, the other an

elegant black satin. Everyone seemed to wear black these days, respecting those lost in the war, but Audrey had decided she just couldn't. What she needed more than anything these days—besides a return of the old Danny—was colour. And since she was going to be on display as an artist, it only made sense that she show off a little of it. She blinked up at the pink gown, appreciating its delicate cut, the folds of the skirt lightly sweeping the floor of the display window. It was absolutely beautiful. But Audrey didn't want pink.

A little bell rang when she opened the door, bright and cheery, and such a welcome change from the grey outside that she couldn't help smiling. A neatly dressed woman came from the back of the store to greet her, though her eyes flicked skeptically over Audrey's coat. Audrey had expected that kind of reaction, and she didn't blame the woman. Danny was right, but he was also wrong. She knew she didn't fit in—not as she was. A change was needed, and if Pierre Antoine wanted to help her make that change, she wasn't going to argue. Yes, she was as poor as a church mouse, but the little card in her pocket was worth more than anything she'd ever owned, including her gold wedding band.

"Good morning," the woman said sweetly. "Can I help you with something?"

"Oh, I hope so," Audrey said, wanting to please her. "I'm looking for a gown for a dinner party." The shadow of a frown crossed the woman's brow, and Audrey pulled out the card. "Don't worry. I came here at Mr. Pierre Antoine's suggestion."

The pale blond brow lifted with surprise, and she took the envelope to her counter, where she slit it open with a letter opener. Audrey waited patiently while the woman read the note, saw her eyes warm with recognition.

"Well, aren't you the lucky lady?" she said.

"I really am."

"A dinner party in your honour? This must be something truly special."

"I painted his family's portrait, and he seems quite pleased with it, I'm glad to say."

"Well, then. We must make sure he's just as pleased with the artist as he is with the art. Let's see what we have for you, shall we? My name is Mrs. Jones, and you must not be shy to ask questions or tell me what you think, are we agreed?"

Audrey tried on five different dresses before she and Mrs. Jones finally found just the right one: an ankle-length evening gown in satin charmeuse, dyed a lovely robin's egg blue. The sleeveless shoulders were draped with a gold embroidered net, and a cluster of rosebuds had been added where the waist drew in over a full, graceful skirt. A matching gold netting fell beneath the hem as well, giving the impression of a golden-laced petticoat. She stepped into a matching pair of shoes and waved away the suggestion of a hat.

"The colour is magnificent, is it not?" Mrs. Jones said, stepping back to regard Audrey's reflection in the mirror. "As if the material were specially made to match your eyes."

She couldn't disagree. The gown was beautiful, and Audrey looked beautiful in it. But such a wave of melancholy broke over her in that moment she had to blink quickly to hide her emotions. Her wedding dress had been blue. She still remembered Danny's flustered expression when he'd seen her in it, and how his eyes had changed as he'd slowly undressed her for the first time. She should choose another dress, one that didn't bring such sadness.

But no. This was the one. She lifted her chin. "It's perfect."

Mrs. Jones misinterpreted the sudden shine in Audrey's eyes. "Sometimes it is amazing to see how a gown can transform a person. Overwhelming, even. You are a very beautiful woman, Mrs. Baker, but it can be difficult to see that when you are forced to hide your beauty beneath lesser clothing. Your husband is a lucky man."

She swallowed back any quick comments, because of course there was nothing lucky about him at all. And "lesser clothing" was all she'd ever known. Besides, Danny wouldn't come to the dinner party; he might never see her in the gown at all.

"And I'm a lucky woman," was all she said.

When she stepped outside the shop again, she pulled up her collar against the blizzard and was instantly drenched in doubt. What on earth was she doing? She couldn't go to a party on her own, could she? By doing this, wasn't she pulling farther away from Danny instead of trying to mend what was broken between them? She had no right to wear something so beautiful, so expensive; though she'd never been told the price, she knew she'd never be able to afford it on her own.

It had apparently been snowing for a while, because little drifts had formed while she'd been in the shop. Walking down the hill toward her house was slippery. She wished she'd stayed inside just a little longer, but after she'd accepted the parcel, conversation between herself and Mrs. Jones had become decidedly awkward.

She had almost passed a café on the corner when a notice in the window caught her eye. Backing up a few steps, she frowned at the ivory sheet of paper, reading it through the rain-speckled window, then she smiled. It was just like the ones she'd seen in London, in another lifetime. A women's meeting, taking place Wednesday at noon in a nearby church. The reminder was bittersweet. So much had been in her head back then, all the changes, the adventure of saving to start a new life. The women she'd met had been her support system, and she decided she needed them again. She memorized the church address and time and headed back to the house.

The brown paper package containing her new gown and shoes slid under their bed. He wouldn't see it there, not if he didn't think to look. And she had a feeling that even if she told him about it, he wouldn't bother. There would be no changing his mind on this.

And now there would be no changing hers. Wednesday's meeting couldn't come soon enough, as far as Audrey was concerned. She survived another silent night on Tuesday, but Wednesday morning she couldn't bear it any longer. She was making his lunch—what there was of it, anyway—while he sat stonily at the kitchen table, sipping tea and eating toast, staring at the plate in front of him.

"Are we ever going to speak to each other again?" Audrey asked quietly.

His gaze rose slowly, as if he'd forgotten she was there. But he hadn't, she knew. He'd just been waiting for her to say something first. He wanted her to think he was unaffected by this tension between them, but she saw it there, thick in the lines across his brow. She read him so well. Knew every desperate thought behind those sad eyes. He was lost. He needed her. But he wouldn't accept even a hint of comfort.

"What do you want to talk about?"

"I don't care. The weather?" she said wryly.

"It's snowing again."

The fact that he hadn't even cracked a smile hurt. "You know I was joking."

His eyes went back to his tea, and she slammed her hands on the counter. "Look at me, Danny."

This time his reaction was a swift glare, shot at her through blazing eyes. Many men would back away from that expression, but Danny didn't scare her. Not in that way, anyway. The only thing that scared Audrey was the fact that he was using it on her.

"What do you want from me, Audrey?" he demanded. "I'm doing all I can."

"No, you're not." She was determined not to wobble. "You're doing all you can to ruin our marriage is what you're doing. I need you to pull yourself out of this, Danny."

"Out of what?"

She rolled her eyes. "You know exactly what I'm talking about. All you want to do lately is moan and groan and drink and be mean to me. You *must* hear it in your own voice."

He leaned back in his chair, stretched his leg out in front. "You want me to pretend? You want me to say I'm happy, you're happy, we're all one big happy family?" He threw his hands in the air. "Oh, that's right. We're not even a family. I can't seem to get you pregnant, can I?"

They didn't often speak of that, and Audrey'd never even think to blame him for it. In fact, she thought it was probably her fault; she'd grown up so poor that she'd starved her body, made it too difficult to have a baby. But she didn't admit to it. Now didn't seem the right time to soften on any subject.

"You are the only family I have, Danny, so yes. You're ruining our family."

"And it's all my fault? While I'm out there working hard to make a penny, you're chatting with the upper crust, rubbing elbows with the rich and famous. Becoming a celebrity of some kind. They're still laughing at you, you know. You're only giving them more to laugh at, going to this party of yours."

He'd been so quiet about the party she'd almost thought he'd forgotten about it. Apparently not. "That's your opinion. I disagree. I feel welcome there. In fact, Mr. Antoine was shocked when I told him I didn't think I could go, that I—" She stopped and her face was suddenly hot. She'd said too much.

Danny regarded her carefully. "That you what, Audrey?"

There was nothing she could do but go on. "I told him I had nothing to wear, so he sent me to the dressmaker's, and he bought me a gown."

His jaw dropped. "He . . . bought you a gown?"

"Y-yes. Mrs. Antoine's clothes are all too big for me, and he said he wanted to make sure I was there, to meet all his friends. Oh Danny, can't you see? He wants to help us! He wants to introduce me to families so I can paint for them. You and I can have a better life after that. You told me a long time ago that you'd be mad to ask me to stop working, that we needed the money. Well, none of that has changed." Her voice had risen steadily now that she felt on solid ground. She knew he'd remember saying that, back at his parents' home. How she longed to be back there! Emotion was starting to edge its way into her words, but she fought it back, needing to stay strong. "You're being unreasonable, and you know it. Well, I'm going to be practical, and I'm going to enjoy myself while I'm at it. I'm going to that party, I'm going to meet people, and I'm going to bring home some money. Maybe then you'll stop all this miserable self-pity. I want you to come with me, but you are just too stubborn."

"You have no idea, do you?" he said quietly.

She frowned at him, taken off guard. "About what?"

"About me. About what it's like to be me, to be a man, to be a husband and watch you doing this. I have all sorts of responsibilities, and you just turn it all around with your parties and your fancy dresses. Life is hard, Audrey. You can't just dance around like a little girl, you know."

"You're making no sense."

"You just don't understand me."

"But I do!"

He held her eyes. "I used to think you did. Now all you care about is yourself."

Words stuck in her throat, and tears overflowed. "What are you talking about?"

Something she hoped was regret flickered behind his beautiful, cold eyes then was gone. "I'm going to work." He hobbled to the counter and picked up the lunch she'd made for him, then he leaned heavily on his crutch and left again. "You go on and have a nice day now," he tossed over his shoulder.

By the time the door had closed behind him, she could hardly breathe. She sank to the floor and hugged her knees to her chest, rocking with sobs, letting them come as loudly as they wanted. She hoped he heard every one of them, hoped they tore at him just as they did her. If she could just be swallowed up by them, melt into the floor and disappear from everything, that would be so much better than the pain that ravaged her heart.

"Danny," she managed to whisper to herself. There was no one else to hear his name, but she needed to say it. "Oh, Danny."

It was a while before she was about to breathe normally again, and she didn't move until she felt sure she was steady. Then she stood carefully, propped herself against the counter, and paused a moment, just breathing.

"I won't give up on you," she promised weakly.

Because if she did, if she followed his directions and left him alone, what would happen to him? How would he survive without the hope of her love flickering at the end of his tunnel? It was a heavy promise to make. It thickened in her chest and she waited for it to settle in for the duration. *For better or worse,* they had said. Please God, let this be the worst.

Taking a deep breath, she pushed her grief away, determined to temporarily change direction and do something for herself. She'd been looking forward to this women's meeting, had even pulled together a couple of posters she'd made for the London women. Maybe she'd show them what she'd done in the past. Perhaps she could be of some help here, too.

The church hall was crowded, filled to capacity with women. Audrey didn't know a soul, and she scanned the crowd, searching for expressions as lost as her own. Instead, she met the hawklike gaze of a beautiful, red-haired woman who gave her a startling grin and stalked toward her. To Audrey's surprise, the woman stuck out one hand, seeking hers.

"I'm Catherine Metcalf," she stated. "And you are new here. Welcome to the club."

Audrey warmed to her immediately. "Audrey Baker," she said, returning the smile and shaking her hand. "Thank you."

"Do you know what this is all about?"

"Oh yes, I think so. I've been to similar meetings in London."

Auburn eyebrows shot up, evidently impressed. Catherine's lips twitched in a conspiratorial smirk. "Really? Well, how positively *international* of you, dear Audrey. This will seem like child's play after that."

"I doubt that. It's all very important, no matter where it's happening."

"True enough. Are you meeting anyone in particular?"

"No. I just saw the poster and thought—"

Catherine grabbed Audrey's hand. "Well, come along then. There aren't very many seats left, but we have an extra in our section."

Audrey went willingly, glowing inside about the first new friend other than Pierre that she'd made since leaving Jeddore. She was led to a spot near the front of the room, three rows back from the standard long table and the customary microphone. Catherine introduced her to four women who welcomed her, saying it was always lovely to see a new face in the crowd. Five other women sat at the table, two in black, one in brown, and the other two in grey. Audrey settled into her chair and pulled out some paper and a pencil, easing her adrenaline rush by quickly sketching some of the faces around her.

"Say, that's beautiful work," Catherine said, leaning closer.

Even now, Audrey blushed with pride when people complimented her work. For so many years her art had felt like a guilty pleasure. Fortunately, now that she was earning a little money she felt more justified, but she still felt lucky to be doing something she loved so much.

"Thank you. I like to paint portraits, and there are some fascinating faces here."

Catherine scrunched her nose with distaste and pointed at one pencil outline. "Fascinating indeed. That's Shirley Hampton. What an old nag."

Audrey giggled and transformed the face of the woman in question into the long, angular outline of a horse, and Catherine let out a hoot. "Priceless!" she exclaimed. "Oh, my dear! That's wonderful."

The meeting was called to order, and a woman in brown stood at the microphone to start the proceedings.

"Welcome, ladies, to tonight's meeting of the Council of Women of Halifax." She smiled broadly around the room. "For those of you attending your first meeting, I would like to personally welcome you to the movement that is changing the world. We believe in equality for women and are successfully waging the battle that will enable us to vote. Many of the provinces across Canada have already seen the light and are allowing women the right we have always been denied, and we feel certain Nova Scotia will soon join their ranks. For those of you who are acquainted with our meetings and our cause, welcome back. We are honoured that you choose to be here with us, and we respect the sacrifices you have made on our council's behalf."

Minutes were read and voted upon, and everyone waited patiently for the new business to start. When it was time, the speaker turned to the table.

"And now I'd like to welcome the president of our local Council of Women of Halifax, Mrs. Agnes Dennis, who will bring us up to date on the upcoming parade and convention."

Agnes Dennis stood and walked to the microphone. "Thank you, Marion," she said quietly. Then she faced the audience, who had gone silent with expectation.

Agnes was a small, sturdy woman. Her long black hair had been pulled back into a bun, and a stiff, white lace collar folded over the high neckline of her black dress. Audrey guessed her to be about thirty, and at first she looked to be nothing more than a gentle motherly type. But before she spoke again, her eyes travelled over the women seated before her, and Audrey saw the intelligent steel shining from within.

"Good morning, ladies, and thank you all so much for being here. This meeting is in preparation for the parade and convention coming up in February, during which we will feature both our inspirational member Mrs. Edith Archibald from the Women's Christian Temperance Union—"

She was interrupted by a burst of spontaneous applause, which she encouraged. "Well-deserved applause for my dear friend Mrs. Archibald. She has been very busy of late and speaking on a regular basis with our province's honourable premier, George Henry Murray. Through her persistence and his own intelligent nature, Mr. Murray has a good understanding of our movement, and as such he has agreed to be a speaker at the February convention. After having spoken with Mrs. Archibald, we have good reason to be optimistic that the women of Nova Scotia will finally achieve our goal and get the vote!"

Cheers and applause broke out again, and she waited calmly for quiet. When it came, her voice was strong and vibrated with reverence. "This is an age of great progress, my friends."

The hair on the back of Audrey's neck stood, and a thrilling sensation swept through her, making her surprisingly emotional. She was suddenly proud to be a woman in this place, in this time.

"Victory is almost upon us," Mrs. Dennis said. "I believe that centuries of inequality will soon be at an end, though the hard work will continue. We have done momentous things over the past few decades, made undreamed-of progress, spurred on by the inspiration and sacrifice of the dedicated women around the world who first brought our cause into the light. Just look at the accomplishments of women across this great country of ours. Women in Ontario, Manitoba, Saskatchewan, Alberta, and British Columbia are all voting in their provincial elections! It is a time to celebrate!

"Now on to the business at hand," she continued. "The event will be on the eighth annual International Women's Day, which will coincide with the celebration being held in many cities worldwide. We will require everyone's participation in the parade, of course, and hope you will each bring a group of like-minded women *and* men with you on that day. As we all know, there is strength in solidarity. We will also need help setting up the conference itself, with speakers and tickets and advertising, among other things, and there will be smaller events going on at the same time, all of which are being planned already. We have a few sign-up sheets here at the front, so if you would be so kind as to line up at the conclusion of this meeting, we're asking you to put your name down as a volunteer. We all have our strengths, so please do not be shy."

She smiled, sharing confidence among the troops. "And now we shall have nominations for various committee heads. I believe we shall start with ticket sellers . . ."

The meeting of the local suffragette chapter went on for another half hour, and afterwards, Audrey went out for a cup of tea with Catherine and a couple of her friends. Since she was new to their group, the ladies asked all the questions one might expect—if she was married, if she worked, if she had any children—but they didn't make her uncomfortable. She told them she'd been married less than a year, that her husband worked at the docks, and that she painted. In a rare moment of self-promotion, she told them about the dinner party at Antoine's, coming up the very next night.

Catherine dropped her spoon with a clang on her dish. "No!" she said, grinning. "It can't be! My, what a small world. *I'll* be at that dinner party. So it's *you* Pierre's been going on about. What a wonderful coincidence. And it'll be lovely to meet your husband as well. I understand he's some kind of war hero?"

Audrey's smile faltered. "Well, he was injured in the war, yes. But . . . unfortunately, he won't be at the party tomorrow night."

"Oh no?"

"He's . . ." Audrey searched frantically for an excuse. She could say he was sick, but then they'd expect her to stay home and tend him. "They've asked him to work an extra shift Saturday night, and he's agreed. Some kind of major shipment coming in, I imagine," she bluffed.

The women exchanged a glance, and their reactions told Audrey they were all thinking the same thing. She knew exactly what that was too. If she were painting expressions of pity, they would look just like that. At least they were pitying her for her lack of money, not her marital struggles. Somehow that would have been worse.

She'd lived happily in Sussex, blissfully ignorant of her station. Life had shipped her to a broken-down farm in France where she'd lived off milk and egg money for years, having little idea that she might someday have the ability to earn more, do more. She'd fallen in love with a crowded old house on the Eastern Shore of Nova Scotia with a small but perfect bedroom built just for them. Now she barely survived in their Richmond "home," working, sleeping, waking in a city where she'd learned that just about anything could be bought or sold. She'd never known real money before they'd come to this place, and only after she'd seen what it could buy had she recognized it as something she didn't have. She couldn't bear it if her new friends saw through her and realized she wasn't one of them, couldn't afford to buy what she wanted.

"That's a shame," Catherine said. "But I'm sure we'll meet him another time. Especially since his wife is about to become such a celebrity!"

Audrey laughed and waved her off. "Hardly that. But I am looking forward to the evening."

Catherine and the others said farewell a short time later, stepping into a cab as Audrey purposefully headed in the wrong direction. There was no way she was going to let them see her walk toward the slums of Richmond.

DANNY

— December 1917 —

TWENTY-FIVE

Danny was losing her. He felt it getting worse every day. And there was nothing he could do about it. He'd taken to going out with Johnny, Red, MacDonald, Franco, and the rest, sucking back drinks and coming in late. Sometimes the boys stayed the night in Danny's little house, flopping on the living room floor, so when Audrey came out of the bedroom in the morning, she'd be surrounded by half a dozen stinking, hungover dockworkers. But she poured tea for them all, even made up some kind of meal, depending on if she'd had time to buy groceries that week. Sometimes when she did that, it reminded him of their first meeting. The way she'd welcomed the whole battalion to the farm and fed them breakfast, her eyes shining with innocence. And in those brief moments he almost wished he was back in France, smelling gunpowder and blood, just so the two of them could go back to those first intimate times together.

She didn't like what Danny was doing. That was no secret. Didn't like the smell of old liquor, the unwelcome men in their house. She didn't like being separate from Danny and didn't like the way he stared at her after she came home from a day at the Antoines. He knew all of that, though she rarely said a word. In fact, she said very little these days.

Danny's heart grew colder over time, chilling the anger within him to a dangerous temperature. The only thing he had ever cared about was Audrey, and now even she was turning away from him. He hated living in the city, freezing cold with barely enough fuel to run a fire in their horrible little house, penned in by other ramshackle buildings, listening day and night to the clunking and shrieking of freight trains, neighbours yelling through paper-thin walls, and the lonely hooting of ships. When he was working he spent almost all his time standing, so the pain in his stump became a constant agony. The sores blistered and burned.

He made a few friends among the dockworkers, but they were never close. Not like his boyhood friends or even the other men with whom he had shared the trenches. These men hadn't been to war, and Danny knew they watched him warily, as if they considered him dangerous. He also suspected they talked about him and his peg leg whenever he left conversations, and his paranoia made him even angrier. He thought about Jimmy and Freddie a lot during those times, pictured them dead in the mud. And sometimes he thought they'd gotten the better end of the stick.

One night she walked in the door on an early December gust, oblivious to the stink of turpentine she brought with her and the short smear of sky blue paint on her nose. Her eyes sparkled with tears from the wind, and her cheeks glowed pink. Part of Danny wanted to kiss that little blue nose, warm those cheeks with his own. The other part wanted to scratch the paint off without mercy, rant at her for staying out late, for smiling as she arrived home from another man's house. A rich man's house. A whole man's house.

Danny noticed something else as well: her eyes didn't twinkle when she saw him anymore. Didn't light up in even the tiniest way. They seemed almost dead when they touched on him at all. Sometimes she turned from him, and if he reached for her she scuttled away like a crab, not wanting him to touch her.

He knew why. He knew she was afraid of the changes in him. He knew he had disappointed her. He knew what he was doing was wrong, that he was dumping his frustrations on her. But he carried on, feeling that if he kept it all inside instead of letting it out on her, he'd explode.

"You know, Audrey," he said that night, just after she'd slipped away from his hand. "Why don't you just go find yourself a real man? A man who could tend to your needs."

At first she looked shocked that he'd even spoken to her, then her cheeks blazed. "Stop it, Danny," she hissed. "All I need is a man who cares enough to clean himself up and take care of business. You feel so sorry for yourself, it's surprising you haven't killed yourself so people could feel worse for you."

He snorted, then took a long, deep drag of his cigarette.

"Danny," she said, stepping closer and softening her voice into a plea. "You have to stop this. Please? You have to believe in yourself again. If you and I are together, we can do anything. But I can't do this alone."

"Sure, sure you can," he said. "You just keep bringing home those big dollars you're getting from Antoine. I bet he pays you even better when the painting's all done and you can give it to him"—he leered cruelly on purpose—"real close and personal."

Her fury was immediate. At least he saw her eyes spark again, and he instantly hated himself.

"You are a bastard, Danny."

He'd never heard her swear. Never. *What the hell was he doing?*

"You sit around crying over your lost leg, drinking what money we make while I'm out trying to make our lives work. Now you accuse me of something you *know* I would never do." She came in close, almost nose to nose, and lowered her voice. "So I'm a whore now? A *whore*? I bring men into my bed so I can buy you beer, do I?" Her nostrils flared with revulsion. "How could you even think that way, Danny? You disgust me."

She turned away, but before she could escape, he grabbed her arm, yanking her back toward him. "I disgust you, huh?"

He heard it in his own voice: a rumbling that came from the trenches, the growl of a hundred Lewis guns cutting men into pieces. He knew his voice was dangerous. He knew it was the last thing he should have done.

But it was in him now: the fury, the revulsion, the desire to hurt something just to prove he was alive.

He didn't remember his hand coming up then swinging down, catching her cheek and snapping her head back on her slender neck, but he heard her cry out as she fell to the floor, covering her cheek and staring at him with utter disbelief. At first he thought she might start weeping, then he saw the hard anger that tightened every muscle in her face. That was worse. Much worse. Keeping her eyes on him, she pushed backwards so she could slide out of his reach, then slowly rose to her feet. She straightened and dropped her hand so he saw the big red imprint of his palm on her cheek. He couldn't speak.

She did. "Goodbye, Danny." Her eyes were like wells. There was no bottom to the pain in them. "I'll come for my things when you are at work."

And she'd gone off into the cool, clear night without another word.

TWENTY-SIX

Danny sat for an hour in total silence, his mind blank. Then there'd come a pounding on the door and Johnny was there, grinning like an idiot.

"Thought you were coming to the pub," Johnny said, then his expression changed. "What's with you? Somebody die?"

Danny blinked slowly, coming out of his daze. "I hit Audrey," he heard himself say, his voice almost a whisper. "I hit her. I hit a lady. *My* lady."

Johnny stared at him. "Why would you do that?"

"Because I'm a bastard is why. I'm a selfish bastard who just blew the last good thing I had going in my pathetic life. She's gone, and she's right."

"Jesus, Danny," Johnny said. He rubbed his forehead hard. "Jesus. You gonna go get her?"

He concentrated on his breathing, on his hands. "No. She's better off. She'll go to Antoine's place and they'll treat her like a queen."

Johnny glanced sharply at his big brother, and Danny fought the fire in his cheeks. He'd kept that juicy little tidbit to himself, not wanting Johnny to know. Johnny and Audrey rarely saw each other anymore, since they both kept so busy during the day. When they did, her life wasn't something Danny let any of them discuss. He knew it was selfish, had known it all along. But there it was. Now, when he saw the expression in Johnny's eyes, he wondered if he should have said something long before. Could Johnny have done something? Helped put out the blaze before it got out of hand?

"*Pierre* Antoine?"

"Yeah."

"The same Pierre who looked at Audrey like she was the cherry on top of a sundae?"

"That's the one."

"Jesus," Johnny said again. "You never said—"

Was Johnny's tone sarcastic? Danny couldn't tell. "His wife and kids are there too, of course," he assured Johnny.

"Of course."

Both brothers stared at the floor, and Danny wondered what was going through Johnny's mind. He knew his own thoughts. He felt sick. He felt as if all the lights had gone out, and he had no idea which way to turn. Audrey was gone. Audrey was his world.

"Christ, Johnny," he said. "I could use a drink."

———

Danny should have stopped drinking as soon as he got started, but he couldn't. The more he drank, the fuzzier Audrey's face became, and he thought if he just kept on going, he'd forget about her altogether. But he didn't. Her face disappeared, sure, but the pain, the iron weight of what he'd done, wrapped around his chest like a chain and just kept squeezing.

They started at one pub and wandered through a couple more, picking up and losing fellow drinkers along the way. At the end of the night, which was the early hours of the next morning, they stumbled back to the pier. They never made it back to the house.

When he awoke, the sky was blue, the air cold and crisp. He instantly thought of Audrey and figured this monster hangover was the least of what he deserved. Where had she gone? Was she keeping warm somewhere?

The sun blazed through one of the doors and sliced into his brain. Must be closing in on nine o'clock, he thought, squinting at some of the men as they trudged in to work. He and Johnny had slept inside the freezing warehouse by the pier since Danny's drunken mind had figured he might as well. He'd just go straight to work anyway.

He pulled his long wool coat tight around him and tucked his frozen fingers under his armpits. The black fisherman's cap his mother had knit him was pulled low over his ears, itchy but warm. Johnny lay beside him on the cold floor of the docks, snoring fit to shake the wooden rafters if they weren't so high up. Damn liquor. *Root of all evil,* their father had always said. Then again, the old man had sipped on sherry and enjoyed an ale once in a while with his friends, too.

Danny suspected evil had rooted itself inside him a little deeper than it had in his father. Set in roots back in France's muddy trenches, and he'd been feeding them ever since.

Johnny muttered in his sleep, and Danny sighed, thinking he should probably wake his little brother up. He started to lean toward him, then felt his stomach curdle. He turned away and vomited whatever he'd eaten or drunk the night before, his head threatening to explode with every heave. As always, he felt temporarily better having rid his system of the poison.

It was damn cold. The warehouse's concrete walls sucked in the chill and never let go. In the summer that would be a welcome thing, but December was frigid enough without that. Danny's back end felt frozen to the floor, and he shifted and struggled upright, moaning as he did so. He was going to have to give up drinking.

"Baker!" he heard.

He staggered out on the dock toward the voice, his hands bracing the sides of his pounding head. "What is it?"

"Come see this. Why, that ship's on fire out there. See? Looks like another ship rammed right into her."

Danny walked to the end of the dock, where he stood with a group of men, staring across the water. It was a beautiful day, not a cloud in sight, and the sun glinted off the ocean like sparks. A burning ship was floating toward Halifax, flames licking out of a huge, blackened hull, a thick column of black smoke funnelling into the sky.

Groups of people assembled along the harbour, watching the entertainment. A steel pedestrian bridge stretched over the railway yard, lined by an appreciative audience and offering an unobstructed view. Not only was the fire large, but an occasional blast shot out from the boat like fireworks, and the people cheered. A fire truck was parked by Pier 6, and the firemen had climbed onto the top of their truck so they could see the spectacle. There wasn't much they could do to put out the fire until the ship got closer, after all.

Another of the dockworkers came to the end of the pier to watch and stopped at Danny's side. He lit a cigarette, breathed in deeply, then blew out a stream of white smoke while he stared at the burning ship. "Kind of a pretty sight, ain't it? I wouldn't want to be one of the poor suckers on board. Think of all that cleanup."

"That a warship?" someone asked.

"Could be," said another. "*Mont Blanc,* it says there. French."

Danny'd heard something about the *Mont Blanc* from a sailor the day before, heard it in passing while he'd been checking another boat's inventory. What was it the man had said?

"She's an ugly boat, ain't she?" someone said.

Danny muddled through his pounding headache, trying to remember. The SS *Mont Blanc*. A French freighter, he remembered now. A three thousand tonne ship . . . whose hull was completely filled with high explosives.

"God Almighty," Danny breathed, forgetting all about his hangover. He shoved at one of the men beside him. "Get outta here, boys. That thing's gonna blow sky-high."

"Eh? It's a quarter mile away. No worry about that."

Danny gripped the man's shoulder, digging his fingers in hard. "See that? That's aviation fuel burning on deck," Danny told him, pointing at the smoke-engulfed ship.

"It'll burn itself out," the man said, removing Danny's hand. "Come on. Get a hold of yourself. You don't get to see something like this every day."

Danny started to run in his uneven, wooden gait. "That's an ammo ship, boys. You run or you're all dead."

Johnny was still sleeping in the corner of the warehouse. Danny grabbed him by the lapels of his black coat and dragged him, kicking and objecting loudly until they were both shoved behind the building's thick new concrete water cistern.

"What the hell you up to, Danny?" Johnny moaned, clutching at his head.

"We have to hang tight here. There's a ship full of explosives out there, and it's on fire and coming this way."

"Jesus," Johnny said groggily, sitting up slowly. "Can we go see?"

"How stupid *are* you? Lie flat and don't bother arguing. Lie face down," Danny yelled, throwing himself flat beside his brother. "God damn, Johnny. I saw the thing and it—"

"Jesus, Danny. Give me a minute." Johnny sat up and hung his head between his knees. "Pretty sure I'm gonna get sick."

Danny sensed an eerie pressure building around him. "Get back here, behind the wall. You can get sick over here, Johnny."

Johnny held up one finger, asking for a minute, then rolled to his hands and knees and scrambled a few feet away. When he figured he was far enough away, he threw up, just like he'd said. He took a moment to recover, then got up and slapped his hands together.

"There," he said. "That's better. Now I can go."

In an instant they were plunged into a pillow of silence, as if all sound had been sucked from the air. Through Danny's tightly closed eyes a light flashed once, then hell slashed through the silence, unleashing its unholy vengeance on the sparkling innocence of the Halifax harbour.

When Danny awoke, dazed and confused, the air was black with oily smoke. Desperate screams came from somewhere—everywhere, it seemed, but they sounded muted, like he'd stuffed cotton in his ears. He was soaked through with freezing seawater, and the floor was puddled with rocks and mangled bits of fish. His ears worked well enough that he heard the metal beams screeching above him, straining to support a roof that no longer existed, and loose bricks fell from the walls, chinking onto new stacks of rubbish. Rubbish that used to be walls. And furniture. And, Danny realized with sudden nausea, people.

Someone screamed, a long, ear-splitting howl of agony that dragged Danny right back to the blood-thick mud of the trenches. He fought to hold the memories back. Keep them separate. He could only fight one battle at a time.

With a groan, Danny turned toward the place where Johnny had been standing a moment before. All he saw was a pile of rubble.

"God, no," Danny whispered. He stumbled toward the mess and started to dig, tossing aside splintered wood and bits of brick and metal. He dug deeper, shouting Johnny's name, getting no response. Broken glass sliced through his hands, but Danny kept digging, blinded by tears.

There was no sign of a body under the pile. He cupped his hands around his mouth for volume. "Johnny!" he yelled. His voice fell flat where it once would have echoed. "Where are you? Johnny!"

Then he spotted something strange in the wreckage, thirty feet away and mostly covered by bricks. He stumbled toward it, trying not to weep, then dropped beside it with a cry. A man's body, crushed beneath.

"*No, no, no,*" he whimpered, heaving a concrete block aside and blinking desperately through tears.

There was nothing he could do. The rock had finished Johnny quickly, taking out the strong young bones of his skull, flattening his face so there was almost nothing left with which to recognize him.

Another explosion went off nearby, and Danny ducked, reflexively curling over his brother's lifeless body as he had in France for Jimmy so long before. When the air stilled again, he pulled back and stared at Johnny, weeping uncontrollably. He ran his bloodied fingers through the short brown waves of his brother's hair, though they—like everything else—were black with soot and grease. Even Johnny's blood looked black. Danny gagged on his tears, then leaned to the side and threw up again. When he was done, he lay on top of Johnny, sobbing until he could hardly breathe.

"What'll I do without you, Johnny?" he whispered. "What'll I do?"

He straightened and gazed down at the remains of his brother. How many men had Danny seen die? How many times had he thanked God for not letting his brothers end up in that foul war? Now here lay Johnny, as dead as any of the boys at the front. What was the point of any of this? Was it God's idea of a joke?

"Go see Big Jimmy and Fred," he told his brother, wiping his arm across his face to blot his tears. "They'll be waiting for you."

TWENTY-SEVEN

❧

Danny had never felt so alone in his entire life. He tugged the cap lower over his ears and staggered off the pile of rubbish. His peg caught on the shattered bricks and he tripped, but he made it to the exit just in time for another explosion to go off. It sounded like it came from outside the pier.

He would come back for Johnny's body. For now he had to get out. Nothing could harm his little brother anymore.

Danny looked out over the sea and froze with disbelief. Spread as far as he could see was the thickest, whitest cloud he'd ever seen, unmoving, untouched, as if it leered over the destruction. It was absolutely beautiful.

Then he turned and faced a world where nothing made sense. He couldn't see even one building still standing on the north end of Halifax. He thought he could pick out where their house had stood, but there was nothing there now.

Audrey. God, Audrey. Where are you?

Flakes of dry, black rain were settling over everything. Ashes, he realized. Black, oily ashes. Glass littered the wet ground like a glossy, crackling carpet. Here and there someone shuffled through the burnt-out street, crying, or they stood stock-still with nothing but a blank stare plastered to their blackened faces. Bodies, or parts of them, lay scattered across the desolation; bits of people, bits of horses, dogs, and fish. Alive, then dead.

Maybe she's all right. Maybe her leaving him the night before was the best thing she could have done, for so many reasons. Maybe she'd even come back and search for him eventually . . .

He saw stranger things with every step. Part of a ship's rudder jutted out from under an icebox that had been thrown into the street by the force of the explosion. He stared at it in wonder. How had that smouldering piece of metal gotten all the way up here?

He looked to the sea, its shores littered with the upturned corpses of ships. The only part of the huge steamer he'd seen the day before, the *Curaca*, was her bow, and it was on the wrong side of the harbour. Metal from ships had flown like shrapnel, cutting into stone walls, slicing through automobiles that had rolled over and over in the street, crushing people beneath. The nearby Pier 6, which had recently been working on two massive schooners, was gone. Disintegrated. The crumpled bow of a sunken tugboat poked out of the edge of the water. Behind the pier stretched miles and miles of rail tracks, the main artery of trade and travel for Nova Scotia. Danny couldn't see the tracks from where he stood but couldn't miss the fact that they were empty of railway cars. How could railway cars simply vanish?

The pedestrian bridge to the side of the rail yards, where spectators had stood to cheer and point at the flaming ship, was gone.

A woman ran past him, her face and hair grey with dust, her body smeared head to foot with blood. Her eyes were crazy black, like glistening holes in a skull. Even her eyelashes were grey. She was screaming, carrying a little boy in her arms. The boy wasn't moving. Danny stared as she ran past and noticed with an odd sense of detachment that part of a windowpane had sliced clean through the little boy's neck.

"Mother?" a soft voice whimpered. Danny turned and saw a young girl, standing completely naked, her face and body caked with dust. She couldn't have been more than six years old, with shoulder-length hair of an indeterminate colour. Her eyes were gone, blown clean out of her skull. Blood drew black lines from her eye sockets in a cruel imitation of a mime. "I can't see."

"I'm here," Danny said, coming toward her. He touched her shoulder, and she grabbed on to him, shaking. But the trembling grew weaker by the moment.

"I'm cold," she said. "And it's so dark."

"Come here," Danny said. She clung weakly to him, and he lowered them both carefully to the ground. Glass splintered under him as they sat, but he cradled the little girl in his arms, tucking her under his wool coat, speaking softly until she died. Then he propped her up against the relatively soft mound of a decapitated horse by the side of the road. He covered her body with a plank of splintered wood and started to walk again.

Dead and dying were everywhere, their bodies tangled, collapsed, broken in any number of horrible ways. The sugar refinery had stood ten proud storeys high, built of concrete and brick. Now it was rubble. A lot of men had worked in that building, Danny thought. A lot of men had died in that building.

Richmond was gone, as if it had never existed. More fires broke out as boilers exploded in the flimsy homes along Barrington Street, igniting one after another, pummelling the air like artillery fire, and the sky was torn by screams reminiscent of so many German missiles. Danny staggered through the street, his eyes stinging, lungs filling with smoke. *Chlorine gas,* his mind suggested. *The Jerries have sent chlorine!* But no. The stink came from the burning ship, and what scorched his eyes now was the smoke, the dust, the oily black rain, and tears.

Other survivors ran past, hollering, "The Germans! The Germans! The Germans are bombing Halifax!" but Danny didn't say anything. Just let them believe whatever they wanted. It wasn't important what they thought, anyway.

But it was hard to keep the war separate from this. So, so hard. It felt as if the trenches had followed him here, were closing in on him, the walking dead from his dreams not far behind.

He squinted up toward the clock tower on Citadel Hill, then all around. It was easy to see why folks thought they were being bombed. The streets of northern Halifax resembled a flattened battlefield, still smoking, the ripped roots of trees sticking obscenely into the sky.

Except on a battlefield, blinded children didn't run naked in the winter streets. Women didn't rush past carrying decapitated babies.

Where was Audrey?

He shook his head, trying to rid himself of the question, and regretted the movement. How ironic that he still had to suffer a hangover through all this. He didn't want to think about that, or the reason for the hangover in the first place. There was nothing he could do for Audrey now.

But here, surrounded by devastation, there had to be *something* he could do.

He didn't have to look hard to find someone who needed him. One of many devastated houses down the glass-strewn street wobbled on three remaining walls, the roof and upper floor already collapsed. A desperate voice, high enough Danny knew it was a child's, screamed from beneath the rubble, trapped in the basement. Danny leaned in and yanked out planks and chunks of rock, as well as more glass and broken bits of furniture. He was able to clear a small hole, and the moment the strange morning light pierced the black interior, small hands reached out to him. He grabbed a pair and, working carefully around the jagged edges of splintered walls, tugged a little boy outside. Though dazed, and white with ash and dust, the child appeared untouched.

Danny turned and reached for the next outstretched hand. He pulled, then let go the moment an anguished scream pierced the ashes. The hand disappeared. After a moment, five small fingers edged back out. This time Danny moved slowly, carefully, carefully sliding another little boy out. This one hadn't been as lucky. A gash had opened the side of his face, leaving part of his cheek flapping, wet with blood and tears. One arm hung at a strange angle, probably dislocated. Danny dropped his coat and ripped the sleeve off his own shirt so he could wrap it tightly around the stricken lad's face. The first boy ran to his brother, and Danny looked closely before realizing they were twins, probably about three or four years old. They stared around the street with incredulous eyes.

"Our house fell down," the uninjured boy told Danny.

"A lot of houses fell down. Who else is in the house?"

"Mother and the baby."

Danny sank his face into the hole he had dug and called in.

"Are you all right in there? Can you hand me the baby?"

There was no answer.

"Hello? Ma'am?"

A sudden yowl burst through the hole as the baby voiced its alarm, but the mother didn't speak. Danny turned to the twins. "Is your mother okay?"

They shrugged, mute, and he thought, What a silly question to ask a couple of terrified little boys. He took a deep breath then started clearing away debris until the hole was wide enough to see inside, though it was still black as night under the collapsed house. The baby was screaming louder, and it wasn't being comforted.

"You boys stay right here, all right?" he said. They nodded and sat.

Danny lowered himself into the hole. His hands were bleeding again, catching on glass, nails, and splinters. His peg was awkward, but he could maneuver it well enough. A loud groan twisted through the house as it shifted, and the wood on which Danny balanced slipped. He had no choice but to ride to the bottom, and he landed by the baby, who cried louder than ever, wriggling in his dead mother's arms.

"There you are. That's right. Tell the world what you think. That's right." He picked up the noisy bundle and set him against his shoulder, then, bracing the little body with one hand, he climbed the constantly shifting footholds. When he reached ground level, the healthy twin was waiting, arms stretched out for the baby.

"That's Norman," he explained.

"Good. Well, I think Norman's hungry," Danny told him.

"Where's Mother?" asked the other twin, his torn mouth barely moving around the words.

"Your mother wants me to take care of you first. Let's get you and your brothers cleaned up, and we'll see what I can do for her later, okay? Here, take my hand. That's a good boy."

The boys stuck to Danny's side as if they'd been glued there. Danny could practically hear their thoughts, feel the complete trust that pulsed in the little hand. This one-legged, black-faced stranger was their saviour. They would stay by him and be safe. Danny watched buildings collapse around them, flinched at the thunder of explosions continuing up the road, tried to ignore the screams of the trapped, and prayed with all his might the boys were right in their naive assumption. The three stepped carefully over thick layers of broken glass blanketed by white ash, like a long-spring trap camouflaged under snow.

The farther south they walked, the sturdier the walls appeared to be, though survivors still stumbled from buildings that looked as if someone had grabbed them and shaken them apart. Most were women. Their men had either gone to war or to the now-levelled factories. Either way, Danny thought, if they weren't dead already, they probably would be soon.

A crowd of women gathered ahead, layered in heavy black coats and hats. They turned toward Danny as he approached, then one of the ladies took the twins and the baby, promising comfort. Danny crouched and told the boys to go with her, saying he would be back to visit soon as he could. For now he had work to do, he explained. The boys appeared doubtful but went with the woman when they heard the magic word "biscuit." After they'd gone, Danny asked where they were taking the children.

"To the Protestant orphanage?" he asked.

"It's no longer standing. There were twenty-seven children living there," she said, her chin quivering. "Two escaped."

Danny tried not to imagine the sight but failed.

"We will find these poor souls a place to be safe and we'll see what we can find out about their family over the next little while," the woman assured him, glancing at the twins over her shoulder.

"I don't know about their father," Danny told her quietly. "But their mother's dead."

Casting weary eyes over the three, she sighed and smiled weakly at Danny. "The new orphanage will be far too crowded, I fear."

TWENTY-EIGHT

Slowly, like the first run of sap in the spring, a relief effort began to mobilize, vague hints of hope whispering through the screaming nightmare. Here and there, clusters of men gathered around stacks of shredded timber that had once been homes, and they dug, calling, always calling. A cheer went up every time someone was wrenched free of wreckage, and stretchers began to appear, carrying the injured to the Camp Hill Hospital or to private homes marked by white flags with red crosses. But the horrors kept coming.

"Whoa!" Danny cried, stumbling out of the path of a runaway milk wagon, its horse white-eyed with terror. The driver slumped dead in the seat, his body riddled with glass. Milk sloshed over the edge of the wagon bed and splashed the road.

An elderly man in a tattered wool coat sat on what must have been a yard—though little remained of the house—his cataract-clouded eyes seeing nothing. Long white strands of hair clung to either side of his blackened face. Beside him lay a woman Danny assumed was the man's wife. Half of her head was missing. The man kept saying, "Don't forget the Christmas oranges, Ethel. Gotta get Christmas oranges. The kids love those oranges."

Every step brought another abomination. Danny walked past the body of a woman whose chest had been impaled by the slivered stud of a house. Her head lolled back so she gazed toward the heavens, and her bare feet dangled three feet off the ground. Beneath her lay the carcass of a dog that reminded Danny of Cecil.

"Where are you, Audrey?" he muttered for the thousandth time.

She had probably been at the Antoines' house, warm and comfortable in their South End home. At least he hoped that's where she'd been. His feet had aimed themselves in that direction before he'd even started coming across the injured and dying, but he couldn't abandon the living, and at first he couldn't look away from the dead. So he stayed with an ad hoc crew, moving from building to building, or rather from one pile of rubble to another. Sometimes it was a hand or foot that gave away the location of a victim, in which case there were very few survivors. One of the men in his group had a dog on a leash, and the animal made himself useful by sniffing for anything that might still be breathing. He unearthed some badly injured dogs and cats, but the men simply removed the rubble and let the animals fend for themselves. They couldn't stay with the animals. There wasn't time.

After a few hours, horse-drawn wagons began to hurry along the streets, their flatbeds loaded with blankets for the wounded or with the wounded themselves. When a different wagon pulled up, loaded more victims, then started moving in a different direction, Danny stopped the driver, confused.

"Where are these folks headed?"

"Train's here," the man said. "Sending some of the injured to Truro right away for help."

Danny was impressed. "They got the trains running? That was fast."

"Yep. One of 'em, anyway," the driver answered. "Word is there are supplies on the way in. Guess we'll see." He tapped the reins on his horses' backs, and they set off down the hill, edging around obstacles heaped on the street, rolling toward the remains of the train tracks.

A pretty young woman sat in the doorway of what had once been her house. Only one wall remained, and it stood unsteadily behind her. She seemed calm. Danny went to her, crunching over glass, and she smiled with welcome. He wondered if she was uninjured, and when she patted the ground beside her, he started to sit, relieved at the opportunity to catch his breath if only for a moment. Just before sitting, he noticed a jagged piece of glass embedded in the woman's back, as big as a dinner plate. Blood stained the back of her filthy blue dress, pooled on the ground at the base of her spine. He wondered if he should try to remove the glass, then decided against it. Oddly, she didn't seem in any pain at all. He wondered if she even knew it was there. He didn't want to do something that might make it worse, but he would get her to help right away.

"Are you all right?"

"I'm the only one left," she said. Her voice was soft. Like a child's. "I was watching the little ones for my neighbours. I had eight precious wee things in my care, and we were all watching the fire. So pretty, wasn't it?"

Danny remembered the men standing transfixed on the docks. None would have survived.

"We were singing songs about the beautiful day, all of us dancing in a circle, holding hands. It was when I had my back to the window that the world exploded. My little angels flew through the wall like they had wings. Only one of them stayed inside with me. She had to, you see? The glass pinned her up against the wall just as neatly as if I'd nailed a picture right there." The woman's eyes began to glaze over, and Danny suddenly feared she was dying before his eyes.

"Hey, let's get you on the wagon, all right?" he asked her.

She seemed to remember he was there, and she gave him that calm, slightly lost smile. Without a word, she took Danny's hand and stood. He led her toward a wagon stopped nearby, filling with the wounded.

"You know," she said as he helped her up. "It's a horrible thing to wish someone dead. But I was ever so glad to see sweet Molly was as dead as could be on that wall. The only thing worse than seeing her dead would have been to see her alive like that. What a cruelty that would have been."

Danny wondered if he would ever, for the rest of his life, be able to get her haunted words out of his head. The relief that a child was dead.

"Watch yourself, okay?" Danny said. "You have some glass sticking out of your back. You don't want to bump into anything or anyone."

"Do I?" She tried to feel around behind her, then gasped when her fingers came into contact with the jagged shard. She stared at the blood on her fingers. "How can that be in my back? I don't feel it."

Danny had wondered the same thing. "Well, I expect you'll feel it soon enough. I imagine the doctors will take it out real easy. Get you back to normal in no time."

She was the same age as Danny, he estimated, but her expression was so much older in that instant. "I'll never be back to normal," she said. "None of us will. But thank you all the same. You're very kind."

Grief tore at Danny's chest, and he tried not to think about the thousands of people wandering, lost and confused, over the devastated land.

"You look tired," the girl said to Danny, as if nothing had just happened. "Come with me, will you? I'd feel better having you nearby. And maybe you could use a bit of time off your feet."

She glanced down and saw the peg leg, splintered and scarred at the bottom of Danny's torn pant leg.

"Oh, I'm so sorry," she said. "I didn't mean—"

"Don't worry, miss. What's done is done. My name's Danny, by the way."

"Thank you, Danny. I'm Esther."

"Wait here, Esther," Danny said. "I'm just going to lend a hand there, and then I think I'll take your suggestion and maybe sit for a bit."

Danny and a few others lifted three more women onto the wagon, accompanied by tiny bloodied children. He made sure everyone was settled and far enough away from Esther's back that she wouldn't get jostled, then he spoke to the driver, who clucked his horse forward.

The shelter was relatively organized chaos. Blankets and cots had been set out in rows, and chairs stood around the edge of the room, occupied by sobbing, bleeding victims. There were uninjured there as well, moving from bed to bed, trying to comfort, wrapping injuries wherever possible, checking for loved ones. Danny was also surprised to see doctors there. He had no idea where they'd come from, but crude surgeries had been set up where they were removing glass, metal, and wood, trying to save tortured bodies. Danny took Esther's hand and led her toward a woman dressed all in white.

"Excuse me, miss?"

The woman, who he assumed was a nurse, turned toward him, eyes wide with alarm. She quickly inspected Danny and Esther, and her expression said she didn't see anything wrong.

"Are you here to help?" she asked.

"Oh, yes, ma'am, I am," Danny said. "But my friend here, well, she needs a doctor."

"Really? What is—"

Danny gently rotated Esther so the nurse could see her profile. The nurse blanched. "Come with me, please," she said, then patted Danny's arm. "We'll take care of her from here. Have you signed your name to the list? Over there, you see? The ladies with the black hats? Please do, would you? We're trying to find out who is . . . still alive, you know." And she was gone, leading Esther away. Danny watched their backs, marvelling at Esther's ability to exist while blood seeped slowly around the blade of glass, leaving a dark, spotted trail behind her.

He headed toward the desk where she'd indicated, then limped toward the women managing the list. He gave his name, and they wrote it down. They asked if he knew the names of any of the deceased, and he cleared his throat before giving them Johnny's name. They wrote it on another list, and Danny didn't like seeing that. He wanted Johnny's name to be right there beside his. He wanted Johnny to be with him, helping rescue people. He wanted his little brother very badly. How was he ever going to tell his family?

"Excuse me," he said. "How do I get word to my family that I'm okay? And about . . . my brother?"

"These lists will be published in the newspaper daily," she assured him. "It's the best we can do."

Danny's eyes blurred. His parents didn't get the newspaper regularly, but he guessed they'd do their best to get their hands on one after this.

He also bet they'd be driving the wagon into Halifax as soon as the roads were clear enough for them to pass.

A group of ladies stood to the side, all in black, one of them with her hand to her face. The others gathered around her, and Danny squinted hard. From across the room, she could almost be Audrey, but it was hard to tell for sure. People kept walking in front, blocking his view. Could it be her? He started to limp toward the group but stopped when he heard a young boy call. It was one of the twins, and his brother sat beside him, almost completely wrapped in bandages. There was no real pattern to the gauze across the little boy's face, and Danny knew the scarring would be bad. He hoped the years would be kind.

He crouched beside their cot and smiled. "How are you, boys? Did you get something to eat?"

"They gave us bread," the first boy said.

Some of the black had been rubbed off the boys, and Danny saw their bright orange hair and blue eyes over cheeks sprinkled with freckles. Black swipes of pain under the second twin's eyes almost hid the freckles, and his lips were pale.

"And how are *you* feeling? Did they take good care of you?"

The bandaged boy blinked, and his brother spoke for him. "It hurts him to talk, so I do it. I know what he's thinking anyway."

"What are your names?" Danny asked.

"Well, I'm Eugene Josiah White," said the first. "My brother is Harry Donald White, and our baby brother is Norman Jefferson White. We have three sisters, too. They are big girls, so they go to school."

Danny had seen the school and the mangled bodies within, dismembered and decapitated, stabbed, crushed beneath walls. He wondered if the White sisters had made it out alive, and doubted it.

"Those are fine names, and you're a very smart boy to remember them all," Danny said, trying to appear impressed. "Those are names for boys who are going to be big and strong one day. Tell me, where's your father?"

"He died at the war. Do you have a brother?" Eugene replied, matter-of-fact.

"I do," Danny said. "I have a few."

"Do they live in Halifax?"

"No, no, they don't. One of them did, but he's not . . . here anymore."

"What was his name?"

Danny stood and gently ruffled the boys' spiky orange hair. He couldn't talk about Johnny. The pain was still a fresh, open wound, not yet ready for exposure to air. "I'm going to go see about a friend now, all right? You two stay together, and you'll be just fine."

They seemed to accept his word, but as Danny walked away, he became painfully aware that their smiles were no longer identical and never would be again. He glanced toward where he had last seen the group of women but could see no sign of them. His eyes raked over the cots as he walked between the rows, searching for Audrey, but she wasn't there. Please God, he prayed. Please let her be alive.

The day was endless. Danny went back out to the devastated city, looking, finding, carrying, comforting. He didn't see even one person he knew. He had only really known the dockworkers, and he didn't expect to see any of them ever again. But he went to the docks anyway. There was one thing he had to do there. He couldn't just leave Johnny like that.

TWENTY-NINE

The sunset happened at six-thirty, but there was still enough light for the searchers. Bursts of orange rose through the pyres scattered around the city, turning homes and shops—and everyone inside them— to ashes. Voices were fainter now, further between. Many of the collapsed buildings held no more signs of life. Close to midnight, the exhausted searchers had to stop for the night.

And it began to snow.

It wouldn't have mattered what the outside temperature was, Danny was cold from the inside out. He had done what he could for his brother, storing his body safely until his family came to take Johnny home. God, how Danny wanted to join them. To go home and lose himself in the hard, uncomplicated life of a fisherman. He started walking to the Camp Hill Hospital, up near the Citadel, with hopes of finding a bed. Some-place out of the growing storm. But the crowds lined up outside the door were enough encouragement for him to move on. Others needed beds more urgently than he, and Danny had slept in much worse places. He went farther, over the crest of the hill where the devastation was some-what less, though houses still burned, their walls buckled like accordions, every window gone. Danny pulled his collar up to cover the back of his neck, as he had a hundred times that day. His stump was numb where it met the peg; it would be a fine mess when he finally sat down to inspect it. But he kept on, sure of his direction now. He headed south, trudging along the dark streets until he came upon the massive home of the Antoine family.

Compared to Richmond, the house seemed relatively untouched except all the windowpanes were gone. Danny climbed up the uneven stairs to the ornate double front door, depending on the precarious banister to keep him upright. When he reached the top, he saw one of the doors had been blown in and was blocking half the entry.

"Hello? Is anyone here?"

No one answered. He tried to convince himself that, since it was after midnight, the family might just be sleeping. After a day like this, everyone needed sleep. But somehow he didn't think anyone was slumbering tonight. The real, live nightmare would keep them awake. Since he couldn't get past the broken door debris on one side, Danny tried the other door, and it eased open under light pressure, the latch barely hanging onto the frame. He poked his head inside.

"Hello?" he tried again. "Is anyone home?" Receiving no response, he stepped inside. The wind had blown snow through the window frames, forming drifts, leaving it just as cold inside as it was outside. The room should have been pitch-black, but the snowstorm lent an eerie grey light to everything in the house. It even caught on the glass crunching underfoot as he walked down the long, narrow corridor.

"Hello?" he called again, louder this time. "Is anyone here? Does anyone need help?"

He glanced around the remains of the family's living area, listening for sounds. He didn't see anyone but would have to look closer. They could be trapped under any type of furniture. Earlier that day they had found a six-month baby girl curled up underneath her family's furnace, warm and hungry. If they hadn't had a dog sniffing around, they'd never have found her.

Danny took the steps slowly, bracing himself against the banister and wall to take some of the weight off his stump. The stairwell was lined with pictures of the family, and Danny recognized Audrey's handiwork. She was so talented, that woman he'd chased away and still loved with all his heart. Sadly, most of the canvasses had been torn by flying glass.

"Audrey?" he shouted, his voice cracking. "Audrey, are you here?"

The stairs creaked under him, and he moved more quickly in case they gave way. One by one he opened the doors along the hallway but saw no one moving within. He kept calling out, listening for a response, but all he heard was the groaning of the boards and the whistle of wind through shattered windows. He stepped up to the beds, the dressing tables, and saw no one. No children, no Audrey.

He got to the master bedroom and hesitated. The door was closed. What if the family was here, sleeping safe and sound? What kind of lout would wake up a family after a day like this? But Danny had to know. He unlatched the door and gave it a push.

"Hello?"

The door jammed, and he had to push against it, squeezing through the opening. A large armchair lay across the doorway, and he shoved the chair out of the way so he could push the door all the way open.

The Antoines had probably spent many hours by their beautiful picture window, watching ships pass in and out of the port. They had a panoramic view of the entire area from this spot, high on the hill. From what Danny could surmise, Mrs. Antoine had seen the fire, and she and three of her youngest children had gathered around the window for a closer look. Now her lifeless body sprawled over the edge of her bed beside two small ones, torn to shreds, frozen in place. In the middle of the room, and straight through a child's body, protruded a jagged metal plate from one of the ships.

Mrs. Antoine had been a large woman, and her body was cold and stiff. It took some effort for Danny to move her around so her head rested on the pillow. After that he lifted one child at a time and laid them on either side of their mother, making sure their sightless eyes were closed. He stood back a moment, considering this little family of strangers. There was nothing more he could do.

Danny backed soundlessly out of the room. He knew from experience he would be of no use to anyone if he didn't at least try to sleep. He limped down the hall, clouds puffing into the cold air with every breath, and went into one of the other bedrooms. Once inside, he tore the blankets off the bed, then carried the bundle to a room at the back of the house. He spread them over a small child's bed he swept free of glass, then he tugged the carpet off the dark plank floor and managed to wedge it up so it blocked the window. The blizzard still raged, but he would be protected from some of it at least. The pillow dropped shards of glass on the floor when he shook it, and he patted it a few more times, just to be sure there weren't any splinters before putting it back on the bed and lowering himself onto the mattress. With a groan, he unstrapped the peg and grimaced at the bruising and blisters he hadn't had time to notice during the day. His stump pulsed now that it met the air, bringing blood back into circulation and making him aware of the injuries. Very carefully, he laid his head on the pillow, trying to ignore everything but the softness of the mattress. The blankets were cold, but his body heat was soon trapped within, and he felt warm for the first time in what seemed like a very long time. He forced his mind to go blank. He had to sleep. Tomorrow he needed to find Audrey.

A few hours later, blinding light seeped around the edges of Danny's makeshift curtain. He squeezed his eyes against the onslaught, unwilling to leave the warm nest he had created, but these blankets were needed elsewhere. Danny shoved himself up so that he sat on the edge of the bed, and used the sheet to carefully clean what he could of his stump. At least it hadn't bled, and the bruising was worse than the blisters. That was good, because he didn't want to trouble anyone with his minor discomforts. He could deal with bruises. He hitched the peg onto his body, then stood and hobbled from room to room, folding all the blankets he could find. He tossed them over the banister along with armfuls of pillows, then he limped downstairs and wandered through the sitting room. As he had anticipated, he found no trace of Audrey or anyone else amid the wreckage of the Antoines' main room. Instead, he found an overturned dining room table, its polished mahogany legs sticking straight up as if it were a dead beast. After piling the blankets and pillows on top of it, Danny rolled one sheet into a thick rope and tied the ends to the table legs. He pushed the knots as low as they would go, then he tugged the entire makeshift sled out the front door, where he stood for a moment, transfixed.

The snow had come with a vengeance, but for now it had stopped. The sun beamed from a cloudless sky, reflecting off a perfect, glistening blanket of white. It was both a beautiful and a horrible sight. The snow would have helped to extinguish fires. Then it would have frozen any remaining victims to death.

Would it be better to die trapped in a fire or frozen solid? Frozen, he decided. After all, he had gone to sleep often enough with his teeth chattering from the cold. Maybe those people had just fallen asleep and never woken up. That had to be better than hearing your own flesh sizzle and pop.

The outside doorframe was still a bit too narrow for his sled, so Danny yanked on the damaged wood and pulled on the remaining door until it gave way, tearing open a wider hole. After all he'd seen, it still gave Danny a perverse moment of pleasure knowing he'd just ripped a hole in Antoine's beautiful house. It didn't bother him a bit that he was leaving with this valuable piece of furniture.

Still smiling, Danny angled the table through the doorway, then left the load on the front stoop and went back inside. The kitchen was chaotic. Glass, ceramic tile, knives—anything sharp had been hurled against the walls and ceiling, and most of it still poked out like the quills of a big, flat porcupine. Danny sorted through the pantry and the icebox, making himself a cold breakfast of ham and bread, which, ironically, had been sliced perfectly the morning before.

Afterwards, he loaded up everything he could find that might be of use and carried it to the dining room. He very carefully slid the entire thing down the stairs, trudged through the mounds of snow, and stepped onto a path already cut on the road by those before him. With his makeshift wagon in tow, he headed back toward the worst-hit part of the city, grateful for Antoine's expensive tastes. The polished mahogany table slid smoothly over the snow, making the journey easier than it might have been with a lesser piece of furniture.

THIRTY

A discarded *Evening Mail* lay in the snow, its frozen pages trembling stiffly in the breeze.

SCENES AT MORGUES AND HOSPITALS
THAT BAFFLE DESCRIPTION

and lower down

TWO CHILDREN ESCAPED ORPHANAGE ALIVE

followed by lists of hundreds of names, either confirmed alive, found, missing, or dead. The paper mentioned a "List of Known Dead" at the undertakers at Snow's Mortuary. Danny tried very hard not to imagine Audrey's name on the list, but he would stop by there later to be sure.

An article lower down mentioned the stage, auditorium, galleries, and all rooms in the Academy of Music had sheltered hundreds of homeless. Camp Hill Hospital was overflowing with victims. Chebucto Road School was acting as a makeshift morgue, and bodies waited to be laid out on the floor. Help was said to be rolling in by train from across Nova Scotia, New Brunswick, and Boston. A great population of relatives of the stricken were from Boston, so that city sent hundreds of doctors and nurses to relieve the exhausted workers who sagged by the cots.

Danny's next couple of days were spent uncovering survivors and helping stack the dead like cordwood beside the road. When he could stand no more, he went into the hospital and checked the name lists. Checked the living, checked the dead, but Audrey never appeared on any of the pages. So many people weren't listed. He wondered if they would ever find all the victims. He helped wherever he could. He got to know some of the slashed faces and missed them when they were gone—for whatever reason.

He was sitting by the bed of a young woman one morning, helping a doctor change bandages around her face, when his father walked in. Thomas and Lionel, Danny's next two brothers, were with him. Johnny filled Danny's mind, and he longed to rush to his father, but the doctor needed him a moment more. Danny kept his hands on his work and his eyes on his family.

Daniel Sr. and his two sons spoke to the woman at the front desk, who gestured to the wall where the lists were posted. Tension strung tight across his father's shoulders as he bent over the lists, which were pages and pages long. The brothers scanned the room with a sort of horrified curiosity, but they didn't see Danny.

Daniel Sr. was just finishing off the second page of "Known Living" when Danny came up behind them and touched his father's arm.

"Father," he said quietly.

His father spun toward him, eyes huge. "Danny!" he cried. "Danny! Praise God! I—we—"

Thomas and Lionel were on Danny in an instant, and everyone was talking at once. All except Danny, who stood back and listened, dreading the inevitable question.

"Let's go outside," he suggested eventually.

"Sure, sure," his father said, lowering his voice. "This is hardly the place for a celebration, is it?"

The December air was cool and crisp, and the family had to shield their eyes from the brightness. But beneath the shimmering crystals of snow lay the frozen dead not yet discovered. Danny would never think of snow the same way again.

Standing in the remnants of a street, Daniel Sr. grabbed his eldest son's shoulders, then pulled him into an embrace. It was something Danny didn't remember ever having experienced before. He felt his father's hot breath against his ear, and he thought of home.

"Thank God, Danny. I thank him for saving you from all of this. Your mother, oh, she will be so relieved."

Danny stepped back and met his father's eyes, heart heavy as stone. The joy in the older man's expression began to fade.

"Johnny didn't make it, Dad."

A silence fell between them. A breath of disbelief, then reluctant acceptance. The younger brothers stared at Danny, then their father, then each other before their postures curled in on themselves.

Daniel Sr. cleared his throat. "Where is he?"

"I knew you'd come," Danny said, fighting the urge to blurt out his sorrow. "He's by the docks. In a kind of storage area. It's the best I could do for him. I knew you'd take him home to be buried right."

"But wasn't he with you?" Lionel asked, chin wobbling madly. "How come he—"

"There was nothing I could do, Lionel." Danny choked on the lump in his throat and looked into his father's agonized face. "It was quick. I don't think he felt a thing."

"Where's Audrey?" Thomas asked.

The question had been looming, but it still took Danny by surprise. A hand gripped his heart and twisted. "I don't know. Truth is I have no idea where she is."

Thomas frowned. "You haven't seen her? Wasn't she with you?"

"No. I was at work. So was she. We worked in separate parts of the city."

"But how can you not—" Thomas tried again.

"I went to the house where she worked. I slept there, waited for her.

But she never came back. And the house where she and I lived is nothing but ash now."

"But—"

Danny felt frustration rise up his throat, tasting like bile. His words lashed out. "Tommy, if I knew where she was, I'd tell you. She'd be with me right now, I promise you that. But I haven't a clue. There are a lot of people unaccounted for around here."

Thomas blanched then looked away. Lionel nudged him, and the boys wandered off, gawking in silent awe at the apocalyptic scene around them.

"It's all right, son," Daniel Sr. said. "You'll find her."

Danny's chest felt tight, like his throat, as if his body just couldn't contain another moment of agony. It would be a lie if he didn't tell his father the truth.

"If she died, it was my fault," he said quietly.

"No, no," his father assured him. "There's nothing you could have done. She wasn't even with you."

"But it was my fault she wasn't with me. You see, we'd had a fight. A big one. And she left me."

Daniel Sr. didn't speak. He frowned at Danny, angling his head slightly.

"Moving here was a mistake, Dad. She and I, we weren't meant to live here. We hated it. And Johnny and I, well, we started getting into the liquor pretty bad." His father dropped his chin, but Danny kept on. "She tried to get me to stop. She—" His breath caught on an unexpected sob, and he coughed, clearing it. His gaze went out to the sea and his view was blurred by tears. "I wouldn't listen. I got worse. I didn't like that she was doing so well, you know? That she was making a new life here, even though that's what we'd both wanted. She came home the night before the explosion and we had a fight and I . . . I hit her."

He heard the sharp intake of breath beside him and knew he deserved it. That and worse.

A tear rolled down Danny's cheek, and he rubbed it off with the back of his knuckles. "Ever since then she's all I think about. I would give my life to have her with me, to show her how wrong I was. She put up with so much . . ." His heart squeezed again, and he forced the words through his aching throat. "She was the best thing about my life, and I threw her away. So yeah. If she died, it's my fault. Nothing will ever convince me otherwise."

"Nothing?" his father asked quietly.

Danny shook his head.

"What if you find her, Danny, and she forgives you? Will you let it go then?"

"She can't forgive me."

Daniel Sr.'s hand curved over Danny's shoulder. "That's true. She can't—unless you forgive yourself first."

"Then she never will. Because I can't ever forgive myself for what I did to her." He looked in his father's eyes. "She was right. She said I took everything pretty and made it ugly. And I know I did. I couldn't stop myself. I'm not worth forgiving. She can't forgive me."

A hint of a smile lifted the corner of his father's mouth. "Of course she can, son. That's what love is."

How Danny ached to believe that. He dreamed of seeing the laughter in her eyes again, twinkling just for him. But the way he saw it, that would be like paying a man for failing at his job.

"I'll take you to Johnny," Danny said. "Watch your step, okay? It's mostly the glass you have to watch out for. It's better now than it was— much better—but it's still not too safe."

Daniel Sr. had his sons unload the wagon, filled with donations of blankets, pillows, and enough bread to feed an army, and they carried everything inside. Danny had the presence of mind to grab one sheet from his father's wagon before the family climbed back on, though. He had tidied up what he could of his brother's face, but Johnny's coat had been whipped away by the blast, as had his hat and one boot, so Danny hadn't been able to use anything for a shroud. Any other blankets or sheets had been required by the wounded.

Daniel Sr. clicked his tongue to the horse, and they headed down the slope to the docks, following Danny's directions to what was left of the shed where he'd left Johnny. When they arrived, Danny bundled the sheet under his arm, then hesitated only a moment before he opened the door. Johnny lay as he'd left him, his body preserved by the December storm. Danny tucked the sheet around his brother's body and face, and no one said a word as they loaded the cold weight onto the wagon bed.

"I'll come back once he's buried," Daniel Sr. said, swallowing hard and blinking back tears. He needed to be strong for his family. "They'll need help here."

Danny lowered his chin to his chest. "Folk sure could use your kind of sermon around here. Seems a lot of them are wondering exactly where God was a few days ago."

Daniel Sr. looked out over the flattened city. "I wondered that same thing myself," he said quietly. "I'm still waiting for the answer. But it will come, son. It will come. Should the boys stay?"

"No, sir," Danny said. "I mean yes, but there's no place for anyone to sleep. We're building homes, but mostly people are living in burnt-out shops. I know of one family living in an empty meat locker. People are tucking in wherever they can find room. Once things are a little more under control out here, I'll send for them, all right?" He gestured toward the blankets. "These are sorely needed, though. Maybe when you get home, you could tell the women along the shore there will never be enough quilts and pillows for all the people here."

"You're not coming, then?"

"I said a proper goodbye to Johnny. He knows I did. I can't leave here, though. I'm in the middle of it all."

His father regarded him quietly, his gaze sharp now that the younger boys were out of hearing. "Are you okay, son?"

"As good as can be expected, sir."

He hesitated only a moment. "I can see you're healthy, and I thank the Lord for that mercy. But you have lived through so much, Danny. How is your mind? Your heart?"

Danny felt his body go weak. He wished so badly he could be a little boy again, that he could weep and wail and admit his pain. He wanted to scream how every nerve of his being was on fire, but he was numb; he couldn't feel anything anymore. His body felt dead. His thoughts felt empty. His heart was in mourning for his brother, for the city, and for the wife he feared he might never find. And beyond everything lurked the haunting emptiness left by the war.

"I'll be fine, sir," he said.

"You haven't had time to heal, son. With everything that happened overseas and now this . . . I fear for you. For your soul."

Danny's gaze went to the ocean, twinkling under the cold December sun. The broken hulls of ships poked through in spots, and he wondered when they'd get around to pulling them out. It'd have to be soon. The harbour had to get back to work. The world didn't stop turning just because Halifax suffered.

"I did what I had to do," he muttered. The weight of all that, of the misery and anguish he'd survived, seemed almost to close over him in that moment, to pull him under, but Danny shoved himself back to the surface. "People here needed me, and I guess the army needed me over there. I'm a man, and a man does what he has to do. You taught me that, sir."

He felt his father's gaze, watching Danny's profile as he spoke, and he wondered what that was like, seeing the boy he'd raised become a man. What was his father thinking? Was he disappointed? Was he proud? Did he even know how he felt?

Daniel Sr. took a deep breath. "I'm sorry you were over there, Danny, and I'm sorry you had to be a part of this, too. Breaks my heart every time I think of how you must have suffered. But I have to tell you something. For me—" He hesitated. "I guess it's even worse remembering what you said to me that day back home, that day when we were working on the new boat. Do you recall what you said?"

That conversation was kind of foggy in his mind, if Danny were to be honest. He remembered being there, remembered that they'd talked, but not much else. He'd been pretty angry, he recalled. Hadn't given his father much of his time.

"You said you wanted me to know that if you hadn't been hurt over there, you'd still have been there. You said it like . . . like I thought you were a coward."

Now he remembered, and he felt a little sick at the memory. He'd been awfully harsh, fresh from the muck, grovelling in self-pity, and he'd lashed out, wanting his father to suffer just as he was.

"I didn't know what I was saying, Dad. I'm sorry about that."

"Son, that was the hardest thing I ever heard, that you thought I was thinking that way about you. Don't you ever think I'm not proud of you, son." He blinked quickly and cleared his throat. "Don't you *ever*. I'm prouder of you than I am of anything else in my life. But son." He put his hand on Danny's shoulder and squeezed. "You need to understand something. I was proud of you even before you went. You're a good man, Danny. Always have been."

Danny stared, disoriented, like a wave had just broken over his head. He wanted to look away. Worse, he wanted to run away. He couldn't stand the hurt in his father's eyes. The hurt he figured he'd put there. He'd been so wrong. So quick to hide behind that thick wall of pride they both had built. In that moment, he dared himself to be as strong and as brave as his father.

"You asked me if I was glad to be back. Truth is, I'm more glad to be home than you could ever know," he admitted softly. "I haven't spoken to anyone about what happened out there. I just couldn't. But it . . . it still hurts, Dad."

"Your leg?"

Danny wished he had a cigarette. Something to do with his hands. He shoved them in his pockets instead.

"Not just that," Danny said. He inhaled, then let his frozen breath out in a long stream. "Everything. Everything hurts. In my head and in my leg. Do you know, I still feel my foot sometimes? I don't even know where it is, and I feel it. Isn't that just the peachiest?" He took another deep breath and the words came faster, like water shoving through stones, rushing to freedom. "I thought of you sometimes, when I was out there. At night it got so dark, so cold, I shook for hours. And when the night was clear the sky sparkled with a million stars. I remembered sitting with you when I was little. Do you remember that? And you'd point out the stars and constellations. I remembered your voice and your lessons. And . . ." A tear spilled down his cheek. His father didn't move. "And I missed you so bad. I wanted to come home and hide from it all. I wanted you to tell me it was all going to be okay."

Danny looked at the moving reflections of clouds in the glass shards. "When I lost my leg, I figured somehow I'd let you down. Like when I got home, I wouldn't be the kind of man I used to be. The kind you needed me to be. I thought maybe I shouldn't even come home. I didn't want to be some circus show freak."

A wagon shuddered past, its driver paying them no attention. Danny heard his brothers arguing on the other side of the dock. But Daniel Sr. said nothing.

"You know, it's funny," Danny went on, surprising himself. "The whole time I was out there, I kept seeing my buddies get blown up, and I thought I was safe from it all. It never occurred it could happen to me. I had a life here on the shore. I was needed here." He shrugged. "Turns out I wasn't safe. Truth is, Dad, when it happens, when God decides you ain't all that special, it really hurts."

Daniel Sr. shuffled his feet. A bird floated by, way out on the horizon. So peaceful.

"I prayed to God," Daniel Sr. said after a moment. "I asked him to—" His voice broke and he cleared his throat. "I asked God to send you home, Danny. I was hearing about what was happening over there, seeing stories in the paper, and I told him I didn't care how you got here. I just wanted you here." He hesitated, and when he spoke again, it was barely louder than the water rustling against the shore. "Sometimes I think maybe that's why you lost your leg. God taught me a lesson about asking for too much, but he did let me see you again. If that's why this happened to you, well, I'm sorry. Maybe it was selfish of me, wanting you back so bad. But Danny, I didn't think I could bear to watch your mother lay flowers on an empty grave. I just couldn't."

Their eyes locked. Blue on blue, hurt upon hurt. Neither mentioned

Johnny, because they didn't need to. His ghost was right there, watching, listening.

"I'm glad to be home, Dad. Even after all this."

Daniel Sr. smiled, but the expression in his eyes was sad. Danny knew what he was thinking. Home wasn't what it was supposed to be. Home had changed, come apart in big gaping wounds.

"God has surprises for us all, Danny. I suppose that's what I should say here. I should tell you that it's meant to be, that there's a reason for all you went through, that there's a plan there somewhere. But I can't say that and still be true to myself. I don't understand what happened to you and those boys out there, and I don't understand what happened here. I don't understand why God would turn away from you all like that. I have been a devout Baptist these many years, preached the Word of God and never questioned how he gives colours and songs to the birds. How the water never stops. How spring always follows winter. But I don't understand any of this. How so many good men were sent to waste their lives and their bodies for no good thing, how the people of Halifax have been blown apart. It has made me question every one of my beliefs, son, and that's the truth of it."

"Yeah," Danny said, giving a humourless snort. "Mine, too."

Daniel Sr. took a few steps away, toward the port, and Danny recognized the walk: the directionless pacing of his father deep in thought. He didn't dare say anything. Because if he did, if Danny said how he felt about God and all this devastation, his father might never forgive him.

Danny was pretty sure he knew the truth about God, and he wondered if his father knew it as well but chose to ignore it. There was no God. No God could allow what Danny had survived. Or if there was a God, the Devil had taken a hold of those desolate fields of Europe while God took a nap. The Devil had followed Danny here to Halifax and slaughtered women and children, left thousands homeless and scarred. The Devil had enjoyed himself thoroughly.

Danny pressed his peg leg deeper into the ground, grinding the end of it into the glass. *Forget the past. All of it,* he ordered himself as a piece shattered under the weight. *Leave it buried. Leave it be. I lived. I lived, goddamn it. The bastard aimed to kill me, but he missed. I shot him first. The explosion should've killed me, but it took Johnny instead. And Audrey too, maybe. That's the way it is. Leave it be. Move ahead, not back.*

His father turned toward him, jarred out of his reverie by the sound made by the peg. Then Daniel Sr. did something that he'd never done before: He asked Danny a question. Not a question like *Will it rain? Will we have haddock for supper?* A real question.

"Have you thought about it, Danny? Have you wondered why God would do that to you? To all those boys?"

Danny stopped hitting the ground and regarded his father. Man to man. "Have I thought about it? Yeah, I did. I've had a lot of time to think, and I wondered about a lot of things. But the only answer I could ever figure out was that it don't matter. Nothing matters. It only happens."

His father didn't move, only held Danny's gaze. The air around them eased. "I am so proud of the man you are, son." His lips trembled, then pulled tight. He glanced at the younger boys, sitting on the pavement and trying to comfort each other. "I reckon we should be going now."

Danny walked to his brothers and gave Lionel a hug. "I'll see you soon, I'm sure. You help out all you can at home, now. You and Thomas, you're the oldest. Hey, Thomas. Come over here. I'm sorry I snapped at you. Things are just . . . kind of difficult for me these days."

Thomas hugged Danny for as long as he could, then turned away, hiding tears.

"Keep well," Daniel Sr. said, shaking Danny's hand.

"Please bring my love to Mother and the others. I would write, but—" Danny gestured toward the city. "I don't think there's much of a post office anymore."

"I shall pray for Audrey every day, son. I shall pray you find her."

"Thank you, sir."

Daniel Sr. studied his oldest son, as if trying to see more, remember more, know more. "And I shall pray you find forgiveness for yourself. Blame and guilt do nothing to heal a man's soul. Make yourself into the man Audrey would be able to forgive. Free yourself, Danny."

Then he turned away, climbed into the wagon seat with his two younger sons and headed slowly down the snow-covered street. Danny watched them go, fighting the urge to chase after the rattling wagon. *Wait for me! I'm coming!* He couldn't look away from the back, where Johnny's bare foot poked out from under his shroud. The wagon hit a bump, and the foot waggled back and forth, as if it were waving.

"Yeah," Danny said with a wry smile that hurt so, so bad. "Goodbye, Johnny. You take care now."

THIRTY-ONE

❧

Soldiers and sailors began to arrive, building temporary shelters as quickly as possible so people could get out of the lethal cold. Day by day the wounded began walking again, often with patched faces and bodies, trying to pull together what they could of their lives.

Danny didn't know if his father was right, about earning forgiveness and all, but he did make a decision after their talk that day. Everything he'd been doing before was over, including the drinking. He'd made a mess of his life, just like this city was a mess. This was his chance to clean up both. He got involved in just about every aspect of the physical recovery of Halifax. It had started with rescue and cleanup, then followed with rebuilding. He joined the work crews, hammering and sawing through frozen days, erecting walls to protect some eight thousand homeless people.

When he wasn't building, he was stopping by the hospitals, checking name lists, always looking for Audrey. He had noticed Pierre Antoine's name listed under "Known Living," but it was a couple of days before he could work up the nerve to go see the man. Found it hard to admit that he'd chased his wife into that night and into the house of a better man.

Once in a while he paused at the beds of people who had lost limbs in the blast. He tried to reach them, to tell them life goes on, even on one leg. But it was hard to convince them of something he only partially believed.

He caught a job for sixty cents an hour with Thomson & Theakston, the big contractor and construction company around town, building new homes and the new orphanage, which, by necessity, would be larger than the original. Dozens of children had lost parents, siblings, aunts, and uncles and had nowhere else to go. The new building was still on Barrington Street but had relocated farther down, to where the Halifax Yacht Club had been.

Pierre Antoine appeared at the job site one day, his long black coat spotless, his narrow eyes just as dark and cold. Nearly shaking with restrained hatred, Danny watched the man as he spoke with the foreman, slapping his leather gloves against one palm. The hammer in Danny's hand seemed the perfect weapon, but he held himself in check. The stuffed peacock might be his only link to learning anything of Audrey's fate. He waited behind Antoine until the meeting came to an end, then he cleared his throat.

"Wondered if I might have a moment of your time, sir," Danny said.

Antoine pivoted in a huff, clearly annoyed. He didn't appear to recognize Danny.

Danny pulled off his cap and held it in his hands, giving the man a quick, obligatory smile.

"Danny Baker, sir. We met when my wife—"

"Audrey!" Antoine's reaction was swift, as if he'd been slapped.

Danny's heart sank. *I will not cry.*

"I am sorry, Monsieur Baker." The dark eyes welled with sympathy, and for a moment Danny forgave the man for most likely being the last person Audrey had ever seen.

"You—" He cleared his throat, determined to know. "You were with her?"

"She arrived at my house the night before, but I left the city to go to Boston early in the morning. On the train, you see. I had a meeting there. But my family . . ." The men stared at each other's chests, unwilling to see the pain in their eyes. "I'm sorry. Everyone in the house was killed."

Yes, he'd seen the man's family, slaughtered and stiff. He'd seen the damage done to the house. But he hadn't seen Audrey there. Could she have gotten out? But why? What could have prompted her to get out of the house before nine o'clock in the morning?

"I didn't see her name . . ."

One black eyebrow rose and fell, admitting fault. "I apologize. I have not had time to do so. I will speak with my secretary about that."

In a daze, Danny went back to work, staring at the nails in the boards, stopping only when tears obscured his vision. *I am sorry, Monsieur Arnold. I'm sorry Fred's not with me. Truly I am. I'm so sorry he isn't here. I'm so sorry, Mrs. Mitchell. I'm so sorry. I couldn't save him. I couldn't—*

He'd handed those boxes to his friends' parents, given them what little was left of their loved ones so they could say goodbye. Letters from home. A Bible. Bits of nothing.

Antoine hadn't handed him anything.

How could Danny ever say goodbye to Audrey? *I'm so sorry, Audrey. I couldn't save you. I can't save myself . . .*

All he could do was work. He put everything he had into those nails.

The city had put together a relief committee, and they supplied all the furniture for the orphanage as well as for other places. The building was put together quickly, and children began moving in. Three of the orphans were well-known to Danny: the twins Eugene and Harry and their baby brother, Norman. Danny tried to visit the little boys as often as he could and found the routine suited him well. He enjoyed their innocence, no matter how scarred it was.

It was during one of those visits that Danny heard a familiar voice. "Well, I'll be. If it ain't Danny Baker himself."

Danny swung around and ended up face-to-face with Mick. Or

rather, face to cap, since Mick was a foot shorter than Danny. Mick didn't seem to have changed much since the war, other than a brand new line of stitches across one cheek which disappeared beneath a black eye patch. How ironic. To survive so much, then end up getting torn apart on your own home soil.

"Mick! Jeez, I never thought I'd see your ugly mug again!"

"I've been back about a month," Mick told him. "You know a newsman couldn't miss a story like this. I got here just in time for the fun." Both men smiled grimly. "You're looking good, Danny my boy."

"So are you. Hey, am I glad to see you."

Mick gave him a familiar, toothy grin, and the new scar lifted with it. "I'm glad to see you too," he said, then winked his remaining eye.

"Suits you, that patch," Danny said. "Makes you even more like the pirate you are."

Mick laughed, though not with quite as much energy as Danny'd seen him do before. "Yep. And now I'm here to uncover buried treasure, I guess."

"You're working?" Danny asked. He spotted the paper and pencil in Mick's hand. "What are you writing about?"

"Oh, this whole thing has made national—even international—headlines, you know. This is a great opportunity for someone in the middle of everything to get himself known. I'm writing all about this, then sending it around the world."

"Jeez. Good luck with that, Mick."

"Yeah. We'll see."

They stared at each other for a moment. As usual, it was Mick who spoke first. His voice, though, was uncharacteristically soft.

"Not sure if I'd rather be here or there, you know?"

Danny closed his eyes for a moment. "At least there's something we can do to help here, instead of just waiting for the next bullet."

"Is that what you're doing?" Mick asked.

"Yeah. Building. You know."

Mick nodded toward the twins. "You know those boys?"

Danny gave the boys a pat on their slender shoulders, then led Mick toward the door, out of their hearing. "A bit," he said. "I found them in their basement right afterwards."

"They got a story?"

Danny snorted. "Yeah. Four-year-old twins with a baby brother, three dead sisters, and a dead mother. The end."

"Can't blame a guy for trying. Hey, can I bum a smoke?"

"I don't have any. That was the funniest thing. When the explosion happened, everything blew out of my pockets. My brother lost just one boot. Just one boot, his hat, and his coat. Imagine that? What kind of explosion does that?"

"Tore a lot of people's clothes off. I've seen far too many birthday suits lately." He chuckled, then reached into his coat pocket. "Of course, you can bum one off me. Nothing new about that."

They stepped outside, and Mick handed Danny a little white cylinder that fit like an old friend between Danny's lips. He leaned forward, and Mick lit the end of it behind his cupped hand as Danny inhaled, long and slow. He closed his eyes, enjoying the sensation as the smoke curled through his body. Danny had always thought the best part of smoking was how the moment seemed to slow as he breathed in. He used that time to ponder what he was about to say. The action calmed him, settled his thoughts. Not for Mick, though. Mick was a talker. Danny knew that well. He enjoyed the differences between him and Mick.

"Quite a thing, this," Mick said, giving him an uncertain smile. "I don't even remember what happened, you know? Started off standing outside the *Chronicle* office, ended up in some woman's garden a block away. Wish I'd been awake for that. Now that'd be a great story." He puffed on his cigarette as if it were a pipe. "They've found over a thousand people dead, you know. All dead in under a second. Think of that. I bet more Nova Scotians died that one day than in the whole damn war."

"What are you doing here, Mick? Why aren't you up front?"

Mick lifted one sardonic eyebrow. "Came home for leave."

Danny waited. Mick got a look in his eye when he wanted to say something. It was there now.

"I ain't going back," Mick announced. "I had thought about that for a while, you know, considered making a break for it. And there were all those worries about getting caught and all that. But this—" Mick spread his hands apart, indicating the disaster. "This makes everything so much easier." He jabbed his thumb toward the eye patch. "They're not going to want me back now." He flicked off the spent ashes on the end of his cigarette. "Trust me, Danny. This explosion'll be the best thing to happen to me and to a lot of other people, too."

Danny thought that over. "Huh. Well, I can't really agree with that."

"Well, no. Of course not. Not the way you're thinking, anyway. But what about the construction boys? All the building right now is being done for free, right? After everyone's got their emergency homes built, they're going to want real houses, right? Not just tarpaper, but brick and mortar. And the companies that get those contracts are going to go through the roof. Imagine window companies! Just you watch. Plenty of people are going to do well as a result of this tragedy."

Danny felt a little sick at the thought, but he didn't say anything. Mick took a long drag on his cigarette, then looked down and kicked at the snow by his feet.

"You know me, Danny. I'm not a bad guy. But I see opportunity. And with opportunity comes so many things—some good, some real, real bad. The next few years are going to be interesting ones." He grinned again and his scar stretched tight across one cheek. "Just you watch, Danny. Stick with me, huh? We'll take an interesting ride, I'm sure."

Danny shook his head, smiling. "You know, I told my little brothers about you," he said. "I told them you never really took the war too seriously. And we all thought you were a loon, but you kept us going when we'd had more than enough of it all. I told them about that Christmas Eve. Do you remember when you—"

"Yeah, yeah," Mick said.

"Well, I thought about you, you know. After I was back here. You were really the only one I thought about. You and Tommy Joyce. I figured the rest of them were probably blown to bits along the way, but you'd pull through. At least I hoped you would." He lifted an eyebrow. "But I never thought I'd see you again, Mick."

"Ah, Danny. There's too much living to be done, I figure, for them to get rid of me that easy. Too many stories to be told that wouldn't see the light of day if I wasn't here to write 'em." He tapped the ash off his cigarette. "Tommy was alive when I left. He wasn't . . . the same, but he was alive."

"Are you going to write about the front?"

"Already started on that. It's gonna take a whole book to cover it all. So many things to write about. Maybe now you're here we can write them down together, huh?"

"Oh, I don't know. I'm not good at thinking about that."

"No?"

"Can't remember much, really," Danny said. "And when I do, I'd rather not."

"Yeah, I guess that's about right. Maybe it's just me. I see it all like a great big bunch of stories that need to be told. Kind of like this one, only longer."

"I wish you luck, Mick."

"Luck ain't got nothing to do with success, Danny. It's imagination and stubbornness that'll get you there. Just never give up. You remember that if you remember nothing else."

"Okay, Dad."

"That's right," Mick said, returning his smile.

A man trudged slowly past, pushing a wheelbarrow along the uneven road. Two children sat inside the bucket. One was missing an eye and everything below one elbow. The other child stared off somewhere no one else could see. The father, or so Danny assumed him to be, used the wheelbarrow as a crutch as well as a carrier. He limped past, headed toward the hospital.

The sight prompted Mick to ask a question Danny'd been waiting for. "How's your leg?"

Danny gave him his standard response. "No idea. Haven't seen it in almost a year."

"Hmm. And how's that been?"

Mick had always been the one to ask questions no one else dared ask. Danny figured that was probably what made Mick such a great newspaperman. He wanted to know stuff, so he just asked.

"You gonna write about me?" Danny asked.

"Only if it's a good story," Mick assured him. "You got a good story?"

Danny snorted. "Not much of one." He dropped the butt of his cigarette and twisted his peg on top to extinguish it. "I got home, felt useless . . ." He shrugged. "Maybe was less useless than I thought, but I felt like it anyway. I couldn't figure what to do with myself. Couldn't really fish. You need two hands, two feet for that. Couldn't hunt because I kept getting caught up in the woods. Ended up working the docks here. Got married to a real queen, you know? But I started feeling so sorry for myself, even she couldn't stand me by the end."

"By the end? Where is she?"

"I got no idea," Danny replied, deciding not to mention what Antoine had said. He still couldn't quite say it out loud. "She left me the night before the world blew up. And I haven't found her on any of the lists."

Mick steepled his fingertips together, like they were formed over an invisible ball. Danny recognized the position. Mick was "formulating thoughts," he had told them once. Formulating thoughts. Who talked like that? Mick did. The whole battalion would be in the trench, knee-deep in mud and shit, and Mick would be formulating thoughts.

"So you did some dock work?" Mick apparently had decided to leave the discussion of marital issues for the time being.

"Yeah. Good money."

"I hear it's dangerous work."

"Can be, I expect. But me and Johnny always pulled through."

"Johnny. He's your brother, right? I remember you talking about him."

"Yeah."

"Did he come to the city with you?"

"Yeah."

Mick gave him a half smile. "What's the story? Why so quiet all of a sudden?"

Danny shoved his hands into his pockets and spat into the snow beside him. "Because Johnny got blown up a few weeks ago."

"Oh," Mick said quietly. "Sorry."

"Yeah. Me too."

"You have a house here?"

Danny suddenly envisioned Audrey as she had been when they moved into that house in Richmond. She was standing in their doorway, looking so pretty in her yellow flower-print dress, her curls soft and sweet where they tickled down her neck. She had still loved him then. Now she was dead, and the last memory she'd carry of him would be the slap of his hand on her face.

"*Had* a house," he said.

"Ah. So where you living now?" Mick asked.

"I've been bunking wherever. Sometimes I stay with the soldiers down at Exhibition Park. They've got tents set up."

"I got a place with an empty room in it."

"Yeah?"

"Yeah. I don't suppose you have too much stuff to move in, do you?"

Danny smiled wryly. "Nope. I ain't got much."

THIRTY-TWO

Living with Mick was like living in the eye of a tornado. Danny felt like he could stand stock-still and Mick would run circles around him. Not physically—though that was true as well—but mentally. Mick loved words. He loved possibilities and what-ifs. He never tired of anything but the act of wasted time. He had more questions than a man had a right to.

Mick brought the newspaper home every day. When he finished reading a page, he passed it to Danny, then quizzed him on the different articles. What did he think? What would he do?

Danny didn't think along thoughts and possibilities so much as practicality. What Danny found interesting was that the newspaper had emerged from the explosion relatively unscathed. There was hardly any interruption between the event and the next paper out.

When he wasn't subjecting Danny to lengthy question periods, Mick wrote in relative silence, punctuated by the odd satisfied grunt. His typewriter's *tick tick tick ding!* was Danny's constant companion. So much cigarette smoke haloed Mick's head that Danny wondered how the man could breathe. Books and papers wobbled in huge stacks, piled from the floor to the top of the desk, and Mick read all of them with such intensity Danny figured another explosion could go off and Mick wouldn't lose his place. The newspaperman would read, then mutter something like "Well, I'll be. Who would have thought? Would you look at that?" then get back to his typewriter, and his fingers flew.

The headlines that grabbed most of Mick's attention were the ones hollering about political change. Especially in Russia. Talk of revolution. Danny didn't know much about politics and didn't care to learn, really. But he got a little interested when he recognized some of the same problems on the streets of Halifax. Worker discontent. Unfair wages. Impossibly high unemployment.

Danny kept hammering, building, picking up work where he could. He was lucky to be living in Mick's comfortable place. Mick never asked for any kind of rent, but Danny needed to make an income, if only to feed himself. Most of the other workers bunked down in the Alexander McKay School, which had somehow survived.

He joined the construction efforts down at the docks, where everything was starting from scratch. The massive Pier 6 was nothing but a hole. Everything in Halifax Harbour had been decimated, but that didn't mean the ocean ships stopped coming. For a while they'd used the Boston port for running supplies, but it wasn't as convenient as Halifax had been. So as soon as the crews could build the means to take in ships and start supplying them again, they did.

Mick had been right about construction contracts. Big money—something like twenty-one million dollars—eventually came in from the federal government, who recognized the importance of Halifax as a major shipping centre. But the money didn't seem so big when it jingled in Danny's threadbare pocket at the end of the week. He worked hard alongside the other men, putting temporary buildings and docks in place as quickly as possible. And every night those same men trudged home, tired all the way through, to see if there was any food in their own houses.

All across Canada women were being given the vote for the first time, though they hadn't gotten it yet in Nova Scotia. That was interesting to Danny because it was something different, and because it made him think of Audrey. She'd told him about the suffragettes in London, about the parades and the meetings. It intrigued him. Women had picked up the jobs when men had gone to war. Fighting their own sorts of battles, he thought. They'd kept the country moving, but from what he understood, it hadn't been fair. Audrey's sweet little voice had risen with indignation, explaining how women workers were paid a fraction of what the men had been paid. Would all those women keep on working after the war? Probably not, because the men would need their jobs back. Plus, if they didn't go back home, who would take care of the kids? Who would cook and clean if the women were out working? Seemed only right to let them vote, though.

It had been almost a month since the explosion. Starting out the new year by living without Audrey, every day was divided between trying not to think of her and trying to imagine what she'd be doing if she were still alive.

He still checked the lists out of habit. Antoine's secretary hadn't seemed to find the time to include Audrey's name on either yet, and not seeing her on the Known Dead list gave Danny an impossible hope. One he needed. Every morning he awoke dreaming this might be the day when he'd find her, and she'd come running back to his arms. Every night he went to bed thanking God that she hadn't shown up on that list.

But the truth was, a whole month was an awfully long time not to exist on any list at all. Danny tried to ignore the voice in his head, telling him to move on. Antoine had said she was dead. Gone. Never again. And the last image Danny had of her was that of her back as she left the house. After he'd hit her. After he'd ruined everything.

Danny gave his head a shake, needing to kill the guilt, if only for a while. If he could get Mick talking, at least he'd be distracted.

"Mick?"

Mick's head was down, the eye patch black as his stubble, cigarette jutting out of one side of his mouth. He was typing hard. How could he work so much? Danny was exhausted, and watching Mick wore him out even more. It had been a very long day in a string of very long days. He needed some air.

"Hey, Mick?"

Mick waved a hand as if he'd heard a fly buzzing around his head. With him unavailable, Danny shrugged on his black wool coat and stepped into the dusk, taking a walk to the orphanage instead. A big poster on the door announced an upcoming charity event for the building, run by some of the society ladies. They were good people, Danny thought. They didn't seem to like getting their hands too dirty, but they did help out with money. This was going to be an auction, he saw. In a couple of weeks. There ought to be some pretty wealthy folks out for that. Well, good for them. The poor had given all they had to their neighbours. The rich could do their part.

Danny pulled open the orphanage door and turned first, as he always did, to the updated lists on the wall. He browsed the most recent additions to both, then walked away, hands deep in his pockets. Still nothing. How could she simply vanish? If only it weren't so entirely possible.

The orphanage was a fairly quiet place, though it picked up energy over the weeks as many of the children recovered. They sat for meals and prayers at a long table set along one wall, and a stove burned constantly nearby. One corner of the room opened to a hallway, which led to a number of small rooms with bunks for most of the children, though some of the younger ones, like the twins and their brother, still slept in the main room. The kitchen was off to the other side, where the volunteers prepared soup or oatmeal, or whatever was on the menu for the day. Right now Eugene and Harry were the only ones in the big room. The twins were crouched in the corner of the main room, their bright hair like a beacon, focused on racing a pair of horses Danny had carved for them. Baby Norman lay on a small cot, sleeping, thumb hanging half out of his open mouth. The boys were very small, he thought, and they didn't seem old enough to get along with other kids. They had each other, but even so, Danny thought they seemed lonely. He made his way toward them, then sat on a bench nearby.

"How are you today, boys?"

"Danny!" Eugene cried. He and Harry roared their little horses over.

"I see they took the bandage off your arm, Harry. Can you move it okay?"

"Yup," Harry said. He was starting to speak a little, and Danny encouraged every word. The boys' voices, at least, were still identical. "I'm hungry."

"Well, that's why I brought you this." Danny presented him with a cheese sandwich, then gave one to Eugene as well. Pudgy little fists closed over the bread, and the boys ate faster than Danny would have thought possible. Even Harry, who had to chew gently in order to protect the slowly healing scars on his face, had finished before he knew it.

"You were hungry," Danny said, looking impressed. "When's the last time you had something to eat?"

"Yesterday," Eugene said, then smothered a burp.

"We had a biscuit for breakfast," Harry reminded him.

Danny frowned. "What about to drink?"

"We had milk this morning," Eugene assured him, reaching for more food. Danny'd brought a sandwich for himself, but now he divided it between the boys.

Danny had heard there had been a donation made just the week before, and the money was designated for the orphans' meals. A biscuit and a glass of milk didn't seem right. He would have to ask Mick if he was aware of any short dealings. Mick knew everything about everything in this city.

"Did nobody eat?"

The boys shook their heads.

"We used to get three meals a day and something sweet before bedtime," Eugene said, his tone wistful. "Hey, Danny, that lady there said we have to live here forever. Is that right?"

Danny stared into two pairs of the bluest eyes he'd ever seen. "No. I don't think so. Not forever. Just until they figure out what to do with you."

Eugene's chin started to wobble. "She said Mommy got killed, and we can't go home."

"Can we come and stay with you, Danny?" Harry asked slowly, labouring over the words. Danny felt his heart give way.

"I, uh, I don't know how these things work," he said. "And I don't have more than a room to myself."

"We're pretty small," Eugene said quickly. "And Norman's a good baby. He hardly cries at all."

Huh. Take the boys home with him. Danny couldn't figure out how he felt about that. It seemed an impossible idea, and yet it appealed to him on a very basic level. He liked the boys. He wanted to take care of them. What would it do to his life if he were to go ahead and bring these children home with him? Was it even possible? He'd been a lousy husband. Could he make it right by being a good father?

"I know he is, Eugene. He's a darn good baby, that's for sure. And you two are very grown-up little boys. But I'm just not sure if I can keep you with me. I work a lot most days. I don't know what the rules are."

"Can you ask?"

Danny leaned forward and put a warm palm on each boy's cheek. The soft, freckled skin was cold to his touch. And though they were clean, the boys still wore the same clothes they'd had on when he'd brought them in, though he knew others had been donated. Was anyone looking after them?

"I will ask," Danny promised. "Now let's see about those horses. Which one goes faster?"

He watched them race, then gradually lose interest in Danny as they played. Danny turned and laid his hand lightly on Norman's little chest, feeling the stubborn little heartbeat pounding away under his thin shirt. He remembered how dark it had been when he'd crawled into the boys' basement to retrieve the baby. He had taken the screaming bundle from the dead woman, and in his heart he had promised to take care of her three children. They'd be taken care of here, he'd assumed. But would they be better or worse off with him? What would Audrey do if she were here?

"You boys have a good night," he said, rising. "Here's a little more cheese for bedtime. Don't eat it all at once or your tummies will hurt."

THIRTY-THREE

Mick was pacing the front room when Danny stepped through the door. The newspaperman's hair was freshly slicked back and his eyes darted restlessly. He'd apparently finished his work, and a stack of crisply typed pages stood on their dining table. At sight of Danny, Mick clapped his hands together.

"Danny!" he said. "I'm feeling fine tonight. Let's go out for supper."

"Oh, I can't do that, Mick. You know I can't afford—"

He winked and jerked his thumb at the paper. "The paper'll pay me a pretty penny for this. Dinner's on me."

"Nah. Come on, Mick. We have some ham in here, I think, and—"

"I feel like going out, and I'll not do it alone. Let's go." He slapped Danny on the back, and Danny gave in, persuaded as always by his friend's contagious charm. They strode into the early evening, moving fairly quickly; Mick had a definite destination in mind. As they walked, Danny brought up his question from earlier on.

"You ever hear of any bad business going on with the orphanage?"

Mick frowned. "Like what?"

"Well," he said, scratching his head. "It's just that those kids don't seem to be getting enough to eat, from what I can see. And they have barely anything to wear, even though I was pretty sure they were getting donations."

"Yeah, they're supposed to be. Government money and all. The committee takes care of most of that. You think there's trouble?"

"I don't know. I mean, well, you know there's always stuff going on at the docks. I get that. It's the liquor and things. But I never thought of it affecting the kids at all. I don't know," he repeated. "Maybe it's just me."

Mick shrugged. "I ain't heard of nothing, but it sure is something I can check into."

"Thanks, Mick," Danny said.

"Think nothing of it, my friend."

Mick led them down the street to a tavern. Its windows had been temporarily replaced by thick planks. As Mick opened the door and they stepped inside, Danny had to admit a warm meal and a cold drink wouldn't go amiss.

It seemed a few other people had had the same thought. Four tables were already occupied by rough-looking men deep in conversation. Danny thought he recognized a few of them.

"Well, there he is," one man said, standing. "Mick, my lad. Won't you and your friend join us for a little supper?"

"Hey, that's Danny Baker," another said, standing up so fast his chair tumbled over behind him. Danny recognized him at once as one of the boys he'd taken on a time or two down on the docks. One of the man's friends grabbed his arm.

"Now, now, Sam," he said. "We're all together now, huh? We're not picking each other apart anymore. That's the way it is. You and Baker should shake hands and make friends now."

That was just fine with Danny, whatever it meant. The last thing he felt like doing was fighting. He'd had more than his share of this day.

Sam's eyes narrowed at Danny. "Yeah, well, he steps outta line and I'll—"

"You'll what?" Danny asked, contempt darkening his sneer. "Go on. What you gonna do, tough guy?"

"Come on, Sam," his friend said. "Sit down. Let's have a whisky."

Slightly mollified, Sam sat, but he kept a wary eye on Danny, who wished he'd stayed home.

"What are you having, boys?" the waiter asked, approaching Mick and Danny. The man was maybe in his mid-fifties, his curly brown hair streaked with white. He had a bandage wrapped around his neck. His knuckles, curled over an order pad, were thick with arthritis, and he had a bit of a stoop to his back. The posture was vaguely familiar, and Danny figured the waiter had once been a fisherman, just like him.

Mick offered his most winning smile, bright in his craggy face. "I'll have a whisky, if you please. And one for my friend as well. And you got any of that steak and kidney pie? We'll have a couple of those, if we could."

"Coming up," he said, tucking a pencil behind his ear and heading toward the kitchen.

Danny frowned at Mick, still uncomfortable at having his meal paid for.

"Danny," Mick said loudly. "I brought you here to meet some of the lads."

"Nice to meet you," Danny muttered, lighting up a cigarette.

Mick grinned at his friends. "Some of you know Danny, some of you don't. He's a man of few words and unshakable integrity. A man who saved my life more than once in France."

"I did not," Danny said.

"You did," Mick said quietly. "You just didn't realize it when you were doing it. Anyway," he said, turning back to the rest of them, "Danny's a dock man like some of you, and now he does construction. Danny works fifteen-hour shifts and goes home with less money every week."

"For Pete's sake, Mick!" Danny cried. "You gotta air my dirty laundry in front of all these guys? What's the matter with you?"

"Hang tight, Danny," Mick said, his voice still raised. "The thing is, these boys are in the same spot you are. They're working harder and getting less money, but they can't quit because there ain't any other jobs around. Ain't that so?"

There were grunts of assent.

"So what?" Danny said. "We're here to whine about our circumstances? Because yeah, I could use the money. But I'm awful glad I can still walk and talk and see and not spend the rest of my life hiding burns from people. I did just fine, Mick. I got nothing to complain about."

"There's a hero, boys. He can still walk, even though he left a leg in France."

"For crying out loud, Mick," Danny said, standing. "I'm getting outta here."

"Okay, okay. Set yourself down, my friend," Mick said, giving Danny a wink. "I'll leave off on you now. But the thing is, we're all here because we got the same problem. We ain't getting paid near enough to feed families, or even ourselves—"

"Except for you, apparently," Danny muttered.

That stopped Mick for only a moment, then he raised his brow in acquiescence. "Well, a newspaperman ain't a dockworker, is he? We got rules about how much we get paid, right? There are systems and things that regulate how a man like me gets paid. You guys hang in there, hoping for work, and no one owes you nothing, because no one has ever said they did. What if someone started talking about that? What if we was to have a union start up around here?"

"A what?" Sam asked.

"Come on," Mick said. "You've never heard of the unions getting power all over the place? Big companies are scared silly after the Bolshevik thing—"

"Heh?"

"Russian people taking power, tossing the czar onto the street," Danny informed Sam.

Mick looked pleased. "You've been reading," he said.

"What else am I gonna do when you keep throwing newspapers at me?"

"So what's this Bowl-shivvy thing? What's it got to do with us?" Sam's friend demanded. "I ain't no Russian."

Other men spoke up at that, making it clear they weren't Russians, no way. Good Canadian citizens, they were. Proud of their country.

Danny studied each man while Mick explained the idea of unionism. Such proud Canadians. Yet other than Mick, he could see only one man, sitting near the back, who carried that cold countenance of someone who'd been in the war, that expression of one who doesn't feel quite connected to the world and might never again. The man glanced up, sensing Danny's eye, and gave him a slow nod of recognition. Danny looked away.

Out of all these proud Canadians, only three had taken up arms to protect her.

He picked through the pie, but he wasn't really hungry after all. He ate because he knew it might be a while before he could have such a meal again. He was getting by with less and less, even though, as Mick had said, he was working harder than ever. If it weren't for Audrey, Danny would have left the whole stinking mess behind. Get back to Jeddore and dig a hole in the ice, try to tempt out a few smelt. Anything but here.

But she was here. Dead or alive, she was here, and he wasn't going to leave without her.

THIRTY-FOUR

Those little boys, he thought wryly. They had planted a seed in his head that germinated and sprouted overnight. They were good little souls. They deserved a good life. A good family.

Danny had plenty to do that morning, what with construction and all, but he went instead to the dark brick Social Services building a block away from the orphanage, where people posted signs and searched for lost family members. A sheaf of papers lay stacked in an open box on one side of the unmanned desk, and Danny grabbed a few of the top sheets. He carried them over to a bench, then sat so his peg jutted out in front. He barely noticed it anymore. It had been over a year since the war had taken that chunk out of him, and since then so much more had been taken from his life. The leg hardly seemed to matter compared to the loss of Audrey and Johnny. He'd give his other one to have them back.

Danny stared down at the papers in his hands, corners curled by so many desperate thumbs. He'd been through them before, but every time he saw new pleas, new drawings and descriptions of loved ones. He had always come in for news of Audrey. Today he had a different purpose, though he still scanned every page for sign of her. Today he started digging deeper, searching for anyone who might know "his" little boys. He knew the orphanage would have sent out notices for all the children, but Danny wondered if maybe he could help in some small way. He flipped through the pages then went back for more, but there was no mention of missing twin boys. Even if their family was dead, Danny figured someone must know of them. Sure, the broken-down homes of the North End had barely been used, since their owners were so often out working, but these two boys would have been hard to miss.

Blank pages lay in another open box with a stack of sharpened pencils beside it. Danny set to work describing the boys and their baby brother, then he left the building and headed down the street toward the newspaper offices.

At the reception desk, Danny asked the woman to please tell Mick he was there. After a moment, the newspaper man swaggered through a door at the back of the lobby, cigarette hanging out of the corner of his mouth. He looked completely at home in the melee of paperboys, reporters, a clattering telegraph, and even a telephone. Danny had only ever seen one of those before. Crazy contraption, he thought. Wouldn't that be a wonderful idea if it were good for anything at all.

Mick clapped Danny on the shoulder, welcoming him to the pandemonium as if he were the ringleader of the entire circus. "Come for a job, have you?"

"Nah," Danny said. "I've come to give you a job."

"Oh? What's that?"

"I've got a little money this week," he said pointedly. "And I think I'd like to—what did you call it? Buy some words."

Mick frowned. "Buy some—oh! Buy an advertisement?"

"Yeah," Danny said. "I'd like to buy an advertisement. For these boys. I want to find them a home." He unfolded the paper he'd tucked into his jacket pocket and showed it to Mick. "They've gotta have family somewhere."

Mick studied Danny's drawing, stroking the line of his chin with thumb and forefinger. "Not much of an artist, are you Danny?"

"And you're not much of a comedian," Danny countered. "What do you think? Can I do that?"

Mick kept staring at the paper a moment more, then muttered, "Well now, I wonder."

Danny smiled to himself. That was a sure sign he'd caught Mick's interest.

"That orphanage is pretty full of these little tykes, ain't it?" Mick asked

"Sure is."

"Tell you what, Danny," Mick said, mind made up. "Your money's no good here." He snagged his cigarette between two fingers and pulled it out of his mouth, dropping a chunk of grey ash on the floor. Mick wagged a finger at Danny, his eyes slightly glazed, as an idea formed in his head. "Here's what we're gonna do. I'm gonna have to pass this by the editor, sure, but he'll say yes. Heck, it's a great human interest angle." His eyes clicked back into focus. "See, here's what it is, Danny. I'll come down to the orphanage and do a story on each kid, then run a series of them. Someone's bound to pay attention if the column is running all the time."

Mick was as good as his word and better. He even brought along a photographer. The stories were a column long, usually on the third page, and they ran the column every day for a month. Beside each of these, they ran a public and private sector appeal, asking for donations for the orphans.

They hadn't expected a miracle, but within the first two weeks, four children had been identified and brought to their rightful families. Mick's editor was so impressed with the results, he started sending the columns out to other provinces and some of the United States. Over time the newspaper began receiving notes from relatives far away, stepping up to do their familial duty. Children were packed up and sent via train to the homes of aunts and uncles thousands of miles away.

But not the twins or their baby brother. No one came for them. Nobody said a word. The boys had no idea what was happening, and Danny was glad about that. They seemed not to notice that the other children were disappearing even though the two of them stayed, but they did seem less and less willing to see Danny go at the end of his daily visits. They drew pictures for him, and Danny brought food and made them more toys whenever he could. They needed him.

All he'd thought about before was Audrey. About finding her, about their life together, and about his part in their own personal disaster. Now there was so much more to think about. The boys, well, he felt them twisting into the fibres of his soul, intertwining with his nerves. Seeing their little faces brought a pulse back to his heart. He needed them just as they needed him.

Social Services was more than willing to give him the paperwork for adoption. What they were less willing to do was consider his application. Not only was he without sufficient funds, he was without a wife. The children would need a mother, they said. If Danny could do something about that, well, then they'd speak with him again.

That made Danny smile, though it didn't make him happy. He could only imagine Audrey's reaction if he finally found her, then asked if she could please come along and adopt these three little boys. It would be too much. Even if she were alive—and Danny had begun to secretly doubt that possibility—she might not be willing to go back to a louse like him, let alone take on three little boys.

Construction around the city was an amazing sight to behold. After the devastation had been mostly cleared, buildings seemed to pop up almost overnight. Streets began to look like streets again, instead of long, bare stretches of flat rock and fallen timber. They began to frame neighbourhoods again, and Danny was able to walk past the buildings without remembering France quite so often.

Life in the north end of Halifax began to resume. A few automobiles puttered through, cutting wide curves around working horses who were back to hauling supplies instead of corpses.

Typically, most of the people from the wealthy south end of the city stayed away from the north. That had always been the way. But recently a few curious southerners had started dropping in, wanting to see what all the fuss was about. Some came with donations, some came to help build. Others came merely to stare with pity and disgust at the hundreds of maimed and blind inhabitants, to tut their tongues at the horrible waste.

The workers toiled on, though it was sometimes difficult to stomach the sight of fur-clad women stepping gingerly from shiny automobiles and into the construction areas, accompanied by gentlemen with fancy hats and walking sticks. Grumbling remarks were made by the workers regarding the new posters that were being hammered up, ordering citizens to stop offering alcohol to the workers. Fortunately, the posters didn't stop the process, only quietened it a bit.

Mick's meetings at the tavern increased in both size and frequency, and he eventually gave up his podium to make way for more forceful leaders. He had to be careful about what he wrote, because the newspaper had some wealthy connections, and there were laws discouraging open dissent. He would be of no use to his cohorts if he were inside a jail cell. He fell into the comfortable position of writing articles, of detailing the troubles the workers faced, the progress they made. While he did that, the labourers made formal complaints to the government about low wages, but those went largely ignored. Danny understood that, in a way. After all, how could the government worry about regulating wages when thousands of people were still homeless? A lot were jobless too, now the sugar refinery and other factories had been destroyed. And then there was the steady stream of soldiers who kept arriving in town, returning from the front, usually ruined either physically, mentally, or both. There was no work for them, either.

Mick's crew wasn't easily dissuaded. Sure, money needed to go to the homeless. But Danny and the other construction workers were busy, trying hard to ensure that soon there would be no problem with homelessness at all. When the workers went home at the end of the day and couldn't afford dinner for themselves and their families, something had to be done.

"You see the boys just gettin' home off the boats?" Mick asked one day.

"What, the lame ones like me?"

Mick gave a short bark of laughter and blew out a puff of smoke. "Yeah. Those ones. Who's lookin' out for them boys?"

Danny shrugged. "No one I know of. They sleep fine, I guess, at the Exhibition Grounds with all the tents."

"Well, I've seen some of them just sittin' around on the street, doin' nothin'. You seen 'em there, Danny? What do you make of that?"

"Why? You think they're lazy? Nah. At least you and I had something to come home to. What's left here for these boys? It's blown apart, just like France, only more women and kids stuck in the middle." One side of Mick's mouth curled up. "I'm gonna go talk with them. I'm gonna bring them on side."

"What, join your group of thugs?"

"Yeah, my group of thugs. That's exactly it. After the war, they're like you and me. They ain't afraid of nothing anymore. They won't be afraid to complain, either. And they look plenty hungry, so they'd have something to complain about."

Danny didn't see much point in it, but he went with Mick anyway. If nothing else, they were reaching out to some fairly lost souls, men who needed at least a friendly voice to keep them afloat.

There was talk of unions, of revolutions, of public protests. From what Danny read, the movement seemed to be happening all across the country. Mick stayed on top of everything and made sure Danny was right there with him.

"There's a town hall meeting tonight," Mick said once.

"Yeah? So what?"

"So we're going, the bunch of us. We're gonna make a noise they can't ignore."

Danny shrugged, then went along. He had nothing better to do.

THIRTY-FIVE

espite his indifference, Danny found the whole process of protests
and "meetings" fairly interesting. Some of the men in the group were
smart, and their tactics at making complaints known were sometimes
pretty innovative. Then there were others, subtle as hammers and just
about as smart. Danny wished they'd stay behind or at least keep their
mouths shut. Every time one of the intelligent ones said something, a
stupid one would say another thing and bring the whole conversation
back a step. When it happened one time, Danny just about hauled off
and slugged the man behind him. The guy wouldn't shut up, just kept
hollering, "More jobs! More jobs! More jobs!" But starting a fist fight
wasn't going to help anything, so Danny just turned away in disgust.

Sometimes Mick's group, which wasn't really his anymore, tramped
across town and camped outside the stately home of someone influential.
They'd carry signs and spend a couple of hours yelling demands. The
people in the house peeked through thick curtains, then dropped the material with a movement that could have signalled either fear or revulsion.
Or maybe both. Danny didn't figure this kind of protest was ever going
to lead anywhere, but as the months wore on, he didn't mind so much. It

wasn't nearly as unpleasant to stand outside now that it was March and getting warmer. And he liked seeing the big houses on the south side, steeped in wealth and tradition. They were nice to look at.

Tonight's planned protest was at a fundraiser, Mick had said. The socialites had gathered for an auction in one of the homes, celebrating the advent of spring, raising money for homeless shelters or something like that. The protesters stayed hidden around the corner, not wanting to raise suspicions until all the guests had arrived. They watched glamorous people alight from automobiles, dressed in long gowns and black suits, arm in arm, laughing as if they didn't have a care in the world. And they probably didn't, Danny thought.

What would that be like, not to worry? He hardly remembered. But if he really thought back, he could recall long, still nights in East Jeddore, where the stars were so endless they seemed to pour into the sea, serving up an infinite shimmering of peace. He vaguely remembered playing around the fire with his friends and brothers when there was no such thing as war or explosives, when the idea of seeing a dead body was something spooky and exciting, like seeing a ghost. The memory seemed to lighten his shoulders. He recalled how he and Johnny—

No. He wouldn't think about Johnny.

The walkway in front of the home had been quiet for a while, suggesting the guests had all arrived. The protesters were getting restless. At a signal from their leader, they walked en masse toward the house, a simmering crowd in tired old greys and browns. Mick liked to walk up front, and Danny liked to walk with Mick, so he was one of the first to reach the front doorway. When they were there, Mick faced the crowd of twenty or so, giving them last-minute instructions.

Danny turned toward the front window and spied movement within, a shifting of shapes unaware of the noise his group was about to make. The people inside had left the curtains open, probably to show off their beautiful view of the harbour, though the night was mostly dark due to wartime blackouts. Candles flickered throughout the room, casting an orange glow, darkening and lightening the shadows of the guests.

A sign was posted just inside the window, displayed on a music stand.

Danny squinted, trying to see the list of items up for auction. His eyes skimmed absently down the tiny print, but he saw nothing because he wasn't really looking. He didn't really care.

Danny was bored. Life was one long, dull day for him now, with no hope of night. Never-ending drudgery. Mick and the little boys provided colour but not enough. He remembered how much Audrey had needed colour in her life, how the city had drained her. She had been right all along, of course. Danny knew he would have to go home to Jeddore soon. That was the only place he thought he might find what he needed. If he didn't, this endless day would go on and on.

Another music stand was set up beside the first one, and Danny shifted to his left to get a better view. It was a painting, he realized, of a soldier. The man was—

Danny stopped dead. It was a painting of *him*, as real as could be. It caught his tall build, the strong jawline and soft curl of brown hair. The way he tilted his head when he doubted something someone had said. The way he tucked his thumb into his waistband. The haunted, distrustful eyes Danny saw in the mirror every morning.

Audrey. Only Audrey could have done this. Danny jerked around, scanning the room beyond the window. Was she here somewhere? Was she—

Their eyes met at exactly the same moment, and their mouths fell open.

No one else was there in that instant, as far as Danny knew. Nothing else mattered. *Audrey.* Audrey was alive, and she would forgive him. Oh, Audrey! He felt a smile rising to his lips for the first time in a long time. He would hold her again, and she would breathe in his ear, and he would admire the gentle curve of her throat as she stretched in the morning . . .

"Audrey," he breathed, and was starting to reach for the door when she dropped the glass she was holding. She watched it fall; he heard it shatter from outside. And in the next instant, Pierre Antoine was there, offering her his handkerchief, patting the wet folds of her skirt in a manner far too personal for Danny's taste, saying something Danny couldn't hear.

Audrey didn't seem to notice Antoine. She ignored his words, only shaking her head briefly once or twice. She stared at Danny, lips still parted. Her hand started to rise, as if she reached for him, but Antoine took it and kissed her knuckles.

The pain that shot through Danny in that moment was worse, in a way, than when he'd lost his leg. When that had happened, he had lost one appendage. Seeing Audrey with another man, he lost all hope. The candlelight caught the shine of tears in her eyes, but Danny didn't wait to see more. He pushed through the throng of protesters, ignoring Mick's shouts. His head pounded, his eyes blurred, and he knew only that he wanted to get away—*had* to get away. He limped down the dark street, aiming for anywhere.

He would leave tomorrow, hide in a schooner, run rum, probably drink it again as well. What did it matter? Who cared? His peg landed in a puddle and slipped a little, but Danny kept on. *Get away. Get away.*

"Danny!"

He stopped but didn't turn. Her voice rang down the street, over the mutterings of the placard-holding crowd, twisting like a knife in his gut.

"Danny!"

She was nearer now, and he heard the quick *pat pat pat* of her shoes on the pavement as she ran toward him. *Please, Audrey,* he thought. *Please don't do this. Please. I can't. I can't bear it.*

"Danny!" She was breathless; her voice sounded choked. He couldn't help himself. He spun back toward her, eyes streaming.

"Oh, thank God, Danny! You are alive!" She ran without stopping until she could wrap her arms around his waist, fitting her body against his, where it should have been all along. "Danny, Danny, Danny," she sobbed into his chest.

He held on to her, breathing her in, rubbing his sprouting beard against her hair, crying along with her. He thought he might lose his balance, but she was there; she had always been there. Always steadying him.

"Forgive me, Audrey," he said. "Please, Audrey. I'm so sorry."

She hiccuped on her sobs. "Oh, Danny. Of course I do. Of course! But I thought . . . Pierre told me you and Johnny were on the . . . the Known Dead list. He told me he saw your name there, and I couldn't bear to see it, so I never checked. He said—"

"Why would the son of a bitch—"

"Danny, hush," she begged. "We have so much to talk about. Don't make it ugly."

She was right. She always was.

"God, Audrey," he said. "Every day I searched for you. I read the lists; I walked through the hospitals and morgues. I went to every place I could think of. You were never there," he said, trying to steady himself. "I thought you were gone. I'd lost hope."

"My name wasn't on any list?"

"No, not a one. And I read so many lists, my eyes just about fell out."

She swallowed. "Pierre said he'd write my name down."

Son of a bitch. "I . . . I talked to him a long time ago. He told me you were dead, that he hadn't gotten around to adding your name to the list. Why would—"

"But he promised me!" she said, horror-stricken. "He said he saw your name on the Known Dead list, and he promised to put me on the Known Living list, in case anyone was trying to find me."

Danny sensed his strength returning. Hope tickled in his heart. "I've missed you so much, Audrey."

But when he touched one soft cheek with his cold hand, she tilted her head self-consciously to the side, turning away just a bit, in a manner he didn't recognize.

"What is it?" he asked.

"Nothing." Her hand pressed on the cheek she'd hidden from him. When he reached for her hand, she resisted. "No, Danny. It was the explosion. It—"

"I'm your husband, Audrey. I love you. I only want to take care of you. What happened? Can I see?"

Her eyes shone devastatingly beautiful and just as pained. She closed them, then slid her hand away, and Danny saw a straight pink scar, the path a piece of glass or metal had taken, cutting a deep gash in her cheek. She was lucky she hadn't lost an eye.

"Oh God, Audrey. Are you all right now? If only I'd known! Oh, please don't hide from me. It's all right. You don't have to cover anything in front of me. You know that. Here, how about we—"

A deep voice called Audrey's name, its source hidden by the dark street. Brisk footsteps came toward them, followed by the muffled shushing and clacking of other shoes, and Audrey stepped away from Danny.

"Audrey! Are you all right? What's all this?" The voice gathered strength with every step. "You can't just leave a soiree like that. People will talk. Here. Who's this?" he asked, his voice hardening to annoyance when he spotted the man beside her, draped in worn and tattered clothing. The outline of shirt and pants was easier to see in the dark than Danny's face. The man stepped up beside Audrey and placed a protective arm around her waist, pulling her tight against him. "Is this man bothering you? Sir, leave the lady alone. How can I help you?"

Danny's blood screamed, battling the restriction of his veins, demanding to be set free. *Antoine.* What was it Johnny had called him? *The fellow who looked at Audrey as if she were a cherry on an ice cream sundae.* Well, here he was with his crisp black sleeve hooked around Audrey—as possessive a posture as a man could show.

Danny stepped into whatever light the moon shared. "Good evening, Mr. Antoine," he said, not bothering to disguise the hatred in his voice.

A small crowd of partygoers gathered, drawing protectively around Audrey. As if she needed protection from Danny. Did she? The group peered curiously at Danny, Antoine, and Audrey, eating up the scene with hungry eyes.

Antoine leaned toward Danny and frowned with suspicion, trying to make out his features. When he did, the Frenchman's face underwent a fascinating transformation. His eyes opened very wide then narrowed almost at once, and his mouth snapped shut. He had gotten thinner since the last time they'd met, and grown a moustache, Danny saw. And a short beard. Behind the facial hair, Antoine's lips were tight, his nostrils flared. Like a dog with hackles raised and teeth bared, prepared to defend its property.

So that was how it was, Danny thought. Fine. Danny was always up for a fight if it called him.

Except . . . how could he fight this?

Months before, Danny had—consciously or unconsciously— pushed his wife into the street through his selfish actions. He'd *hit* her. The explosion had obliterated any possibility of discussing and mending the problems that had plagued their marriage. She had been alone and injured, both physically and emotionally. And she was perfect for Antoine, whose entire family had been destroyed on that crisp December morning.

Danny's expression revealed nothing. He stared stonily at Antoine, measuring the man, wondering what he could possibly do to pry his wife from the grip of those wealthy, influential fingers. She was small beside the pristine black suit, hugging herself against the night chill, though Antoine held her tight. A glimmer of something on her chest caught the moonlight, and Danny saw what he thought was either an emerald or a sapphire. Something Danny would never have been able to afford over his entire lifetime. Her hair was curled into shiny coils, her makeup fashionably done. He'd never seen her wear makeup before. It made her seem a bit like a stranger.

"Danny," she whispered.

She seemed torn. As well she might. With Antoine she reaped the benefits of society and all a wealthy man could provide. With Danny she would maybe share a tiny apartment with Mick and his typewriter. Right now she was living a life of luxury, knowing no want, needing no one.

He took a breath, then blew it out quickly, mind made up. "I'm glad you're okay, Audrey," he said, then turned and walked away, hands sunk in his pockets.

"Danny?" she called, his name almost lost in a sob.

Danny kept walking and didn't look back. If he stopped he might never move again, he thought. God, why hadn't the explosion killed him, saved him this pain? His throat thickened with dammed tears, and he held his breath to avoid swallowing. Tears started down his face, but he didn't brush them away. She would remember his straight back, his head held high. Sure, she'd see his limp. There was nothing he could do about that. But she wouldn't see him cry.

AUDREY

– March 1918 –

THIRTY-SIX

꧁

He hardly limped anymore, she noticed. He walked as fast or faster than any other man with someplace to go. *Where was he going?*

Pierre cleared his throat. "Well, it appears he's made his decision. Wise man." He pressed his hand against her back. "Let's get back."

Danny's solid shape swept past the regal row of houses, not slowing to breathe, never looking back. The light of lanterns in windows shone yellow as he passed, lighting his hair, briefly bleaching the black from his coat. She heard the *step thump step thump* of his passage echoing off the road and thought she might die.

I thought he was dead!

"Audrey. Pay attention."

The fog in her brain began to clear, bringing her back to her own feet, which were wrapped in the latest uncomfortable fashion. Pierre took her elbow and smoothly led her away from Danny's receding form. Most of the crowd had dispersed and were walking back to the house, laughing among themselves, building tonight's episode to such a height that it would soon be the more talked-about piece of gossip on everyone's lips.

"You're making a fool of yourself, Audrey. Come."

She stared at Pierre, seeing a completely different man from the one she'd known the past few months. The one who had taken her in when she'd run from Danny on that frozen, horrible night so long before. She'd stayed in the maid's room on the first floor, and in the morning the world had exploded. *The war had found them! They were being bombed!* She thought she might have lost consciousness for a moment, though she would never forget the deafening pressure of the explosion in her ears. Her window shattered, as did her mirror, and her mother's teasing spirit whispered, *That will bring you seven years of bad luck, my girl . . .*

Pascale. So many times Audrey had pushed her mother's teasing gaze from her mind, but now it was laughing so loudly she couldn't ignore it. Ever since she'd figured out her mother's "barter" system, living from bed to bed to support them both, Audrey had been determined she would not follow that path. Danny had been her one and only love, and she'd never thought farther than that until it all started to fall apart. What had Pascale done when Richard Black disappeared? She'd mourned him, certainly. Audrey remembered the silent sobs in their dark tent and the pain in Pascale's eyes whenever Audrey asked about him. She'd mourned him, then moved on. Ultimately, she fell ill, and when Audrey grew old enough to understand such things, she realized Pascale's way of life, her method of surviving, had been the cause of that illness. And she'd died.

Audrey had mourned Danny after the explosion. She'd thought she would perish from the loss of him and the knowledge that they'd left each other so horribly. She hadn't died, but the emotions ripping through her chest made her wish for it. But then she'd moved on.

I understand, Maman. We do what we must, oui?

Pierre hadn't been in the house when the world exploded. He'd left earlier that morning on a train to Boston for business. When she felt brave enough to trust the floor beneath her feet, Audrey struggled out of bed, using the walls to brace herself. She was dizzy, her legs unsure, and she had the strangest sensation on one side of her head—opposite to where Danny had struck her the night before: freezing cold air where it shouldn't have been. A persistent buzzing noise vibrated in her ears. But without the mirror, she couldn't check to see.

She listened for any kind of sound besides the buzz but heard no voices. She didn't hear an air raid siren, either.

She clung to the banister as she climbed the staircase, calling Mrs. Antoine's name, listening for the children, but the house was still. At least the three youngest should have answered, since they were too little to attend school yet. The only sound she heard was the tinkling of loosened glass falling to the floor around her. The smaller, individual portraits she'd so lovingly painted hung in shreds along the staircase.

It was in the master bedroom that she'd found Antoine's family, and she'd run from the house as if the devil were chasing her, unwilling to believe what she'd just seen, unable to rid herself of the image. She burst outside and squeezed her eyes shut, trying to control her reaction. *Breathe, Audrey. In, out.* Eventually, her heartbeat slowed, and she became aware of the chill in the air. She opened her eyes, hugging herself, and blinked into the glare. The sky was a pure, breathtaking cerulean blue, and it contained the largest white cloud she had ever seen. It seemed to extend for miles, soft and welcoming and harmless. But when she lowered her gaze, taking in the world below the beautiful cloud, she saw an entirely different story.

It hadn't just been the Antoines' house. The damage was everywhere. Very few windows remained in the buildings around her, and she was painfully aware that these structures were sturdier than where she'd been living just one night earlier. She didn't want to imagine what might have happened to her house. The image of the Antoines' bedroom came to mind, complete with small mangled bodies, and she choked on a sob.

Danny! Where are you, Danny?

She should be with him. She *had* to be with him. *Oh God, Danny.* In a daze, she started walking toward downtown, feeling tiny and vulnerable between the neat line of damaged buildings.

She'd seen smoke and heard explosions, but she hadn't expected to meet with such desolation. Emerging from the sheltered, wealthier streets, she peered down toward the sea and realized there was nothing left. The ground had been flattened for miles, and anything still standing either wobbled or burst into flame as the furnaces of collapsed buildings combusted. Ugly, broken hulls of ships poked through the water where there once had floated majestic, unsinkable vessels manned by sailors, carrying soldiers.

Placing one foot in front of the other, she inched her way down the hill, following her heart toward the harbour, toward their sad little house, though her head screamed at her to stay away. The slope was too much, and her legs followed its angle until she was suddenly running, unable to stop. She reached out, wishing she had a cane to brace her—even better, Danny's arm—but there was nothing. Then it was as if she were floating, the ground beneath her feet swaying like the sea on a cold, grey day, and a roar filled her head, sounding like the ocean on those thrilling, terrifying, stormy nights in Jeddore. When the sensation offered to carry her away, she let herself go.

She awoke to the gentle prodding of leather-gloved hands. Concerned frowns loomed over her, and the voices started to make sense.

". . . hear me? Are you all right? Look, Jeffrey. Her eyes are open. Where's that blasted wagon?"

Audrey's eyes rolled up, seeking darkness again, but the gloves shook her awake. "Come on, girl. Hold still a moment. You're losing a lot of blood."

Her head pounded, and she cried out when someone cradled the back of it, lifting her neck off the ground. Another pair of hands joined the first, and she whimpered helplessly as they wrapped a scarf around her head, covering her eyes. The pressure both soothed and irritated the searing pain on the side of her head. And now that she could see nothing, she wanted to see it all.

"Where are you taking me?" she demanded, trying not to struggle as they lifted her and laid her on a hard surface. It rocked, and she heard the jingling of a harness. A wagon? "What's happening?"

"It's all right, Audrey," came a familiar voice. One of the husbands, she remembered. She'd painted his family. What was the name? King, she recalled. Donald King. She envisioned him as she'd painted him: tall, lean, and bald, decorated only by a pencil-thin black moustache. "You're safe now. We're taking you to the hospital."

She assumed it was King who had brought Pierre Antoine to see her a few days later. She'd had to go through painful reconstructive surgery at the busy hospital, where they'd tried their best to sew her torn cheek back into place. It had been almost entirely ripped from her face when she'd arrived in the wagon. She wondered vaguely if she'd left a terrible bloodstain on the Antoines' sheets, then she shoved the idea away, not wanting to envision his family's fate ever again. Except she knew it would always be in her mind, the violent colours, the torn and terrible bodies, the peace on the children's faces now that they were gone.

But it would remain in her mind. She would never, *never* put it to paper.

The women came to see her, Catherine and some other friends, all feigning concern in their big black hats and high collars. She kept the side of her face out of their view, though she saw them trying to get a glimpse. There was nothing she could do about it. She was deformed now. Ugly beyond belief. It was probably good that Danny couldn't see her like this.

But Pierre hadn't seen it like that. He had come to the hospital and sat beside her for as long as the Red Cross people would let him. He held her hand, and she let him bore her with his stories, first of Boston, then of having to clean up the mess when he got home. His face had tightened at the thought of his family, but he hadn't dwelt on their demise. She told him how sorry she was, and he'd squeezed her hand, thanking her graciously for her condolences. When she was well enough, he brought her to his home, which was quickly being reconstructed. She wasn't surprised to see its steady progress, since Pierre seemed to own most of the construction contracts in the city. He offered her his wife's bedroom, but she'd slept in one of the children's rooms instead. She said she'd prefer a smaller space, not wanting to offend him. The truth was that she never again wanted to open that door and remember what she'd seen. It was all too much.

And then he'd come to her, his dark expression miserable, and confessed that he'd found Danny's name on the Known Dead list. She'd told him it wasn't true—*couldn't* be true—but he'd taken her hands in his and assured her with complete empathy that it was. Danny was dead. Audrey was a twenty-year-old widow.

They'd had no more than months together, she and Danny. Less than twenty-four hours in France, a few months of letters, less than a year of marriage. Did it all even add up to a year?

She'd excused herself, she remembered, then stumbled to her room, neither eating nor speaking for two days. She just sat on her bed, staring at the flowered wallpaper or pushing her good cheek against the tear-soaked pillow. How easy it was to forget the most recent months, to excuse the strain Danny's depression had put on their marriage. How easy it was for her to recall only the tall, handsome soldier watching her from across the road.

But in moments of lucidity, she felt the fire of his hand hitting her cheek, recalled the impact of her body on the floor when his fury had sent her sprawling at his feet. Oh, she'd known he hurt inside, burned with guilt and self-hate, but she had never imagined it might come to this. Never thought him capable of hurting her. Not her Danny.

As the print of his hand on her cheek softened, fading from red on impact to a yellow bruise, she realized it was the last touch of his she would ever feel. That would be the last time he would ever touch her with any kind of emotion. With any kind of . . . anything.

She couldn't go back to his family, because they'd want to know what had happened. How had she survived while he hadn't? Why weren't the newlyweds safe and sound in their own little house, holding together when the world had come apart? If she went back now, she wouldn't be able to lie when they asked what had happened. And that meant she would always be a reminder to them of how their son had changed, how he had shamed them all in that one weak moment. No, she couldn't hurt them like that. She decided it would be better if they thought she'd died along with Danny on that awful morning.

Over time Pierre persuaded her, helped her see how lonely they both were, and how they could help each other with that particular pain. He'd fed her, kept her under his reconstructed roof, given her the best brandy, dressed her in the most beautiful things she'd ever seen. He bought her new, expensive painting supplies, and when the society people started coming together for parties or dinners, Audrey became a fixture on his arm, often wearing a new trinket he'd given her.

With one hand, Danny had slapped her into a whole new world. She'd never consciously chosen this life, but here she was.

Whether she was painting, attending meetings, or going to parties, Audrey was now in the middle of whatever was happening in Halifax. In the past she'd admired these wealthy, influential people from afar, both intrigued and intimidated. Now she had only to walk into a room and someone usually wanted to speak with her. Was it what she wanted? Maybe. And maybe, on some level, she'd needed it—or at least needed to experience it for a while. But for the rest of her life? Of all the life changes she'd struggled through, all the ups and downs, she still wasn't sure where this one fit in.

She was safe, dry, fed, appreciated, even celebrated. Would she give it all up if Danny walked through that door?

She'd known all along that she was Pierre's prize. After all, she was just over half his age, she was still beautiful—despite the scar—and her art made her something exotic. When he offered her the world, she accepted. And when he came to her one night, his breath heavy with whisky, she felt she couldn't turn him away. She closed her eyes and did all she could to imagine herself somewhere else, and she never once objected to his advances.

Because he was right. She was lonely. To the bottom of her soul. Empty. If Pierre noticed the tears on her pillow every night, he made no mention of them.

Pascale would be proud. Audrey had done what she'd had to do to survive. She'd survived the war, the munitions factory, Danny's violence, the explosion, and now she would survive Pierre. She had to.

Over time she came to realize Pierre Antoine was a selfish man, one with a cold heart and little time or regard for others' feelings. She didn't think he'd always been that way, but it could have been that she'd just chosen not to see it. At first she'd only seen him as a kind, interested man, one always curious about her painting, her life. He'd seemed enthusiastic and genuine about helping her and Danny, insisting on sending home clothes his family no longer needed, food they didn't eat—though there had never been any chance that Danny would accept those gifts. He'd paid attention to her as a woman, eventually threw her the party, bought her pretty things. Most importantly, he had believed in her as an artist—or so she thought. As Danny had drawn farther away, Antoine had welcomed her, given her hope and opportunities.

It had been apparent from the first time they'd met that he was a hard man when it came to business, and he hardened further after the explosion. He'd barely taken time to grieve his own family before launching right back into work. In fact, he was busier now than he had been before, as far as she could tell.

Tonight changed everything. Now she knew this man before her was much worse than she'd thought. All the time he'd been showing her off, puffing up with pride around her, making her believe he was rescuing her from a terrible, lonely life, he'd been lying.

"Why didn't you tell me?" she asked softly.

His face darkened and the lips beneath the black moustache tightened. He didn't speak.

"You lied to me, Pierre. He . . . he wasn't dead."

How could this be happening? How could she have trusted him with the most important thing in her life? He'd said Danny was dead, and she'd swallowed the lie. She'd never even checked the lists, not wanting to see the truth of those words. Rage built in her chest and rose up her throat, though she knew it came from anger at herself as much as blame for him.

"My . . . my *husband*, Pierre! My husband has been alive and searching for me all this time, and you told me he was dead! You told him *I* was dead! You watched me grieve for him. How . . . how could you do something like that?"

Pierre scowled at her, then glared furiously at the dwindling onlookers. They caught his warning and shuffled away, but Audrey saw their curious backward glances. *Let them see. Let them know what kind of man he is!*

He put a hand under her elbow again, tried to lead her away, but

Audrey's feet were planted. Seeing the fury in her expression, he adjusted, grabbing her arm tighter and yanking her in the direction he wanted to go. She tried to pry his fingers from her arm as she stumbled down the street beside him, but his grip was like a vise. There would be bruises. When Pierre deemed they were far enough away, he pulled her again so that she whirled around to face him.

"I saved you," he said through his teeth. He shook her with every one of his statements, and her curls bounced. "I rescued you from a terrible life. A waste of a life."

"It was *my* life. Not yours," she hissed.

His eyes were cold. The fingers tightened, and she lifted her chin, determined not to cry. "No, not exactly. Not anymore. I sheltered you. I fed and clothed you. I introduced you to Halifax and made you famous among the well-to-do. You owe me."

The truth behind his words was unavoidable, but she turned her face away, trying to escape it. She'd known all along that he was using her, but she'd chosen to ignore it. In her hopelessness, in her weak, frail attempt to move on without Danny, she'd let herself be sold into becoming a piece of his property. She'd thought she needed him. Thought she was safe and content in his home, surrounded by the best life had to offer. But she'd also thought she was a widow. Then she remembered all those long nights in bed, the quick, often rough way he had of using her body, and she met his eyes.

"I owe you nothing," she said, her voice low. "I gave you more than enough."

He sighed and lifted one corner of his mouth. He was trying to placate her, she could see. Trying to ease this new situation. He wasn't familiar with confrontation. No one argued with Pierre Antoine and got away with it.

"Come now, *ma petite*," he said gently, releasing her arm. He dropped his hand to his side and rubbed his fingers against his thumb as if he felt something sticky. "You must understand. What I did was for the best. You came to me as little more than a gutter rat, and now you are a swan. Would you throw it all away?"

"Yes."

"You would go back to a man who beat you? Who drove you into the street?"

Another truth, and one just as difficult to acknowledge. She fought the turmoil building inside. This was no time for emotions.

"Yes."

He blinked quickly, his smile tightening. "You have a lot to think about. Come back to the soiree now. Have some wine and some food, and let all this settle in your mind. I cannot see a woman as intelligent as you simply walking away without going through all the options." His eyes went to the street, in the direction Danny had taken. "Then again," he said with a shrug, "maybe you have nothing to think about. Your dear, devoted husband appears to have left you here with me. Maybe he no longer wants you after all."

And that was exactly what she feared most.

DANNY

— March 1918 —

THIRTY-SEVEN

❦

The next morning was like any other over the past few months, except it wasn't. Danny woke up, pulled his coveralls over a faded blue shirt, and tugged his grey slouch hat over his hair. He needed a haircut. The brown curls that flicked from under his hat were getting unruly. He poured himself a cup of tea and lit a cigarette, then headed out to the latest site, falling into a rhythm alongside the others, measuring, cutting, hammering, measuring, cutting, hammering.

With every cut of the saw, every pounded nail, Danny thought of Audrey. Saw her there, small and shocked within the shelter of Antoine's arm. She had looked so pretty. So comfortable in the rich materials she wore, with that sizable gem hanging from her neck, surrounded by the cream of society.

The women who emerged from their shiny automobiles in the mornings, bringing food for the orphanage and eventually for the workers, they would know Audrey.

The businessmen who came with contracts and fat cigars, they would know her.

Danny wondered if he still did.

On the other hand, he was fairly sure the children didn't. Danny was somewhat of a hero in the orphanage these days. He brought as many treats as he could afford for the children, then sat and played cards or tiddlywinks with the older ones. With the younger ones he raced hand-carved toy horses around chairs and tables. Anything to entertain them and lighten the monotony of his days. It was impossible to be bored in a roomful of children. These little souls had lost everything. They had no families, no homes, no concept of a future, and yet they laughed and played together. They moved past their injuries, got used to each other's scars, found a way to get along. In their eyes, no one was better or worse than any other.

Mick came by the construction site later that morning. He tugged Danny out back and produced a bottle of ale for each of them. They hadn't spoken the night before, after Danny's hasty departure from the protest. Danny had gone home, gone to bed, then pretended not to hear Mick's noisy entrance a couple of hours later. But he couldn't avoid the questions forever, and questions there would be. Mick was king of those. If only Danny were half so good at answers.

"You gonna explain last night?" Mick asked as they leaned back against a new wall.

"Why?"

Mick barked out a laugh, then coughed. "Okay. Right you are. None of my business. It's just I turned around and all of a sudden my buddy's gone and there's a well-dressed lynch mob on his tail. Come on. A fella's got a right to be curious, don't he?"

"Yeah, yeah," Danny said, giving him a tired smile. "I guess you do." He took a long swallow from the bottle. "Thanks for this. It's thirsty work." Danny stared at his palms, then concentrated on picking a sliver from the tip of one thumb. "Saw Audrey last night."

Mick choked on his beer. "Audrey? Your wife, Audrey?"

"One and the same," Danny said. "Seems she's alive after all."

"Okay," Mick said slowly. "So why didn't I see her in our apartment when I got home?"

"She had a better offer."

Danny didn't bother keeping anything from Mick. He figured the newspaperman would figure out the answers anyway. So he explained everything, including the wreck he'd made of his marriage, and his question of why on earth Audrey might ever want to come back to him.

Mick listened in silence, which was strange because Danny was used to Mick's endless peppering of questions. At the end of Danny's story, Mick was still quiet. He sipped from his beer, and for a few minutes all they heard was the monotonous rhythm of saws and hammers.

"Antoine's not a great choice," Mick finally said. "From what I've been hearing, the man's not exactly clean, if you catch my meaning."

"No? Not a model citizen?" Danny's voice twisted with sarcasm.

"Word is he ain't averse to getting his pretty hands dirty."

"Yeah, well, I don't want to think about his hands right now, Mick, thanks all the same. They were taking good care of my wife last time I saw them. Aw, hell. I don't know what to do. If I were a good man, I'd just leave her with him. Let her live the good life. Let her forget about the mistake she made marrying me."

"What a bunch of hogwash," Mick said, shaking his head. "I gotta say I'm surprised. I never would have taken you for that kind of fella, Danny."

"What kind is that?"

"You know. The fella who's always going on about how everybody else is better than him. That kind of fella. Sure, I know the war took a lot outta you. It took a lot out of most of us, and you got hit hard because of your leg and your buddies. I know all that. I know it's been hard, finding what you're good at, and I figure you're still finding it. But look at what you're doing now. Half these homes have your handiwork nailed into them. You've helped kids no one else had the time for. You're always the guy people go to. Someone needs something? I tell 'em, 'Go to Danny.'"

Danny snorted, then finished his beer. "Yep, that's me. At least I'm good for something." He stood, ready to go back to work. "She's better off without me. Anyhow, that's why I took off on you last night. Sorry about that. And thanks for the beer."

Mick glared at him with such disgust, Danny felt the sting of Mick's words before they hit the air.

"You leave her with Antoine, you're not half the man I thought you were. And you know what? You can get your own damn beer next time."

"Yeah, well, maybe I deserve that, and maybe I don't," Danny said, starting to bristle. "I don't need your opinion on my character, thanks. Why don't you go stir up some trouble? When you're ready, come get me and I'll be your tough guy. In the meantime, don't you worry about me."

Mick tossed a grimace of disappointment over his shoulder as he walked away, and Danny tried to ignore it. He didn't need to see it. Truth was, he was disappointed enough for both of them.

He resumed his place, nailing up a wall alongside a crew of equally silent men. What was it, he asked himself, that had made Audrey love him in the first place? Why would the girl have left everything to come to him? Well, sure. They'd started with physical attraction. He could still recall the quick focus in her eyes when they'd spotted each other by the broken-down wagon. Then the letters—all those words back and forth between them, all the things he'd never say to anyone else. And she'd actually been interested in what he was talking about. That was one thing he'd always found amazing. And when she'd seen the mess of his body, she'd still loved him. Every time she touched him, he thought he might burst into flame.

So when had it gone wrong? Danny knew why, just not when. He'd felt self-hatred building from the moment he'd woken up in the hospital missing a leg. The cloud had grown heavier every day, blocking any possibility of sun. But Audrey'd stuck with him, even when he snapped at her. She'd come willingly enough when he picked up their lives and moved them to the city. Then again, he could lie to himself and say that had been partially for her benefit. Her art was so good, he reckoned she'd outgrown East Jeddore and all those little places. But she'd never been truly content in Halifax. He guessed maybe it was because they'd gone there together but ended up spending so much time apart.

Poor Audrey. Followed her heart and it had led to a dead end. Apparently, she'd found an escape route, though.

So now what? He figured what he really needed to do was answer the same questions he'd just thrown at Mick. Which was the better idea: go after Audrey and bring her back, or leave her in the rich comfort of Antoine's care? If only they'd had more time the night before. If only he could have spent more time reading her eyes before Antoine appeared like a knight in shining armour.

Damn! Danny stuck his thumb into his mouth and sucked on the spot he'd just hammered. He had to stop thinking like this. It wasn't helping any.

THIRTY-EIGHT

For the next week, days came and went, one house rose beside another, and Danny tried every day to move on and forget Audrey. But how could he, when she was part of every breath?

Then one afternoon she was there. Danny was up high, working on the rafters of one of the new houses. He had taken a break to catch his breath, wiped his brow with the back of one hand, and peered down at the site's visitors. Planners and reporters came every few days, watching the progress and taking pictures for posterity. Women didn't come as often. They needed special clearance in order to get into the construction area, and one needed influence to get clearance.

Audrey climbed out of a big black car in the company of three or four similarly pastel-clad women. They wore large hats that were the style of the day, and Audrey's brown curls were tucked underneath her wide brim. She didn't see Danny, so he took the luxury of staring.

She was the smallest, and she stood back a bit from the main group of women. They pointed and gestured, discussing something inconsequential to Danny. One of the women touched Audrey's arm and she nodded agreeably, then turned away.

Danny knew what she was seeing, even if no one else did. She was noticing the shapes and expressions of the buildings, the lines and colours. Like the trees and grasses along the Eastern Shore that had always captivated her. Audrey found beauty in everything around her—including him, he thought bitterly. After today she would go back to wherever she was living and recreate this scene, infuse the brush strokes with her emotions. She'd see the neat row of houses, their cottage-style yards and fences, the individual designs they'd given each home. She'd notice the men working, backs to her, concentrating on their work. Would she see him? Would he appear in her art again?

It became a game. He watched her, noticing every gesture and expression, and willed her to notice him. *If you look up and see me, it means you still love me. It means you want me to bring you home.* It was a terrible game to play. If she never looked up, then—

She glanced sharply to the side and up, locking eyes with Danny's.

He wondered what he should do. If he truly wanted her to live a comfortable life, he should tap the brim of his own hat in greeting, then turn back to his work. But he was terrified of doing that. She'd never come after him. She'd be afraid of his temper. And this might be his last chance. *Love me, Audrey,* he thought. *Please love me.*

Her lips moved, and he saw his name. She was thirty feet away when he saw the first teardrop trickle down her cheek.

What did she see? The cruel man who had broken her heart? Or could she see a man changed, which Danny certainly was. He rarely drank anymore, and never to excess. His insecurities—or most of them at least—had burned to ash inside one of the Richmond houses, just after he'd rescued a little girl from the flames. He had found the three little boys in the collapsed basement, trapped with their dead mother. Every spare moment he'd spent with them, trying to make their lives—and his—a little more bearable. He'd gone to Mick and they'd run that national campaign trying to find homes for all the orphans. It had been his idea, his desire to help that had made it work.

The truth was, he had done well—and he had done good.

But Audrey couldn't possibly know all that about him. Antoine hadn't even told her Danny was alive.

Suddenly it seemed Danny's entire life depended on getting to her, telling her how wrong he'd been, how much he needed her. He reached for the ladder and threw himself onto the rung, his peg leg knocking like an out-of-control clock as he made his way down. He turned to run toward her, and she met him halfway as she always had.

Neither of them spoke. It was enough to take in each other's presence in the daylight. So much had changed. In the sun, the darker shade of pink at the side of her face was more obvious, a scar she would bear forever, though the wide-brimmed hat shadowed her disfigurement.

She sniffed, then hid her mouth behind a delicate hand. Her fingertips were dark, stained by oil paints. He liked that she wasn't wearing gloves. He stepped closer but was afraid to touch her.

"Can we talk, Audrey? Can I tell you—"

Her chin quivered, lips pressed tight together for control. Her eyes pleaded, and he hoped he read them right.

"I've changed," he blurted. "And I'm sorry. So, so sorry."

He took another step and dared himself to reach for her hands, now tucked under her arms. She took a deep breath that hitched a couple of times, then lowered trembling fingers onto his palms. He curled his hands around hers, wondering which of them was more nervous.

"Audrey, I need to tell you that I think I understand your life. You are beautiful and healthy, and, well, except for right now, you seem happy. I wouldn't blame you at all if you decided to stay with him, to live a good life. If you stay with him, you can have whatever you want." Her cheeks blushed a little, and he hated that. It bolstered him for the next bit, though. "If you come back to me, Audrey, if you come back, I can't offer anything he can. But . . . but I can tell you no one will ever love you like I do. No one."

He became aware that he was squeezing her fingers hard, and he relaxed his grip.

"Danny—"

"Wait, Audrey. I gotta tell you. You'll understand, I think, you with your paints. I'm not saying this for pity, because you know how much I hate that." They exchanged a cautious smile. "I just need you to know that my life without you is blacks and greys. You took all the colour when you left. And when I thought you were dead, well, I couldn't see much that would make me want to go on. Then I saw you that night, and ever since then I can't think straight."

"Oh, Danny," she said quietly. "I am sorry for all your pain. But I've been hurting, too. For a long time. I have always loved you, and you have always hated yourself. I did what I could, but it was too hard. All you did was hurt yourself and push me away. I can't live that way any longer."

"But you wouldn't have to," he said. "I've changed."

"You look well," she admitted. "Still living rough?"

"Rough, but healthy. And rough for a reason. I work hard, Audrey. I work and I make money, and I do what I can to help."

She wasn't going to make it easy for him, he could see. She gave him a skeptical scowl, but her lips were soft. "And when work is done at the end of the day? What then? The other men come over and drink away your money? You go out to visit the ladies in the taverns and get home in time to go to work? What kind of life is that? Yes, I've lived well these past few months, just like you say. I've lived with people who like to talk about art and music, not just pretty girls, or which man is the strongest. These people like me. They value what I do. They make me feel . . . special."

He was losing. He could feel it in the urgency of her words. *No, no, no.* She couldn't leave him again.

"You and I, we aren't the same people we were, Danny. Neither of us. I'm not the same innocent young farm girl you married."

"You are, Audrey. You're good and sweet and full of life. You're everything. Don't push me away."

She bit her lower lip. "I . . ."

"What? What has you . . . Oh. Antoine." She nodded, and he swallowed his pride. "Does he love you, Audrey?" he asked, his voice gruff. "Would he die for you? Because I would. I would give everything I had if I knew I could have you with me." He tucked one finger under her chin and lifted her gaze to his. "Look at me, Audrey. Tell me you love him and

I'll walk away. I'll never bother you again. I'll leave the city and disappear. Tell me that."

Tears spilled over her cheeks again, but she didn't hesitate. "I have only ever loved you, Danny."

A woman approached from behind. Danny saw her come closer, observing him with wary eyes. "Are you all right, Audrey?" she asked.

Audrey dropped his hand and whirled toward the woman. "Hello, Catherine. Yes. I'm fine."

Catherine squeezed her lips into a tight little circle of distaste. "He's not bothering you, is he? I've seen him, you know. He's one of those protester types."

Danny snorted and held out a hand. "Nice to meet you, ma'am. The name's Danny. Danny Baker."

"Catherine, I'd like you to meet my husband," Audrey said quietly.

Catherine took a startled step back, ignoring his offering. "Really? Well. Isn't that something. I thought Pierre said your husband was dead."

"He did," Audrey said.

"Apparently he was mistaken," Danny said. "I'm well enough."

"So I see," Catherine said, studying his peg. "And you've come for your wife? Take her back to . . . wherever you come from? Maybe she can carry one of those signs you folks are so good at carrying."

"Actually, I'm working here. And if she comes back with me, it's up to her."

Catherine laughed. A short, derisive sound that raised Danny's hackles. She wiggled her well-shaped eyebrows. "I have a feeling Audrey won't be leaving Pierre any time soon."

Audrey gasped. "Catherine!"

"What?" Catherine asked, feigning innocence. "He is your husband. He should be told."

Danny became aware of a definite shift in the air. "I should be told what?"

"You may leave now, Catherine," Audrey said coolly. "You've done enough."

The woman gave Danny a smooth smile, then waltzed back toward the other women, all of whom watched with owl-like expressions from a few feet away.

"I can't come with you, Danny," Audrey whispered.

"Why not?"

She took another long breath and blew it out between her lips. He felt it tickle his cheek and couldn't help inhaling.

"Because I'm pregnant with Antoine's baby," she declared, lifting her chin. "And I'm sure you don't want to spend your life with a woman who fell into bed with another man as soon as she thought her husband was dead. Especially one who is pregnant."

Danny felt dizzy. "You're going to have a baby?"

"I am."

"And you . . . You won't come back to me because you think I wouldn't want you like that?"

"That's . . . part of it, yes."

Danny tapped the bottom of his peg leg against the ground, trying to think. He fought back the mental image of Antoine on top of Audrey, his black beard scratching the gentle slope of her belly, his thick hands pawing her body. The pain of her betrayal was like nothing he'd ever experienced. Closing over him, suffocating him, leaving him dizzy. But if he wanted her back—and *oh,* how he wanted her back—he'd have to say just the right thing. Now it was she whose pride hung in the air, and he knew first-hand how heavy that burden was.

"You thought I was dead," he reasoned.

"I did." Her voice was tiny but brave. Her eyes, though, they were so full of regret he couldn't stand it. "And I did—" A little sob cut through the words. "I did what I had to do."

He swallowed, battling the ache in his throat. He would *not* cry. *Stand up for this woman for once in your life,* he thought. *Be the man she needs you to be.*

"I could hardly expect you to stop your life. You're beautiful, and intelligent, and talented. Any man would want you," he managed. "I've always thought it was too good to be true, that you loved me."

"But I did," she said, confused.

"Yeah. That always amazed me. But the thing is, Audrey, I still do. I want you back, and if it means Antoine's baby comes with you, I'd welcome the little tyke and love it like my own."

"No, you wouldn't," she said slowly. "You'd always think of Pierre when you saw the baby."

Danny blinked hard. "I can't say I'm not jealous. I'll never be able to say I'm okay with the thought of you with another man. That'd be a lie. But I do understand. Things happen. And now you're pregnant. You and I, we were never able to get you pregnant, and I know how bad you wanted to have a kid. You may have trouble believing this, but if I get to be the one to see this baby grow in you, to watch you become a mother, well, yeah. I'd love the baby. Because it would be half you."

"But what would your family say?"

He mustn't get too excited, but it was difficult to keep hope from lighting his eyes. If she could even think about his family, maybe she'd think about coming back. "They'd be overjoyed to see you," he assured her with a casual shrug. "They all think you're dead."

"But—"

"Audrey, you know my family." Except maybe she didn't. Maybe she hadn't contacted them because of the baby, because she'd been so ashamed. "It wouldn't have mattered to them. They'd love you no matter what."

Something changed in her face. At first it was as if she wanted to bring up something else, but she decided against it. In that moment it was as if all the tension in her body suddenly let go. She looked like she had when they'd first met, only more fragile. Very young. Every muscle in his body wanted to hold her tight, take care of her, but he waited. He'd waited this long. He could wait a little longer.

"Do you think we could go back to Jeddore?" she asked quietly.

She was so beautiful. So trusting. Like she had been before. Before he'd ruined it all. Now here she was, offering him a chance to save his life.

"Is the ocean wet?" he asked gently. He'd asked her that same question when she'd first arrived in Canada. When she'd asked if he wanted to take her home.

"Oh, Danny," she said, any hesitation in her expression dissolving. Her eyes, dark with misery, filled with tears. "I am so sorry."

"Not nearly as sorry as I am," he said. His hand stroked her damp cheek, his thumb smudging away her tears. His fingertips reached the scar on her cheek and she instinctively withdrew, looking embarrassed. He smiled, but kept his fingers on the smooth pink skin, skimming across the scar in a soothing movement.

"What was it someone very wise once said to me?" he asked, thinking back to a warm, mellow morning, the sunlight pouring through the bedroom window and spilling over his young wife's face. "Ah yes. I'm touching you because I want to give you pleasure. And it gives me pleasure as well. And your cheek? Scarred or not, I'm touching a part of you that's still there."

He leaned closer, and she met him halfway. Their lips touched, and Danny forgot everything but Audrey. She was his again. He could breathe.

THIRTY-NINE

❧

"I have to speak with Pierre," she said when they stepped apart.

Danny swallowed his disgust. He was going to have to move past this if he was going to keep her. "What'll you say to him?"

Her hesitation was over quickly. "I'll tell him . . . I'll tell him he should have told me you were alive. He should have done what he promised he'd do. I'll remind him that you're my husband."

"He won't be too happy about all that. What about the baby?"

Audrey chewed on her lip. It was a new habit he had noticed. She seemed almost . . . frightened. "Well, I'll have to tell him anyway."

"What does he say about the baby?"

She puffed out a breath and glanced to the side, avoiding his eyes. "He was quite angry about it, actually. He said he didn't want any more children. He said—" She scraped one of her boots against the road, uncomfortable, but he kept his gaze on her face. "He said I would become fat and useless like his wife."

What an honourable man, Danny thought. "Why did you stay with him, then?"

Her liquid eyes blinked against the late-afternoon sun. "Where else could I go?"

"I'm coming with you," he decided. "I'll make sure you're safe."

"Oh yes, Danny. Please do."

"Tonight?"

She took a deep breath and shut her eyes. "Yes. Tonight."

Danny collected his things and spoke to the foreman, who let him go early. The women with Audrey stared at her with disbelief when she said she wasn't going back with them. They bustled into the back of their car, exchanging glances and words.

"I won't have to tell him much," Audrey said, sighing. "Catherine and the others will speak with him first."

"Maybe you won't have to go at all."

"Of course I will. It's his baby, after all."

"Right," Danny said quietly, suitably scolded. "But for now, come on along to Mick's place, will you? I want you to meet him. And I'd like to put on a fresh shirt if we have time."

She smiled and went with him. He wanted to wrap his arm around her, where it belonged, but there was still a lingering crevasse between them he couldn't yet cross. A solid space. He would have to figure out how to get around it.

———

Mick was home when they walked in. He came out of the back room all businesslike and gruff, rolling up his shirt sleeves. He had pulled his newsman's hat down low, half covering his eye patch so he appeared more disreputable than ever. When he caught sight of Audrey, he stopped short and slid off his hat.

"Ma'am," he said, offering a little bow.

"Mick? This is my wife, Audrey."

A grin spread across Mick's face. "Oh, is it? Well, Daniel my boy, I'm so pleased to hear that." He turned to Audrey. "Audrey? I'm not sure I've ever been so happy to meet someone. The boy's been a mess without you.

Practically useless to me around here."

She chuckled. "Well, I do hope things will improve now."

"Mick was in the battalion with me," Danny said.

Audrey tilted her head to the side and squinted. "I thought so," she said. "I thought I recognized you. We didn't speak at the time," she assured him when he seemed confused. "You would have no reason to remember me. It was a busy time."

"I'm sorry? I—"

"Mick, do you remember the farmhouse where we went once, and Audrey was there with her grandmother? We fixed their wagon and—"

"I do!" Mick exclaimed, eyes wide. "I do! Well, and if that ain't the craziest thing. So you and Danny—the two of you . . . Well, I'll be!" He slapped his thigh, then Danny's shoulder. "Good for you! He always talked about you in the trenches, you know. Couldn't stop talking, showing us your picture." The newspaperman's expression changed from one of friendly recognition to one that carried a little suspicion. "So you did survive the blast. We'd heard you didn't. Where have you—"

"Mix-up somewhere along the road," Danny said. "Her name was . . . left off the lists."

"I have been living with Pierre Antoine," Audrey admitted.

There were a few beats of surprised silence as Mick took that in.

Audrey chewed her lip. "I know how that sounds. He found me at the medical centre and brought me home. Poor man lost his wife and children, and he tended me when I was ill."

The men exchanged a fleeting glance.

"What was I supposed to do?" she demanded, clenching her fists at her sides. "I was alone with no money. He told me you were *dead,* Danny. He told me you died at the docks."

"I know, Audrey. I understand. It's all right."

"No, Danny. It's not all right." She turned away. "None of this is all right."

"Audrey," Mick asked, interrupting their quiet conversation. "Did Antoine talk about his work a lot?"

She glanced toward him, startled, as if she'd forgotten he was there.

"No, not really."

"He never mentioned anything about contracts?"

"No," she said, frowning. "Not to me. I heard him talking with the other men when they were all sitting around blowing cigar smoke. Sometimes I heard him on the telephone."

"He has a lot of friends, don't he? A lot of well-dressed fellas, I mean."

"I suppose. And yes, everyone near Pierre dresses well." She pulled a gold chain from under the top of her dress and revealed the gem Danny had seen before. Blue, he saw, like her eyes, and rimmed by an ornate gold frame.

"He gave this to me," she said. "It belonged to his wife, he said. He used to say he'd have liked to give me earrings, but they only made my scar more obvious." She snorted softly. "He thought that was funny."

"Nice guy," Danny muttered.

"So now you're coming back to Danny, huh?" Mick asked. She nodded. "Good. That's good. Tell me, did Antoine ever give you anything else besides the necklace? Any money?"

Audrey's jaw dropped with disgust. "I would never take money from him! He paid me in the beginning to paint, but after that I was lucky to be given a place to stay and food on my plate."

"A place to stay. That's right," Danny said under his breath.

"Give the girl a break, Danny."

Audrey glanced uneasily between the two, then sighed. "Mick, you should know something. Danny's giving me a very big break. He wants me back . . . even though I'm pregnant."

Mick's eyebrows shot up. "Pregnant! Well, now, I don't know how to answer that." Danny turned away. "Should I say congratulations?"

"I've always wanted to be a mother," she said, her smile tremulous. "But I only ever imagined it would be Danny's child. I never meant—"

Danny snorted, avoiding both their gazes. "But surely you knew, going with him like that—"

She whirled to face him. "What was I supposed to do? I was alone. You were dead! I had no money, and my face was all cut up. Pierre lost his family and took me home. He cared for me."

"And you got pregnant," Danny said.

Her cheeks instantly reddened. "Yes. I got pregnant."

"And how does Mr. Antoine feel about that? About the baby?" Mick asked.

Her gaze dropped to her hands in her lap. "He's . . . he's not happy. He wants me to . . . give it up after it's born."

"Nice guy," Danny said. "Adding to the orphan population."

Her voice dropped dangerously. "Danny, you said you could handle this. I can't change what it is. What is done is done."

"But still. You stayed with him."

"Where was I to go? The street? Penniless and pregnant? I may not be very smart, but I'm not stupid, either. I know a good thing when I have it."

It would have been so easy for Danny to rant, then storm out, to leave her as she'd left him. But leaving was the easy part. After that there would be living to do. And Danny knew he couldn't live without her.

Mick broke the uneasy silence. "Did Antoine have a lot of meetings in his home?"

"Yes, he did." She blinked a few times, regaining her composure.

"Do you remember the people who came to the meetings? Their names?"

"Some. Why?"

Danny looked at Mick, who said nothing, only returned his gaze. Words passed between them, though. *Go ahead,* Danny urged. *Tell her.*

Mick tapped the end of his pencil on the table, and Danny had a feeling he knew exactly what he was thinking. How exactly was he going to break it to Audrey that she'd been living with a louse? That she'd slept with a snake?

He sniffed and leaned back in his chair, gauging her reaction. "It's only Antoine's no choir boy, you know? He's got quite a reputation around the financial markets."

"Of course. They say he's an excellent businessman."

"And quite a character."

"He is," Audrey said. "Very entertaining and charming. But he has a bad temper, too. Unpredictable and vicious. Like a tiger. You should stay out of his way, Mick."

The devil twinkled in Mick's eyes. "I love tigers."

"We're headed to his house tonight," Danny said. "To tell him she's coming back to me."

"That's bound to meet with a friendly reception," Mick said with a chuckle.

"I don't care how he reacts. Audrey's my wife." He darted a nervous glance her way, and she smiled, reassuring him. "He has no right to keep her there."

"Sure, sure," Mick said. "I'm only saying he won't be real happy."

"I don't expect he will be, but it has to be done."

Mick winked. "Watch your back, pal. He has some pretty big friends to go along with his tiger temper."

"I ain't scared."

"Oh, I know you ain't. Only too well, my friend. I'm just saying to be on the lookout."

Danny assumed Mick's earlier grin. "Who's going to warn him about me?"

FORTY

At about six o'clock Danny and Audrey arrived at Antoine's front door. The sun still shone on its polished wood surface, and the couple stood side by side, staring at it.

Danny tugged her coat sleeve. "You're sure, right? That you want me instead? Because this sure is a pretty house."

"It is," she agreed. "And it's warm. And he always serves delicious meals and fine wine."

"Seems like you could have been happy, here with the rich folks. Won't you miss it?"

"Of course. Some of it. I've done things I never imagined while I was here. I met the mayor! I've tasted champagne, Danny—"

"It'll be hard to go back to beer."

She peered up at him from under her lashes, mischievous. "I prefer the taste of beer."

"What about the painting?"

"I'll never stop painting," she said. "But maybe we could just visit the city once in a while, and I could paint on special occasions. People here really like what I do."

"So . . . you're not sure?"

She didn't smile this time. In fact, her expression was unhappy. Danny's palms went slick.

"You're not, are you?" he asked. "You're looking at me like I'm making you do something you don't want to do. Like you're sad. If you'd rather stay here, I'll understand. I have nothing to offer. Probably never will."

She let out a long breath, and Danny's heart rate soared. Then her hand went to his arm, her little fingers latched on to his sleeve. She wanted something from him, he could see. Was she going to bargain for something? Because whatever it was, he'd do it.

But her voice wasn't demanding. It was soft, almost pleading. "Danny, you spend every minute telling me you have nothing to offer. Nothing to give me. But tell me this: did I ever ask you for anything? All I ever asked was that you promise never to leave me. And you did promise me that." He swallowed hard, and she went on. "Can you never see yourself like I do? I don't want to spend the rest of my life with someone who is always making excuses. I want *you,* Danny. You are all I ever wanted. Not this," she said, hooking her necklace with one finger. "Not this house, either. I'd live in a fish shack with you, Danny, as long as you believed in yourself."

She was right. She was always right, and he could kick himself for all the wasted time. He held her gaze. "I'll be the man you think I can be, Audrey. I'll be the one you came here for."

"Don't do it just for me."

"No. I understand. I do. I've changed a lot since you left, and I'll prove it to you."

Keeping her eyes on his, Audrey leaned forward, then lifted to her toes so she could kiss him lightly on the lips. His pulse raced like it used to, before she'd left. He wanted to pull her against him, take her in his arms, and escape into the bright solstice night with her. But they had a job to do. He stepped back, all business.

"Let's do this." He knocked on the door and waited, admiring the new doorframe. They would have had to replace all the stolen blankets and pillows as well, he thought with a secret smile. And that beautiful dining room table. He wondered if Antoine had ever recognized his own things when they'd shown up at the hospital.

The young maid who answered the door scowled at Danny, letting her eyes drift from his head to his shabbily clad toes. He almost thought she might shut the door again, but Audrey stepped forward with an authority Danny hadn't seen in her before.

"Good evening, Margaret."

The girl's eyes widened. "Good evening, Mrs. Baker."

She'd kept his name. Danny practically swelled with pride.

Audrey stepped past the startled Margaret. "Is Mr. Antoine in the sitting room?"

"He is. With Mr. Callahan. He's been asking about you, and he isn't happy. Suzanne kept your supper warm for you."

Audrey gave her a short nod and tilted her head forward as she removed her hat. Danny's cap was already in his hands. He stood back, careful not to interfere in her business, and noticed her nibbling her lip. Ah. She wasn't nearly as confident as she appeared. He brushed a hand against her back for reassurance.

"Shall I tell him you're here?"

"Don't trouble yourself, Margaret. You have other things to do. I'll show myself in."

Margaret cast a doubtful glance at Danny, and Audrey grabbed his hand. "This is my husband," she said.

Danny wanted to laugh at the little maid's open-mouthed reaction, but he didn't. Only squeezed Audrey's damp fingers.

She led him down the hallway, and a strange memory swept through him, bringing back that unforgettable day. He had been in this house before. There was a master bedroom over his head here, he recalled, and down from there was the child's bed in which he had slept on that frozen nightmare of a night. Plush new carpeting sank beneath his foot and his peg with every step—a far cry from the crunching of glass that had been there before. It was warm in the house, almost stifling within the velvet-papered walls, and Danny remembered the whistling urgency of the wind that night, the small snowdrifts that had piled inside the absent windows just as it had inside those lesser homes. And the way that same snow had piled over the remains of other houses, like dirt on graves.

He wondered how long it had taken Antoine to replace the big, impressive windows, to repaint the damaged walls, to send his servants out to purchase more quilts and pillows. He wanted to tell Audrey how desperately he had searched every room in the place that night, searching for her. He wanted to share the loneliness that had never quite gone away, that gut feeling that she was gone, swallowed up by the wind and the fire and the snow.

She had dropped his hand by this point and was walking with purpose, shrugging back her shoulders so she stood taller. Her silhouette faded in and out before him as she passed by lamps and dark spots in the hall.

He could share all that with her later. It felt good, knowing there would be another time.

The wall of defence to Antoine's sitting room was a heavy oak door, but there was also a small vertical window in the wall where Audrey stopped, just out of sight. Without taking her eyes from the man inside, she spoke to Danny in barely more than a whisper.

"Don't say anything, Danny. Let me speak. He won't want to discuss this business with anyone but me."

"Is it all right I'm here?"

"I'd be too frightened to do this without you."

Antoine sat across from the window, leaning back in a navy armchair, cigar smoke curling from the brown stub between his fingers. He appeared to be speaking with someone, and the low rumble of men's voices carried through the walls. When Audrey showed her face in the window, Danny saw a shadow of irritation cross Antoine's expression. He said something to excuse himself, then strode toward the door. He flung it open, appearing in a flash of gold-embroidered waistcoat and slicked black hair. A surge of blood rushed into Danny's fingertips at the sight of the man.

"Where the devil have you—" He stopped short at sight of Danny, and his words slowed. "Well, Mr. Baker. What an unexpected pleasure. Thank you for escorting Audrey back safely. The streets can be a dangerous place for a beautiful woman."

"They can indeed," Danny said cordially. He would have been happy to jump in and say more, but he had promised Audrey he would keep quiet. Danny was limited to playing the role of observer.

"I apologize for making you worry, Pierre, but I've been with my husband," she said, giving Danny a tiny smile. "There was really no cause for concern, because I'm always safe when I am with Danny."

"So I see," Pierre said, eyes narrowed. He turned toward Danny, as if dismissing her altogether. "Thank you for returning her to me. I shall have my man drive you back to your—"

Danny laughed, surprising himself. "*Returning* her to you? Excuse me? I ain't returning her to anyone. She's mine."

Beside him, Audrey bit her lip, but she didn't try to shush him. Her gaze shifted to Pierre's face.

Antoine's expression was like steel, but it didn't bother Danny. He'd met up with much worse, and he'd beaten them all. He might have lacked a leg, but he stood a head taller than Antoine and ten years younger.

"You see, since she's found out I'm still alive—which you chose to lie about—she wants to come home with me. We're just stopping in to collect her things and say thank you very much." He gritted his teeth, holding back the pressing urge to crush the man's face between his hands. "Thank you for taking such . . . good care of my wife."

"It has been my *pleasure,*" the little man finally said, his words dripping like grease off bacon.

"I imagine it has been," Danny replied.

Audrey glanced nervously between the men, then stepped into the conversation. "I am very sorry, Pierre. I know this is difficult, but I obviously can't stay here with you. I'm married, and I have missed my husband very much."

"Is that right?" Pierre said, cocking an eyebrow. "You didn't seem to miss him much when you were here. Indeed, I thought you were quite . . . satisfied with the arrangements."

She blushed, and a growl rumbled in Danny's chest. "Regardless of how things might have been," he said, "she's coming home with me."

"I'll go get my things," Audrey said, backing uneasily from the room. "I'll be right back."

The men stared at each other after she had gone, the air thick with fury.

"How dare you?" Pierre hissed. Danny raised his eyebrows. "How dare you take her from all this so she can live in squalor in a filthy hut somewhere? She deserves better. Especially . . . now."

Danny closed his eyes. He had been wondering how long it would take before Antoine came to this. When he opened them again, he let them sparkle with a hint of mockery.

"She decided she would rather live in a hut with me than spend another moment with you."

"And now she'll have the bastard—"

"Whom you didn't want. And who will become my child," Danny answered readily. "What's mine is hers, what's hers is mine, after all. That's part of a wedding contract, I believe. Although I'd heard your own understanding of marriage was somewhat different from that. I always wondered: did your wife turn a blind eye to all those sweet little honey pots so's you'd leave her alone?"

"Why, I should have you arrested—"

"You could, couldn't you? Make my life miserable, I mean. You have so many people in your pockets. It's impressive, actually."

Antoine's grim mask hardened, and Danny felt a tremor of concern. "Oh, I could indeed, Mr. Baker. I could make your life very unhappy. In fact, I wouldn't start feeling too comfortable if I were you."

"Thank you for the warning." A creak from the top of the stairs alerted them both to Audrey's arrival. Danny's blood sang with victory. "Ah. Here she is. My lovely bride."

Audrey padded down the plush runner covering the wood stairs, following a maid who carried one of her bags. The other bag, which he could see contained her art supplies, Audrey carried herself.

"Got everything?" Danny asked Audrey. She faced Antoine, taking the bag from the maid.

"Pierre, thank you for all you did for me. I hope you understand this is best for all of us."

"I fail to see how this benefits you, Audrey," he said roughly.

"I told you about Danny."

"Yes, you talked about him constantly. To the point of annoyance. I know all about his drinking, and how he hit you."

"You also know I missed him every minute."

"Not every minute," Antoine reminded her, staring pointedly at her belly.

She swallowed hard, her mouth twisted with disgust. "Yes, Pierre. *Every* minute."

FORTY-ONE

Mick was scarce that night, and Danny knew it was because he wanted to give his friend room to get reacquainted with Audrey. They walked into the quiet kitchen and Danny felt as if he had to dust off the chairs before offering one to her. This new Audrey was so sophisticated, with her hair all curled, her lips still carrying a light tinge of red lipstick. She wasn't quite meeting his eyes yet.

He set the kettle to boil because he knew she'd want tea. When it was boiled, he set Mick's best china cup in front of her, and she sipped daintily through the steam. He sat across from her, blowing on his own cup before drinking the entire thing down and scalding his tongue in the process. He did it on purpose, needing something to shock him out of his daze. Her eyes were down, her fingers tracing lines on the table. So many questions. In a way, he knew exactly how she felt.

"What happened that morning, Danny?" Her voice was soft, afraid. "What happened to you? Our house is gone. Where were you?"

"At the docks." He cleared his throat. "After you left, I . . . lost my mind. Johnny came home, and he and I went to the tavern. We slept in the warehouse. Never made it home."

He could tell from the tightness of her expression that she hated remembering that morning—and the night before—as much as he did. "So Johnny was with you?"

"He was. But he's not anymore. The explosion, it—"

"Oh no." Her words were barely more than a whisper, and her whole face squeezed tight with grief. "Oh, Danny."

"He was right there with me, you know?" Danny didn't need to work hard to summon Johnny's face. His hangover had left the skin dark under his eyes, but life had still shone in them. "One minute I could have reached out and grabbed him, the next he was gone."

She closed her eyes, then covered her face with her hands, and he fought back his own sobs as she gave in to hers. "Oh, poor Johnny," she breathed. As the worst of it eased, she wiped away what she could of the tears. "I'm so sorry you had to go through that alone."

He couldn't speak for a moment. "I miss him," he finally said.

She'd reached across and grabbed his hands before he could cry, and the hot tears streaming down her cheeks could just as easily have been his. But he'd already cried so much. He needed to move on. Audrey was back. He had to move forward.

"What about you?" he asked. "You're okay now?"

She told him how she'd gone to Antoine's house that night after their fight, devastated and lost. He'd welcomed her in, and she'd fallen instantly asleep in the quiet room on the main floor.

"In the morning . . . I forgot where I was. It was like the war had come to find me, and my face was bleeding but it was too dark to see. Antoine had gone away for a business meeting, taken a train early that morning, so I was alone with his family." She faltered. "And they—"

"I know," he said. "I came to look for you later and I saw them, covered them up. Oh, if only I'd found you there!"

"I left right away. I needed to know what was going on, and I was so afraid after I found them there . . ."

"I didn't get there until late. I waited, stayed the night there, but you—"

"I was in the hospital. Someone found me and brought me in."

The months of separation, of questions, of hopelessness, hung between them, bringing back the pain all over again. He knew she felt it as he did, and for just a moment he was tempted to give in to the frustration, to rant and yell and get everything out. But her eyes told him she needed him to be strong, because she needed help.

It had always been her in the past, saving him. She had brought him light and sweetness and hope when he had tried to push it all away. Now it was almost as if their lives were reversed. She was the one in need. He tightened his fingers around hers.

"It's okay now. We found each other."

The grief didn't entirely leave her face, but he saw relief there as well. Hope, even.

"Can we . . . can we go to bed now, Danny? I just want to lie down, hold on to you in the dark."

After she'd finished her tea, he led her through the paper-strewn front room and upstairs to his bedroom. Unlike Mick's half of the apartment, his was neat as a pin. He had no real possessions to litter the place, and having a clear floor helped him move around more easily. He had purchased a four-drawer dresser to keep things tidy, and he quickly emptied two of the drawers for Audrey. A couple of jackets hung on a rack by the door, and his crutch hid behind them, for use on those days when his leg ached too badly. He hooked her light summer coat over one of the spare hangers, and she placed her hat on their dresser, where it seemed so cheerful it was almost out of place.

"Can I help you with your buttons?" he asked. They were small, in a line down the centre of her back.

She whispered, "Yes, please."

He was almost as nervous as he had been the night of their wedding. She seemed like someone new. As if he were cheating on his wife by being with her. And she was equally shy. He took his time, ignoring the adrenaline pumping through his bloodstream, trying to disregard the trembling in his fingers. When he'd finished, she turned shyly toward the closet, where she hung her dress. He took the opportunity to admire her back, veiled by an expensive new shift.

"Are you staring?" she asked, still facing away.

"I am," he admitted. "Can't help it."

She turned toward him. "Everything is different, Danny. How do we start again?"

"Like we started the first time, I guess. Come here."

She wasn't obviously pregnant, but her curves were rounder, her breasts a little tight against the shift. He was suddenly and painfully hard. Her eyes danced with delight.

"You did miss me, didn't you?"

This time it was he who flushed, but he couldn't deny what was so obvious. "Every day."

"Forgive me?" she whispered, pressing her hands over her belly.

Danny had promised himself that no matter what she did, he wasn't ever going to let her go again. But every time he thought about the new life growing in her womb, he felt a stabbing in his own gut. It should have been him that got her pregnant, not some pompous, overblown snob with short, stubby hands. Not some black-haired Frenchman with too much money and not enough integrity. Forgive her? Yes. Of course. But could he ever forgive Antoine? No. And could he ever forgive himself? He doubted that very much.

Which was too bad, he thought. Because that was exactly what she wanted him to do.

"I forgive you," he whispered back, pulling her close and burying his nose in the perfumed coils of her hair.

"I never meant to—"

"Hush, Audrey. Kiss me, would you? Kiss me like you used to."

He thought it'd be uncomfortable, kissing her now that he knew another man had tasted these lips, touched this body. But the moment she was back in his arms, with her breath caressing his cheek, her eyes begging for forgiveness then clouding over with desire, it felt like home. Like he'd never left. God, how he'd missed her.

When they lay in the dark afterward, the awkwardness returned, and he hated it. The only sound in the room was their breathing, and he wished he could be more quiet about it. Who was she now? What was she thinking? Was it as difficult for her as it was for him? Did her heart ache like his did?

He rolled toward her, folding one arm under his head. "How do you feel? I mean being pregnant and all? Are you sick?"

"No," she said quietly. "I guess I'm lucky. Some ladies talk about how sick they got. I feel fine."

"That's good. I'm glad."

The image of another baby came to mind, clear as the last time he'd seen him. Danny hesitated, nervous all over again, but he had to go on. There was something they had to discuss, and it wouldn't help to put it off. He cleared his throat to buy a little time. "You said you always wanted to be a mother, right?"

"I did."

"Well, I might have a little surprise for you," he said, dipping a toe into dangerous territory. "Three of them, actually."

She frowned and rolled toward him. He pulled his eyes from the view, then told her about the two little boys and their baby brother.

"It was that very first day. Maybe an hour or so after the blast. I heard these little voices coming outta nowhere. At first I couldn't figure where they were coming from, because there was nothing left of their house. But they never quit yelling. So I dug in the house and found them in their basement. When I think about that day, about how surprised I was to see those little boys—" He swallowed. "If no one had heard them, they'd have died that night. They'd have been trapped with their dead mother, and they'd have frozen to death. But I was there at the right time, I guess. And after that, well, I went to see them every day. They waited for me, and when I thought I couldn't stand another day without you, I'd go to them and forget for a while. I saved them, sure, but they saved me, too." He locked his eyes on hers. "I've applied to adopt the three of them," he finished.

Her eyebrows shot up in surprise. "What?"

"Yeah. Well, I'm sorry to spring this on you. It's just, well, it's real important to me and the boys. And I was hoping you might approve."

Joy spread across her face. "I do, Danny! I do! Tell me more."

No one had ever been able to make him feel as good about himself as she did. She watched him with adoration, listening to everything. She'd always loved his stories. Couldn't get enough.

"The original orphanage was destroyed. It was horrible. I helped with the cleanup of the place, and it darn near broke my heart—if it hadn't already been broke, that is," he said self-conciously. "Then after the blast there were so many more orphans than before. We had to build it bigger, with more rooms, more beds. And the kids, they weren't accustomed to it, you know? I know a lot of orphans start out as babies, left by their parents, and they don't know any better. But some of these kids lost their mothers, fathers, brothers, sisters, the family dog even, and all in one moment. They were old enough to remember what they'd had. Now they're all alone. And when I stopped in, it seemed like they needed me. Feeling that, well, it helped me get over you a little. Because I figured you were gone, you know."

"But you checked the lists. Every day," she said dutifully, repeating what he'd told her so many times.

"I did. But nobody checked on these kids. I mean, there were nurses and volunteers, but no one came for the kids. Like their families were all gone. So I figured Mick might be able to help, and soon we had ads in newspapers across the country, looking for relatives. It was fantastic. About a dozen of the kids ended up with families. But my boys never did. And right from the start, it was like they were with me. So I've been waiting for paperwork to go through. It's been a while because, well, because I was a man without a wife. And a crippled man at that."

"But you're not on your own anymore," she said softly. "Will it help that I'm here?"

"Everything's gonna be better now that you're here." He grabbed one of her hands. "You're sure it's okay? I mean, I know it's asking a lot, bringing home a pair of four-year-olds and a third little fella almost ready to walk."

"Oh, Danny. And we can bring them to Jeddore? Can we have a real home again?"

"I'd sure like that. I've put some money away so we can at least put a start on building a house out there, if you want."

Tears of happiness, of regret, of hope glittered in her eyes. "I've been saving, too. Oh, Danny. You have no idea how much I want that. Living in Antoine's house, well, I cried every night." She sniffed and blinked sadly at him. "What happened to us?"

Danny touched her cheek with one callused thumb, wiping away a tear. "It was me, and we both know that. But I've changed. You'll see."

She kissed his thumb. "I already do."

Danny guessed dawn was just a few hours away. He'd have to work soon. He was exhausted, and Audrey's eyelids drooped.

"Audrey, I want to fall asleep beside you. Hold you until the sun comes up. Like we used to."

She smiled dreamily at him. "I would like that very much."

"And tomorrow you can come with me, and we can sign the papers for the boys."

"I would like that, too."

Sleep carried them away. In the morning they awoke and made love again, then they dressed and headed toward the Social Services building. Danny led her to the desk where he'd been before, and they stopped in front of a frumpy, middle-aged woman, dressed all in black. She sat slightly hunched, pen in hand.

"Good morning, Mrs. Munroe," Danny said, doffing his cap. "You're looking lovely today."

"Good morning, Mr. Baker. How can I be of service?"

"I'm here about the boys, ma'am."

"I assumed that. Has something changed in your application? Because at the moment it is still under consideration, which we have already discussed."

"Of course," he said, grinning. "But yes, my situation has changed considerably. Mrs. Munroe, I'd like to present my wife, Mrs. Audrey Baker." Mrs. Munroe slid her spectacles up her nose and peered at Audrey. "I see. Well, this does change things. You are his wife?"

"I am," Audrey replied. "I thought he was dead."

"Congratulations to both of you." Mrs. Munroe's face twisted abruptly into a painful grimace. She reached to the side and pulled a well-seasoned handkerchief from her bag, then blew her nose loudly. "Please excuse me, will you? I—"

"Mrs. Munroe lost her husband," Danny murmured into Audrey's ear. The couple waited patiently until the woman had herself under control. She sniffed, tucked the cloth into her sleeve, then focused on them.

"Now," she said. "Let's see your file." She thumbed through a box of envelopes, finally coming across one labelled Baker. She slipped the pages out and laid them on the table in front of her, then skimmed over the words with a finger just beginning to bulge with arthritis. "Ah, yes. Right. Eugene Josiah White, Harry Donald White, and Norman Jefferson White. All three, was it? You wanted to adopt all three?"

"I wouldn't split them up."

Mrs. Munroe squinted critically at the couple. "You're awfully young to manage three young boys, but if you think you can handle it . . ." With a shrug, she signed something at the bottom of the page, then gave Danny a warmer smile. "I will expedite these forms so you will hear by the end of the week. I'm doing it as a thank you, Mr. Baker. You have done wonderful things for those children. For all of them."

"No more than they deserved," he said. "Thank you very much for taking care of that. So we'll be back here next Friday? To meet with you?"

"Yes. Bring your marriage certificate when you come. That's how it's done," she said.

FORTY-TWO

❧

They walked into the street, their footsteps accompanied by the constant pattern of hammers and saws, noises that had taken over for the songs of birds and schoolchildren. Those other sounds were slowly returning to Halifax, but they had a long way to go. A woman walked by with a train of rope-holding children behind her, somewhat like a duck with tethered ducklings, and Audrey and Danny squeezed each other's hands with sympathy. The children were blind and scarred, staring but seeing nothing. They would never see their own scars. Perhaps that was a blessing.

Danny held the door open when they reached the orphanage, and Audrey stepped ahead of him. He knew what she saw because he saw it just about every day.

"Danny!"

The boys—*his* boys, he liked to think—were on him as soon as they looked up from the little toy horses. They wrapped their arms around his legs and squeezed. Behind them, little Norman wobbled on his feet. He was growing like a weed, that little fellow, reaching for the wall and daring himself to stand.

Danny led the boys back to their brother, then squatted between them. "Boys, I have someone very important for you to meet."

All eyes went to Audrey, standing beside him. Norman crawled over and grabbed a fistful of her skirt, struggling to find his balance. When he gazed up at her, eyes full of wonder, chin shiny with drool, Audrey sank to her knees and took his little hand in hers, helping him up.

"This is Mrs. Baker," he told them. "She's my wife."

"You're pretty," Eugene said, staring at her. "Like my mom."

Danny and Audrey exchanged a glance. The little boy's words tugged at Danny's heart. "I think she is, too."

"And you all seem like very fine gentleman," Audrey assured them. She tapped Norman on the tip of his messy nose. "Even you."

Norman gurgled something, waved one arm wildly as his balance abandoned him, then plopped down to the floor.

"Danny made us horses," Harry said helpfully, holding out one of the toys for her to inspect.

"Well! Aren't those lovely," she said.

Danny saw a deep, desperate hope shining in her beautiful eyes. It struck him that she'd never known little children, really. And now she stood before these three, quite possibly the salvation they all needed, and Danny realized she was afraid of rejection.

"May I hold it?" she asked Harry.

The twins' expressions were sober but trusting. "You can hold mine too," Eugene said. "Mine's bigger."

"Is it?"

"No, it isn't," Harry said.

"Yes, it is," replied his brother.

"All right, all right," Danny said. "Enough of that or I'll take them both back." He considered Audrey, hoping he was about to ask the right question. "Mrs. Baker, I have to go to work. Would you like to stay here a while?"

"With these little gentlemen?" she asked. "Oh yes. Would you like that, boys?"

In reply, the boys hopped around, thrilled at having made a new friend.

"That's settled then." She reached for Norman, who curled his hand around her finger. Danny loved watching her fall in love with them, just as he had.

"Good," he said, rising. "I'll see you all later."

She stood for a kiss. "Are you still doing construction on Barrington Street?"

"I am. Guess I'll be there a while yet."

"I'll bring lunch later."

Danny's heart sang all day. In the evening he came home, and Audrey had supper ready. It was like before—no, it was better than before. There was no reek of scotch clinging to the air, no bickering over small things. She made them a simple stew, which Mick practically inhaled. After supper the men lit cigarettes while Audrey cleared the dishes.

"It's a strange thing to say," she said, pouring boiling water into a basin for the dishes. "But I've missed this. I've missed cleaning up and feeling like I'm doing something useful."

"Yeah?" Mick asked, blowing a perfect circle of smoke toward the ceiling. "I would've thought you'd have been too busy with parties and stuff."

She kept her back to them, but they could hear the contentment in her voice. "Well, it was busy. I don't remember the last time I had a quiet day. When Pierre wasn't having people over, he expected me to host teas, and we went to a lot of parties. It was all about business, really. He needed to keep up the impression that he was in charge of all the business in Halifax, you know? I met some interesting people. A lot of them asked me to paint for them." She glanced over her shoulder, one eyebrow raised. "I still have most of that money, Danny."

"That's my girl," he said proudly. "We'll need that to build our house."

"So you're gonna move back up the shore?" Mick asked. "Why

anyone would want to move away from this town is a mystery to me. This is where the action is, folks! Everything you could ever want is here. Then again, I guess if you prefer reeking of fish and manure, well, you'll find it out there."

"That's right, Mick. I'm headed back for the manure. Just can't get good-enough shit out here."

"Danny!"

"Sorry, Audrey. Only teasing."

"Well, I'll miss you. Won't be the same around here without your snoring," Mick said.

"You could come with us . . ."

"Ha!" Mick guffawed, smacking his thigh. "I ain't no fisherman, no way."

When the dishes were put away, Audrey sat at the table with them and brought out some scribbled drawings the boys had done for her. She traced her finger along the messy lines, describing how the boys had fared, and Danny could see how proud of them she was. Just like a mom should be.

When she was done, Mick jumped right in with his intended conversation.

"So, Audrey. Let's hear about Antoine."

She frowned and set the pictures to the side. "What?"

"The man behind the money. He's somewhat of a mystery to us newspapermen—loud and slippery, but still a mystery."

"Slippery?"

"Sure, sure. He's sneaky."

She thought about that, then she gave Mick a hard stare. "He isn't sneaky."

"Sure. Sure, he is." Mick chuckled. "He'd take his grandmother's last penny, and she wouldn't even know it."

"Why do you say that?"

"Well, interestingly enough, I've been doing some investigating of the man lately. He's hardly a saint, as I've said before, and there's some real quiet things happening that shouldn't be happening. His name's all over those things. Did he ever talk money with you?"

"No. I guess he didn't think I would understand." She shrugged. "He was probably right."

Mick peppered her with questions then dove back into his office, where he kept newspapers stacked against his typewriter. He emerged with his hands full of paper, a pencil tucked behind one ear.

"Can you remember any of the men's names?" he asked, swinging into a chair and plopping his supplies on the table. "The men he talked with?"

Audrey frowned. "Ralph Whelan was often there. And Harry Shelton. Fred and Joseph Warrington sometimes came, but they never spoke. They just sat in the corner of the room." She turned to Danny. "They're twins. I'd never seen grown-up twins before. It was very interesting."

Mick kept busy writing names as she spoke, scribbling words beside each one. He apparently knew these fellows. Or knew of them, anyway. When he'd finished writing, he looked up and stared silently at her for a moment, making Danny wonder if he'd finally run out of questions. Of course not. He was only thinking up more. But Audrey stopped him before he could say anything.

"Will you say awful things about Pierre in your story, Mick? I don't know how comfortable I am with that. He was kind to me."

Danny sighed and dropped his forehead into his hand. "He was so kind to you that he lied and told you your husband was dead. He was such a good man that he let me believe you were dead, too. He was such a terrific guy that he got another man's wife pregnant and wanted her to get rid of the baby." He lifted his gaze to hers. Her face was bright red. "Why did he take care of you? Not because he's a good man. No. Johnny saw it a long time ago, and I didn't listen. He said I never should have let Antoine be alone with you. Antoine saw you as a pretty little decoration, and one that perfectly matched his social circles."

She took a deep breath. "I used him, too. I'm no angel, Danny. I needed to build a new life, and he offered a good one. He isn't fully to blame."

"Maybe not," Mick interrupted, stubbing out his cigarette. "But this guy always knows what he's doing. He's sneakier than you'd think,

Audrey. I haven't told anyone about this yet, but I'm working on a really big story. Really big. If I can get all the evidence I need, I can prove he's stolen thousands of dollars from innocent people."

"Really?" She sounded shocked.

"I'm sorry to be the one to tell you, but Antoine's been making his fortune on the backs of orphans and homeless. Not a nice man."

"How do you know about all that, Mick?" Danny asked.

"All I can tell you right now is that you have to trust me, and you both have to keep this to yourselves for now. I'll fill you all in as soon as I can."

"We won't say a word," Danny promised, turning to his wife. "Come to bed, Audrey."

Her eyes, clouded by Mick's revelations, cleared. "All right."

Mick cleared his throat. "I'll just get back to work then. Hey, Audrey?"

"Yes?"

"Thanks. This is going to be a heck of a story."

———

At dinner that night, Audrey was subdued. She pushed her leftover stew around the bowl with her spoon, staying mostly out of the conversation, seeming distracted. Danny tried to give her room but was dying to know what was eating her up.

"I had a visitor," she said when he asked. "Catherine. You remember her? She came to the orphanage, and she didn't seem the least bit surprised to see me there." Audrey set down her spoon and rubbed her hands together as if they were cold. "She talks a lot, Catherine does. She said she and her husband had supper with Pierre last night, and he was very angry." She swallowed, looking nervous. "Pierre does not like to lose."

"So?"

"She told me we should be careful. That was all she said."

"Sounds fair, coming from Antoine," Mick said.

"Yeah, well, he should be careful too," Danny said.

Mick chuckled. "Sounds fair, coming from Danny."

FORTY-THREE

❧

Thursday night, Danny and Audrey stayed up for hours, talking about Eugene, Harry, and Norman. She seemed just as excited as he was, and she had visited the orphanage a few more times that week, just to get to know them better. She'd brought along some scones she'd baked and even bought them some new shirts and trousers. As they lay in bed that night, Danny kept gripping her hands, telling her not to get too excited. If the answer was no, they'd both be terribly disappointed. But he was having an awfully difficult time listening to himself.

If the answer was yes, he was going to sit down and write his mother a long-overdue letter. If the adoption went through, he and Audrey would head home immediately to start building their new home. He'd been saving up what he could, and now that he'd had so much practice, he figured he might be able to make some money in construction back home. Maybe the boat market would pick up again. Maybe something would come up. Somehow they'd make it work. They had to. And when the new house was all done, the boys would come out. He hadn't told them what he'd been doing, because he didn't want to disappoint them. Not until he had the answer he wanted to give them. Not until, he hoped, today.

It was a big day, so Danny had asked the foreman for time off. He and Audrey were up early, preparing and laughing like children. When they were ready to head to Social Services, Audrey wore a pretty pastel blue dress with matching hat, and Danny wore his cleanest shirt and pants. Audrey helped him with his tie, which he tucked under a black vest and jacket. Mick gave him the once-over, then vanished into his room, returning seconds later with his newsman's fedora, minus its usual "Press" card tucked into the front. Danny patted the hat on, offered Audrey his arm, and they stepped out into the street.

The late spring sun lit the city and warmed the air. Sweat snaked down the back of Danny's neck, but he wasn't sure if it came from heat or anxiety. The heavy black door outside Social Services seemed somehow larger today, more imposing, but it also seemed like a symbol. Like he and Audrey were opening the door on a bold new life. He turned the knob and ushered Audrey ahead of him, removing Mick's hat as he went. Bells hanging over the door chimed cheerily in welcome.

"Good morning, Mrs. Munroe," Danny said.

The woman was in her accustomed chair behind the desk but was bent over, picking something up off the ground. At the sound of his voice she sat up quickly. "Oh! Mr. Baker. Good morning to you, too. And to you, Mrs. Baker."

On the opposite side of Mrs. Munroe's desk were two chairs. Danny pulled one out for Audrey, then took the other one, smiling broadly.

"Well, ma'am," he said, "it's Friday, and we're back, just like you told us to be. How did everything work out with the paperwork? Anything more for us to sign?"

Mrs. Munroe started to say something, then bit her lower lip. She frowned strangely at him, then reached for the files and pulled his from the stack marked Completed. The bold lettering jumped right off the page and stamped itself onto Danny's heart. This was the most exciting thing he'd ever done.

Just as she had before, Mrs. Munroe slowly slid the papers from their envelope and spread them in front of her, but this time she didn't even look at them.

"Denied," she stated flatly.

"What?" Danny and Audrey cried together.

"Yes. You see? It's stamped in red right here." She pointed at the obvious word, and Danny felt all the blood drain out of his face. Audrey, in contrast, went bright pink. Mrs. Munroe frowned at Danny as if he were a recalcitrant schoolboy. "Seems you are not what you say you are, Mr. Baker. Not quite the upstanding citizen you claim to be."

Danny's blood pounded in his ears. "What?" he cried, leaning forward to read the page. "What does it say?"

She pulled one sheet closer and adjusted her spectacles, her eyes huge behind the lenses. "There is quite a list here, provided by a prominent member of Halifax society. Let's see."

Danny felt sick. He only knew one prominent member of Halifax society.

"Says you have a disreputable character. You have an unpredictable temper, a drinking problem, and"—she shot him a furious glance—"you have been known to strike a woman."

"No," Audrey whispered, sounding horrified. Her face went from pink to white as a sheet.

"Obviously, Mr. Baker, we cannot allow you to adopt our children. That would be a crime." She waited, lips pursed together, but Danny said nothing.

He seethed. Antoine. It could only be Antoine. He rose slowly and replaced his hat. Audrey stood silently beside him, like a shadow.

Despite his wooden leg, Danny set a pace that had Audrey practically running beside him. She had ceased apologizing after the third or fourth time, when he'd growled at her to stop. Now she stuck grimly to his side, begging pardon as they pushed past people at the side of the road. Danny barged through the newspaper office door and stopped at a front desk.

"I'm here to see Mick," he said to the woman there.

"Certainly, sir. One moment, please." She stood and opened a door behind her, filling the quiet room with clacking typewriters and the voices of men, then vanished inside and took the noise with her.

Having reached his destination, Danny's heart began to slow again. Reason started to trickle back into his brain. Audrey stood beside him, staring straight ahead, looking absolutely miserable. He noticed the lace on her little hat was trembling.

"Aw, Audrey. None of this is your fault."

"But it is."

"Well, if it is, then it's mine, too. Don't be unhappy. We'll get this thing fixed up, and we'll be teaching those boys to fish in no time."

Her eyes didn't believe him, but she smiled nonetheless, and he was grateful for the attempt. He didn't believe himself, either.

Mick stepped through the door, striding purposefully around the desk toward them. "Well, if it ain't my two favourite roommates," he said, grinning. He stopped and frowned. "As the bartender said to the horses, what's with the long faces?"

"We need your help, Mick."

Audrey chipped in. "I'll give you whatever you need to get Antoine."

Mick's brow shot up. "Oh? What's the word then? What's the old man done?"

"Blocked the adoption," Danny said flatly.

"Blocked the adoption? On what grounds?"

Danny snorted. "Antoine believes I have a 'disreputable character,' and Social Services says his word is better than mine."

"Well, well, well. He's messing with Social Services now? Wonder who—Oh! That'd be Joe what's-his-name. I'd heard that he—Audrey! This is great! I mean, I'm sorry this is happening to you two, but it's fantastic news for me. And don't you worry. We will get all this sorted out and you'll be chasing after a couple of four-year-olds before you know it."

Mick's excitement was contagious—almost enough to dampen Danny's anger, but not quite. "Can you really get him?"

"Certainly can try," Mick said, and very clearly winked his one eye.

The next morning Danny tucked his hammer into his belt, then kissed Audrey goodbye as he set off to the work site. She said she wanted to go to the orphanage, see the boys, and perhaps meet one of the other ladies later on that morning. Both were doing their best to think positively. Mick hadn't come out of his office that morning, and Danny took that as a positive sign.

Despite everything, this was nice, he thought, as he walked through the streets. Like a regular marriage. It was just about the first time he could claim that. The first few money-strapped months of their marriage had been wrapped in deliciously romantic nights and days in his parents' house. The next bunch were ugly and confrontational, with neither of them being themselves. Neither of those two situations seemed like real marriages. Now they were pulling it together. And their plan to move back to the shore was bringing them closer still.

She had made him a sandwich, which he'd tucked in his overalls pocket. His leg was doing pretty good, and he no longer felt even the slightest craving to have a drink. He still got down on himself some-times, but lately it was more because of his losses than his disabilities. He missed Johnny terribly. His little brother should have been there to cheer them on as they made these big family decisions. He'd be Uncle Johnny. Just think of that. Johnny might even have been making his own family plans by that point.

Danny arrived a few minutes early and headed toward the most re-cent wall. The boards were dark from the rain, and drops slipped off the peak of his cap. He took a moment to stretch as tall as he could, finger-tips reaching for the endless grey sky while he let out a healthy yawn. Then he pulled the hammer from his belt, stuck a few nails between his lips, and started to work.

He hadn't gotten very far before he felt a tap on his shoulder. He turned to see the foreman, Guy, who was twisting one finger in his ear and looking annoyed.

"Morning, Guy," he said. "What's up?"

"Changes, Baker. Changes. Orders."

"So we're moving on? Where to?"

"Boss says I gotta cut you."

Danny blinked. "What?"

"We gotta make some cuts. Not enough money to pay all the guys. You're on the list to go. Sorry, but that's the way it is. I hear they're hiring on the Eastern Passage. Some kinda cement factory."

"Why me?"

Guy shrugged. "I only bring the news, you know? Sorry, man."

Danny watched Guy's back as he walked away, steeling himself as a leaden mixture of fear and anger curdled in his stomach. This could only be Antoine's doing. Again. Danny let his head loll back on his neck, then he glared up at the sky, letting the air cool his face. After a moment, he dropped his chin, stuck his hammer back into his belt, and headed to the street.

This was going to go on forever. If he went for the cement job, whatever that was, Antoine would find out and block that one as well. In the past, when nothing had mattered, the solution would have been obvious. He would have given in to the pounding in his fists, the urge to drive one of them through the man's face. And he likely would have been tossed unceremoniously into a cell until the end of time. But now things mattered. He had to find answers that came from his head, not his hands.

He would go home. Take Audrey and go. Damn the money. They'd figure something out. He'd have to make enough for the baby, too. The irony of that hit him, but he didn't laugh. Antoine was preventing Danny from providing for his own baby. In any case, they'd get by. The Bakers always did just fine. And his parents would be happy to have them home again. Even the baby.

He started toward home, barely conscious of the ache where the peg met his leg. The pain was a constant, but so many other things hurt much more. Like his pride. His shoe slapped on the ground with every step, sounding loud in his ears. He should have been working, not walking.

Somehow, it didn't seem the slightest bit strange when his direction changed. He headed toward the streets in the south, where the buildings stood farther apart from one another, their walls more solid, their gardens neat and tended. It struck Danny again how large Antoine's home was. How the woodwork around the front door and the four windows facing the street had been worked in meticulous detail. He liked that. Maybe one day he'd fashion wood frames like that for his own home. Danny didn't hesitate at the door. He rapped hard, waited a couple of seconds, then knocked again. He heard the sound of approaching steps from within and stood back a bit, waiting.

"What is it?" Pierre demanded as he yanked open the door. It took only a beat before he recognized Danny, and his expression of irritation flared to one of outright hatred. "What the hell are you doing here?"

In contrast, Danny was cold as metal. "Came to pay my regards, Mr. Antoine. Let you know we're leavin' and you'll never see her again. Never. Oh, also, if you ever come near her again, I'll kill you."

Antoine's mouth twisted into a smile, but his eyes shone with hostility. "Oh, really? Have you asked her about that? Made sure she still wants a useless cripple as a husband? No. I think there's a different reason you're here. Come to beg, have you? Got no job? No money? No . . . little boys? Maybe you'll have to live off your wife's income, fisherman. She's a very . . . talented woman, Audrey is."

Danny's fist smashed into Antoine's cheek, knocking the smaller man to the floor, and Danny was on him, punching again and again, riding the fury as it roared through his head. He was grabbed roughly from behind and thrown into the air, landing in the middle of the street. He felt the crunch of boots on his ribs, the beating of fists on his face, hard and purposeful, like when a butcher tenderizes a cut of meat.

"Get rid of him," he heard Antoine say, just before he blacked out.

FORTY-FOUR

They dumped him by the docks, where he blended in with other fallen men. When he awoke, he managed to force his swollen eyelids open, and he thought it might be dusk. The faintest hint of orange still shone on the grey sea of the harbour. Danny rolled to his hands and knees, spat blood from his mouth, and swiped an arm carefully across his face. It hurt to touch, and blood stained his sleeve. Groaning with effort, he stood and wrapped an arm around bruised ribs—one or two might even be broken, he thought. At least they'd left him his leg. It could have been worse. He could have been dead.

He limped slowly to the water, grunting with every movement, then cupped his hands and dipped them in the unforgiving cold of the harbour. Bracing himself, he splashed salt water over his torn face. It burned like acid.

He had nowhere to go but home now, and he'd go there a beaten man. He had lost. He had wanted so badly to prove he was the better man, the victor, but Antoine had won again.

All around him, rivers of rain trickled down the pebbled slope of the road and drained into the ocean. He looked toward the pier, now rebuilt over the spot where Johnny had died. Just another pier. Another drab building without character, welcoming in the big ships from Europe, where men were being blown apart every day.

Danny had a sudden urge to step in the water, feel the grit of sand between his toes. Trying to ignore the throbbing of his ribs, he sat on the edge of the dock and slipped off his shoe. He took off his sock, tucked it inside the shoe, then set it to the side. Standing again, he folded his pant legs and waded in. The water wasn't clean and clear like it was when it flowed past the peace of Jeddore, but just knowing at one point this same current might have wandered past his home made it feel good. He had an impulse to sink into it, sit chest-deep in the ocean current and watch the boats, like he'd done as a little boy.

It was time to go home. Home to the Shore. Tomorrow. Tonight he needed Audrey.

———

She wasn't home. When he stepped into the empty house, Danny thought about visiting the orphanage, but it was too late. Besides, he had a feeling the condition of his face would scare the boys pretty bad. Danny wandered into the kitchen and slumped over the sink, rinsing off the dried blood and salt. Everything hurt. What would Audrey say? Where was she?

A couple of hours later, Audrey came home. He had gone to bed and dozed off but awoke when he heard her latch the front door behind her. He visualized her moving smoothly through the entrance, the sitting room, the kitchen, followed the sound of her feet as they shuffled across the floor. He knew when she came closer and was surprised to hear her hesitate. She didn't normally do that.

The bedroom was dark, and a sliver of light from the outer rooms peeked in when she opened the door.

"Audrey?"

"Oh, Danny. It's late. I didn't mean to wake you."

"Where have you been?"

Again that little hesitation. Danny felt a tingle of fear at the base of his neck.

"I went . . . out," she said. He sensed her hanging her coat in the corner of the room and remembered it was raining outside. She slipped off her shoes and started to unbutton her blouse.

"Audrey, come here, would you? You're makin' me nervous."

She came to the side of the bed and stood a moment, looking down. The darkness hid all evidence of Danny's beating, but not the angle of her face as she dropped her chin to her chest.

"I . . . I went to see Pierre," she said.

Bile rose in Danny's throat, and he knew. Despite everything she'd said, she loved Antoine. He and Audrey were through. Danny didn't say a word.

"Danny," she whispered. She tried to sit on the side of the bed, but he put a hand up, holding her back. If she touched him, he wasn't sure what he would do. "It is not what you think," she said. "I went to thank him, yes, but also to ask him to leave you alone. I was just so afraid he'd hurt you! And I thought—"

His voice was rock-hard. "Why, Audrey? You don't think I can take care of myself? I'm such a cripple?"

He saw her flinch and knew Pierre had used that term—again.

"No, it's not that. You know it's not that. But lots of men work for him, and well, he pays them to hurt people. I didn't want him to send them after you."

"Oh, really," he said dryly, running his tongue over his split lip. "Did you kiss your lover goodbye?"

She sniffed. "Of course not. Don't even say that. I realize now that I shouldn't have gone. I should have left it as it was. I only wanted everything to be fine with all three of us. Make it all go away so that no one gets hurt."

"Too late." He snorted. "No one gets hurt. That's a good one, Audrey. Did you tell him you loved him?"

"I told him goodbye."

"Did you tell him you loved him?" he insisted.

The tiniest of hesitations, then she took a deep breath and let it go. "No. I never loved him, Danny. Never. But you have to understand that he did a lot for me. He took care of me. He made me feel good about myself, and to be truthful, he made me feel beautiful. He was good to me." Her voice hardened a little. "I had to say thank you, didn't I? I had to thank him for everything he'd done for me. This is not about you, Danny. It's about him and me. That's all. I don't understand why you are so hurt that I went there for that."

"How could I not be hurt, Audrey? How could I not feel betrayed when you go, in secret, to the one man who almost destroyed us? To beg for my sake? You think I'm so useless that I need you to sneak around and defend me? Because I'm not, Audrey. I can handle myself. It's you I can't trust."

The darkness seemed suddenly complete. She didn't move. It was like she'd stopped breathing, though her slender shadow still stood beside the bed.

"Please don't," she whispered. "Please, Danny."

She reached a hand out, but his eyes were closed, and he didn't sense her there until her cool, wet fingertips grazed his cheek. He hissed at the pain and pulled away. She was instantly at his side, leaning over him.

"What's happened, Danny? What have you done?"

"It's nothing."

"What is that? You're hurt! You're hurt badly! What—"

She spun around and left the room, then returned moments later with a lit candle, its flame dancing in a bright yellow circle before her. Danny stared at the ceiling, arms crossed. This was going to get complicated.

Her gasp was quick, her fingers light when she saw the damage. Danny kept his eyes open but lowered his gaze, watching hers.

"Who did this, Danny? Why?"

"Why do you think?" His words were like venom. They were out before he could stop them, even if he'd wanted to. "Guess you didn't get there in time."

She was quiet for a moment, brushing dark strands of hair back from his brow. God, he loved her. It hurt how much he loved her. Through the candlelight he could see the pain in her expression, knew she ached to find him again through the jumble of broken promises, but he did nothing to help. She was on her own.

And she knew it. Audrey set her jaw and spoke in a low voice. "That's why I went, Danny. That's why I had to go and ask him to stop. I wanted to make him promise to leave you alone. I thought if I could only make him see reason . . . You know I don't think of you as a . . . as a . . . cripple. It has nothing to do with your leg. It has everything to do with all the thugs he has working for him. They could have killed you!"

"I ain't dead."

She pressed gently against his brow, and he hissed through his teeth. "No, thank God. You're too stubborn to be dead." Her fingers continued to caress his forehead, tracing soft lines that made him want to close his eyes and disappear into the sensation. "Oh, Danny. I can't stand this. What happened to us?"

He ignored the question. "How could you?" he demanded. "How could you go to him after everything we talked about? It wasn't up to you, Audrey. It's up to me. I'm the man. I'm the one who is supposed to protect you, take care of you, make you so happy you don't need anyone else. He can't go away feeling he's won. I'm the one who has to come out on top. It's the only way I can feel all right about this. But now . . ." He closed his eyes and breathed, waiting for emotion to die down before he spoke again. "Now you've taken that from me, Audrey. You took our trust, and you took my pride by doing that today. You took our future by doing that."

"No, Danny," she breathed. "No. You can't say that. I went because I needed a future with you. I needed you alive."

"I might be alive, but I've got nothing left."

"Not true," she said. Her voice wobbled into the beginning of a sob. "You have me. You'll always have me."

"Ha!"

"Please, Danny. Please!"

The rain picked up again, hard enough that it sounded as if someone had thrown a bucket of nails at the window. The house shuddered.

"How do I know?" he finally asked.

"Know what?"

"How do I know I can trust you? How do I know you don't love him? How do I know it's not just obligation that's brought you back here?"

"Oh, Danny! How can you say that?"

"How can I not?"

Tears ran down her cheeks, golden in the candlelight. "Because I love you, and you know that. I have never loved anyone but you."

She sounded tired and defeated. Danny wasn't sure how he felt about that. He had to admit it was good to hear the honest pain in her voice and know he wasn't the only one suffering. But everything in his heart burned to comfort her. To pull her against him and breathe her in.

"It was a mistake," she whispered. "The biggest mistake I've ever made. But it's in the past, Danny. It's nothing compared to you and me. I love you, Danny. I've always loved you. I can't imagine living without you. Please forgive me. Please?"

A gust slammed the rain against the trembling windowpane. It made him cold. It made him want to hold her tight and believe. God, he wanted to believe. In her, in them, in himself.

"Blow out that candle and come to bed, Audrey. We'll see how we are in the morning."

She lay naked beside him almost instantly, leaving her clothes in an unaccustomed heap by the side of the bed in her urgency. Her fingers touched his shoulder, her thigh pressed against his, and he rolled toward her, closing his eyes against the tears. Her head lay on his battered chest, her curls cold and wet against his skin. She gripped him like a lifeline, and it hurt. His bruises, his heart. It all hurt. She shook in his arms, sobbing, and he held her, but he couldn't quite get past that hole in his heart where trust used to be.

"I don't know what to do, Audrey. It's all wrong."

"Give it time," she whispered. "Please. I promise. It will be fine again. Please."

His fingers brushed the soft skin of her breast, tracing the slope he knew so well. She pressed closer against him, and he held her to her promise.

"Love me," she begged.

"I never stopped loving you, Audrey."

His lips found hers, and he inhaled her breath, the sweet scent that always made his heart skip. They kissed and touched and breathed together until he could wait no longer, then he melted into her warmth and fell in love all over again. He leaned down and nuzzled into the curve of her neck afterward, relishing the taste of her drying sweat. Her pulse was steady and promising under his lips. He sighed and lowered his ear onto the pillow beside her.

"I'm ready to go home," he said softly. "Are you?"

She breathed deeply and he felt her cheek tighten in a smile. "I just need to pack a few things and I'll be ready. Let's go, Danny. You and I, we're not meant to be city folk."

"I think you're right. We'll go in the morning. Nothing to keep us here."

FORTY-FIVE

Danny slept lightly, his mind caught up in so many circles. He awoke finally at five a.m. to the sound of the front door slamming shut.

"Everybody up!" he heard. "It's a day to celebrate!"

From the sound of it, Mick had been out all night. Danny hopped out of their room, not bothering to attach his peg. His head pounded. He scrubbed his fingers through his hair and glared at Mick.

"What's this all about?"

Mick looked at Danny. "Whoa. Can't say that's much of an improvement to your face, pal. Horse kick you or what?"

Danny grunted and cocked an eyebrow, but it hurt to do it, so he let it drop. "It's nothing. What are you going on about? Better be important. You've woken Audrey, and she needs her sleep."

Mick shrugged, then swept off his hat and plopped it on Danny's head. His coal black hair was pasted down against his skull, which told Danny the hat had been in place all night long. "Oh, it's important, Danny, my boy. Bring that pretty lady out here, if you please."

Danny turned toward their room, but Audrey was at the door

already, wrapped in Danny's dressing gown. He loved when she wore that. She looked tiny, almost drowned in the long sleeves.

"Good morning, Mick," she said, her voice a little groggy. "Have you been out all night?"

"I have, I have," he said, grinning broadly. "Take a seat, would you? Do we have something to drink? Tea?"

"We were sleeping," Danny growled.

"No? Oh, well. Maybe I'll just—"

"I'll get it," Audrey said, turning toward the stove.

"No, no, no. Come here first," he said, indicating two chairs by the table.

They sat close together, always touching. Danny leaned forward, frowning, his elbows on the table. Audrey leaned toward Danny, her fingers on his neck, his back, his bruised and swollen face, flitting everywhere. When they were comfortable, Mick opened the black leather bag he always carried and pulled out a folded newspaper, which he laid flat on the table in front of them. He smacked the front page with the back of his hand.

"Right. Well. What is it my grandfather used to say? If you lie down with dogs, you're liable to wake up with fleas. Well, I can tell you right now, this dog has had his day."

HALIFAX BUSINESSMAN PIERRE ANTOINE: FRAUD.

THOUSANDS OF DOLLARS OF DONATED SUPPLIES SKIMMED AND

SOLD FOR PROFIT. AT LEAST SIX LOCAL BUSINESSMEN TO BE IN-

DICTED ALONG WITH ANTOINE.

"Mick," Danny said, his voice low, heart racing. "You've done it."

Audrey was staring at the newspaper.

"Nice guy, huh?" The words escaped before Danny could stop them. Fortunately, she didn't seem to notice. Her eyes followed the lines of type, skipping from line to line.

"He did all this?" she whispered

"He did indeed," Mick said. "And more. Sorry, Audrey."

"How'd you figure it all out?" Danny asked

Mick chuckled. "Oldest trick in the book. Follow the money." He opened both hands, palms up and lifted one, then the other, as if they were part of a scale. "Money comes from somewhere, and it goes somewhere. It kept going to Antoine. Actually, Danny, you got me going on it."

He explained how Danny's comment a while back about missing donations to the orphanage had raised Mick's interest. He found out that Pierre Antoine's business had garnered practically every government contract for rebuilding the city, including managing the incoming supplies off the docks. Mick had gone down and spent time at the docks, watching food come in, counting boxes, watching distribution.

From what he'd seen, Antoine hadn't been satisfied with government money alone. The businessman paid off everyone he could think of at the docks, but the simple employees whose job it was to unload and load crates were overlooked. Those fellows had been more than happy to accept Mick's offer of cash for anonymous information. Everything they told him pointed to Antoine skimming off the incoming donations. After that, all Mick had to do was watch the ball roll. In time he discovered that the items Antoine's hired men stole were being sold to buyers on the other side of the border.

Mick burrowed deep into an investigation of Antoine's side projects, and there were a lot of those: construction bribes, bootlegging, fraud, and more. Pierre Antoine was not the great, community-minded man others had thought he was. Using friends and contacts, he had won contract after contract to distribute goods donated by the government to aid the victims of the explosion. One shipment here, one shipment there, and no one seemed to notice. No one but Mick. But Antoine was devious, and his deeds were often difficult to reveal. It was frustrating, because Mick knew they were there. Just couldn't quite reach them.

Audrey's unexpected connection had been a gift from heaven.

"What will happen to him?" Audrey asked.

"Well, he cooled his heels in a cell last night, so we'll see how he feels about that. He'll be indicted this morning, locked up again, and to be honest, I hope they throw away the key. He took food off a lot of people's plates."

Audrey was quiet, and Danny drew in beside her. "I feel stupid," she admitted.

"Everyone makes mistakes, Audrey," he said quietly. "You needed someone to believe in, and I wasn't there."

She sat back, looking deflated. One hand rested on her stomach. "What have I done?"

He laid his hand over hers, though it took effort. "You've given us a head start on being a family. That's all."

"Bet this changes the story on the rest of your family plans," Mick said.

The wheels in Danny's head started spinning, thinking about what his old friend had said. "You think . . ."

"Can't hurt to check." He gave Danny his one-eyed wink. "But you might want to wait a few hours. Sun's not even up yet."

———

Mrs. Munroe's cheeks flared red when Danny and Audrey approached her desk about five hours later. Despite the pain in one of his front teeth from the beating, Danny tipped his hat and flashed her his widest smile. Her mouth dropped open, seeing the variety of bruises and cuts covering his face.

"Good morning again, Mrs. Munroe. I hope you had a pleasant evening."

"Em . . ." She was flustered, trying to peel her eyes from his damaged face and pull her paperwork together in front of her at the same time. Her discomfort made Danny feel strangely satisfied. "Mr. and Mrs. Baker. Good morning to you both. I'm . . . I'm glad you've come back this morning. It seems, well, I'm in a bit of an embarrassing position. I hope you understand."

"Oh, really?" he said, feigning innocence.

"Seems I spoke in haste the last time we met. Your papers have been reviewed." Her grimace was painfully bright. "And I'm very pleased to inform you that you have been approved to adopt all three boys."

Joy filled Danny's heart, and he squeezed Audrey's hand.

"Fancy that," he said, calmly.

Papers in hand, the couple stepped into the street minutes later, their lives changed. A mist hung over the city, but the sun was trying hard, burning the fog in places. The air seemed clearer by the big black door to the orphanage, as if someone had swept the gloom away.

"After you, my dear," Danny said, holding the door open for her.

The boys sat side by side at the big table, munching on crackers and cheese. Danny took a seat across from them, and Audrey sat by Harry.

Danny gave them a serious look and started right in without even saying hello. There didn't seem any need for formalities with these two.

"Do you fellas like fish for supper?" he asked.

The boys' heads bobbled with assent, disregarding the crumbs that dropped from their mouths. Their matching eyes stared at him. "What happened to your face?" Eugene asked.

"Aw, it was nothin'," Danny assured him. "Do you like fishing?"

"Never fished before," Harry blurted out, shooting bits of cracker across the table.

"Don't speak with your mouth full," Audrey said, and Harry obediently snapped his mouth shut.

Danny scratched his head, appearing to consider something of the utmost importance. When he spoke again, his words were deliberate. "Do you think you'd like to try fishing? A couple of strong boys like you would be a big help up at my house."

The nodding started again and both pairs of eyes widened further.

Eugene swallowed hard. "Can we come live with you, Danny?"

He leaned toward them, still frowning. "Would you like that? Would you like me and Audrey to be your new mother and father?"

"Can you?" Harry squeaked.

Audrey beamed. "We would like that very much. It would be a big change for you—"

"And Norman, too?" Eugene glanced at the little boy, slumped comatose against the wall, snorting with baby dreams.

"Of course Norman, too. Couldn't very well go without him, could we?"

"Can we go on a boat?"

"I might even let you steer."

"Can we go right now?"

He leaned back. "You'll have to be a little patient, Harry. Audrey and I are going to go to Jeddore to build us a nice big house on the ocean. You fellas would like that, right? And we'd live right by your new grandparents. Can you wait that long?"

The boys' eyes simultaneously filled with tears. The impossible question rose in Danny's mind, and he held Audrey's gaze, asking. It would be the two of them, after all.

"Well, we'd be pretty busy building that new house. Do you think you'd be good helpers?"

"I can hammer," Eugene said, then glanced doubtfully at the sleeping Norman. "He can't do much, but we'd take care of him and keep him out of your way."

"I can carry stuff," Harry said quietly.

Audrey hugged the little boy. Danny was speechless, watching the sweet round face squeeze against her. This was everything he had wished for and more.

"Yeah," he decided. "You know what? Let's go home today."

The boys stared without speaking, hardly daring to believe, then they jumped to their feet and ran in circles, chanting, "We're going fishing! We're going fishing!"

But there was something Danny had to do first. He drew Audrey close against him.

"What?" she asked. Those blue eyes blinked up at him with that beautiful, open expression of trust he lived for.

"I gotta go do something first, okay? Take care of something."

"All right," she said. "Where are we going?"

He kissed her forehead, then stood. "Alone, Audrey. I gotta go alone.

You stay with the boys and see if we have to do anything with papers or whatever. I'll be back soon."

He liked the shadow of worry that flitted over her face. It meant she cared. "Where are you going? Why can't I come?"

"Just gotta visit an old friend is all. Don't you worry."

She walked toward the door with him, her expression full of concern. "You're not going to—"

Her face darkened, a cloud blocking the sun. "Don't ask, Audrey. You don't want to know."

"Oh, you fool!" she cried. "Leave it alone. He nearly had you killed the last time."

Danny held her face between his hands so she couldn't turn away. He felt her instinctively pull back, but he held her close. "Listen, Audrey. This is something you have to understand. I am a man. I have a man's sense of honour. And in order to keep that honour, I have to believe I am still strong. That I am not a coward. This man took everything from me, then you went behind my back and tried to make it all right. Well, it's not all right. It will never be all right. But at least if I finish it my way, I will be able to move forward. Do you understand?"

"No, I don't."

"Do you want to be married to me?"

"Of course, Danny! But look at you! Your poor face—"

"It'll heal. But you gotta let me do this. Even if you don't understand why, you have to understand that it's important to me. You don't need to worry. I'll be safe. I'll be careful, and I will come back here for you. But you have to let me do this." He hesitated. "If you don't, we're done. Because I won't be me anymore."

A single tear trickled down the side of her nose and clung to one of his fingers. He felt her careful movement of assent between his hands.

"I'll be back in an hour. Maybe you could see what needs doing here so we can cast off later today."

"Okay," she said, then closed her eyes when he kissed her.

"I love you, Audrey. Always have, always will."

"I love you too," she whispered into his ear. "Come back soon."

FORTY-SIX

No one at the desk said much when Danny arrived at the jailhouse. He signed in and an officer accompanied him down a long cement hallway. His peg was loud; its familiar *clop clop clop* echoed off the walls. But for the first time, Danny wasn't ashamed of the sound. For the first time he realized the chunk of wood at the bottom of his leg wasn't anything to hide. Sure, it was ugly and uncomfortable. Sure, he would have done just about anything to get his original leg back. But what he had, well, it was like a medal of honour. He had gone over there and given all he had, and they'd given him this kind of a life in return.

Pierre Antoine? Well, he had a beautiful house and a lot of money. And now he was ruined. He had a criminal record and a reputation that would stay with him for as long as Danny's peg leg stayed with him. There were consequences to everything a man did, and for the first time Danny was satisfied with his.

Antoine sat alone in the back of a cell, elbows on his knees, face to the floor, but he lifted his head when he heard Danny's steps. Danny probably felt more satisfaction than he should have, seeing that Antoine's face wasn't much better than his own, blooming into layered bruises of black and purple, which Danny'd put there before the goons had grabbed him and dropped him at the docks. That made Danny smile. The man bruised just like any other mortal. Now, Antoine scowled at Danny through the bars. Danny stuck his hands in his pockets and gave the Frenchman the smile of a saint.

"I gotta say, you don't look too comfortable in there, Mr. Antoine."

Pierre's eyes narrowed. His voice was a growl. "What are you doing here?"

"Just came to visit. Like I did last time, before we were so rudely interrupted." Danny touched his cheek gingerly. "By the way, that bald man of yours has a mean uppercut. You can tell him that from me." He shrugged. "I know some guys with better ones, though."

"I'm sure you do. Should be you in here, you son of a bitch. You probably know most of the scum in this place personally."

Danny stepped back and scanned some of the other cells, recognizing a few men.

"Actually, I do," he said. "And if you'd like a little advice, well, you might wanna treat them a little nicer than you treated me. They aren't as well-mannered as I am." He winked. "And not so patient with sucker punches."

Antoine sneered. "So what? Who the hell asked for your advice? You think I care why you're here? What is it you want? You come here to gloat?"

Danny rocked a bit between his foot and his peg. "Uh, yeah. I guess I did. See, because I got the girl. She chose me, despite everything you've got. You can't ever have her again. And I got the kids and the home and the life I always wanted. And you, well, you got this." He rubbed the back of his neck. "Wow. I wish I could say I felt bad for you, Mr. Antoine, but I sure don't."

"Yeah? Well, that's just fine. You've said what you wanted to say. Now get out of here."

"Oh, I'm sure there's more."

Pierre spat to the side. "Get outta here, Baker. Run along now, fisherman. Oh, that's right. You can't run like other men can. The thing is, you'll never run, you pathetic, crippled *boy*. You're a sorry excuse for a man is what you are. So you can say all you want, but you'll never, never be the man I am."

Danny tightened his jaw and met the man's eyes with his own fury. "And I thank God every day that I won't. You are a stupid man, Antoine. And very, very small. I hope you never get out of here. But if you do, I've got a message for you."

"Yeah?"

He lowered his voice to the dangerous tone he kept hidden behind the wall in his heart. The dark voice rumbling in the trenches, cold, forbidding, and lethal. "Stay away from me and my family. And stay away from the orphanage."

"Or what? You gonna kill me?" Antoine's eyes were jet black in the swollen lids. "Listen up, Baker. Listen good. When I get outta here, I'm gonna mess you up bad. And then I'm gonna mess up Audrey. I'm gonna come after your entire bloody family. I'll make your lives hell. You're gonna regret you ever met me."

Danny grabbed the bars of the cell and pressed his face against the cold metal. The contact thrilled through the cuts and bruises, feeding Danny's energy. Antoine had risen to the bait and now stood only a few inches away. He could smell the ripe stink of the man's fear and fought the urge to spit at him.

"Doesn't surprise me you should feel that way. After all, you're the one on the other side of the bars. You got nothing left but threats. But you might soon wish you'd never threatened me like that."

"Oh yeah? Why's that? I'm not scared of a half man."

Danny chuckled, then leaned back again. "Hey, Franco!" he yelled down the corridor.

A deep voice called back, "Yo, Danny! Dat you?"

"Sure is," Danny replied. "Who's down there with you?"

"Well, let me see," Franco said. Danny could picture the big man counting off on his massive fingers. "There's Jimbo, Maddy MacDonald, Chains, Bruce . . . they's all here. Oh, and Red, too, I think. You here, Red?"

"I'm here, Franco. Nice to hear your voice, Danny my lad," came the response.

Red was a huge Irishman. He loomed over everyone at the docks and was built like a bull. His nickname naturally originated from the colour of his stiff brush cut but also applied to the deep shade of red that seeped up his face when he was the least bit roused. Danny'd never seen a man with tougher knuckles than Red. The image of those fists introducing themselves to Antoine made him smile inside.

"Good to hear yours too, Red. You comin' out to play sometime soon?"

"Oh, sure I will. Just catchin' up on some sleep is all. Three square meals a day here. A fella can't complain."

"What are you all in here for this time, Franco?" Danny watched Antoine's face. He already knew the answer to his question, and he had a pretty good idea of how the answer would affect Antoine's confidence.

He imagined the big Italian's careless shrug. "Somethin' to do with dat altercation at the rail yards th'other night. Slight disagreement is all." Scattered chuckles bounced off the walls. "Red put three fellas in the hospital. Crazy Irishman. Why you here, Danny? You need somethin'?"

"Oh no. Thanks. I'm just here visiting. Hey, did you boys meet the latest jailbird? My old friend Pierre Antoine? Seems he stole stuff from the orphanage. Let the kids starve. Some kinda hero, huh?"

Pop pop—the trademark sound of Mad MacDonald cracking his knuckles. "I read about that guy in the paper this mornin'. Tell you what, lad. I'd sure like to meet that new friend of yours face-to-face. He's some kind o' celebrity."

Danny looked down the corridor. "He has some big plans for me and my family, apparently. Did you hear what he said?"

"Every word," came Red's voice.

"No' a real polite lad, is he?" asked MacDonald. "Threatenin' our friend an' all."

"Don't worry," Franco's voice rumbled. "We'll look after Mr. Antoine for you, Danny."

Pierre paled to a sickly white under the bruises. "Am I gonna kill you?" he asked. "Nah. I won't have to. The tides have turned, and now I'm the one with influential friends. Enjoy your stay, Mr. Antoine." He stepped from the bars and tipped an imaginary hat toward the men down the hall. "See ya round, fellas. Take care of yourselves."

FORTY-SEVEN

Danny did as he'd promised, returning to the orphanage to collect Audrey and the boys, but he did so only after he'd stopped in at Mick's house and packed all the couple's belongings. That way they could just leave the city once and for all. He borrowed a wagon and carried all their things to the docks, then arranged for passage. Danny didn't have a boat in Halifax, and he hadn't set this up in advance so his father could bring one down for them, so Danny paid a man to sail them, and all their meagre possessions, up to East Jeddore.

When he arrived at the orphanage, Audrey was watching, concern wrinkling her brow. Her expression cleared when she saw him, and as soon as he was close enough, she wrapped her arms around his neck and stretched up for a gentle kiss.

"Is everything all right now?" she asked.

"Yup. Everything's fine."

"What about Pierre?" she asked carefully.

"You don't need to worry about him ever again." She frowned, but he only shook his head. "It's all taken care of. End of story, Audrey."

He knew she wanted more information, but it was his. He didn't want to argue, didn't want to answer questions. He'd done what he'd had to do. He could move on now.

"Hey, boys," he said, turning toward them. "Who wants to go on a boat?"

Mick came to the dock to bid them farewell. He accepted all the invitations they issued, promising to visit when he could. "The boss'll be sure to offer me a few days' holiday after this story blows over. But I'll be plenty busy until then."

"Hey, Mick," Danny said, holding out a hand. "Thanks for everything."

Mick gripped Danny's hand, giving it a shake. "Watch yourself up there, eh? Don't get lost in the stink of fish. But if you do, I'll probably still have room for you here." He cast a dubious eye over the little boys running in shrieking circles around the bags. "Whenever you want."

"Thank you, Mick," Audrey said, hugging him. "For everything." From over her shoulder, Danny watched his buddy's eye close, his hands press against her back.

Mick stepped back. "I'm glad it all worked out. Take care of him, will you? He tends to get himself in situations."

She sniffed. "I promise I will."

"Good. Then let's get this boat moving. Ain't gonna be daylight forever."

The little boys climbed into the sloop and sat close to each other, trembling with anticipation.

Danny turned back to Mick. "Hey, Mick. If you need a story in a week or so, you might wanna check on Mr. Antoine over there in the jailhouse. See how he's getting along with Franco and the others."

"Oh?"

"Yeah. I introduced him to them, you might say."

Mick grinned. "You always was full of surprises, my friend. I'll watch out for that and keep you informed on his situation. Thanks for the heads-up."

"No. Thank you," Danny repeated. "I mean it. For everything."

Danny gave the little boys strict instructions about exactly how far they were allowed to lean over the edge of the boat, but he let them touch the water as they floated up and out of Halifax Harbour. Audrey held Norman on her lap and pointed out sights as they went.

The wind picked up as they pulled away from the dock, and the captain gestured to Danny, who let out the jib until it barely luffed, then he tightened the sail and tied it off. The captain did the same for the mainsail, then sat at the tiller. The saltwater wind whipped Danny's hair against his face, blowing cool and clean, healing so much more than just his cuts and bruises. He leaned against the mast and closed his eyes. The weight of the past year began to slide off his shoulders and sink into the sea.

For five hours the sloop passed by nothing but water, sky, and trees. Danny knew it all seemed the same to the others, but not to him. Every inch of the shoreline was etched into his mind, and he was soothed by its fingers, its constantly changing patterns of green and grey. The explosion had stripped the north end of Halifax of most trees, and now the familiar whispering of leaves at the water's edge was like a lullaby. Branches had lengthened over time, new birds flitted from tree to tree, but it was the same. It was home.

"We're almost there," he told them.

Audrey sat between the children, who were now half asleep, silently watching the shore. The creases he'd seen so often crossing her brow were gone, like the waves of the sea when it calms after a storm. She smiled in that young girl's way, sweet and trusting. But no longer quite so innocent. Not quite, he knew, as naive as she had been. But she was still his girl. Deep down he knew that.

"Here, little man," he said to Eugene. "Go and sit with your brother so I can talk with your mother."

Eugene wobbled to his feet, then joined Harry on Audrey's other side. Danny took his place and wrapped his arm around Audrey. He searched her eyes for regret, for something that might take away the magic of this moment, but saw nothing but love.

"We can do this," she said.

"Yeah," he replied. "We can. We'll be just fine." He grinned. "It'll be crowded at first, but we'll get the house built eventually, and life will go on."

The water lapped at the hull and the captain ordered everyone down so he could come about. They all ducked and watched the big sails swing to the other side. Almost immediately, the wind filled the sails and pushed the boat faster up the shore.

"Danny," said Audrey. "I have a little surprise for you."

He grimaced. "Not sure I can handle too many more of your surprises."

She leaned over and kissed him. "You'll like this one." She pulled a small purse from her bag and held it out to him. "I wasn't sure when to give it to you, but now seems like a good time. Open it."

Frowning, he did as she said, then stared at its contents, suddenly dizzy. "What is this? Where did you—"

"I sold the little necklace Pierre gave me."

Danny pulled out the money, savouring the feel of it in his fingers. He chuckled. "Nothing 'little' about that necklace."

"No, but he didn't want it back." She shrugged. "I thought we should use it ourselves. I reckoned it was only right. After all, he tore down our house in a way. Now he's helping us build one."

Danny recognized the scurry of his nerves as hope filled his heart. There was enough money here to make a good start on their new home. A very good start. They'd get building right away. He and his dad and his brothers, his wife—and his sons.

It would be all right. Everything would be all right.

"Look, Danny," Audrey said. Her eyes were blue as the sky, her soft pink lips open with happiness. She was pointing ahead, toward the rooftop of his family's house where it peeked through the trees.

The boys drooped against each other, exhausted. Well, they were about to wake up in a pretty big way. So were his parents. He couldn't help chuckling to himself, imagining how they might react.

Danny kissed the tip of Audrey's nose and wrapped his arms around her, filled with the wonderous certainty that he was right. Everything *would* be fine. He kissed her again, then put his lips against her ear.

"Welcome home, Audrey."

A Note to Readers

In 2008, my family and I made the move from Alberta to Nova Scotia. We didn't have family here or jobs lined up, we just wanted to explore more of Canada and experience a different way of life and living. I grew up in Toronto, lived in New York for a few months, then Calgary for about seventeen years, and having now lived in Nova Scotia for almost fifteen years, I can tell you that each place has its own unique pulse. The heartbeat of Nova Scotia rises and falls with the tides, up at four a.m. with lobster fishermen like Danny Baker, then back down after all the chores are done, long after sunset.

When we moved here, I was in my early forties and just starting out on my journey as an author. At that time, I was writing Scottish historical fiction, inspired by many of my favourite books, most of which were based in Europe—particularly Scotland and England—or America. I suppose I thought Nova Scotia might provide more Scottish inspiration for my books, since the name translates to "New Scotland." Instead, I found myself in a place with its own history, only vaguely influenced by its namesake. And for the first time in my life, I felt physically surrounded by history. Just up the road stood houses well over a hundred years old, and small communities marked areas where families had lived for generations. The cemeteries were filled with their stories as well as those from the *Titanic* and the Halifax Explosion. Suddenly, I no longer had to seek out history from overseas, because it was right on my doorstep.

I had never heard of the Halifax Explosion before, which astounded most of the locals I met, but I didn't remain ignorant for long. The facts of what happened at 9:04:35 a.m. on December 6, 1917, blew a hole in my heart and left a permanent scar.

The morning had dawned crystal clear and cold. It was a perfect December day in the sparkling city of Halifax, and its streets and walkways were busy with women and children on their way to school, soldiers freshly returned or about to head overseas, and sailors taking well-earned leave.

Out on the water, the French ship, the *Mont-Blanc*, floated through what is called "The Narrows" of Halifax's busy wartime channel, lazily approaching the shore. The *Mont-Blanc* was loaded with about 250,000 kilograms of explosives, including picric acid, TNT, guncotton, and benzol. She had been waiting to join a convoy that would escort her to the war.

Also waiting to leave the harbour was the Belgian relief ship, *Imo*. *Imo* carried no cargo because she was on her way to New York to pick up emergency supplies. Her captain was impatient to leave, since they were already delayed, having been forced to wait a couple of days for coal. He accelerated to seven knots, then stayed to port, the "wrong" side of the channel, avoiding a passing tugboat. This put her directly in the *Mont-Blanc*'s path. The *Mont-Blanc* blew her whistle, reminding the *Imo* that she was in the wrong lane, but the *Imo* replied with two whistle blasts, informing the munitions carrier that she wasn't going to give way. After almost forty-five minutes of arguing back and forth through whistles, the *Mont-Blanc* eventually turned hard left and *Imo* reversed her engines: hard astern. But it was too late.

Imo struck the *Mont-Blanc*'s bow and sparks flew, igniting benzol fuel and the highly unstable picric acid. Thick black smoke filled the sky, and the crew of the *Mont-Blanc* abandoned ship, diving into the freezing water and swimming as fast as they could. No one could put out that kind of fire, they knew. They fled to the Dartmouth shore, screaming warnings to people like young Percival and his friend who were watching the spectacle from the waterfront or their windows, but since the men were yelling in French, no one understood what they were saying.

Twenty minutes later, the *Mont-Blanc*'s temperature reached approximately 5,000 degrees Celsius. When it exploded, its steel hull shot sky-high as if it weighed nothing at all. Part of its anchor landed more than four kilometres away, and a gun barrel was blasted in the other direction, landing five kilometres away in Dartmouth. The explosion flattened Halifax and the surrounding area, incinerating anyone and anything in its path unless they were lucky, like Danny Baker. It obliterated all of Richmond, Tuft's Cove in Dartmouth, and the small Mi'kmaq settlement of Turtle Grove. Windows shattered a hundred kilometres away from the epicentre, and the impact was heard clearly on Prince Edward Island.

Caption: Taken at Bedford Basin, looking south down Halifax Harbour, this photo was purportedly taken fifteen to twenty seconds after the explosion. The estimated distance from the blast is 2 kilometres (1.25 miles); the height of the blast at its peak was measured at approximately 12,000 feet (3,657 metres). Library and Archives Canada / PA-166585

The blast instantly killed approximately 1,600 people, but four hundred more died soon afterwards. Most of the buildings not leveled by the explosion burst into flame, their wood or coal stoves having been shaken or toppled by the blast. Since many of the firefighters were dead, there was no one there to put out the fires, and people were trapped inside what was left of the structures. Mere hours later, a nasty blizzard struck, burying those who hadn't been able to escape.

In total, it's estimated that out of the 2,000 people who died during and in the immediate aftermath of the explosion, five hundred were children. There were probably many more, since the frigid tsunami of seawater that followed climbed as high as eighteen metres above the harbour's high-water mark, and it would have dragged some bodies out to sea, never to be found. There were also a lot of undocumented soldiers and sailors on leave or en route to deployment who could have disappeared without a trace. In addition to the dead, hundreds of people in and around the city of Halifax, Nova Scotia, were maimed, blinded, and burned, and 25,000 were left homeless in the middle of a cold Canadian winter.

Caption: Parts of Halifax were completely leveled; here is an example of one house that was affected but still somehow standing. Library of Congress / George Grantham Bain Collection / 1917 / LCCN 2014706063.

The first trains to arrive with aid came from nearby communities, but the explosion had twisted the tracks so badly that the trains could go no farther. Medical supplies had to be carried in by hand, slowing progress. Eventually, two trains fully loaded with doctors, nurses, and medical supplies arrived from Boston, bringing desperately needed help.

The Halifax Explosion was the largest man-made explosion in world history (until Hiroshima), and remains the biggest disaster in Canadian history. And yet that day has, for the most part, been forgotten by the rest of the world. Of course, that has to do with the fact that it was overshadowed by the terrible repercussions of war; however, local author Janet Maybee said in a CBC News interview in 2017 that "some of the returning soldiers said they had not seen worse destruction on the fields of Flanders."

During World War I, more than 60,000 Canadians perished. Danny Baker was one of the 140,000 or so wounded men who returned to Canada via Halifax, the busiest port in the country, one of the 3,741 with at least one amputated limb. He was also one of the more than 9,000 reported cases of shell shock. When it came to the invisible wounds of shell shock—what we now know as post-traumatic stress disorder, or PTSD—doctors were at a loss for what to do. Vague treatments of talk and physical therapy alternated with electric shock therapy, in which the patient was electrocuted in an effort to stimulate paralyzed nerves, limbs, or vocal cords. As it turns out, electrocution was the most effective treatment, enabling two-thirds of all patients to return to the front.

When Danny set his one remaining foot on Pier 6 in October 1916—a pier that would be obliterated just over a year later—he entered a very busy and relatively prosperous city, one that had benefited greatly due to the war industry. A port with so much value needed to be protected as well as could be, so once the sun set, it was as if someone hit the "off" switch on the entire place because anyone violating the evening blackout could be fined up to $5,000. The city was never attacked; however, submarines were spotted in Halifax Harbour.

Women found purpose, self-confidence, and a new sense of pride during World War I. Like the munitions factory where Audrey Poulin worked in England, the ones in Canada hired more than 30,000 female workers, more than a thousand were employed by the R.A.F. driving ambulances or trucks or taxis, and about 6,000 found work in the civil service. Thousands more Canadian women worked in regular jobs in banks, offices, factories, and farms, proving they could do so much more than raise children and keep a tidy house. Female suffragettes seized the opportunity and moved steadily toward victory, and the first Canadian women to vote in an election were the Canadian Nursing Sisters, or "Bluebirds," whom you can read more about in my novel *Bluebird*.

In this book, I cover the tragedies of World War I and the Halifax Explosion, but I should note that two major long-term benefits resulted from these historical events.

First, the demands placed on doctors and innovators led to amazing medical progress. In March 1915, French physician Alexis Carrel gave a talk entitled: "Science has perfected the art of killing: Why not that of saving?" and given the carnage they were seeing from the war, the medical professionals put all their energy into that front. Orthopedic and facial prosthesis (including dentistry) underwent astonishing progress, as did new forms of surgery and antiseptic to cut down on life threatening infection. Anesthesia was introduced in the form of a nitrous oxide-oxygen mix, there was widespread vaccination for typhoid and tetanus, and a greater overall awareness of the importance of good hygiene, among other breakthroughs.

The other benefit was the founding of the Canadian National Institute for the Blind (CNIB) in 1918. The Halifax Explosion was the world's largest "mass blinding," since so many people in the city had been watching through windows as the burning ship drifted closer to the pier. When it blew up, they suffered terrible wounds, including shards of glass in their eyes. Many soldiers also returned from conflict blind, and like the victims of the Explosion, they needed to learn how to "see" again, but without their vision. The CNIB taught people to read Braille, to knit, and to operate important daily tools like washing machines and bread mixers. A century later, the CNIB still operates under the slogan "Seeing beyond vision loss since 1918."

Tides of Honour was my first historical fiction novel that focused on a chapter of Canadian history. It was a fascinating project and an emotional roller coaster, but as soon as I was finished, I knew I couldn't stop. I began looking into more parts of Canadian history of which I knew very little, if not nothing, like the Acadian Expulsion, the Klondike Gold Rush, the British Home Children, and more. My favourite, most rewarding reviews are the ones that say, "I had never heard of this before! Why wasn't I taught about this?" because that's exactly how I feel every time I begin a story. Canadian history is full of amazing stories, and I can hardly wait to dig into the next one.

Acknowledgments

Thank you to all the generous people living along the Eastern Shore of Nova Scotia who helped me learn about this area's history and culture, and how they lived through so much trauma. In particular, I'd like to thank Harold Baker (Bakers Point Fisheries), Linda Fahie (fishermans life.novascotia.ca), and Thea Wilson-Hammond (HeritageVillage.ca). I would also like to thank Annette Fulford (ww1warbrides.blogspot.com) for her help on researching Audrey's journey.

Thank you to Nova Scotia author Jon Tattrie for letting Tommy Joyce hop briefly from his brilliant novel *Black Snow* onto the pages of *Tides of Honour* so he could help Danny along the way.

As always, thank you to my advocate and agent, Jacques de Spoelberch. I am so grateful to you for making your first foray into Canadian publishing on my behalf.

I'm so thrilled and privileged to be working with Simon & Schuster Canada, a committed, excellent publisher thriving under the stewardship of President Kevin Hanson and Vice President, Editorial Director Nita Pronovost. When I sent my manuscript to my editor at that time, Alison Clarke, she truly opened my eyes. Every time she sent me a question about this book, it felt as if she opened another window, and my story grew exponentially. Since then, I have a new editor, Sarah St. Pierre, and with her guidance and brilliant creative suggestions I learn more every time.

I also thank Shara Alexa (Director of Sales, National Accounts), Adria Iwasutiak (Vice President, Director of Publicity and Canadian Sales), Felicia Quon (Vice President, Marketing and Communications), Lorraine Kelly (Manager, Library and Special Sales), and Jessica Boudreau (Designer). Very, very special thanks to the wizard of a woman who keeps me organized, Mackenzie Croft (Marketing Associate and former Publicist).

I am particularly thrilled that two very special members of the Simon & Schuster team in the United States, Paula Amendolara (VP Director, Retail Sales), and Lexi Dumas (National Accounts Manager), have put so much effort and dedication into bringing my books to our American friends. The Halifax Explosion might not be very well known in the United States, but many of the people in Boston will know about it. Bostonians were among the first to arrive and offer aid to the shattered city of Halifax, sending doctors and nurses and two fully loaded trains right away. Ever since then, Nova Scotia has sent the people of Boston an annual reminder of our gratitude: a big, beautiful, white spruce Christmas tree.

Tides of Honour would not be the book it is today if not for Dwayne, my beloved husband of almost thirty years. He is my most demanding reader, and his insistence that I dig into the core of every story means I cannot rest on my laurels at any point. He loves me and understands me when I have trouble doing that for myself, and he is the reason I believe in true love. Thank you for being my happily ever after, Dwayne. Forever and ever.

TIDES OF HONOUR

GENEVIEVE GRAHAM

A Reading Group Guide

Topics & Questions for Discussion

1. During World War I, the role of women changed drastically—from homemakers to munitions factory workers—but when Audrey remembers her own mother's choices to abandon tradition and acceptable norms of women's work, she understands that her mother did what she felt was necessary to provide for her family. Discuss Graham's different portrayals of Audrey, Audrey's mother, and Danny's mother in light of the suffragette movement occurring in London and Halifax.

2. In the prologue, Graham sets up the morning of the Halifax explosion, then jumps back in time to Danny's return to Nova Scotia. As you read the novel, did you realize that the plot was building up to that event? And given what you knew about Halifax's history, how did the description of the horrors of that December morning change your understanding of the explosion?

3. Danny Baker is an example of what many wounded veterans faced when they returned from the front. Like so many others, he is jobless, depressed, and disillusioned—and without resources to help him integrate back into society. Do you feel Graham captures the need for organizations for returning veterans? What do you know about the creation of Veterans Affairs Canada and The War Amps after World War I?

4. Given the mounting tensions between Danny and Audrey, what does the explosion symbolize in the novel? Thinking of Mick and Danny's suspicions of Pierre Antoine and their organized protests, can you speak to the explosion's impact on socialist reform?

5. How would you characterize Danny before the Battle of the Somme? Why do you think Graham uses firsthand accounts of Danny in 1916 instead of flashbacks?

6. Audrey's art is central to her identity and a language itself. Does her art bear any similarities to Danny's carpentry? How are both mediums used in the story?

7. Given Danny's downward spiral and his neglect of Audrey, how did you feel about Audrey and Pierre as friends, and then as a couple?

8. Danny's relationship with his father seems fraught with the expectations of what men and husbands must do to provide for their families. How does this reflect the role of men in this time? How does the war complicate these ideals? Compare the motivations of Danny, his brother Johnny, and their father.

9. How do Audrey and Danny's physical disfigurements reflect their emotional trauma? Why do you think Graham prevents them from surviving the war and the explosion unscathed?

10. Earlier in the novel, Audrey is introduced to the first strains of feminism with the suffragette movement in London. How does her relationship with Pierre complicate her growth as a feminist? What do you think Audrey's character arc throughout the novel says about women of this era?

11. Why is Danny unable to open up to Audrey when he returns home from the war? How would you describe their early love, given the obstacles they must overcome together?

12. In the media today, there is a lot of discussion about PTSD, especially in relation to veterans, and the practice of companion dogs to help alleviate many of the long-lasting effects of the disorder. What did you think about Danny's relationship with dogs, both in the trenches and at home?

13. What do you think the title *Tides of Honour* refers to?

1. To learn more about the Halifax Explosion, check out these two videos made by the CBC for the hundred-year anniversary of the catastrophe. The city remembers, including one of the survivors: https://www.youtube.com/watch?v=V0g2dSX6YyM. A moving, digital 360-degree reenactment of the event: http://newsinteractives.cbc.ca/halifaxexplosion.

2. Read about the courageous railway dispatcher Vincent Coleman, who sacrificed his life to alert an incoming train on the morning of December 6, 1917, on the Maritime Museum in Nova Scotia website, which also includes an online gallery of objects salvaged from the explosion: https://maritimemuseum.novascotia.ca/what-see-do/halifax-explosion/vincent-coleman-and-halifax-explosion. Vincent's story was further commemorated in a Heritage Minute: https://www.youtube.com/watch?v=rw-FbwmzPKo.

3. For insight into the history of prosthetics, one of the legacies of World War I, see this video produced by the *Wall Street Journal*: https://www.youtube.com/watch?v=M4NgZON8wb0.

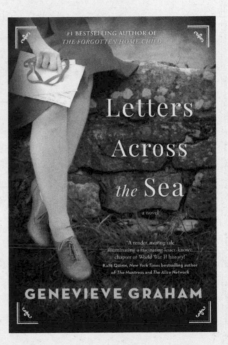

ALSO BY
GENEVIEVE GRAHAM
NATIONAL BESTSELLERS

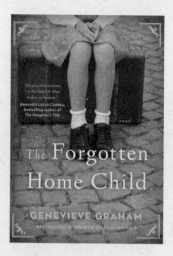

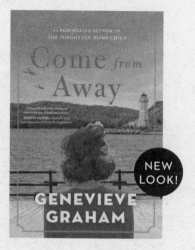

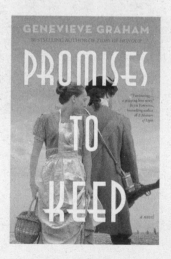

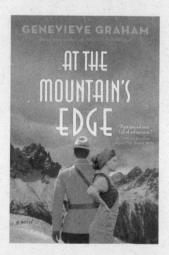